HEARTS
ON FIRE

Hearts on Fire

Paris
1968

BILL PEARL

Fifty Years Late Publishing

To my wife, Joann

USA Copyright Registered #TXu2-003-156
ISBN: 978-0-692-06566-2
Genre: Historical Novel
Adopted from French edition published by Harmattan, Paris, May
2018
Editors: Amy Belding, Chris Noel, Marcus Trower, Ellen Brock and
Jay Neugeboren

Contents

Foreward

My fellow Americans,

At least fifty years have passed since I wrote this letter. That's how long I instructed Robbie Samberg to wait before releasing it, and I'm confident he kept his word.

Four years and two days have passed since I left the White House, on January 20, 1969, and the memory of the last casualty list sent to me is still fresh on my mind. In 1968, 14,835 American boys died in Vietnam and 95,798 were wounded.

I tried to end the war before leaving office, but I failed, and I never told you why. I never told about the treason of Richard Nixon and how he delayed the peace talks just long enough to win the presidential election of 1968.

I never told about Robbie Samberg, the American student studying in Paris who bravely confirmed that Nixon was guilty of violating the Logan Act. I kept these things secret because my most experienced advisors thought it too shocking for a nation already rocked by assassinations, civil unrest, and war.

Robbie Samberg was a junior in college when I met him, and he impressed me as an honorable young man, finding his way through turbulent times. He witnessed this untold part of our history, and I knew one day he would want to write about it. I prepared this letter to attest to his story.

I had genuinely hoped the unrest in our nation might subside after I left office, but as I write this, we are on the eve of yet another shock to our political system, called Watergate. I profoundly regret that I did not act to prevent the election of the man responsible for this.

As you read this, I am long since deceased. In my grave I still see the faces of the boys who died in war under my command. I also see the face of Robbie Samberg, and I vouch for what he is about to tell you.

Lyndon Baines Johnson
January 22, 1973

Chapter 1

The Press Conference

Rosemary Rork was not happy. I was her star intern and walked in just as Senator Hankie entered the ornate semicircular Old Senate Chamber and took his place in front of a portrait of George Washington. I was too late to help set up, hand out the press releases, or replenish the coffee supply.

Rosemary had a weather-beaten face, with wrinkles that had her frowning even when she wasn't. She glared at me; I knew right away she was not pleased with my late arrival. I shrugged my shoulders and opened my hands in an "Ah, shucks" manner while mouthing the word, "Sorry." But it didn't work. Rosemary's piercing glare continued. I was relieved when she finally looked away toward Senator Hankie.

She was, after all, the consummate Capitol Hill professional, and had probably never been late a day in her life. I recalled sitting across from her in the senator's office on the afternoon she hired me. She wore her customary black dress its hemline down to her calves, was tall and slim, with short, jet black, and perfectly coiffed hair, and black, thick-framed glasses that accentuated both hair and dress.

We had just started talking when I spotted a string of wires on the outside window ledge and asked if it was an antenna

used to secretly communicate with the White House or the
CIA—Senator Lance Hankie was chairman of the Foreign Relations Committee and a close ally of President Johnson—and
she responded without hesitation, "No, Robbie, that's to keep
pigeons off the ledge."

It was my first important lesson about Washington—things
are not always as they seem. Or more exactly, things are often
less than what they seem?

By now the press had taken their seats, the most important
reporters in the front row. The senator stood at the podium,
smiling as always. Hankie was a pudgy, avuncular man from
the Midwest—everybody's uncle, a guy who always had a kind
word on his lips and a smile on his face. He was one part Walter
Cronkite, one part Walt Disney, and a loyal servant of his men-
tor, formerly his leader in the Senate and currently president
of the United States. Hankie wore a dark-blue pinstriped silk
suit, a red tie, and an oversized gold United States Senate pin
on his lapel. I sat on the aisle in the second row in case I was
needed to fetch something from the office, or adjust the sound
system.

"Well, boys," he began, rocking back on his heels and holding to the edge of the podium for balance. "We've got a bit
of a situation brewing . . . the war, the protests, and so forth,
the unrest among the Negroes . . . Feels some days like it's all
falling apart, but I know this president, and I know he'll get us
through, and today I want to talk to you about the progress we
are making in Vietnam. I just finished a meeting with General
Westmoreland, and he shared with me the body count over
the past few weeks, and I can assure you that at the rate we're
killing the communists, if we just hang in there and don't cut
and run, they simply cannot prevail. In fact, in just the first two
weeks of this year we have killed four thousand four hundred
and six enemy troops." He paused, and looked out across his

pince-nez glasses resting on the tip of his nose. "We cannot allow Southeast Asia to fall to the communists," he said. "Now I'll take some questions."

"What about the bombing halt?" *New York Times* bureau chief Tom Wicker asked, his six-foot-two-inch frame jolting up from his chair, spiral notepad in hand, a take-no-prisoners look on his face. Wicker was a star reporter who wrote the influential "In the Nation" column.

That got everyone's attention.

"Well, I spoke to the president and to Westmoreland about that and, you know, we've tried that, and every time we've tried it, the North Vietnamese have shown their gratitude by sending more men and supplies across the DMZ to kill American boys."

"So, it's not true! He's not considering a bombing pause?" Wicker followed up.

"The president wants to stop bombing. He's anxious to stop bombing, and he has done it eight times, the last time for thirty-seven days. He stopped it on Buddha's birthday. He'd be glad to stop it again if they tell us they won't use it to kill more of our boys."

"What about the protests, the antiwar movement?" David Lamb asked, jumping up from his seat a few rows behind me. He was the United Press International foreign affairs reporter.

"If the American people understood our position, they wouldn't be mad at us. They would support what we're doing. I need for you reporters to get that out there, all right?"

I looked over at the other reporters, most of whom were crouched in their chairs, heads down, taking notes on what I had increasingly come to believe was so much rubbish. Did Hankie really believe the only measure of victory in war was the body count? These numbers were announced by the military and regurgitated by an uncritical press as if some invisible referee would declare America the winner of the contest when the count reached high enough. I questioned how the army could accurately count bodies in any case after massively carpet-bombing battlefields in remote parts of the jungle with napalm. How could they really know how many people we killed? And how many innocent civilians burned beyond recognition got counted as enemy soldiers?

Suddenly, I was jolted by a prod from Allen Hoffers, sitting just behind me with the senator's other legislative and foreign relations staffers. He tapped me hard on the right shoulder and whispered, "Go get the senator a glass of water."

The senator had started coughing, and he signaled Allen, who was sitting just behind me. I ran to the back of the room, grabbed a glass off the refreshment table, filled it from the icy-cold pitcher, and ran it back down to the front of the room, handing it directly to the senator, who interrupted his remarks to say, "Thank you, Robbie," with a smile that conveyed the impression he knew me well. In fact, those were the first words he ever spoke to me. I was surprised he knew my name.

I returned to my chair, agonizing as the reporters continued to ask questions about the war and other issues. The president's position on a bombing halt contingent upon assurances that the enemy would not use the pause to kill our soldiers made sense to me, but the overall policy did not. *Where are we going with all this expenditure of blood and treasure? Can we really quell a popularly based liberation movement? Can we do it without staying there longer than the American electorate will tolerate? And if we withdraw, isn't it obvious what will follow?* I trusted my instincts about this, but at the same time I wrestled with the disloyalty it represented. I had been taught to support our government, especially in times of war. My father lectured us about this. My mother agreed. My friends at home and at school did not share my doubts. They did not question our policy and did not approve of my speaking out against it. They saw antiwar protestors as treasonous long-haired radicals endangering our national security.

Squirming in discomfort, as most of the reporters around me doted on every word the senator spoke, I watched attentively but my mind wandered to a recent visit home.

"Shut up already about the war," my father said, standing to reach the plate of blintzes. I had just explained my opposition in the most careful and thoughtful way I could at a Yom Kippur break-the-fast dinner with the entire family in attendance.

"Leave him alone, Irwin." My mother cut him off before he and the others could pile on.

I cringed. She agreed with him but she protected me. I fell silent. This was how it would go every visit home.

As the senator took the last question and closed the press conference, I felt a now-familiar knot in my stomach. It was a sensation I lived with more and more at school, at work, and especially on my visits home. I struggled with my opposition to what so many around me accepted without question. I worried about the draft.

The work for Hankie was exciting. It was three days a week, which permitted time for classes at George Washington University and the hours were flexible. His legislative assistant, Allen Hoffers, liked my writing and assigned me the task of preparing the first drafts of speeches and constituent letters about the war. It was a big responsibility for an intern. Hundreds of letters would arrive each week from all sorts of people—workers, mothers, company presidents, even governors.

Allen provided me a large loose-leaf notebook with tabs delineating topics—colonial history, legislation, the Gulf of Tonkin Resolution, the China threat, the Thiệu government, the domino theory, and more—each of which contained approved language I was supposed to use to construct the senator's correspondence. The problem was that the prepro-grammed paragraphs did not always fit the questions asked, and when the letters came from an important constituent, a mayor, or a governor, I did not feel comfortable providing a less than fully researched letter of response. I asked Allen if I could supplement the answers in the book with some inde-pendent research at the Library of Congress, and to my sur-prise he said yes. Allen knew I opposed the war but as long as I towed the party line in my work, he did not care. I spent many happy hours working at the Library, where the staff catered to me as a senator's staff member despite my youth, my scruffy beard, and less-than-professional attire—usually blue jeans and a baggy sweatshirt.

Allen was a frumpy, potbellied political junkie who looked ten years older than he was and who took me under his wing, providing an insider's education about politics and govern-ment. His tie always loosened, his clothes always appearing as if he had long ago grown out of them, he nonetheless appeared to know everybody in Washington and would happily regale me with stories as we lunched at the Senate staff cafeteria. We both loved the bean soup and would laugh at the risk we took eating it, working in the tight quarters of the Senate of-fice building.

As a key Senate staffer for the Foreign Relations Commit-tee, Allen was privy to classified information, which to my astonishment he occasionally shared with me. "Watch for Mc-Carthy or Kennedy to jump into the race," he offered in a whis-per well before it was public knowledge. "Things are heating up out there, and the forces seeking to oust LBJ are growing stronger. I got the inside scoop from Allard Lowenstein."

Kennedy and McCarthy had already begun to speak criti-cally about the war in private and had been approached by fac-tions in the party to challenge LBJ, something unprecedented in Democratic politics, but Allen would tell me again and again that 1968 was going be a year unlike any other.

The year had opened with a Day of Peace, declared by Pope Paul VI, and a truce in Vietnam, which lasted only minutes before it was broken by a Viet Cong surprise attack. I remember when we heard about the attack on the radio, driving to dinner in my father's station wagon during winter break. He slammed his hand against the steering wheel. "Bastards!" He looked at me and shook his head as if I were a coconspirator with the Viet Cong.

He reacted the same way when he heard about the race riots. In the prior year there had been inner-city riots in Boston, Kansas City, Newark, and Detroit—and by 1968 a new term, "blacks," was replacing "Negroes," which became a pejorative used to mock those who did not support the Black Power movement. My father hated it when I called Negroes "blacks." It was like I was personally responsible for tearing down the social order. He and my mother thought if things continued the way they were headed, we would be facing race riots in Trenton that could threaten our home and his business.

"You're not going to tame those savages by calling them 'blacks,' my father would say. He thought the police ought to be issued military grade weapons. "We got to make sure police have the firepower to put them down if they rise up!"

As if the rampant fear generated by racial tensions were not enough, the antiwar movement grew more intense as 1968 began. At the end of 1967, there were seventy-one demonstrations on American college campuses directed against the war in Vietnam and against Dow Chemical, maker of napalm, first developed by scientists at Harvard for the army during the Second World War. I remember coming out of Thurston Hall on G Street and running into the first demonstration we had on the GW campus. I wanted to stop and join them. I believed in what they were trying to do, but I quickly moved on to make my next class, ever mindful of my grades, my job with Hankie and what my father would say if he found out I was protesting.

"I'm not spending all that money on tuition to have you marching against our country," my father would admonish every chance he got. "Mind your studies and leave the war to the generals, who know what they are doing."

Antiwar sentiment had grown at George Washington University and college campuses around the nation and the globe, with protests erupting like brush fires, sparked by a shared antiwar, antiestablishment sentiment and the rapid spread of news by the new phenomenon of worldwide television coverage. "Robbie," Allen would repeat, "our country is about to face headwinds the likes of which we have not seen since the Civil War—the divisions among us are that great—and I don't think anybody has a clue how we are going to get out of this."

The antiwar and the Civil Rights Movements had come together at the most radical fringes of both. When Hubert Rap Brown replaced Stokely Carmichael as head of the less than aptly named Student Nonviolent Coordinating Committee (SNCC), he famously quipped, "I say you better get a gun; violence is necessary! It is as American as cherry pie." And antiwar protestors screamed, "Up against the wall, motherfuckers!" the words of playwright LeRoi Jones, who was sentenced to jail and fined $1,000 for illegal possession of two revolvers during the Newark riots.

"I'm not sure even the leadership of a Kennedy or a King can contain this," Allen warned as he slurped his bean soup, and handed me an AP wire story about the riots. "It's going to be a freakin' crazy year," he said with a look of consternation. I nodded as bean soup splashed from my spoon onto my white shirt. I frantically dipped a napkin into my water glass to wipe away the stain, but my shirt was now soiled and wet where I had attempted to clean it. I felt a mess in a nation that felt a mess.

Chapter 2

Paris

Like many inspired ideas, this one originated in the bathtub.

Winston Churchill dictated inspirational prose from the tub, calling a wary secretary to the bathroom door to record his verbal gems. So it was for the idea of taking my junior year abroad, only Andi (short for Andria Smith), my girlfriend, did not sit outside the door. She sat naked on the edge of the tub, her brown eyes peering down through her round tortoiseshell glasses, scribbling notes on a yellow legal pad inscribed with the insignia of the United States Senate. She tended to me in this fashion every afternoon during the hot baths, prescribed by the doctor for my recovery from a recent surgery.

"Robbie, I can't believe you wrote that speech for Senator Hankie and it made the front page of the *New York Times*." She tossed aside the notepad, her smile turning mischievous, her hands moving playfully across my clean, wet skin, her fingers slipping down to where I had wanted them to be for the past half hour. "A front-page story in the *New York Times*," she whispered.

"Andi, aaah, that feels so good . . . Actually," I said, struggling to repress the pleasure she was by now briskly providing, "I'm bored writing speeches for Senator Hankie. Aaah . . . the policy people take out half the good stuff, and the lawyers take out the rest. Oooo . . . By the time the speech is approved it's gutless, and I don't like gutless," I offered in a halting, staccato voice, masking ecstasy.

"You're all guts, big boy," she said, speeding up her strokes, the water splashing over the bathroom floor. I moaned in the loudest voice, and it was the very next moment, the calm restored, that the lightning struck. "I need a new challenge, Andi."

"Want me to invite Sylvia over?" she asked, sliding her hand from the tub and tossing me a sultry look.

Andi liked girls and boys and was trying to figure out which she liked more. I think she wanted to see how she would feel doing both at the same time.

"No, I'm talking about work." I threw the washcloth at her, and she caught it, laughing. "Seriously, I've gone as far as I can go with Hankie, and it's time to move on. I'm stagnating. Do you realize they cut out the entire section I wrote about body counts? Hours of research down the tubes!"

"Body counts?" Andi stood and shimmied her torso.

"And I'm sick and tired of everyone thinking I'm some kind of traitor just because I think this war policy is shit! Christ, even my family is against me!"

"Your father is an ass," she said, noticing the hollow look on my face.

I babbled on as Andi listened, jumping from thought to thought, not entirely oblivious to her gentle strokes and pats on my torso with an oversized terry-cloth towel. I climbed out of the tub and sat on its edge as she fell to her knees and started drying my midsection.

"I'm going to Paris," I said softly but firmly as the thought spilled out from someplace deep within me.

"Right after I send you to the moon," she said, giggling and casting me a wicked smile.

My face lit with pleasure as I anticipated Paris, an idea that seemed attractive, exciting, and possible in equal measure. George Washington University had just announced an exchange program with the American Institute in Paris. I could transfer there. I could escape. No more mocking by my father; no more bad dreams of a gruesome death in a far-off jungle, and awakening the next morning in sweat soaked pajamas. No more cringing at Hankie's inane press conferences!

Suddenly, Andi looked up. I could feel the storm of her displeasure.

"You're serious?" she said.

It had been just one week since she broke her engagement to Peter Straight—a rising star, Harvard intern at the Pentagon, from the mainline Philadelphia Straights—who offered her a three-carat diamond and a lifetime of security. Two weeks before that she had seen me in the lounge of my dorm and recognized me as the boy with whom she had fallen madly in love at a prep school graduation party two years before. I had been so stoned and so deeply enthralled by my blond escort that night, I did not remember meeting her. She walked up to me and started talking about the graduation party as if it had just happened yesterday and resumed her flirtation, standing ever so close, looking me over, biting her bottom lip and raising her eyebrows. I played along, turned on by the cleavage of her amazing low-cut dress.

For the next two weeks Andi and I were inseparable, she living out her prep school fantasy while I went along for the ride. Her idea of our relationship quickly became something more serious than had ever occurred to me. She was a hot Shiksa (that's a non-Jewish girl, or to us Jewish boys, forbidden fruit) in rebellion against a strict Catholic upbringing and doing just about everything contrary to what she had been taught. I, on the other hand, was a nice Jewish boy who believed that the only girls I could take seriously, or who might one day be serious contenders for marriage, would have to come from a Jewish family. It was the tribal thing impressed upon me by my parents, our rabbi, and just about everyone else in the family.

"Jews stay with Jews," my father would say. "The goyim will never accept us." He was forever telling me tales of anti-Semitism, which he thought lurked in almost everybody who was not Jewish. I struggled with this and with him, but more about that later.

It was also in the tub that Andi broke the news to me about ending her engagement to Straight. Speaking with all the solemnity of a president announcing a declaration of war, she told me that she had given back the diamond, the dimensions of which might lead one to think that no sane girl would ever return it, and from that moment she set out to draft me as his replacement.

The tub faucet in my studio bathroom dripped, the only noise to be heard as Andi stood before me silently digesting my words about going to Paris, her face contorted in a building rage. She had hinted that I was "The One," and I had wanted to let her know that I did not feel the same way, but I could never find the right words, or place or time, and I was enjoying her uninhibited affections too much to spoil such a good thing. I felt her pain, but I thought she would just have to learn that a two-week white-hot affair did not necessarily mean a binding commitment . . .

"Andi," I beseeched, "you've got to understand that a two-week—"

She threw a bar of soap, then the washcloth, and finally the towel at me, ran from the bathroom, put on her clothes, and stomped out, no doubt angry at herself for her blind submission and angry at me for my dishonesty. I could have told her up front that she was not The One, but I did not. *Am I such a*

bad guy for not hanging out a sign saying "Just Out for a Romp"?
Guys don't do that! Besides, a Shiksa could never be The One,
right? In a remarkably few moments, the guilt subsided and
gave way to exciting thoughts of my escape to a new life in
Paris. I had never been out of New Jersey before coming to DC
for college, and my work for Senator Hankie had fueled my curiosity and longing for adventure. Lost in daydreams of time-
lessly beautiful French women, I ran the hot water, climbed
back in the tub, and soothed my wounds.

My reverie ended abruptly when I realized I had only fifteen
minutes to dress and get back to the office for a legislative
staff meeting. This was something I could not miss, so I ran
more than a few red lights, parked my well-worn Volkswagen
Beetle on the grass outside the Capitol, and raced up, taking
the elevator marked "Senators Only," which was fortunately
operated by a friend. I made it, though just barely.

Following the meeting, I returned to the office, where I
found my inbox filled with a new stack of Vietnam letters and
requests for constituent tours. In addition to my other du-
ties, I served as the senator's tour guide in chief, shepherd-
ing constituents through the Capitol while briefing them on
its history. My script included a reference to the design of the
Capitol, which was derived from the Paris Pantheon, the east
side of the Louvre, and the dome at Les Invalides. I would
explain to each group the French influence on the layout of
Washington, DC, designed by a Frenchman, Pierre L'Enfant.
When I had time, I would research more about the French influence on Washington and America and add to the script. The
more I read, the more excitement I felt about going to Paris.

The day was hectic, with three tours scheduled after lunch.
As I spoke to the visiting groups about French influence on
the Capitol, my thoughts wandered to preparing for my year
abroad, selling the idea to my parents, finding and applying for

a study program, and clearing the trip with the draft board. There was much work to be done, and thinking about it and working on it took my mind off the war, the draft, the protests, and the race riots.

That evening, at the Library of Congress, I found a book about Jefferson in Paris. He wrote, "A walk about Paris will provide lessons in history, beauty, and in the point of life." I was hungry for all three. I asked the library staff to pull books on Americans in Paris and spent the next few afternoons comfortably perched in one of the library's cozy window nooks, my feet up on the desk, reading about the unique allure of Paris. I also gathered my textbooks from three years of French in high school and studied the grammar and vocabulary as if I were cramming for a final. I bought a set of French language tapes and polished my pronunciation. I imagined myself speaking French on a Paris street, ordering food at a café, reading the street signs and taking the Métro.

For two centuries Paris was where young American artists and intellectuals had sought an inspirational rite of passage, drawn by the intoxicating appeal of the ancient city, which had served as the cultural, political, and scientific capital of the old world. I read about the travels to Paris by Franklin, Adams, and Jefferson in the eighteenth century, and by Charles Sumner, John Singer Sargent, Augustus Saint-Gaudens, and Samuel Morse in the nineteenth century. I reveled in the powerful mystique of the "lost generation," the Paris of F. Scott Fitzgerald, Ernest Hemingway, John Steinbeck, Ezra Pound, Sherwood Anderson, Waldo Peirce, Sylvia Beach, T. S. Eliot, and Gertrude Stein . . .

The epoch may have changed, but the allure lived on, no less strong a gravitational force than in generations gone by. Paris was a place I needed to go even if I could not fully understand why. Perhaps it was the writer in me searching for inspiration, or the nascent political activist craving historical perspective, but mostly it was a place to escape an America that felt increasingly in disarray.

Chapter 3

Interlude

It was up to me to turn the inspiration of studying in Paris into reality, and that meant navigating parental permission, transfer requirements, program selection, vaccinations, passport procedures, and, in 1968, a draft board review. It also meant resigning from the senator's staff, which I really did not want to do. The more I worked to prepare for the trip, the more excited I became, although not everybody whose support I needed initially shared my sentiments.

My father looked at me and without hesitation said, "No way." His thought was that I could get just as good an education in the United States as anywhere else in the world, and he pointed out again and again that the president had asked Americans to curtail travel to help with the nation's worsening balance of payments.

One night during a weekend home, I entered the den and found him watching the news. The reporter announced that the Vietnam War was costing the United States $30 billion a year. He looked at me and pointed to the black-and-white TV screen as the reporter dryly spoke about how the war was financed by the sale of gold reserves, which were now at less than one-half their postwar record level and fast declining. He went on to report the $3.6 billion annual balance of payments deficit was considered so enormous that some economists speculated about it destabilizing the world economy and setting off a worldwide depression.

"See, I told you! Where's your sense of patriotism?" he demanded, conveniently avoiding the need to admit that he did not want to spend the money on sending me abroad. Then he got up from his chair and sped off, as he usually did when criticizing me—hit-and-run. He had to collect money from a jukebox in a bar in Hoboken, so he hurried out, wearing his usual khaki pants and red plaid shirt. I was left sitting in the den thinking I might never get to Paris unless I could convince him it was not unpatriotic and would cost no more than if I stayed in school in Washington.

What a candyass! But I've got to get him on board. I've got to get out of here!

I prepared a detailed budget showing that with the lower tuition cost at the American Institute, the good exchange rate for the French franc, and the student housing available through the school, my father would save money compared with the cost of college at home, even accounting for third-class round-trip passage by boat. I presented the budget to him and to my mother. I think the cost figures caught his attention, but not as much as the pictures I showed them both of the Che Guevara posters plastered all over the walls of the student center at George Washington during the last antiwar demonstration. The campus police had to intervene, and one student fell in the melee and broke his leg.

"That's sickening," my father said, looking at the pictures. "That's what I pay tuition for? To send you to school with posters of communist revolutionaries?"

"What about the boy who broke his leg?" my mother asked.

"He's in the hospital," I said.

"Irwin, it's dangerous there!" my mother said. "Maybe Paris is safer, far away from this madness, and you'll save money!"

"Well . . ."

"We'd be the only couple in town with a son studying in Europe," she said. "I think those bankers at Trenton Trust you want to approve your loan will be impressed," she added.

"You think so?"

"Only very successful men can afford to send their sons to Europe to study," she said, casting him a look that was equally affectionate and flattering.

That did it.

It was important to both my parents to provide their children with the education they did not have themselves, but they also enjoyed letting others know that they could afford to do so. Paris fit the bill, and my father could revel in what my carefully prepared budget revealed. He was saving money!

"I want this for you, Robbie," my mother said later that same afternoon, "but I can't bear to see you go so far away." She looked at me lovingly, her brown hair coiffed up in a bun, her face beaming as she stood in the doorway to the kitchen. She had a terrific sense of style and looked fashionable even when dressed for housework. "You'll have to send me some of those fashion books from Paris."

I was happy at last to have parental approval, but in 1968 a year of study abroad could not happen without the blessing of the draft board. The day after I'd won my parents' approval, the Selective Service announced that three hundred and two thousand men were to be drafted into the army, an increase of seventy-two thousand over 1967. That figure was later increased to forty-eight thousand a month. In addition, the Johnson administration abolished the student deferment for graduate studies and announced that one hundred and fifty thousand graduate students would be drafted in the fiscal year beginning in July 1968. This did not bode well for me.

I walked into the office of Selective Service Draft Board Number 35, on Front Street in Trenton a loyal, patriotic American with respectfully short hair, beard responsibly trimmed at my mother's insistence, and impeccably attired in a new charcoal-gray, three-piece pinstriped suit. For that final touch of respectability, I carried a slightly worn leather attaché case. It was a gift given by a customer to my father, who wouldn't be caught dead with a real leather bag, preferring the old, cracking, vinyl-covered briefcase of the same shape and size he had used forever.

"Leather bags are for your uncle Hymie in the big office," he would say. "Not for me!" He worked out of a cubicle just behind Hymie's secretary, Rose. Hymie, his oldest brother, was the CEO of the family vending company, the guy who dealt with the banks and the suppliers while my father wrestled with the bar owners, bowling alley managers and restaurant operators, collecting money and making payouts and loans from the coins in the jukeboxes, cigarette, and candy machines. He was the street guy, and that was how he saw himself. My mother couldn't get him to put on a suit, much less buy a new one in the latest style.

No such inhibitions affected me. I strutted into the draft office, expecting to be treated with the deference accorded to members of the leather-bag-toting establishment. I wore a red tie, just like Senator Hankie's, and of course a Senate lapel pin, which I had bought in the Capitol gift shop to signal my importance as a Senate staffer. I looked calm on the outside, but my heart raced and my palms were soaked in sweat.

The draft board office was barren, with creaking wood floors seriously lacking in varnish, camouflage-green walls like an army barracks, and a few scattered surplus wooden chairs—a bleak landscape. A heavyset, rude-looking woman dressed in a calf-length military uniform sitting behind a large, unpainted, scratched-up wooden desk beckoned me to take a number from a small gray metal dispenser on a table by the door and to sit down on one of the chairs and wait until my number was called. She looked at me with a coldness and insensitivity that could only have been matched by a medieval henchman. Everywhere her face seemed to come to a rigid point without the slightest flow of grace or charm. Her words were caustic—spewed, not spoken—and penetrated my ears with ferocity.

Surrounding me on the hard, plain chairs were gentlemen of obvious distinction with local police and truant officers. Nervously combing their ducktail haircuts with a passion for order in the rear, where they could not see, each grumbled his circumstance of woe to another, exchanging moral support and on occasion partaking in group laughter. The mention of anything that, however remotely, served as an excuse for the release of nervous tension became riotously funny. I felt like I was in a foreign land where I didn't speak the language.

Towering above the scene—the only concession to decorum on the drab, vacant back wall, and a complement to it—was a princely photograph of Lyndon Johnson standing erect by his chair in a Louis XIV pose, a *l' État, c'est moi* look on his face. I recalled the story Allen had told me about LBJ. A military aide offered him directions at an air force base, pointing straight ahead, and told him, "There's your helicopter, Mr. President," and LBJ snapped back, "Son, they're all my helicopters!" I looked at the portrait, imagining the moment he might have posed for such a picture, a thousand more pressing matters on his mind. You could see the impatience in his eyes.

Suddenly, my number was called, and I awkwardly rose before the intimidating stare of this magisterial woman as she approached me. No names were used here, not mine, not hers. I felt lightheaded.

"This way," she barked, spinning her flabby body in military fashion and marching back to her desk.

I followed and sat down in the metal folding chair next to the desk, and in a quivering voice I began to present my case for a deferment. As I spoke, my eyes were drawn to the peeling varnish on the side of her desk, which bore a distinct resemblance to her flaky skin. I could feel the idea of Paris, whose time I thought had come, beginning to slip away.

"Hello, my name is Robbie Samberg, from Trenton, and I work in Senator Hankie's office in Washington," I said with feigned confidence. I paused to absolutely no effect. "I am planning to spend next year on a study program in Paris. I would like to report this to the draft board and to make arrangements with the board for my departure."

"Here is the application form for a deferment," she snapped, completely unimpressed with my Capitol Hill credentials. "Young man, I don't care who you work for. You're not going anywhere until this form is approved."

"Okay, I'll fill out the form, mam," I responded, trying to regain my composure.

Stay cool, Robbie! She looked at me, eyebrows raised, as if to deny me the privilege of acting like a perfect gentleman. I sat, shifting uncomfortably in the metal chair, and filled out the form, wondering how many healthy males this woman must have castrated in her day.

"Nice weather today," I meekly volunteered, pasting on a flimsy smile and handing her the completed form.

She carefully reviewed it, along with other papers in my draft file, finally lifting her head from what seemed to be an interminable pause, "You will be notified about the Board's decision in three weeks."

"Mam," I inquired, "what are the criteria for granting—?"

"We don't disclose or discuss how we make decisions, young man. There's a war going on, you know. If you are approved, you will be able to leave the country in time to begin school in September. Take a copy of this form, too," she added in a scolding voice, handing me the paper. "It's for your school to fill out and send to us as proof that you are enrolled in college." She raised her voice at the word "proof" and gave me a look of suspicion that instantly accused, tried, and convicted me of draft evasion.

"Proof?"

"Yes, we need proof that your body is enrolled in the college."

"Mam, I intend to enroll at the American Institute in Paris, and I will give them the form," I responded. *And mam,* I thought as I rose from the chair, *should I lose a limb somewhere in my travels, I will be happy to report to you immediately its whereabouts.*

As I turned to leave, I caught a glimpse of the locals, still standing at the back of the room, whose numbers had swelled, and eyed a group of Negroes who had just walked in and stood as far as they could from the whites. *These are the guys who will be going to war.* Unlike me, they probably could not afford college, much less a study year abroad.

My mother was waiting for me outside the draft office. She asked me how it went and I told her I had no idea. When I removed my jacket, she glanced at the wet patches around my armpits.

"Oh, I can see it went well," she said. Earlier that day President Johnson had announced another escalation of the war. That night, we had family over for dinner and my cousin Michael bragged about his plan to enlist in the army to help defeat the communists.

"Just hand me an M-16 and I'll show those commies," he said while munching on a well-done hamburger. "We need to stop them from taking over the South. If we don't—"

"That's great." My father patted Michael on the back and scowled at me.

"Michael, it's not that simple," I said.

"Oh, it will be really simple," he responded, lifting his arms as if aiming and shooting a rifle. He was a tough guy, football player, and all-around jock who was as good-looking as he was brash.

"Michael, this war is more complicated. It's a struggle that goes way back to a history of colonialism and the occupation of Vietnam by the Chinese, the Japanese, the French, and now by America."

"Oh, there he goes again, my educated son," my father said. "You think too much and you talk too much, Robbie."

"But I have studied—"

"And you are dead wrong."

I shut my mouth and silently prayed for a positive response from the draft board. *I will spend 1968 in the safety of the City of Lights. I will! I will!*

As the antiwar movement grew, my reaction was to read every book I could find about the history of Vietnam. I threw myself into a frenzied effort to figure out why this war happened and how to end it, and my growing collection of books about Vietnam was a testimony to the effort. I bought, read, and highlighted each book, my favorite the biography of Ho Chi Minh by Jean Lacouture, which I read again and again until the book disintegrated and its pages fell from the binding. I studied the war and wrote articles about it for the university newspaper the *Hatchet*. That's how I found solace in the tumult. I avoided the chaos on the streets and the mockery I would endure at home if I openly joined the protests. Paris would be my shelter from this storm, a shelter of beauty, civilization, culture, and light. *I will spend 1968 in the safety of the City of Lights. I will! I will!*

I worried about the draft board decision. The news from Vietnam continued to be bad, and the president steadily increased the buildup of American troops.

"Not looking good," my mother told me one evening a few weeks later as she slid pasta into boiling water, preparing her delicious spaghetti and meatball supper. She was worrying, too, and praying her son would be off to Paris instead of the jungles of Vietnam.

"Hey, there's a letter here from the Selective Service," my sister Dottie said as she came in the side door to the kitchen clutching the day's mail, which my mother usually brought in but that day had forgotten.

"It smells good," she added, lifting the lid of the pot with the slow-cooking tomato sauce.

I grabbed the letter from Dottie, and my mother hurried over and we sat down at the table. She snatched the envelope from my hand and ripped it open, shielding the contents from me as she read.

"So?" I asked.

She looked up and smiled. "You're going to Paris!"

My father came home an hour later, changed into his home clothes—baggy pants and plaid shirt—perused the letter, and after complaining about the brown spots in the salad my mother had prepared, said, "Good thing I already told the boys at the bank I was sending you." "Oh, so that's the only reason you're happy about it," I said.

"No, I'm saving money, too, right?" He smiled.

A few weeks later the letter came from the George Washington University admissions office. My transfer was approved. My transcripts had been reviewed and accepted by the American Institute, and I was cleared to become the first student to study abroad under the new exchange program between the schools.

With the draft board and school transfer approved, the next chore was deciding what to pack. I was determined to bring as much of what I conceived to be modern America as possible. This included four pairs of new shoes, a present from my cousin in the shoe business; three new suits, one of which was the three-piece pinstriped beauty I wore to the draft board; nine packages of brand-new, shiny-white Fruit of the Loom underwear, three to a pack; a powerful shortwave portable radio; a stereo record player with a full set of discs; my Kodak Brownie 127 camera and a year's supply of film; my entire library of books on the Vietnam War; and because I had read that the toilet paper in Paris was especially coarse, sixty-four rolls of extra-soft, two-ply Charmin, all carefully and strategically packed in two large steamer trunks.

"Mom, be careful what you put on top of my tape recorder. It will break!" We sat together in my room and packed the trunks. I was bringing the recorder and my Brownie 127 to document my experiences and to send tapes and photos back to my parents. *One day I'll use this material to write a book about my year abroad*—a bestseller. I fantasized about book signings at mall bookstores throughout New Jersey.

"You'll mature in Paris, Robbie," my mom said again as we stood together in my room, the trunks now nearly filled, except for the last-minute items, which were still strewn about the room. You will come home a man," she repeated, speaking as much to herself as to me and tossing me a look of affection.

"Mother, enough already."

That night we had yet another heated exchange at dinner about long-haired war protesters, my father warning me to keep my hair short and neat while I was away at school. He hated the protesters and how they dressed and especially their long hair. The more he ranted, the more I prayed the day of my departure would come quickly. I couldn't wait to get out of there.

I decided to spend most of the summer in DC in order to continue working at Senator Hankie's office and to avoid the strife at home, except for the occasional weekend and holiday. It was hot there, muggy hot and, having sold my car, I would ride my bike to work each day, arriving soaked in sweat and happy to jump into the office bathroom shower, where I left a change of clothes hanging on a hook on the back of the door. I would emerge from the bathroom a picture of sprightliness and head over to Rosemary's desk to check on my tasks for the day.

On my last day of work, an especially hot August morning, Rosemary greeted me in her customary curt manner, handed me a list of constituents scheduled for tours, and a final stack of correspondence with responses due by close of business. Just as I turned to head toward my cubicle, she invited me to a staff meeting at 4:30 p.m. in the senator's office, warning me not to be late.

I had a lot of mixed feelings that last day. Sadness about leaving work that I enjoyed so much, excitement as the day of my departure approached and regret about the way my relationship with Andi had ended. I thought about calling her to see if she had calmed down and might be willing to talk about what had happened. I wanted to apologize and say goodbye, but I couldn't quite get there. The day was exceptionally busy and the senator's guests for the tours were not merely constituents, but his sister, brother-in-law, and their children from Indianapolis. I allowed them to linger in the Capitol for as long as they liked, which put me behind schedule.

I skipped lunch to get the correspondence completed, consulting only briefly with Allen about the draft of a letter to Roger Branigin, the governor of Indiana.

"He's a tiger," Allen warned, "so you better have it right," he added, waving the letter as he handed it back to me.

"It's good, don't worry. What's the meeting about?" It was rare for Rosemary to call a staff meeting in the senator's office.

"Just some office stuff I think."

I wanted to have some time to say goodbye to Allen, but he was slammed that day as well, so I thought I would call him and stop by his place before I left town.

I continued to work through the afternoon at my cubical and at about 4:20 p.m. walked to the kitchen to grab an ice tea. That's when I noticed that the office was exceptionally quiet for a Friday. *Where is everybody?* I made my way through the empty cubicles, down the central corridor to the senator's interior office door, the one that connected his office to Rosemary's workspace just outside. She was gone, too. The door was closed. I looked at my watch and it said 4:30 p.m. so I walked over to the senator's door and opened it.

"Bon Voyage!"

The staff cried out, gathered on the royal blue carpet facing me. Everyone held up a glass. Rosemary rushed over, handed me a glass and filled it with French champagne. "To Robbie's adventures in Paris!" Allen exclaimed.

"To Paris!" the staffed responded.

"The city of light is about to go dark," he added, teasing me in his customary manner, followed by laughter.

Next it was Rosemary: "To the best intern on Capitol Hill! You'll always have a place here when you return. I just hope they are not hiring at the French National Assembly so we get you back!"

And lastly the senator himself entered the room and came over to shake my hand. "Good luck in Paris, my boy. You stay out of trouble over there!"

"I will, Senator! Thank you, Senator! Thank you!"

After that, the days flew by, but the memory of the office bon-voyage party lingered. I was unaccustomed to praise. I never got it at home, especially from my father and it felt good. I vacated my dorm room and returned home, where I was soon to experience a second bon-voyage party, this one organized by my parents, an extravaganza held at our home, which was carefully prepared for the grand occasion. Nearly one hundred people were invited and came to say goodbye to me, most of whom did not know me. My parents took this as an opportunity to show off the education they were providing their son, so they invited everyone on their lists, especially those they sought to impress.

They came from everywhere—from my father's business, from the temple, from our old neighborhood—to devour my mother's trays of smoked salmon, caught by my father and smoked by his key employee, Sandy Kandrack, to drink my father's vodka Gibsons and to offer me inane advice about the French and especially about French women. It was incredible how many self-proclaimed experts on French women attended the party, filling my head with thoughts about their beauty, their sculpted facial features and thin waistlines. There was also advice, usually whispered to the sounds of tinkling ice cubes and couched amidst clouds of cigar smoke, to beware of French wheeler-dealers, who might otherwise cheat me. Such was my introduction to the myths that abound in America about the French . . . especially the most prevalent one—that they were cold and didn't like Americans. I had never heard such things before.

"They don't really like us!" warned a familiar voice. "They'll take you for everything, Robbie boy. You got to watch the bastards."

I had to clear the smoke surrounding his head by waving my right hand before I could see it was Uncle Sidney speaking. He was never without a cigar in his mouth, inspired, I'm told, by wartime memories of Winston Churchill. He looked a bit like Churchill: the portly stance, ruddy cheeks, slightly crooked mouth. A top hat and cane would make him a dead ringer.

He was the family expert on French affairs, since he had visited Paris after the war, awaiting a military transport back to the States. Questioned more closely, Sidney revealed that his experience with the French was meager at best. Quite a wheeler-dealer himself, he admitted that his entire time in France was spent at the bar at Le Bourget Airport. This was our French expert.

I had read that food was important in French culture. They dined rather than ate—more a sensual experience than a filling up of the tank—but food was also a big deal in my family, although not in a good way. My mother was always talking about dieting and weight. If any of us gained weight, she would be all over us, especially Dottie, whose nightly dessert parties at some point crossed the line from the amusing to the unhealthy. And then there was my older sister, Lorraine, whose family survival tactic was to eat as little as possible. She would pick at her food, leaving most of it on the plate.

In 1968, the most popular female model was the five-foot-six-inch Lesley Hornby, who, at 112 pounds, had earned the nickname Twiggy. To Ellen, Lorraine, and Dottie, Twiggy was the supermodel of choice. Lorraine jealously guarded the three issues of *Vogue*—April, July, and November—which featured her on the cover. She also carried a Twiggy lunch box, wrote with a Twiggy pen, and applied fake Twiggy lashes to her eyelids. All this was devastating to Dottie, who had no chance in the competition for thin.

By four o'clock the party was over and the house empty, except for my sisters, parents, and my two best friends, Howie and Ricky, whom I invited to sleep over and accompany us to the boat in New York City the next morning. With the house quiet at last, it started to sink in that the very next morning I would depart for the other side of the Atlantic.

As I lumbered down the stairs to my bedroom on the ground floor, Howie and Ricky in tow, I passed my mother, still cleaning up. "I'm going to miss you, Mom!"

I reached out to embrace her. She had been rock solid all night about my going away, but, hugging me goodbye on the stairs, she let go. We embraced and cried, and Dottie, putting down her bag of sweets, came out of her room to join us and she cried, too. Lorraine didn't cry, but she joined us for a rare group hug.

My father saw us on the stairs as he disassembled the dining room table, paused momentarily and demanded, "What time are we leaving tomorrow?"

Chapter 4

Boat Ride to Cherbourg

The next morning was a kaleidoscope of confusion. Everyone in the house burned excess energy getting in everyone else's way. Mother, Father, two sisters, and friends scurried about, all attempting to take charge at once.

Our maid, Mary Anderson, came in early to help. She'd had a benign influence in the house ever since my mother hired her as our nanny just after Lorraine was born, and while my parents were often busy with their business and social schedules, she was always there to offer an understanding ear to us kids. She was a large woman, her hair up in a bun, covered in a white head cloth, always a smile on her round black face, except when any of us stepped out of line, when she would bark us back into place without mercy. You didn't want to be on the receiving end of her scolding, but she was always fair and always loving. She was really the disciplinarian of the household, admired and respected by us all, and she was the only Negro person I knew.

Despite the chaos that morning, under Mrs. Anderson's watchful eye every item on the final packing list was identified, checked off, and locked away in the two steamer trunks, and we lugged the heavy trunks outside and placed them in the back of my father's yellow Chevy station wagon.

When at last it was time to leave, we traveled in two cars, Mom, Dad, and my sisters in my father's car, and Ricky, Howie, and I in Howie's car. It was a hot and humid morning, and Howie's car did not have air-conditioning, so we sweated the entire way to New York City. I was relieved to be riding with friends instead of with the family. It would spare me the bickering between my parents and the hard work in my customary role as marital referee.

The ride from Trenton went by quickly, and before long we caught the first sight of the Queen Elizabeth in the distance. The red stacks of the great ship stood out against the skyline at that point on Route 7 where drivers got an unobstructed view of the city. We had passed this view many times on family outings to New York to have Chinese food and see a movie. From here, the ship appeared small, like a toy model glistening on the horizon. I strained to keep it in my sight as the car moved on and the skyline disappeared behind us.

As the car sped toward the docks, I found myself thinking about Andi again. I had never reached out to her, and this still bothered me. *I should have spoken to her. I should have explained. I should have apologized.*

Andi was the first non-Jewish girl I had ever dated. My parents warned against bringing home a Shiksa, as if they were a dangerous species. But my experience told me otherwise. Andi took care of me. She valued my ideas and my work. She went out of her way for me. She listened to me. She made me laugh. She was the first girl I knew who enjoyed ripping off her clothes, who couldn't wait to get her hands and her lips all over me—zero inhibition—and despite what I read in my well-hidden copies of *Playboy,* I was never sure such girls really existed.

Here I was about to board the ship that would take me to Paris, and I was still feeling guilty.

We boarded the *Elizabeth* through a tunnel ramp, at the end of which was one of the ship's many ornate lobbies. Nobody spoke as we boarded. None of us had ever set foot on an ocean liner before, and I think we were all feeling the awe and excitement. Once on board, I had my ticket checked by a tall, slender, mustached officer dressed in a white uniform. He directed us to a corridor, which in turn led to an elevator, which in turn led to another corridor, which in turn led to a side corridor, where with some luck and additional assistance we at last found my cabin.

This was a third-class cabin, the cheapest on the ship, or "steerage." It looked like a converted mechanical closet, heavily painted angular iron supports all around, gunmetal gray, with very little to soften the look. My sisters, two friends, and both parents stuffed themselves half in and half out of the cabin for some final words over a glass of champagne, dutifully poured by a cabin steward. This was the *Queen Elizabeth of the White Star Line,* so even third-class cabins had white-gloved stewards though the champagne in steerage was sparkling wine.

The steward reentered the cabin, squeezing himself among us to offer some hors d'oeuvres. He had a smile and a kind word for everyone as he passed out the goodies. My mother loved all this. She could hardly wait to tell her friends about the ship's White Star Service, even as she snapped at Dottie, "Don't eat too many" right in front of Ricky. I glanced at my sister's face, and she looked like she was going to die right there. My father said very little, which was typical of him in the presence of the entire family. What conversation he had was almost exclusively with Howie, whom he favored and would lavish with attention, to my dismay.

"I'll bet there's Roebling steel in this ship," he whispered to Howie, a distant relative of the Roebling's, slapping him on the back and adding a compliment about Howie's pastel-blue sweater.

"Dad, I think the ship was built in England."

"So?"

"I don't think they would have used American steel."

"You don't know anything about shipbuilding, Robbie," he said with disdain.

"I think Robbie is right about that, Mr. Samberg," Howie interjected.

"Well, then, I stand corrected," my father said. "You would know these things, Howie!"

Of course, this was not a private cabin, and just after the steward left, in marched my roommate for the voyage, a robust, red-bearded Scotsman, fiftyish, with glowing eyes and an infectious smile.

"Hello, lad, my name is O'Higgins, Bernie O'Higgins. What's the matter, little chap? Why aren't you smiling? Plenty of women to be had on this ship, that's for sure. Why don't you come up and have a drink with me?"

My mother looked shocked and cast a disapproving glance at O'Higgins, who appeared not to notice.

"Irwin, I told you to get him a private cabin," she whispered, irritated, her voice resonating in the small space enough for everyone to hear.

I hadn't realized that I wasn't smiling, but O'Higgins sure exposed that in blunt fashion.

"Well, my parents are here and—"

"Jewish, aren't you? Ah, I can tell a Jew a mile away, but don't worry, I love Jews," he proclaimed. And, turning to my mother, "Don't you worry. I won't let him fall in love with a

Shiksa, not on my watch," he said, saluting her. "I'll see you all later."

My mother's jaw dropped, her shock turning to anger.

"Irwin, will you please do something about this . . ."

Bouncing about with impunity to his every outlandish word, O'Higgins grabbed something from his bag on the lower berth, turned, and abruptly left. Before my father had a chance to react, the steward again entered to announce that all non-passengers had to leave the ship.

"Well," my father said, glancing at his watch and putting his hand on Howie's shoulder, "it's time."

He had been looking at his watch for the past half hour and appeared anxious to leave. He glanced at my mother as if there were nothing further he could do about the roommate.

"Give him some money, Irwin," my mother snapped.

He dutifully handed me a sealed Chase Bank envelope and pulled a fifty-dollar bill from his wallet.

"In the envelope is an international money order which you can convert to French francs at the Chase branch in Paris. It's for your rent, food and spending money. Open a checking account at the branch and pull out what you need each week."

"And let us know if you need more and your father will send it to you," my mother added, eliciting a look of shock on my father's face.

"Of course I will," he said, looking at my mother for a whiff of approval.

I guess I won't have to worry much about money on this voyage!

"And give this fifty to the steward if there's anything you need on the ship. They dance to the tune of money," he said. "Good luck, Robbie." He paused a moment, then disappeared into the hallway.

Mom took time for hugs but tossed me a guilt bomb about how lonely the house would be without me. My sisters emerged from their respective states of self-absorption just long enough for each to give me a dutiful hug and kiss goodbye. Howie and Ricky smiled, awkwardly feigned a hug, and followed my father, mother, and sisters out into the hallway.

Suddenly, they were all gone, and I sat in the room staring at my bags on the upper berth and feeling a little lost. My mouth was dry; my cup of sparkling wine empty. I wondered, why no excitement? Instead, I felt anxious and alone. The room was silent except for the creaking of pipes. I could feel the vibrations as the ship's engines started. I could hear the whistle blow many decks above and decided to leave the windowless space where I would be sleeping.

I stood on the deck, sipping a sparkling wine as the great ship wound its way up the Hudson River, surrounded by New York's skyscrapers. It was a sight to behold. As I leaned on the rail, the wind rustling my clothes, the sun warming me and illuminating the scene, my mood at last shifted to excitement and anticipation. I remembered from high school the picture of the *Isle-de-France* in my second-year French textbook, not to be confused with the larger *France*, later to become the *Norway*. *Isle-de-France* was a sleek steamship, the picture of which, also on the Hudson, with New York in the background, was used to instruct on the vocabulary of travel. I thought about how my French teacher, Madame Gautier, born in Nice, would pronounce *paqueboat Île-de-France*. It had such a nice ring, replete with her French pride in their national engineering prowess. She would always compliment me on my authentic-sounding French accent.

"You sound like a Frenchman," she would say. "*Magnifique!*"

By now I was fired up, and a little tipsy from the wine. I decided to explore the ship. I climbed the exterior stairs to the highest point on the boat on the upper deck, from where you could see the giant stacks belching black smoke into the air. The sea winds blew stronger. I stood there bracing myself on the rail and looked out at the endless swells of the sea. I imagined the waves crashing against the French coast still six days away.

On my way back to the cabin I happened upon a metal door which had apparently been unintentionally left ajar. Overcome with curiosity, I yanked it open and quickly found myself in the inner sanctum of the first-class steam room. Everything on the ship was divided by class, and as a student on a cheap third-class ticket, I was not entitled to be where I was.

A Chinese steward in a red jacket approached me and bowed respectfully. "Right this way Mr. . . ."

"Samberg," I quickly added.

I dutifully followed him, not knowing what to do and never having been in a steam room. He led me to a small but ornate compartment and drew back a red velvet curtain with finesse.

"You may leave your clothes in here, Mr. Samberg," he said as he again artfully drew the curtain and waited outside for me to disrobe, leaving behind a thick, white terry-cloth towel with an embroidered gold White Star emblem. Once undressed I emerged wrapped in the towel, and he led me to the first in a succession of steam rooms, each one progressively hotter and more densely filled with hot steam accented with menthol aromas.

The first room was comfortably warm, with cushioned seats and a magazine rack, where I found the June issue of *Life* magazine. I read the cover story about Barbra Streisand's live concert in Central Park before a hundred thirty-five thousand fans.My mother had begged my father to take her.

"Fuck you, Irwin," I heard her say under her breath. It was the first time I had heard her curse. She had offered to have the concert serve as her birthday, anniversary, and Chanukah presents all in one!

"I don't do crowds in Central Park, even for Streisand," he said.

"But it's for me!"

"Not even for you!"

The steward returned to escort me to the next steam room, which was smaller and too hot for magazines, and after a few minutes I began to feel faint. I wondered how I was going to extricate myself from this situation without blowing my cover. Suddenly, the steward returned again and smiled as he led me out of the torture chamber.

"Now room three." He handed me a glass of water with what looked like a cucumber in it. I gulped it down, nearly imbibing the cucumber, my body craving the hydration.

"A third room? How nice," I mumbled, trying to think of some way to excuse myself, but alas, his rigid manner and quick pace did not leave an opening, so there I was, closeted in room number three as the faithful steward turned up the steam. Now I was really wilting—no, burning—in what felt like purgatory and, after a few moments, hell. I have no idea what the temperature was, but I felt like a turkey roasting in an oven.

It seemed like an eternity until the steward returned, bestowing upon me that certain obsequiousness to which those who paid many hundreds of dollars for first-class passage were apparently entitled. He helped me up and steadied me as we walked to the final room, which thankfully had no steam. It was the massage room, where I climbed onto a long narrow table and lay face down just as an attractive woman in her mid-twenties entered to rub my body with scented oil. I caught a glimpse of her before I placed my head into the cradle at the end of the table. She stepped right up and without a word placed her hands on my lower back, holding them in a stationary position as if to gauge the energy running through my body before beginning the massage. Slowly she worked her fingers deeply into my back and shoulders, asking in a whispered French accent if the pressure was okay.

"Okay."

This was my first professional massage, but I felt compelled to pretend it was not, thinking this must be a routine experience for wealthy first-class passengers. It was as intimidating as it was relaxing, but I mustered the courage to speak to the masseuse, whose look had intrigued me and who by now was working her way down my back to my anxiously awaiting gluteus maximus.

"My personal masseuse was not able to join us for the voyage, so I'm glad I found you."

No response.

"Yes, she had a family commitment and could not come."

Here I am lying again to make hay with a woman, just like I did with Andi! Robbie! The inner voice admonished.

Thankfully, she again did not respond, but her hands were speaking clearly enough, working their magic on every square inch of my buttocks without inhibition, and I loved what they were saying. If Andi's touch was a warm, welcoming instrument, this gal's hands were the full orchestra playing the *1812 Overture*.

Soon it was time to turn over, which I accomplished while she held up a towel to shield me from view, quickly laying it back down once I'd flipped and sliding a pillow under my head and a roller beneath my knees.

"Are you comfortable, monsieur?" she asked, her accent melodic.

"If your touch were a person, I think I would be falling in love," I blurted, eliciting a giggle. *At least that is no lie!* I asked her for her name.

"Christine René," she said with another giggle. "I am so happy you are pleased with my work."

"Yes, very happy," I responded, wondering how far her hands would drop below my stomach, which she was caressing with aplomb. *So, this is first class*, I thought.

"How is the pressure now?" she asked as she lightened up to a soft, flicking tingle and moved her fingers around the edges of my stomach, dipping to just above my hairline.

"Ah . . . fine, very fine!"

"What is your name?"

"Robbie."

"Well, Robbeee, my contract is over when we reach Cherbourg, and then there won't be any rules."

"Rules?"

"*Oui*, I am not supposed to become—how do you say?—familiar with the passengers."

"Familiar?"

"You know, to date. I have not been permitted to do this for the past two years at sea. It's the rules."

"Have you always followed the rules?"

"I am a good girl, Robbeee, so yes, I have followed the rules." She giggled again.

"And now that you are leaving?"

Another giggle. "Well." She sighed and moved her sensual touch to my upper right thigh.

"Maybe weee can forget the rules tonight. If you like, I will meet you on the cabin deck by the lifeboat number three at midnight."

"Okay, yes," I said, my arousal boldly evident.

"It's time to turn over again, Robbeee."

She lifted the towel, holding it high and giggling again as I awkwardly obeyed, finding it difficult to position myself on my stomach in my current state. I managed, and she began to work her hands for a second round with my lower back and buttocks, which were now exposed. She evidently saw no further need for the towel. She continued to work her hands deep into my muscles, and I could feel my body relax.

When the massage ended, Christine helped me up, and I could see her fully for the first time. She was beautiful, slender, with long brown hair falling to her shoulders, breasts full but not oversized, filling out her light-blue uniform as if it were for a Playmate photo shoot. She gave me a look that spoke volumes about what a night it would be. *Here's my real-life "Playboy Advisor" story.*

"*À bientot.*" She smiled.

"*À bientot,*" I said, returning the smile.

"Good accent, Monsieur Robbee! Very good!"

I showered, dressed, and left via the front door to the spa, where I was greeted by the steward, who inquired what sitting I preferred for dinner. I choose the eight o'clock, late for me, but evidently an acceptable European hour for dinner. He handed me a gilded card with my name written neatly at the center.

"Present this card to the maître d' in the first-class dining room at 8 p.m.," he instructed. "And thank you for visiting our steam rooms today." He offered a final bow.

I hurried back to the third-class area and descended to the metal closet where I lived. I was alone again, but this time more relaxed than I had ever felt. My body moved in slow motion, my breathing was deep, my mind clear, and I was excited about Christine's come-on and her invitation. If this was how all French ladies behaved, maybe good old Sidney was right. I could not wait to find out. I pulled out my gray three-piece suit, which I thought would be appropriate dress for dinner in first class. If I couldn't sleep the part, I could certainly dress and eat the part, I thought, bravely but foolishly deciding to continue the charade. *What can they do? Arrest me? Throw me in the brig? No, they will just send me back to third class, so why not take the risk? The door to the first-class steam room was open for a reason, and I want to see where this good fortune will lead next.*

Just then, before my next thought, which would likely have been of my father admonishing me that dining in first class was stealing, I heard the key inserted into the room door, and when it opened, there was Bernie, a blond bombshell on his right arm and an opened bottle of champagne in his left hand. The blond carried the glasses, and it wasn't long before they both slid onto the lower bunk, the champagne spilling, and the lady's skimpy top askew—or should I say half-off? —as Bernie's charm and his hands worked overtime. This was clearly not their first bottle this evening, and they offered me a glass as I hurried to get ready, trying to ignore the show.

"Here you go, lad," the blond said, reaching up to hand me the glass. "My name is Tina," she said seductively, her words slurring.

"Hey, thanks," I said. "I'm Robbie, and I'll be leaving in a few minutes," I added, refusing the glass.

Bernie and Tina exchanged glances and giggles.

"Yes, I'm invited to first class to dine tonight," I said, holding up the three-piece suit.

"First class? Way to go, my boy, way to go!" Bernie raised his glass to congratulate me.

Of course I neglected to mention it was a charade and a scam.

I stepped into the small bathroom to wash up and put on the suit. Moments later I emerged.

"Goodbye."

I waved as I walked to the cabin door, but Tina and Bernie did not respond. They were going all the way. Bernie managed to turn around just enough to wave back. It was an image right out of Playboy.

I headed up to the first-class area of the ship. The décor improved dramatically as I approached the ornate dining room, the carpet thicker, the wall sconces gilded, violins playing in the background. Entering the gilded room, I stood at the maître d's table behind a couple inquiring about a change in their table. I felt uneasy, thinking that at any moment someone might tap me on the shoulder and scold be for being where I did not belong. At last I handed the uniformed maître d' my dining card, which he carefully reviewed, looking up at me and down at the card before breaking into a warm smile and saying kindly, *"Bienvenue,* Monsieur Samberg." He checked his table listings and handed me off to a steward, who promptly led me to my assigned table. I was in.

The steward sat me at a round table adjacent to a starboard-side picture window with an English family returning from a New York vacation. Harrison Pelham was a banker, tall and thin, with high cheekbones, a slender mustache, rosy cheeks, and the overall deportment of a nineteenth-century military officer in a formal portrait. He wore black tie and tails. It was the first time I had ever seen such formal attire, which appeared to be the standard dress for most men in the room. The steward pulled out my chair and introduced me as Mr. Samberg of New Jersey to the assembled Pelhams, who did not appear enthusiastic about having a stranger join their family table. Suddenly my three-piece suit felt rather inadequate. I smiled at everyone, offering that it was a pleasure to meet them and thereafter falling into silence as I studied the serious array of silver cutlery, china plates, and crystal goblets before me. Mr. Pelham ignored me, which was somewhat uncomfortable as my chair was next to his. On the other hand, his wife, Elizabeth, dressed in a black Victorian ball gown with lace flourishes all around, was a fountain of chatter, going on about how Lord So-and-So and Baron Somebody were going to love the trinkets they were bringing back from New York. She spoke at length about their country house near Gatwick, describing her latest renovations and recounting the guest list for the final two weeks of September, worried that she may have excluded someone her husband may have wanted on the list. The third family member at the table was their daughter, Catherine, whose name in my American naïveté I shortened to Cathy to the consternation and scowling looks of her parents. I quickly switched back to Catherine.

A chip off the old man's block, Catherine, too, never uttered a word in my direction, not even in response to my oft-tender beckonings to pass the salt or bread. Catherine wasn't exactly a knockout, but her looks grew on me, and her body was a marvel of genetics, thin at the waist and awesome at the chest, the kind of chest a boy could just sink into and lose himself in for an eternity. She wore a beige silk dress that accentuated her shape and complemented the shiny long brown hair, which fell below her shoulders.

The meal was served at a leisurely pace. First there was the *amuse-bouche* of caviar wrapped in bite-sized pastries, then a terrine of foie gras, followed by a vegetable soup, then a chicken dish, followed by fish, then a salad—served incongruously after the two main courses—then dessert, followed by cheese (not just one but three), coffee, and sweets. *How do they eat this much every night without gaining a thousand pounds? My mother could not handle it*, I thought, *and Lorraine, she would be gone. Dottie would be in heaven.* This was what the Europeans called "dining," not just eating, and I must confess that I loved it—the subtle tastes, the relaxing pace, the silver and fine china, the candlelight, linen tablecloths, the fresh flowers, and the serene, dignified ambience of the service.

"So, I see your president is finally increasing taxes to pay for the war," Mr. Pelham uttered, for the first time turning my way. "Looks like you can't have guns and butter without paying the price," he offered, as if this were a lightning bolt of genius. "I am a banker, and I believe balance sheets don't lie, but I don't think you Yanks are going to be too happy with the war now that you are going to have to pay for it."

"I know—the balance of payments thing. My father told me all about it and the price of gold and so on," I faked it, reciting information I had seen on the TV news. *Here I am lying again!*

"Ah, so your father is a banker like me?" Mr. Pelham said, warming up to me as he turned his declarative statement into a question.

"No, but he does business with many banks, and he worries that destabilization in the markets could lead to a world depression," I answered, parroting more of what I had seen on the news. *I have no idea what I am talking about.*

"He must be an industrialist," Mr. Pelham concluded, lifting his cut-crystal champagne glass to take a sip.

"Well, I guess you could call him that." I feigned modesty, suggesting in my manner that it was not good etiquette to brag about one's wealth and connections. "I think a lot of Americans are already unhappy about the war, Mr. Pelham. Students in the SDS would rather see the money we spend on the war redirected to the unmet agenda of the Great Society, rebuilding the slums of the inner city, for example. That's a big part of what the student protest movement is about. They oppose the injustice and the waste of the war and how it limits our ability to achieve progress at home, especially with the Negroes."

"That's the Students for Democratic Socialism?"

"No, Students for a Democratic Society—SDS."

"You're a member?"

"No, but I know a few members, and I agree with them on a lot of things."

Pelham was remarkably up to date on what was happening in America, and not simply because he had just been there. He followed our politics closely, and he knew about the draft card burning, the arrest of the activist David Miller in New Hampshire, even the Port Huron Statement, the manifesto of the student protest movement, issued by the SDS a few years earlier, which "in an ideal world," he noted, "has much nobility to it. But alas," he concluded, "it is not an ideal world in which we live."

I did not agree, but I held my tongue, noticing that our conversation had attracted Catherine's attention, although she remained silent.

I could not help myself. "Which part of the Port Huron Statement do you favor?"

"I'm certainly not a fan of Tom Hayden, who, as I recall, wrote the statement, but I thought he was correct when he said that the goal of society should be human independence, and I agree with his call for participatory democracy. The rest of the statement is rubbish!"

"Well, I guess we'll just have to agree to disagree, because I thought Hayden pretty much captured the thinking of my generation." I glanced at Catherine, who was listening intently, and I surmised from her expression that she agreed with me. For a moment I thought she might speak.

With the serving of dessert, a crème brûlée, some two hours after the start of the meal, followed by coffee and some little pastries the waiter called *mignardise*, the meal was finally coming to an end. As we got up from the table, Mr. and Mrs. Pelham were very gracious, welcoming me to return to their table the next day for lunch and inviting me to visit them at their country house if my school schedule permitted. Catherine kept her silence but managed a half smile as I said good night to her.

With time to kill before my date with Christine, I returned to the cabin, changed clothes, and decided to take a walk on the deck. Bernie and Tina were gone—probably back at the bar—but the cabin was a wreck, with empty bottles, champagne glasses, and assorted undergarments strewn all over and the smell of cigarettes and marijuana. *They must have had one romp.*

I continued to walk, still satiated from the ten-course meal. After a few turns around the deck, I sat in a padded chair, enjoying the ocean breeze and anticipating my date with Christine. I had had countless conversations with friends about sex in high school and in college—it was the number one topic of conversation—but I never thought of girls as having a sex drive of their own. I thought they just reacted to boys, but Christine seemed different. It was as if she knew what she wanted. It was pretty amazing.

As midnight approached, I set out looking for Christine on the boat deck. I thought about her gentle hands all over my body during the massage and, although tired from the long day, I wondered what those hands might do once off duty. As I approached lifeboat number three, there she was standing at the rail in a light-blue strapless dress, her hair pushed up in a bun secured by a silver clip and her cleavage exposed just enough to excite, looking far less a masseuse than femme fatale.

"Hello, Robbeee," she whispered. "*C'a va?*"

"*Superbe, maintenant que je te vois. . .*" I smiled and took her hand as we moved away from the rail and walked along the thousand-foot deck stretched out before us. By now I had come down off the high but was still feeling good. The winds had picked up again and whitecaps appeared on the waves below. The deck was empty.

"So, you're going to leave this life at sea?" I asked.

"Yes, it's time. The money has been good, and now I can pay for school in Paris, which my parents could not afford. I have seen much of the world, but it's time to go home." She squeezed my hand as if to communicate her comfort in the moment.

"Is Paris your home?" I asked.

"*Oui*, my parents are there, my grandmother, and my friends, and I want to see them again. I want to spend time with them. The work on this ship is very hard and lonely. It is a great luxury for the first-class passengers like you, but it is a great labor for the crew."

"About the first-class thing. . ."

"Someday I will travel first class like you," she said. I felt a twinge of guilt.

"Right." I hesitated.

"In a few days my contract expires," she added with a coy look.

"No more rules," I said.

She smiled, spinning on her heals in the moonlight. "Yes, and I am breaking them right now!" She laughed.

"Robbeee, did you see the film *In the Heat of the Night*?" she asked.

"No, I haven't seen it."

"I saw it when the ship was docked in New York. It is with your actors Rod Steiger and Sidney Poitier. Robbeee, do the whites in America hate the Negroes? Is the racism as bad as they showed in the film?"

Her question caught me off guard, and I thought for a moment before responding. "I haven't seen it."

"Do whites in America hate Negroes as much as they hate the French?" she asked.

"What?" I looked at her with shock and surprise, concealing my thoughts about Uncle Sidney.

"I have heard that you think we French are anti-American," she said.

"Are you?" I asked.

"Would I be here walking along this deck with you if I was?"

"No, I guess not. I've got an uncle who thinks you French don't like us," I admitted.

"Does it run in the family?" she asked, poking me with her index finger.

"No, not at all!"

"And the Negroes?" she asked again. "I know about the radical groups and riots in the inner cities, about the looting and rampaging. I am happy to be returning to France where it is peaceful," she added.

"I feel the same way," I said. She looked at me with surprise and squeezed my hand. "I think racism in America is real, especially in our south, but I don't think the majority of whites hate Negroes or that the majority of Negroes hate whites."

"You should see the film," she said.

"I will put it on my list."

"In France we do not fear African people, and we do not consider them inferior. We are a society without racism, and I think that's why your Negroes who come to France find it so welcoming. I read a quote by the New York City mayor, John Lindsey, who said 'America is moving toward two societies, one black and one white, separate and unequal.' Is this true?" She looked at me pensively.

"I don't really know. Maybe," I said. "One of the reasons I'm on this ship is to get away from the strife in my country, the racism, the war, the protests. When things seem hopelessly screwed up, getting away is not a bad idea."

"Paris is always a good idea," she said, "like Sabrina told Linus in the movie," she added, a smile lighting her face.

"Yes, I saw that one. Loved it."

"Me too." I pulled her closer, leaned over, and kissed her passionately.

"Do you want to make love, Robbeee?" she asked.

"Ahhhh . . .Yes, yes, I do, I do."

She tightened her grip on my hand again and led me back inside and through a maze of not-for-public corridors, down winding stairs, deep into the ship, below my third-class cabin, to the staff quarters.

"Now we are really breaking the rules," she announced with a wicked grin. She pulled me close and kissed me on the lips, her mouth opening and inviting me inside.

"I am so horny," she whispered, now nibbling my ear. It was the first time I had heard a girl say that and it was an incredible turn-on.

"Time to go to inside my cabin, beeeg boy," she moaned, fumbling with her keys to the door.

The cabin was tiny, with two cots separated by a curtain. Christine's roommate was sound asleep. We tiptoed and lay on the empty cot.

"Hush," she whispered, raising her index finger to her lips. We lay on top of one another, which was the only way we could fit on the bed. Christine deftly unbuckled my belt, pulled down my zipper, and lowered my pants, simultaneously slipping down her underwear. We kissed passionately but silently as she reached down to guide me inside her with a determined efficiency. *This was mega "Playboy Advisor" material.*

"So much for the rules," I whispered as we both struggled to mute our laughter.

"You are so good, Robbeee," she moaned.

We made love again. After, we lay wrapped together, gently caressing one another, drenched in perspiration. It was warm in the cabin. We could hear the heavy breathing of the roommate through the thin curtain.

"Now do you believe I'm not anti-American?" she whispered, smiling rakishly, her face illuminated by a tiny night-light.

"Robbeee," she whispered, "I was once in love with a Negro. He was from Nigeria, the son of a tribal chief and a student at the Sorbonne. He was my first love, and he left me to continue his studies in America. He was killed in the Los Angeles riots and it broke my heart." Her face turned serious, her eyes showing the pain.

I didn't know how to respond. I lay there silently. *No wonder she asked about race relations in America.*

"I'm sorry!" I sat up and looked at her, balancing myself precariously on the tiny bed.

"I'll never get over it," she said.

I lay back down and thought about what she'd told me. I wanted to talk about it, to ask her questions, but I thought her wounds were still too fresh and too deep. *Better to wait for another time.* At last, with a glance of mutual consent, we quietly rose from the bed and departed as surreptitiously as we had arrived hours before.

Christine took my hand and led me back to the upper deck. She kissed me good night on both cheeks and ended with a long, lingering kiss on my lips, her tongue reaching into my mouth one last time. By now it was well past five in the morning, and I was exhausted, happily exhausted. I returned to the cabin, where in spite of Bernie's heavy snoring I fell asleep in an instant.

The next day, which arrived all too soon, when the purser discovered the error in my dining arrangement, he immediately called and transferred me to a dining table in third class, charging my ship board account a steep $75 upgrade fee for the first-class meal. I had to smile. *"How are you going to keep him back on the farm once he's seen Paree?"* After that, I could no longer visit the first-class spa or dining room and though I kept an eye out for Christine on the decks, I never saw her again during the rest of the voyage.

Of course, the décor and the meals served in third class were somewhat different from those of the night before, more mashed potatoes than potato gratin—no fine silver, caviar, foie gras, or *mignardise*—but truth be told, it felt more like home.

Chapter 5

An American in Paris

Stepping onto French soil that cool Saturday morning was like coming home to a part of me I had never met. Perhaps it was the noise of the harbor terminal, the din of comings and goings, of carts of luggage passing in all directions, the odor of a thousand bodies rushing to find their way, the muted colors, everything in a state of maturity, the cracks and rounded edges from aging you didn't see in vastly younger America. I couldn't explain why, but I felt like I belonged. I felt lighter and brighter as the sun illuminated the stone pillars of the wharf and its cavernous terminal, the seagulls squawking and swirling above like official escorts. My plan was to pick up the luggage, catch a bus to the train station, take the train to Paris, and then find a cheap hotel until my appointment at the college housing office on Monday. I also had to go to the Chase Bank to set up a checking account with the money order my father had given to me. It was enough for me to cash a check for 250 francs a week—about $50—for rent, food, and spending money.

I struggled to translate the signs leading to the buses outside the terminal, and once there, faced more confusing signs, but eventually I found the right bus thanks to my much-improved vocabulary and apparently native sounding accent which were helpful in asking for directions. I climbed aboard the faded silver bus to Le Havre train station and took a seat at the back just behind a shapely long-haired blond girl and her friend, a jock—big build, huge arms, and tightly cropped hair—whom I could hear speaking English.

"Can I see your *Green Guide?*" the girl turned and asked, spotting the book sticking out of my well-worn knapsack.

"Sure." I handed it to her.

"I'm Jan Miller from Chicago, and this is Rick Ryan," she said, her voice raspy.

"Robbie Samberg."

I reached out to shake hands. Jan's was soft and warm, and she moved her forearm slowly, gracefully up and down. Ryan's was hard, and his firm handshake confirmed my suspicion that he was some kind of football star. They had also come from the *Queen Elizabeth* and were headed to Paris for their junior years abroad, Jan at the American Institute and Ryan at the Sorbonne.

She leafed through the book, while he leaned in close to read with her. She was tall and wore tight blue jeans, a button-down plaid shirt, and boots. Her shiny blond hair fell all the way down to her butt, but not exactly in a flower child way—more like that of a goddess atop a white horse riding along a sandy beach. I noticed that her hand trembled slightly as she held the book.

"What are you looking for?" I asked.

"A hotel in Paris."

As the bus pulled into the station, I stood up to get off, with Jan and Rick in tow. We grabbed three well-worn luggage carts and fetched our steamer trunks from the baggage compartment. We rolled the heavy carts across the uneven stone floor of the station and got in line to purchase our train tickets.

When we reached the ticket window, Jan realized she did not know all the words to ask for the cheapest tickets to Paris. Rick's travel vocabulary wasn't much better and he stood puzzled by her side. I jumped in with my pseudo-perfect French accent to locate three seats together on the next train at the lowest possible price. It felt good to take charge.

"Way to go, Robbie," Jan said as I handed her the tickets.

At last we found our platform, Number 5, and our car, Voiture B. We climbed the steep metal stairs, lugging our trunks up the narrow passage and into the car. My first thought upon entering the passenger compartment and seeing its wide, plush seats, generous legroom, and spacious overhead bins was that it seemed too luxurious for third class. We sat together in a group of four seats, two pointing forward and two back—I in the chair facing the rear of the train, and Jan and Rick in the two seats facing forward. I smiled at Jan, who returned the smile with the brightest pearly whites I had ever seen. It was good to be sitting down and on our way.

Moments later, an unsmiling uniformed ticket collector arrived at our seats and demanded our tickets. He all but seized them from our hands and studied them and us, but as he pulled his silver puncher from his black leather belt, he suddenly stopped and cast a deep frown.

"*Messieurs et mademoiselles*, you are in zee wrong car," he announced, his voice stern and inflexible. "Your tickets are *troisième* class and this is a *premier* class car. You must move."

Again?

There was no point in arguing, so we gathered our things, exited the car, reloaded the baggage carts, which fortunately were still where we had left them, and found our way to the car where we belonged.

On the way, I told Jan and Rick about my steam room adventure on the ship. We laughed and accepted our fate to occupy less comfortable third-class accommodations, where the seats were narrow, the legroom limited, and the overhead bins tiny. By the time we loaded the trunks and bags in the new car, there were no three seats left together in the crowded passenger compartment. Jan and Rick sat together several rows ahead and I sat alone at the back of the car with a single empty seat facing me on which, happily, I could put my feet up for greater comfort.

I expected the three-hour train ride to be uneventful, a nap, beautiful countryside, a snack, until to my surprise Jan came over to take the empty seat directly in front of me. She faced me, mumbling something about Rick falling asleep, took off her shoes and placed her right foot between my legs, resting it on the front edge of my seat. The passenger next to me, a smartly dressed elderly lady, noticed but quickly shifted her eyes.

"This seat taken?" Jan asked with a wink.

"No, it's cool. Where's Rick?" I asked, grabbing a blue blanket left on the empty seat so she could sit down, then throwing it over my legs.

"Asleep and snoring. I hate his snoring!"

Jan's candor made it easy to talk to her, and we shared stories about the boat, mostly about drinking too much and carrying on. We were surprised that with six days on board, we'd never seen one another. There was no way I would not remember seeing someone who looked like her. She told me about the night she had imbibed one too many whiskeys at a party in the suite of a wealthy German couple and had climbed up on their coffee table to perform a striptease, only to be pulled "off stage" by Rick.

"I got all the way to my panties before he stepped in and ruined a good thing. It was the first time I had ever done the exhibitionist thing, and I was enjoying it. I wanted to stay up there and take off the rest of my clothes, and that tight-assed jock wouldn't let me! I've had enough Catholic school morality, and it's my mission in life to put that shit behind me," she declared emphatically, as if inviting me to join her.

"I understand. I dated a girl in Washington who felt the same way."

"For me rebellion is pure fun, but for my parents it's a nightmare. They hate me, hate the way I live, hate what I stand for, hate my politics and my hippie friends. The youth rebellion is happening all over the planet, and that has never happened before in history. It's a new era, and I don't plan to calm down and become a housewife or an ad exec at thirty, just like my parents and the establishment expect of me. I'm fed up with shallow and unworthy authority running things on a platform of bullshit!"

"Wow, you're a wordsmith," I offered.

"Ha! I stole that from William Burroughs!"

"I read his short stories," I recalled.

"Did you know he was a heroin addict?"

"No way!"

"And that he killed his wife?"

"No!"

"Did you read *Naked Lunch*?" she asked, her rapid-fire questions an effort to shock or test me in some way.

"Yes. Genius!"

"I tried heroin last summer and it was crazy, but then I read about Burroughs and his wife, and I swore I wouldn't do it again."

"Got it," I replied, taken aback and wondering if I might be pulled into the next act of her acting out.

The hours passed in conversation which never waned until we felt the jar of the train's brakes as it slowed to pull into the Gare du Nord.

We walked back to a still-sleeping Rick, whom Jan awakened with a stern poke to the shoulder blade. He shook his head, blinked his eyes, and gave forth a powerful yawn as he looked up at the two of us standing over him, holding our bags. His face was chiseled and angular in a way that defined male good looks.

We got off the train, replenished our backpacks with fresh clothes to last a few days, stored our trunks for later pickup, and hailed a cab at the front of the station. The driver informed us that the hotel Jan had chosen from the *Michelin Guide* was closed for renovations, so we asked him to take us to a nearby hotel that was not too expensive. He smiled and suggested the Hotel des Gobelins on rue des Gobelins, a short drive away. We huddled together in the backseat of the cab, Jan in the middle, her long legs resting awkwardly on the large bump in the center of the floor. No one spoke. Upon arrival we shared the cab fare, and entered the lobby of the hotel.

The three of us stood together at the front desk. The clerk was busy on the telephone but signaled us to wait and pointed to the rate card taped to the top of the counter. He was an older man, about sixty, with short white hair, his eyes large and round like those of a hawk and his nose curved like a beak. He was dressed in a bulky blue sweater with a white stripe around the collar. I volunteered to speak for the three of us.

"*Bonjour*," I said in my most authentic accent. "We would like to rent two rooms without a shower or bathroom and without breakfast."

"*Anglais?*"

"*Non*. American."

"Ah, so you know that you save the money without the bath and the breakfast. Very good," the clerk said in English. "*Très bien*."

I felt good about accomplishing the savings, and my comrades looked on with admiration, especially Jan, who by now was paying an uncomfortable amount of attention to me and ignoring Rick. The clerk informed us that we would have to pay in advance for the first night, which we promptly did. He handed us our keys and told us the elevator was out of service, pointing to another sign on the counter, so we grabbed our bags and headed for the stairs to the third floor.

As we walked across the lobby to the stairwell, I noticed the freshly painted walls and simple décor, accented with newly framed photos of the Eiffel Tower, the Arc de Triomphe, and the Palace of Versailles. Hotel des Gobelins appeared to be the picture-perfect low-budget Paris hotel and a credit to the cabdriver who'd led us there. I was sure he was already off on his next mission of assistance to equally ill-prepared foreigners.

My sense of appreciation did not endure, for as we rounded the first turn in the newly carpeted stairwell we came upon walls that were burned charcoal black, and we instantly realized that restorations from a fire had been limited to the lobby and lower stairwell, the charred walls conveniently kept outside the line of sight of new customers paying in advance at the front desk. I ran back down to the lobby, my eyes wide with outrage, where the clerk informed me that refunds were not possible, pointing to the fine print on the counter sign.

"No, *monsieur*," he said dismissively, his index finger lingering on the sign, his expression unwavering. I wondered what we would find when we reached our rooms.

Thankfully, the third floor was above the fire line, although the hall and the bathroom we would share with the other rooms still reeked of smoke. I entered my room where the walls looked as if they had not been painted since the last century. The furniture was made from dark laminated wood and had Formica surfaces—vintage 1940s—with cracks and swelling from water damage to the flimsy pressed-board construction.

But my focus on the decrepit furnishings and the hotel's deception quickly faded as I walked up to the classic floor-to-ceiling French windows at the far end of the room. I pulled back the tattered drapes to a pristine view of the city below. The window handles must have been a hundred years old, but when twisted they effortlessly withdrew rods from the top and bottom of the windowsills, which made it possible for the windows to swing wide open. It was a marvel of French engineering, and before me now lay Paris, all the noise, the movement, the color, the odors wafting up from the street below, everything right there— beckoning, enticing, enchanting. Sitting on a bench across the street, a black man kissed a white woman, something you did not see at home. Just behind them on the sidewalk, I spotted Rick Ryan charging ahead as if on a football field. He appeared upset and in a big hurry.

With my attention focused on the view outside the windows, I hadn't noticed that Jan had moved her luggage to my room until she walked up behind me, and slipped her arms around my waist.

"Jan, the view . . ." I uttered.

"You have a more beautiful view right behind you."

Paris notwithstanding, she was right about that.

"You are one stone fox," I observed, turning around.

"And what about Rick?"

"I broke up with him," she whispered. "He didn't take it well."

"Is he going to come here to beat the shit out of me?"

"No, he's gentler than he looks. It's not about you, Robbie. We were done when he pulled me off that stage and put his puritan bullshit ahead of what I wanted. He doesn't have a clue about who I am or what's important to me."

"I do?"

"We'll see. My gut tells me you're a lot more sensitive than most guys, and that's what I'm looking for."

"Paris awaits!" I smiled. "What should we see first?"

"The Eiffel Tower, of course."

"Let's go. There's a restaurant on top and I'm hungry," I exclaimed.

We marched down the burnt-out stairwell, and exited onto the bustling street to hail a cab. I prayed we would not run into Rick, who was twice my size and, no matter how gentle, could not be too happy with me.

Our cab sped through the narrow streets of the quartier, windows wide open, the fresh air invigorating, and the sights and sounds of the city intoxicating.

"*Vous êtes Américains?*" the taxi driver turned to inquire with a friendliness that was unexpected.

"*Oui, nous sommes Américains,*" I offered in my best French accent.

"*Bienvenue à Paris!*" the driver said as he began a running commentary on every historical building we passed, speaking in as much English as he could muster. "You have a very good accent," he added. *"Extraordinaire!"*

"There eees the Assemblée Nationale, our version of your congress," he said, pulling over and slowing down to point out a statue on the side of the road. "There eees your Monsieur Jefferson, who was zee ambassador to France. We admire Jefferson as much as we admire Rousseau." I grabbed my Brownie camera, which hung on a strap around my neck, and quickly snapped a shot through the open window.

Jan and I looked at each other, surprised by the driver's warmth and courtesy. This was not the cool reception Uncle Sidney had described at my going-away party. *So much for the*

French not liking Americans. The cab zig-zagged through the dense Paris traffic along the River Seine.

"*Vous* young Americans may not remember, but we remember," the driver said, carefully turning his head back toward us so we could hear his words.

"Remember?" I asked, raising my voice so he could hear me.

"The war! My father was eeen the Resistance. He was killed in '44." His voice choked as he turned to look back at us while maneuvering the cab. "We shall never forget what America deeed for us! We shall never forget what your soldiers deeed. They died for our *liberté*!"

Jan and I looked at each other again, surprised by driver's emotion. He spoke as if we were the very soldiers who had saved France. Neither of us knew how to respond, so we sat silently in the backseat as the car hurtled on.

"Without your soldiers' sacrifice at Omaha Beach," the driver continued, "my family would not have survived, and France would not have survived!"

"*Merci*," we responded together, feeling the inadequacy of the word.

"*Non*, it is we French who must thank you! And we must never forget our gratitude even as the years pass. Zat is what my father would have wanted."

The cab arrived at the Eiffel Tower and the driver pulled over and turned all the way around in his seat. He was a large man with a genial face, a mustache, and long hair that fell down upon both sides of his head in tangled curls. He smiled at us and held out his hand, reaching over the seat.

"I am Pierre Laboutte."

We introduced ourselves and shook his outstretched hand.

"We are students at the American Institute, and this is our first day in Paris," Jan explained.

"I can see eet in your smiles and your bright eyes," he responded. "Paris does thees to those who see it for the first time. It's a place of wonder."

Pierre handed us his card and told us that if we ever needed anything, we should call him and he would come.

"Now go enjoy our Eiffel Tower," he said, shooing us from the taxi. He turned off the meter.

"How much do we owe?" I asked.

"Zis ride is a gift from the Laboutte family! Now go. Enjoy Paris!"

"*Merci, merci beaucoup!*" we replied, exiting the cab, delighted by Pierre's generosity.

Pierre waved goodbye as he drove off, and we watched as the cab merged into the torrent of city traffic. We stood together on the sidewalk at the base of the tower, with its four gigantic feet, and looked up at the colossal iron structure looming above us.

"How did they build this in 1889," I asked Jan, "before power tools and cranes?"

"Most Americans don't realize the French are world-class engineers," she said. "I read a book about this tower."

"Bravo, Monsieur Eiffel!" I cried out, excited to stand before this great symbol of France.

"Everybody credits Eiffel, but the tower was actually designed by two little-known French engineers whose names have been left out of the history books," Jan said, her tone professorial.

"Who were they?"

"Maurice Koechlin and Émile Nouguier."

"You're kidding! So it's the Koechlin-Nouguier Tower," I responded, struggling to pronounce their names.

"Yes, it is," she said, moving closer and taking my hand.

"Are you as hungry as me?" I asked, interrupting the history lesson.

"Starving. Let's go up."

We moved through the crowd and got in line to buy tickets. Jan put her arms around me and cast a mischievous grin.

"That kind of hungry?"

"Starved," she whispered.

"But the crowds," I observed, scanning the tower above us.

"Don't worry. I've got an idea."

The line moved forward, and we entered a tiny elevator standing at the front by a small window as it began to move at a steep angle up one of the tower's enormous legs, then straight up the interior structure. The rivets on the iron beams were clearly visible at close range, and the view became more spectacular as the cab climbed the tower.

The elevator jolted to a stop at the first observation deck. We emerged still hand in hand. The view of the city was breathtaking—the Louvre, the Arc de Triomphe, the Grande Palais, Sacre Coeur, the Seine, the grand boulevards, and a maze of narrow streets, the arteries of a thousand years of city life. We walked from one side of the deck to the other, mesmerized by the view in the moonlight. We entered the restaurant, aptly called 58 Tour Eiffel, as it was fifty-eight meters aboveground, found a corner table, and ordered two croque monsieurs—toasted sandwiches with ham and melted cheese—and a bottle of red wine. We sat silently taking in the view of the city as we waited for our food to arrive.

Jan broke the silence. "Why are you here?" She cast her eye to the city below.

The waiter arrived with the wine and filled our glasses.

"To experience new things, I guess."

"That's it?"

"When I return, I'll put to work what I learn, whatever that may be."

"Good answer."

"What about you?"

"I'm going to learn French and become America's Joan of Arc."

"I think you'll do it."

We finished the *croque monsieurs* and the wine, and Jan motioned for me to get up and follow her. I knew by the look on her face she was up to something. Watching carefully to make sure we were not seen, she led me to the ladies' room, pulled open the door, yanked me inside, threw the dead bolt, and tore off her clothes and mine. This was no easy maneuver, as the bathroom was tiny, just a toilet and sink, like on an airplane.

"Make love, not war, right?" Jan whispered, kissing me, her voice raspy, a spasm of coughing taking her over, then leaving as quickly as it came on.

"Yeah, the world could blow up at any moment," I said, returning her kisses anywhere and everywhere I could fit my head in the cramped quarters.

We ignored the knocks at the bathroom door, and when we finally emerged, flushed and laughing hysterically, we faced a line of irritated French women, legs crossed, offering us pained looks of disapproval. We moved quickly, left our money on the table, and exited the restaurant, returning to the tower observation platform.

"We just had sex on the Koechlin-Nouguier Tower," I said as we sat down on a bench, our laughter subsiding.

"I know. I was there," she said.

"I thought that was Joan of Arc."

"Haha."

"Should we be thinking about protection?" I asked. *Better late than never.*

"From what?"

"You know."

"You sound like my mother."

"Maybe we should find a pharmacy."

"I'm not worried," she said, looking at me as if she were holding something back.

We took the elevator down and walked through the winding, inspiring, and romantic streets of the city. We arrived at the Avenue des Champs-Élysées and strolled along its enormously wide sidewalks, slowly making our way toward the Arc de Triomphe, a monument honoring those who fought and died in the Revolutionary and Napoleonic Wars. Inscribed on the monument were the names of every major French battle and every victorious French general, and beneath its great arch lay the Tomb of the Unknown Soldier from World War I.

"I think I'm ready to take the Métro back to the hotel," Jan said, a pained look shooting across her face.

I noticed her hand trembling again.

"Come on, old lady, the night is still young."

"I'm tired and my feet hurt."

"But we've got to climb the Arc!" I urged.

"Another time."

"How about a half-hour rest and then we climb?"

"What are you afraid of?" she asked.

"Afraid?"

"What are you afraid of?" she asked again.

"I'm not afraid."

"Oh yes you are. Everybody I know is afraid of something."

I stopped to think. She was serious and staring intently, expecting an answer. I could have turned the question back on her but said instead, "Nuclear war."

"Ah, those duck-and-cover drills at your desk. Did you do them, too?"

"Of course."

"What else?" she asked.

"I don't know."

"Really?"

"What else?" she persisted.

"Getting drafted when I get home and dying in some rice paddy in Vietnam."

"Right but what else?" She kept up the pressure.

"Well . . . making mistakes that will mess up my life."

"Anything else? Now dig for it."

I hesitated as I thought, trying to be straight with her.

"Not measuring up and not being successful," I said.

"Good one!"

"Now it's your turn."

"I'm not afraid of anything."

"Joan of Arc, right?"

"After what I've been through, Robbie, there's nobody who can hurt me, and I don't give a shit if I succeed or I fail."

"Are you going to tell me about it?"

"Let's head back. When I'm ready, I'll tell you."

We sat on a bench to rest. Jan pulled down her long blond hair, which had been folded into a bun hidden beneath a wool cap, and shook her head side to side to straighten the falling hair. She was beautiful, smart, and such a live wire. She uncharacteristically blushed as she noticed how I was looking at her.

"I once did Abbie Hoffman and Jerry Rubin at the same party," she deadpanned.

"You what?"

"I did, and it was fun."

"At the same time?"

"You've never done a threesome?"

"No, I was offered but turned it down."

"Afraid?"

"I guess."

"I was at a party celebrating the founding of the Youth International Party. Hell, we were Yippies, and that's what Yippies did when we weren't busy administering shock treatments to the establishment. I did them both. We were so stoned!"

"You are one stone fox," I said again with a hint of envy and admiration.

The more I learned about Jan, the more I liked her and how she lived her life at full throttle. "*Une vie à plein bord*," she said, quoting her favorite sculptor, Auguste Rodin: "a life filled to the brim." That's how I wanted to live, too.

Chapter 6

A Ride on the Métropolitain

The next day Jan took off to spend time with a friend of her family visiting the city and I decided to check out the American Institute. I entered the Métro near the hotel and headed for Place de l'Alma, a busy square on the bank of the Seine, not far from school. It was one of those cold, rainy days more typical of winter in Paris than early spring. There was a chill in the air that went right through me. I didn't take a jacket that day and I was happy to descend into the protective warmth of the underground.

As I climbed down the stairs to the tracks below, I breathed the slightly sweet and rancid air with its unique odor from the accumulation of the sweat of multitudes and decades of dust, mold, and mildew. At the bottom of the stairs, I stopped at the tiny ticket booth with its narrow window, behind which I could see the ruddy cheeks of La Femme du Métro, who promptly sold me a ticket.

The Métro had a well-thought-out map system, with electric lights that would come on to show riders the shortest route between any two points. I stood before it, pressed the buttons to light up my route, and headed to the track to wait for the train. Within moments I heard the screeching noise of the iron wheels as the conductor applied the brakes to slow the train to a stop. I reached out to flip the shiny brass hand latch that opened the door to the third-class car and entered to look for an open seat.

As I sat down, I noticed a large, unshaven, disheveled man enter the train. He had a muscular chest and long arms and wore a tattered French soldier's coat, a leather pouch hanging at his side. He limped slowly up the aisle toward me. The car was nearly full and he could not find a seat, so he stood in the aisle next to me, grabbed the rail to steady himself, and turned around to face the direction of the train's travel. The weather-beaten pouch that hung down from straps around his broad shoulders lay against his left hip, close to my right arm. I noticed the ivory handle of a hunting knife sticking out from the corner. He was so close I could hear his heavy breathing. He had a bad cold and a nasty cough. I could smell his foul body odor.

Just before the train departed, as the piercing siren warned that the doors were about to close, a tall slender Asian girl hurried into the car and took the last open seat on the aisle, just next to the exit door. She was several rows ahead of us, and I only saw her for an instant, but the large, scruffy soldier standing next to me could see her very well. She was dressed in a richly embroidered silk robe covering her from neck to toe. As the train pulled away, she stood up to consult the map of stops, which was posted on the wall of the car. I noticed her flawless skin, which appeared perfectly smooth, luminescent, glowing. I had never seen such perfect skin—no marks, no lines, no contours, nothing but fleshy silk and a remarkable glow. I caught the expression on her face—a determination and confidence that she would find her way in this foreign land, a gentleness and optimism reflected in her bright eyes as she focused on the task at hand.

I was watching as she appeared to calculate the correct stop to exit the train, when suddenly she turned toward me to sit back down and her eyes met mine. Unexpectedly, in a moment whose profound impact was yet to unfold, she smiled, her eyes wide and on fire in a way I had never seen or felt before. I was captivated.

The soldier became agitated at the sight of the girl, whom I realized was Vietnamese. At first he spoke angrily under his breath, then raised his voice to a shout, and before long lifted his fist in the air and taunted her. He blurted obscenities and railed about dead comrades from the French war in Indochina. Though I could not understand his every word, I sensed that he was becoming increasingly hostile, vulgar, and threatening. Each time he screamed, he lifted himself up on the toes of his boots in order to better thrust his invectives at the hapless girl, and each time he did this he brushed up against my right arm. As the taunts grew ferocious, the soldier reached over with his right arm and shoved his hand into the pouch, grabbing the handle of the knife. I was bracing myself to intervene, when for no apparent reason he suddenly stopped and stood silently, his hand letting go of the knife, which slid back into the pouch. I breathed a sigh of relief and slowly rose from my seat to glimpse the girl, whose dread was now as apparent on her face as the serenity had been moments before. Her eyes met mine again as I slipped back down into my seat. She understood she was in danger.

I was careful not to invite the soldier's attention as I steadied myself to intercede if his assault on the girl resumed. He was larger than me and appeared stronger and had shown himself to be as unpredictable as he was hostile. I was afraid that if I confronted him he would stab me. I had to get the knife away from him before he could use it on the girl or on me. I decided that when the train stopped at the next station, I would grab it from the pouch and toss it away.

I rose from my seat again to look at the girl. She was standing in front of her seat, her smooth skin now white and her brow furrowed. She saw me looking at her and returned an expression that pleaded for help.

The car shifted on the tracks and leaned to the side as it hurtled around a curve toward the next station. I could hear the brakes applied and dreaded what would happen next. When we stopped and the doors opened, the crazed soldier suddenly renewed his screaming and reached for the knife. I grabbed the handle, finding it before he did, and hurled it to the floor, where it came to rest several aisles behind us, safely out of reach. The soldier swung at me, missing my head and striking his fist on the metal frame of my seat. He winced in pain as the crowd of passengers pushed him forward. He lurched ahead to grab the girl, who, shielded by other passengers, quickly dashed out the door onto the platform and entered the adjacent Métro car. The soldier followed her.

It all happened so fast. I tried to follow too but was blocked by the crowd entering the car and could not make it to the exit before the doors again slammed shut and the train pulled away. I pushed my way through the standing passengers to the front of the car, where a small interior window permitted me to see into the adjacent car. I watched through the window as the girl hurriedly sat down next to an old man in an aisle seat just a few feet away. The old man was no match for the enraged soldier, who, having followed the girl, now stood perilously close to her—a mere arm's length away. I felt helpless as I saw that the old man and the passengers around him in the adjacent car had no idea of what was about to unfold.

I looked on in horror as the soldier screamed and his face contorted with rage. I could not hear his voice through the thick glass window and the noise of the train, but I could see everything. The other passengers appeared stunned and frozen in place. The girl trembled but remained stoic in the face of the onslaught. The old man sitting next to her stood up and thrust his left arm forward to stop the soldier, admonishing him by wagging the index finger of his right hand in the soldier's face. No sooner than the downward stroke of the second wag, the soldier grabbed the old man's finger and yanked it backward, breaking it in an explosion of rage that instantly had the two of them wrestling in the aisle, fists, teeth, and blood flying all over the girl, the passengers, and the train. A passenger pulled the emergency stop cord, and the train veered off to the nearest platform. Throughout the melee, the girl stood erect, serene, and ready to defend herself. She looked over through the interior window and saw me watching her. Her distraught look again beseeched my help.

Another passenger stepped into the aisle to confront the soldier and assist the old man, who now lay bleeding and motionless on the floor. He was joined by three others, who together wrestled the soldier to the floor and held him down, screaming and writhing. As soon as the train stopped, I rushed to the exit and ran into the adjacent car, stepping over the bodies of the wounded old man and the screaming soldier as the four good Samaritans struggled to hold him down. I reached the girl, still standing in front of her seat, took her hand, and led her away. We ran to the station exit hand in hand. I pulled and she followed as if in a dance of flight up the steep concrete stairs of the Saint-Paul Métro station and onto the sunlit plaza at rue Saint-Antoine. We crossed the busy street, dodging cars, buses, and bikes, and dashed into the courtyard of the Hôtel de Sully, skipping up the ancient, uneven stairwell at the end of the courtyard and through the narrow barrel-ceilinged hallway to the spacious gardens behind the great house.

At last it seemed safe to stop. We were both out of breath and still holding hands.

"Are you all right?" I turned to look at her as she caught her breath and let go of my hand.

She leaned forward, placing her hands on her knees, then pulled herself back up, erect, with her head held high, her breathing returning to normal, her posture retreating from hypervigilance to a more relaxed state. She was even more beautiful face-to-face than she had been at a distance.

I studied her facial features—high cheekbones; dark, sparkling eyes; jet-black eyebrows—and her hair, offset by the porcelain-like glow of her skin and pulled up into a bun, held tight by ornate ivory hairpins.

"I'm frightened," she whispered in a soft, melodic voice.

"Let's sit down." I motioned toward a nearby stone bench under a tall box tree at the side of the courtyard. "You're safe now."

"My father will be so angry with me," she said. "He will punish me for going out without the security," she added, her voice trailing off.

"The security?" I asked.

She did not respond.

I could see the fear begin to melt away from her face, her skin tone once again flawless and luminescent. I retook her hand, noticing how natural it felt to touch her. We looked at one another on the way to the bench, and she signaled her comfort, glancing down at our hands, joined at the palms.

"That was a close call," I observed, letting go of her hand as we sat down.

She did not respond, taking more time to gather her composure, eyes scanning the surrounding courtyard.

"The rage in that soldier is the horror of war which torments those who survive," she whispered in a dulcet voice, her vowels softened, her gaze still fixed on the expanse of the courtyard.

I was impressed that she spoke in perfect English and that her first thought was to understand the soldier who had victimized her.

"I think you are right," I said.

"I must forgive him. He has likely endured far worse than I have."

I was again struck that she would focus on forgiveness so soon after a vicious attack. *This girl is special.*

"You are brave and your willingness to forgive is—"

"I was lucky brave men stepped in to protect me."

"True, but you were brave, too."

"And you? Would you have protected me, too, if you had been able to follow me to the other car?" she asked, looking at me, her voice still soft, melodic, her accent less pronounced as she calmed down.

Her directness surprised me, and I didn't hesitate to respond.

"Yes, I would have."

"I know. I could see it in your eyes." She glanced at the bloodstains on her dress, then looked at me, as if a reminder to us both of how much worse things might have turned out. I was awed by how she could communicate with her eyes, her expressions.

"I'm Robbie, Robbie Samberg."

"I am Le My Hanh. Le is my family name. My Hanh is my given name."

"How do you pronounce it?"

"'My' in Vietnamese is pronounced like 'me' in English. Le 'Mee' Hanh. Are you American?" she asked hesitantly.

"I am."

"I have never met an American," she said, looking away.

I sensed a strain, a rupture of the bond I had felt between us that began when our eyes met on the train.

"Thank you for leading me to safety," she said stiffly, her manner now more formal, her voice lower. "I can see you are a boy with a generous heart. I did not think I would ever see this in an American," she said emphatically.

"So I am an exception?" I gently provoked.

"Yes, perhaps," she said, nodding.

"There are two hundred million Americans. Perhaps there are a few more exceptions."

"Okay," she said, her concession communicated with her eyes and her body language.

I was impressed at how gracefully she corrected herself. I thought it strange that with nearly a half-million Americans in Vietnam, she had never before met one. *Maybe she grew up in France. But her English is perfect.*

"Do you live in Paris?" she asked.

"I am a student at the American Institute."

"What do you study?"

"Political science and diplomatic history. I study the war in your country."

"Have you visited my country?"

"No, I have a student deferment to complete my studies here in Paris and to graduate next year, so I was not required to join the army to fight in your country. What part of South Vietnam are you from?"

"I am from Hanoi."

"Hanoi? But Hanoi is in—"

"I am the daughter of Le Duc Tho, the foreign minister of the Democratic Republic of *North* Vietnam."

"Oh my . . ."

"You are shocked."

"We are at war, and you are the enemy," I responded, dumbfounded.

"Maybe I am an exception, too," she said, punctuating the statement with her luminescent smile and a laugh.

"Why are you in Paris?" I asked, returning her directness with my own.

"I am here to help my father."

"Your father is in Paris?" I thought about the rumors of a bombing halt and peace talks. *Perhaps it is true.* "Is he here for peace talks?" I asked.

"Robbie, you ask too many questions," she said.

"You don't understand. I am a student of your history. Understanding this war is my passion. I have read many books about it, and I brought them all to Paris. I used to answer letters about the war for a United States senator!" The more I spoke, the louder I raised my voice.

"You *are* an exception," she said, looking at me as if I were from Mars.

"Please tell me! You must!"

"Robbie, I am not permitted to speak about this."

"Please, just let me know if there are peace talks!" I asked, casting the look of an innocent beggar. "I promise I will tell no one else."

"I can't speak about this, Robbie."

"Okay, you don't have to speak. I will count to five, and if there are peace talks, simply get up from the bench, and if there are no talks, remain seated. You don't have to say a word."

"Robbie, you are an impossible exception," she said, smiling.

"One, two, three, four, five . . ."

She rose from the bench, gazed at the garden, and sat back down.

"My father is going to disown me," she said. "How do I know I can trust you?"

"Well, I risked my life for you. Does that count for trustworthiness?"

"Watching as I was attacked through a window from another car?"

"Wait a minute," I protested, and explained how I had pulled the knife from the soldier's pouch and tossed it away. She had not seen me do this.

"You did save me," she said. "And you risked your life to do it."

"No problem. I knew you were an exception," I rejoined with a laugh.

"My father is here," she continued slowly, looking around to make sure there was no one nearby who could hear, "to prepare for meetings with your president's representative. He hopes they can agree on conditions to bring an end to the bombing of our country and begin talks to end the war. Robbie, you must not repeat this to anyone," she implored.

The rumors are true. I wonder if Allen knows about this. "Of course I will keep this between us. Thank you for trusting me," I added, having a hard time containing my excitement.

"I'm going to suggest to my father that the meetings be held here in this house because it is so beautiful, and perhaps from that beauty will come the inspiration necessary to achieve understanding."

"The talks have not yet begun?"

"There you go again with your questions!"

"I'm a student. I'm curious. It's how I learn."

"There are many preliminary issues to be decided," she said, "and this takes time, with all the parties involved. My father is working on this."

"Where did you learn to speak English so well?" I asked.

"Thank you for the compliment. It took years of training to learn English, especially the pronunciation. I struggled with word tense, vowel sounds and with the rhythm of American speech, which is so different than Vietnamese."

"You got it," I said.

"I have been trained in five languages. I speak French, English, Spanish, Mandarin, and Vietnamese. I attended high school here in Paris, and I am now enrolled at the Peking University. In my last semester, I took an advanced class in English pronunciation as part of my diplomatic training. I took leave from my studies to assist my father. To be truthful, I did not want to come, but I could not refuse to help him."

"Why didn't you want to come?" I asked. "Helping your father negotiate a peace agreement is pretty exciting, and you got Paris as a bonus."

"Paris is always a bonus," she said. "I am happy to be here again, but I was happy in my life at the university, and I didn't want to give that up. No one knows how long we shall be here, and I miss my classes and my friends, and by the time we return they will have moved on and I may need to repeat my classes."

"That's a lot to give up, but it will be worth it if you can help your father succeed."

"He really doesn't need my help, and besides, I want to define success in my life and not just do what my father decides."

"A liberated girl?" I asked.

"This is a delicate matter, because in our country girls are not supposed to think this way."

"Why didn't you just refuse to come?"

"Because a Vietnamese girl does not refuse a request from her father."

"American girls refuse requests from their fathers all the time," I observed.

"I would not do that, especially in wartime. It was my familial and my patriotic duty to come here. But it is something I did from duty, not because I wanted it. Do you understand?"

"Yes, I understand."

She looked at me uncertainly.

"I am surprised that I have told you this, Robbie. I do not usually share such thoughts, even with my best friends at school." She gazed at me as if trying to understand what was happening between us, her smile once again overwhelming me.

I felt strangely off balance, alert and vulnerable at the same time, a combination I had never felt before and didn't understand. I sat on the edge of the bench, eager and excited to continue our conversation.

"My father asked me to join him in his business when I return home," I said. "He plans to buy a radio station, which is his dream, and he told me he needs my help. I don't think he really needs my help, and I don't want to do it, but I feel as you did that it's a family duty. I'll probably do it, but it's not my dream. It's his dream."

"You do understand," she responded with excitement, looking at me with renewed warmth and what appeared to be nascent affection. "I do not understand what is happening here between us," she said. "You are so different from any American I had imagined." She looked away, retreating to silence and gazing at the beautiful garden.

"A penny for your thoughts," I whispered.

"What?"

"It's an expression in America for when you want to know what someone is thinking."

"I thought American capitalists were very rich, so I would expect that you would offer more than one of your pennies for what I am thinking."

"It's just an expression—you know, a gentle way to prod, to get someone to open up about themselves."

"Robbie, I think I have already opened up to you more than any respectable Vietnamese girl would to a boy she had just met, and a million times more than a North Vietnamese girl would to an American," she said, smiling and looking me over, her eyes searching for an explanation of what was happening between us.

There was something about her. Her words resonated as if she were an old friend whom I had not seen for years. I felt as if we had nothing to hide, that it was safe to share every thought and feeling. I did not understand how this could have happened, but there it was, and I sensed that she felt the same way.

"Look, Robbie," My Hanh said, pointing to the upper portion of the great house, "there are statues of women, one carrying flowers of the summer, and the other carrying wheat of the spring. These are the symbols of changing seasons and sustaining life. This is a good place to search for peace."

"Ending this war will take more than a beautiful garden and symbolic statues," I observed.

"Of course, I know that," she said. "But symbols are important, because they can inspire, and inspiration can affect behavior and choices, and I think peace is a choice. It will also take good luck."

Perhaps she is onto something.

"Hanh in Vietnamese means 'luck,' and I think this garden will bring good luck to the peace talks," she said, shifting her weight to the back of the bench and stretching out her legs, the shape of her body visible beneath the dress, with its intricate patterns in shiny silk. Her eyes lit up and she spoke with enthusiasm. "My father believes that one day your American political system will adjust and adopt a more rational conclusion about our struggle. He believes that in time our nation will be unified, and America will be our friend, even a partner in commerce."

I shook my head. "No way."

"I know this sounds impossible, but I have heard my father say it will happen."

"We're talking here about America," I said incredulously. "Anticommunist America. Hasn't your father read LBJ's speeches? Hasn't he noticed a half-million American soldiers fighting in South Vietnam?"

"Robbie, you are being sarcastic!"

"Yes, I am."

"My father knows what we are up against," she said, "and he understands your political system. He recognizes that your president cannot appear soft on communism, especially when he is under political attack by his opponents."

"That is true, but I think there is more to it than that."

She turned toward me, curled her legs up underneath her, and sat in the lotus position.

"He believes your president thought it would be good politics to take the strongest position against us, even if it meant making up stories, like he did during the Gulf of Tonkin incident four years ago."

"Can you prove that?" I asked.

"I swear, Robbie, our naval forces were not even in the Gulf on that day. The attack by our forces never happened. It was a fiction used by your government to justify expanding the war. History will prove this."

"Maybe it was just confusion on the battlefield that day," I said.

"My father thinks your president wanted to escalate the war for political reasons. Your ships were inside our twelve-mile limit. Your puppet-regime torpedo boats were attacking us. This was not confusion. It was a deliberate fabrication, one that in an American election year was good politics."

"A friend told me about this," I said, "but it's hard to believe."

"The proof will come in time," she said. "Your leaders are mistaken that our Vietnamese communism is a threat to your country. My father says we are Vietnamese nationalists first and communists second, and we have absolutely no aspirations to expand our economic and social system beyond our borders. Your domino theory is a fiction, too."

"It may surprise you, but I agree with your father about the domino theory. Many Americans agree, but it will take time for our political system to correct itself and reflect this."

"I never thought I would hear an American say this," she said, nodding her approval.

"More exceptions?" I asked.

She smiled. "Your polls show a majority of Americans support the war," she said, citing a poll her father had shown her.

"This will change in time," I responded, realizing that my assessment would be regarded at home as at best controversial and at worst treasonous. *It would be treasonous to my father.*

"Robbie, Ho Chi Minh is our Lincoln, not our Hitler," she continued, "but your government treats him as if he were an evil Nazi bent on world domination. It's more of your anticommunist hysteria."

"You know about McCarthy?" I asked.

Yes, I have studied this period in your history and the damage that was done to so many innocent people," she said. "It was shameful."

"I agree."

"It is equally shameful how your country has treated mine. Once we are permitted to unify Vietnam, I assure you that we shall live in peace with our neighbors, with your nation, and with all nations," she said. "It saddens me that so many must die before this comes to pass."

"I understand."

"Forgive me, Robbie, but I don't think you really understand. As an American you cannot understand."

"What do you mean?"

"Your America has acted so foolishly, and when I read the words of your political leaders I see that their ignorance is camouflaged by a certain pride and a blind sense of superiority," she admonished, her tone resigned and angry. *"Lời nói không đi đôi với việc làm.* Their words don't match their actions."

"There you go again generalizing."

"Look, I lost my younger brother to napalm dropped by your air force. This is not just a political discussion for me, it's personal, and it takes all my life energy to restrain my anger and my anguish, to understand and to forgive. Perhaps you can forgive me if I generalize."

We sat silently. I thought how extraordinary a person she was to be struggling to forgive and contain an anger she had every right to feel. *Is every American somehow complicit in the death of her brother?* Every day we read stories in the papers about our air force carpet-bombing Vietnam with napalm, but to most Americans and to me this was more an abstraction than a reality, something far-off and far from anything over which we had control. We saw pictures of the jungles burning, but the pictures did not show the people burned alive below the tree line. The pictures did not show the agony of her brother and her family. I realized My Hanh was right. *Maybe I can never really understand.*

"I also have two sisters, one younger and one older, and I do not want to lose them!" she said. "We must end this war."

"I have two sisters, too—one younger and one older," I said.

"Does your older sister watch over you like mine does over me? Older sisters in Vietnam are like second mothers, always protecting, even when you do not need or want it."

I was relieved to see her smile again.

"No, my older sister does not do that. She keeps her distance."

There is no way I can explain my sisters.

"That's too bad, for as much as it annoys me when my older sister is overprotective, I know she is doing her duty to our family, and I love her for this."

"I like that family and sense of duty are important to you," I said.

"Not always," she said. "I struggle with this. I have read that girls in America are liberated and willing to break away from their biological role as caregivers for their men and their families. This must be exciting."

"It's also confusing," I observed.

"For the girls?"

"Yes, and for the boys."

"In Vietnam, there is no women's liberation movement or sexual revolution like in the West. Our girls are encouraged to be submissive, protective, and to care for their families. Our girls grow up to become women and mothers who are noble, hardworking, and chaste, but I have sympathy for girls in the West and their struggle. I share their struggle."

"Another exception?" I asked.

"Yes."

"What is chaste?"

My Hanh smiled again and gave me a funny look. Her face turned red. "I have to translate English to an American! It means 'virtuous.'"

"Aaah!"

"There is a Vietnamese proverb, 'Virtue is much better than beauty,'" she recounted.

"If you are more virtuous than beautiful, you must be a saint!" I smiled at her.

"Thank you, my Robbie, but at risk of disappointing you, I am not exactly a saint." She looked at me coyly.

"My Robbie?" I asked.

"The letters *m-y* with an accent over the *y* mean 'American' in Vietnamese, so I have called you Robbie the American," she explained.

"And without the accent?"

"*M-y* spelled without the accent means 'bird' in English, and as I told you, Hanh means 'luck,' so I am lucky bird," she explained.

"Tell me about your dress. Is it a native costume?"

"Yes, it is called *Áo dài*."

"Maybe after today it would be a good idea to wear something less traditional in the Métro," I suggested.

"I am not going to change my behavior because of what happened today."

"Well, that's brave, but don't you think it's also foolish? There may be more deranged French soldiers out there. I admire your courage, but you need to think about your safety."

"Now you sound like my father, who will be very unhappy that I left our hotel without a security detail."

"He won't be able to scold you if you do as he asks."

She did not take this well and it showed on her face.

"I can give advice, too," she barked. "Your country's bombers drop fiery death on our people every day. If you're concerned about my safety . . ."

"I get it! I get it! I'm sorry. I was just thinking of your safety—your *personal* safety."

Whatever our connection, it appeared she would not forget that our countries were at war.

"I am sorry, too, my Robbie. It's just—"

"It's cool. This is going to take a little getting used to," I observed at the risk of presuming we had a future.

"You think you can get used to me?" she asked, her sense of humor returning.

"I don't know. I'll have to see you in jeans."

"We don't have jeans in Vietnam, but I have bought them on the black market."

"So you're not a saint."

"I told you. And I think you will like me in jeans."

"Maybe more than I do in *áo dài*."

"Then I shall wear only the jeans," she proclaimed.

"Even on the Métro?"

"Yes, even on the Métro." She laughed heartily.

"You'll look like a cool chick from the West," I added with a sly twist of the eyebrows.

"Yes, groovy, as your hippies say in America, and I'll let my hair down, too!" She reached up, pulled out the ivory pins that held up her bun, and shook her head, her shiny black hair tumbling down on either side of her beautiful face. "How's that?" She ran her fingers through her hair.

I sat stunned, amazed at her beauty and her sheer joy of being. It was contagious. "Fab, as we say in America," I said.

She looked at me warmly, her eyes penetrating mine. "Aaah, you are a difficult American to dislike, my Robbie. It is confusing to be at war and find that you very much like one of your enemies, but when I listen to you, when I look in your eyes, I do not see the ignorance and the cruelty of your country's war. I see a young man who is generous, understanding, and funny. I see a man worthy of my affection. Am I right about this, my Robbie, or am I being a foolish girl with wishful thinking?"

"You are not a foolish girl."

"I think everyone in my country would say I am a very foolish girl," she said with another blockbuster smile. She sat back down on the bench, moving closer to me.

"Somehow, My Hanh, though we have just met, I feel like you know me. In fact, I think you knew me the moment our eyes met on the train. Does that sound foolish to you?"

"No, because I feel this, too. Do you have a steady girlfriend?"

"No, I don't. And you, a boyfriend?"

"No," she said. "Have you ever had a girlfriend who knew you the moment you met?"

"No. And you a boyfriend?"

"No, never this way, never from the moment we met."

"The girls I have dated have been in love with the idea of rebellion, position, wealth— something external to themselves and to me. I don't think any have ever known me the way I think you know me."

"Did you open up to them, listen with your heart to them, and take time to know them?" she asked.

I considered her question. "Maybe I needed to do a better job at that."

Again she got me thinking.

"Aristotle said, 'Wishing to be friends is quick work, but friendship is a slow-ripening fruit,' so I think understanding others takes time," she said. "This is true for individuals and for nations with different cultures."

"I think that's what's happening in America. There is a transformation underway, a process we can see in the words of our poets, like Robert Lowell and Allen Ginsberg."

Her eyes lit up. "I know these poets, Robbie. I have read them."

She recited Lowell's "Children of Light": "'Our fathers wrung their bread from stocks and stones and fenced their gardens with the Redman's bones.'"

She pronounced each word as if English were her native tongue.

I picked up: "'They planted here the Serpent's seeds of light; and here the pivoting searchlights probe to shock, the riotous glass houses built on rock.'"

Amazingly, we had each loved and memorized this poem while living eight thousand miles apart on opposite sides of the planet in cultures and with backgrounds that couldn't be more different.

"The transformation is also taking root in our political system," I observed. "We hear it in the voices of Eugene McCarthy and Robert Kennedy. There are many people less well known who are demonstrating to bring our nation to its senses about the war."

"I know McCarthy and Kennedy," she exclaimed, her eyes lighting up again. "They have spoken out for peace!"

"But the majority of our leaders still support the war," I added. "They may understand that your country fights for its unification and independence, but their focus is on the ideological struggle between the Soviet Union and the United States, between communism and freedom, and yours is a communist country, so they are convinced that America is doing the right thing."

"So, it is all about communism."

"Yes, that's exactly the problem. American leaders don't want to lose face. The Russians and Chinese would take advantage of any perceived weakness. No one wants nuclear war."

"So Vietnamese die instead?"

"Yes. It's the lesser evil."

"The lesser evil," she repeated, her voice sarcastic, her tone defiant.

"I'm just trying to explain why this is happening," I insisted. "I'm not agreeing with it."

"It's your leaders who are evil. They are driven by fear. Look at your inner cities, your college campuses, and the jungles of my country. There is no love, no tolerance, no understanding, only fear. Power obtained by fear will always fail. It is the law of the universe."

"My Hanh, you are wise—wiser than any girl I have met."

"*Cái khó ló cái khôn,*" she spoke in Vietnamese, her voice softening.

"What does it mean?"

"It means 'adversity is the mother of wisdom.' My father always says this."

"What else does he say?"

"*Một câu nhịn chín câu lành.* It means 'better a lean peace than a fat victory.'"

"I like that."

"It may be all we can hope for." She looked at me affectionately.

I took her hand. We sat in silence, gazed at one another, our eyes locked, our hands clasped. I basked in her warm glow. I tightened my grip of her hand. A light breeze blew across the garden, and the warm rays of the setting sun fell upon us from the west. She tilted her head slightly and I tilted mine. I let go of her hand, put my arms around her, and pulled her close. I moved my head ever so slowly to hers. Our lips touched, and I could feel her breath moving with mine. Our kiss lingered with lightness and gentleness.

"Oh, Robbie!" she cried.

"My Hanh, I . . ."

Suddenly, she broke away, still looking into my eyes.

"In my culture girls do not move as quickly as they do in America or in France. Am I too old-fashioned, my Robbie?"

I answered her with an understanding look.

"Did you ever think you would kiss a communist and a Buddhist?" she asked, another smile breaking out on her lovely face.

"No! Never! You're Buddhist?"

"Yes, I practice the six perfections of Buddhism: generosity, morality, patience, energy, meditation, and wisdom. I try to do no harm in this life, Robbie, to live as an enlightened being true to my own nature, and I apply these teachings when I am distracted by feelings of anger, greed, or fear."

"If you could bottle that, I would drink some," I joked.

"Maybe we could get your American policy makers to drink some."

"If only it were that easy."

"In Buddhism," she said, "we try to live as a lotus blossom, floating in the muddy waters of life, which not only adds beauty but by its very actions makes the water cleaner."

"Maybe when you are done helping your father you should move to America and run for political office," I joked again, feeling giddy and sharing in the glow of My Hanh's effervescent joy.

She reached up, placed her soft hand on my cheek, and stroked it gently.

I was delighted and enchanted in equal measure by this girl, whose spirit I could feel lifting mine.

"Tell me about your religion?" she asked.

"Okay. I'm Jewish, but in my family we ran away from our religion. My grandparents, who came to America from Russia and Poland, wanted to be seen as Americans, not as Jews. They shortened their name to sound less Jewish and gave up many of the rituals of Judaism. They dressed and acted like the ma-

jority of Americans, who are Christian. I guess I am not a serious person when it comes to religion."

"There are no Jews in Vietnam, except for a small group of
French expatriates," she said. "Do you practice *tikkun olam*?"

"How do you know about *tikkun olam*?" I asked, amazed.

"I wrote a paper about this during high school. I love the
idea of a shared responsibility to heal, repair, and transform
the world. I think we need more people who live this way."

"You wrote a paper on *tikkun olam*?"

"I remember this quote by a rabbi—I think his name was
Herschel—that living is not a private affair of the individual. It
is what man does with God's time, what man does with God's
world. He also said that the meaning of a man's life lies in his
perfecting the universe, that he has to distinguish and redeem
the sparks of holiness scattered throughout the darkness of
the world. These words impressed me."

"They are powerful and beautiful," I agreed.

Tikkun olam was the only thing that had stuck with me
from all the years my parents had sent me to Saturday religious
school. I couldn't believe that My Hanh knew about this, coming from a country with no Jews!

"Ah, so you are not such a bad Jew after all," she observed.

I shook my head in disbelief that we shared another common interest, the chances of which were so remote.

"I guess I'm just another lotus blossom floating in the
muddy waters of life," I deadpanned.

"So that makes you a good Buddhist, too," she retorted.
"Like your Abbie Hoffman, half Jew and half Buddhist."

"How the hell do you know about Abbie Hoffman?"

"He's half Buddhist, so I have kept up with that half."

"Probably better than I have kept up with the Jewish half."

"Yes, I read that he married twice, first at a Buddhist ceremony 'in holy mind blow' to the *I Ching*, and later that day at a Jewish temple on the Upper East Side."

"You are really something!" I exclaimed.

"I would like to teach you more about Buddhism, Robbie, for all of us require a teacher. And you must learn more about your Judaism and teach me."

"Deal," I said, holding out my hand.

"I believe that when used wisely, spiritual practices can carry us across life's difficulties like a boat across a river, but you should never use them as a ram to smash other people's beliefs," she instructed. "Promise me you will never do that, my Robbie."

"I will not do that," I said. "After all, we are in the same boat, right?"

"Yes, I think we are in the same boat. A simple Vietnamese junk sailing in smooth waters."

"I was thinking a technically advanced American cabin cruiser with a cozy stateroom."

She laughed and slapped me on the arm. "Aaah, you have a really bad sense of humor!"

I grabbed her hand and pulled her to me. We kissed again, lost in our mutual attraction, and this time we kissed until we were both breathless.

"I cannot tell my father about us," she whispered.

"My parents would freak out, too. We are again in the same boat."

"The junk?" she asked with a smile.

"No, the cabin cruiser—more stable in rough seas."

We laughed and kissed and talked nonstop until the sun went down, the air cooled, and the darkness fell around us. We would not have noticed were it not for the guard who approached and informed us that the garden was about to close.

My Hanh asked me to walk her back to the Métro so she could return to her hotel. I asked her if she wanted to take a cab, but she refused, saying she had forgiven her assailant and let go of the past. She repeated that she was not going to permit the incident to affect her behavior and would never let her time in Paris be intruded upon by a security detail.

Hand in hand we walked back to Saint-Paul, and I stayed with her, helping her find the right Métro line, and walked her to the platform. We stood on the platform and embraced until the Métro arrived, a fitting tableau in the city of light and love. We kissed and did not take our eyes off each other until the Métro pulled away.

Chapter 7

American Institute
in Paris

Home for me in Paris was the sixth-floor apartment of Madame Gueumier, a single lady of some distinction whose contribution to Franco-American relations was to rent the extra room in her grand apartment to an American student each year. The rent was 120 francs a month, less than half of what a small apartment cost and included a weekly dinner. The room was separated from the rest of the apartment by a long hallway and had its own back stairwell, convenient for sneaking girls up for the night, although I rarely managed to do that without being caught by the eagle-eyed concierge, the iron-fisted Marionette Dubois.

I found the room at the school housing office the Monday following my arrival, checked out of our temporary quarters at the Hôtel des Gobelins, and moved to Madame Gueumier's apartment at 54 rue de la Bienfaisance, just down the road from the Gare Saint-Lazare. Jan found a place at Cité University. Madame Gueumier's apartment was located in a wonderful upper-class neighborhood, fitting for a woman who had worked her way up the corporate ladder of a large international insurance company and now ran their operations in France. She was well dressed, with perfectly coiffed gray hair, and always wore one of her many stone-encrusted pins on the right shoulder of her dress. She spoke English with an accent that made many of her words sound French.

"*Enchantée*," Madame Gueumier said with a half-smile and a look of interrogation when she met me for the first time.

"Nice to meet you," I responded, eagerly offering my outstretched hand.

She hesitated, then grabbed it for a single shake.

At first Madame Gueumier treated me warily. She grimaced when she saw my library of books on the Vietnam War and raised her hand to her forehead in dismay when she saw me unpacking the sixty-four rolls of toilet paper. "*Mon Dieu*," I thought I heard her exclaim under her breath. It looked to me like she immediately concluded I would be trouble.

Our weekly dinner, part of the school housing package, was at first a formal affair. We would meet in her dining room; the door connecting my room to the apartment would be opened in advance, on that evening only. We dressed up for the occasion, and Marionette was hired to prepare and serve the meal, which, although not quite up to the quality and volume of first class on the *Queen Elizabeth*, more resembled that fare than what I had come to know as dinner at home or at school. Marionette always served at least four courses and presented each artfully and graciously, responding promptly to Madame Gueumier's bell when we were ready for the next course.

At these dinners I would often bring up the topic of Vietnam, and Madame Gueumier would react the same way: a pained look, a shaking of her head, and an admonition that she just could not understand why this was so important to me, why I kept reading all those books, and why I'd bothered to bring them all to Paris. "*Tu es un peu fou avec le Vietnam*," she would say, meaning roughly, "You are a bit crazy with Vietnam." Actually, I was a lot crazier with Vietnam than she realized. I could not stop thinking about My Hanh.

"Your French army could not win there, and I don't think we can either," I offered as she twitched her eyes, chewed faster, grimaced, and squirmed in her chair, the body language equivalent of *Shut your ignorant mouth, kid!*

Then, one night, when I mentioned the French war, as she deftly moved a slice of foie gras to a piece of toast with her knife, looking down, stone-faced, and seemingly annoyed, as she always became when I brought it up, she suddenly lurched from her chair, walked over to the open window on the other side of the room, and stood there, her back to me. I could hear her weeping—so out of character. I was shocked to silence and didn't know what to do. In a moment, which seemed to linger, she turned around and spoke wistfully in English, "Robbie, I lost my husband in Vietnam."

She had never spoken of him before. He was a colonel in the French army.

"I loved him so. . . Losing him broke my heart, and although it was years ago, my heart, it is still broken. Every time you speak of Vietnam it opens the wound."

"I am so sorry! I had no idea!"

"I ask you, Robbie, please do not speak of this again.

"I understand," I responded, feeling remorse at having added to her suffering.

After that, I never brought up the war and even took my collection of books off the mantel in my room, storing them in boxes, which I slid under the bed. Then one day a few weeks later, following rumors in the press of a possible bombing pause and peace talks to be held in Paris, Madame Gueumier surprised me by bringing up the subject. Of course I said nothing of what I had learned from My Hanh.

"I pray they will settle this," she whispered as she lifted her spoon from a steaming bowl of potage de légumes. I did not respond. "It is time for this war to end, and I am happy the talks may take place here à Paris. *C'est à propos.*"

She spoke about her late husband, Armand, and how he died at the Battle of Dien Bien Phu. Her words and her gestures revealed the suffering that war creates in its aftermath, the wounds of the families who lose loved ones. She told me that like so many of her generation, she was convinced that the use of military force was necessary to stop the spread of communism, and that de Gaulle's authoritarian rule was the only thing stood between France and chaos. She fully accepted the domino theory of American foreign policy. If we didn't stop the communists in Saigon, they would show up one day in Marseille or Milwaukee, and our way of life in France and in America, liberty and a free economy would be lost.

"Nonsense," I told her, wondering if I was speaking too bluntly.

"You are so naïve, young Robbie. You and your books. You don't really know how the world works, and I don't think you appreciate the dangers."

She paused before continuing, glancing at me, then looking down. "When I think of the pain, my pain, and the pain of so many in France, in America, and in Vietnam, the suffering all these years, I pray this bombing pause takes place and leads to an end of this war. So, I agree with you, Robbie. There has been enough killing, enough pain."

She told me Armand had had his own doubts about the war, something she had never admitted to anyone.

"As much as I don't like to admit it, the arguments he made to me were not so different from the arguments you have made against the American war."

"And I thought you thought I was, how do you say in French? *Plein de merde*—full of shit."

"*Non, non.* Come to think of it, you are a little like Armand," she said with a wry smile. "Another idealist who thinks the world can be remade for the better."

"One roll of toilet paper at a time," I added.

We laughed.

Looking back, the lessons I learned talking with Madame Gueumier at our weekly dinners were as important as any I gained in the classrooms at the American Institute, except perhaps in the extraordinary political science class, taught by Dr. Franz Nastovich. He was something of a legend at the school, and it was not uncommon to face a waiting list to sign up for his class.

"Mr. Sambergerrrr . . ." he called out when I entered his class two minutes late on the first day of school, adding an *-er* to the end of my name and stretching out the *r*, calling me by the three-syllabled last name as it was before my grandparents shortened it to Samberg. "You are late, young man," he admonished as he stood, straightening his corduroy blazer with leather patches at the elbows, putting down his pipe, removing his wire-rim glasses to wipe them clean with a white hanky, and lifting his head to loosen the plaid bow tie he wore every day.

Nothing like this had ever happened at George Washington, where professors could care less if you walked in after the class started. I scurried to the closest empty desk, but he would not let me off the hook insisting I provide an explanation for my tardiness to the entire class.

"I was in the toilet," I explained

"Mr. Sambergerrrr, really?" He scowled at me and shook his head back and forth.

In Nastovich's class, I found myself defending the America I often criticized to others. The harder he poked at the foundation of my traditional beliefs about America, the more I rose to the defense.

"Mr. Sambergerrrr, I am editing the manuscript of Monsieur Servan-Schreiber's new book, *Le Défi Américain*, in which he documents the insidious threat of American economic imperialism."

America, according to Nastovich, was hell-bent on taking over Europe, something that the presence of a McDonald's on the Champs-Élysées bore witness to, and as he would say, "In the clear, cool light of dispassionate reason, unless the juggernaut is stopped, Europe as we know it will be lost."

"Sorry." I stood at my desk. "I just don't see any threat to French culture from the sale of American hamburgers in Paris."

"Oh no?" he glared at me.

"I may be only a student from New Jersey, son of Irwin and Ellen Samberg, not Samberger, of Trenton, and straight from the middle class of torn-up, screwed-up, messed-up America, but I really don't think there is a plot afoot to take over Europe. Free markets will bring cultural and economic changes to both sides of the Atlantic and throughout the world, but that change will go both ways. Lots of Americans eat French fries!" Jan winked and tossed me a discreet thumbs-up. I sat down.

"Mr. Sambergerrrr," Nastovich roared, leaning over the lectern, his bow tie slightly awry, "are you really that naïve? Don't you know that when you enter a hotel here in Paris and hear the music in the elevators and the hallways, it is the same insidious Muzak produced in America and is part of the same process of cultural subjugation? The culture war is on, Mr. Sambergerrrr, and Europe is in the crosshairs! In the cool, clear light of dispassionate reason, what do you say to that, Mr.

Sambergerrrr?" he goaded, pushing his glasses back up to the base of his nose.

"Well, actually, professor," I responded, rising up again, "you must not be aware—I am sure you are not—that my father makes his living as a Muzak franchiser in the state of New Jersey."

By now the two of us were going at it, adrenaline pumping, while the rest of the class observed like Romans at the Coliseum. No one dared make a sound in disfavor of Dr. Nastovich for fear of reprisal, except for Jan, who enjoyed the class as much as I did and engaged similarly with Nastovich. She smiled encouragement.

"Before you conclude that my poor father is guilty as charged," I continued, "a cultural provocateur and musical terrorist of the first order, I must tell you in his defense, as a frequent witness to the running of an actual Muzak franchise, that I never once heard any conversation about a goal of cultural hegemony here in France or elsewhere in Europe, or anywhere for that matter!" I concluded with the self-congratulatory smirk one happily casts on an opponent when they are clearly on the ropes.

Not a stir could be heard in the class, except for the staccato rhythm of Dr. Nastovich nervously tapping the podium with his Harvard ring, shaking his head back and forth, his look menacing, then suddenly transformed by a smile of resignation.

We would argue back and forth, most of the time playfully, mock heroically, and at times passionately, and to our mutual annoyance in what became one of the most stimulating and important experiences of my education abroad.

I thought for some time that our verbal jousts might morph into a personal relationship, and I really wanted this, but Nastovich remained aloof and, unlike some professors, who encouraged personal contact, inviting students for coffee or to their homes for a meal, he kept his distance. He remained a mystery, a confounding, challenging, stimulating, articulate mystery who kept us all off guard, even as he opened our minds to new thinking.

One Friday afternoon, following a testy exchange about General Motors—he thought it was about to take over the European auto market—I asked Dr. Nastovich if he would join me to meet my friend Danny Cohn-Bendit at the nearby University of Nanterre. Danny had invited me to a meeting of a new group he was forming to challenge the French university system—"To shake things up," he said—and I thought that with Nastovich's influence in academic and political circles he might be the perfect American to bring along.

"No, Robbie. I have no interest in sticking my nose into the affairs of the French Ministry of Education. I'll leave that improbable task to you students, but you better be careful," he warned. "Don't go getting yourself into trouble."

Trouble? I thought. *Why is he warning me about getting in trouble? It is only a student meeting. No big deal.*

"Robbie, you need to understand there are some serious problems there and a lot of pent-up frustration," he warned, waving me out of the classroom.

I had the feeling he knew more and cared more deeply about the problems in the French university system than he let on.

Danny was also Jewish, born just two years before me to a German father and a French mother in postwar France. We met at the apartment of Charlie Siebel, a fellow student, whose family lived in Italy and rented him an apartment in Passy, where he hosted nonstop parties.

One night I headed to Charlie's for a party and couldn't get in the front door. Charlie had locked it because an inebriated freshman, Terry Barnhart, was balling two guys in the dining room, and Charlie didn't want anyone coming in to interrupt. I waited outside the apartment door, knocking on occasion and enjoying the sounds of the fun taking place inside, which were clearly audible in the hallway. Danny arrived while I was waiting and sat down next to me. He was also a friend of Charlie's.

"You're at the American Institute like Charlie?" he asked.

Danny had wavy, thick red hair, large ears, puffy cheeks, and a ruddy complexion with lots of freckles. His wide eyes protruded from his face. He wore baggy pants, a black golf shirt, and a blue windbreaker without a collar.

"Yes, and you?"

"I'm at Nanterre." He curled his legs up to his chest and placed his arms around his knees.

"What are you studying?" I asked.

"Sociology. You?"

"History and poli-sci."

"Like Charlie," I said.

We laughed as a climactic moan emanated through the door.

"Want to trade places?" Danny asked.

"Why?" I thought he wanted to switch places on the floor, though I couldn't imagine why.

He grinned and chuckled. "Because your school is only screwed up, while ours is a hopeless fucking disaster."

The moaning stopped, but the door remained closed. I got up to knock again. No response. I sat back down.

"No, I'm okay at the American Institute."

"You and Charlie are lucky," he said. "We have to wait in line an hour and a half for a hot meal. It's ridiculous!"

"The food's okay where we are."

"We've got two hundred forty professors for twelve thousand students," he whined. "Our buildings are dingy. Our dorm furniture looks like it came from a flea market, and we can't even visit our girlfriends in their dorm."

"We live off campus, no dorms, so our school doesn't get into that. Why don't you take your complaints to the student government?"

"You're kidding," he said, looking amused and a bit exasperated. "We don't have a student government."

"You guys need to find a professor to sponsor one and get things going," I suggested.

"You don't understand. At Nanterre there's zero communication between students, faculty, and the school administration. The professors just lecture from on high and grade papers without mercy. They don't give a shit about us, and the school administration cares even less."

He was amazed to hear about my classroom debates with Dr. Nastovich.

"That's baaad, really awesome!" he said. "We don't even talk to our professors."

The moaning started again.

"Now there's good communication." I nodded toward the door, and we both broke out laughing.

"I guess we're going to be here for a while," Danny concluded, an infectious smile on his face.

"Nastovich told me the French system sucks."

"It's worse than that. The system is overcentralized, bureaucratic, and what's taught is hopelessly outdated and jammed down our throats in a tyranny of exams. Our students have become so frustrated, they're ready to revolt."

"That's been happening a lot," I responded. "I saw an article in the *Herald-Tribune* about a student march in Prague for improved heating and lighting in their dorms. A small group—no more than a hundred students—marched to Prague Castle carrying candles to symbolize their cause, and the police blocked their path and clubbed them, wounding fifty of the protesters."

We both shook our heads.

"Can you believe that shit?" Danny exclaimed.

"It makes no sense."

"No, it doesn't, but that kind of insane overreaction and the press it generated probably helped the students get what they wanted."

"Crushed skulls for brighter lights and warmer rooms," I said. "It's crazy!"

"The protests are contagious, "Danny observed. "They just seem to pop up spontaneously around the world."

"Charlie thinks the communist party is behind it and is trying to gain ground by infiltrating the student movement."

"Charlie blames everything on the communists," Danny said. "His family is filthy rich and right wing. I haven't seen any communist influence at Nanterre."

"I think we need more influence to get in this door," I said, jumping to my feet and knocking again. The moaning suddenly grew louder. "I think they're all swapping spit in there," I said, looking at Danny as we both laughed again.

"It's cool that the protests are happening worldwide," he continued, his laughter subsiding. "We've had protests in Spain, Brazil, Japan, and England. There's something going on out there that nobody is talking about. The movement is spreading like a prairie fire."

Danny told me he had studied in the United States a year before I graduated from high school and had attended a memorial service for Andrew Goodman, Michael Schwerner, and James Chaney, the civil rights workers murdered in Mississippi in 1964 by the Ku Klux Klan. He knew all about the Congress of Racial Equality (CORE) and the Student Nonviolent Coordinating Committee (SNCC), for which Goodman, Chaney, and

Schwerner had volunteered to register Negro voters in rural Mississippi.

"Looks like somebody forgot the 'nonviolent' part," Danny observed. "Come to think of it, your system is as fucked up as ours. What kind of country strips Muhammad Ali of his world title for refusing to kill Vietnamese?" he asked, shaking his head. "Two white Jews, Schwerner and Goodman, heading into the Deep South to fight for racial justice. I'm not sure I would have signed up for that," he added, clearly admiring their courage.

"What about Nanterre?" I asked. "Any prairie fires spreading there?"

"Yes, and I've been busy fanning the flames."

"What have you done?"

"I led an occupation of the girls' dorms to demand men be allowed in," Danny responded, quickly realizing this was not much to brag about and hurriedly adding, "I also interrupted the dedication ceremony of a new swimming pool to read a manifesto on sexual freedom."

"Not exactly Mississippi moments," I observed.

"Well, no, but it took guts to seize the microphone at the pool dedication and lecture the Minister of Education, who was presiding. At least I did something. It's absurd that male students can't visit female students in their dorms. We're not children."

"Yes, I agree, but it's worse in puritan America. That's where you should have seized the mic and read the manifesto. They would have sewn a scarlet letter on your chest."

We laughed again. Meanwhile, the moaning continued, loud and unabated.

As we sat on the floor sharing our thoughts on school, girls, sex, the war, and everything in between, Danny told me about the new group he'd founded at Nanterre to challenge the status quo and organize protests. It was called the March 22 Movement. He invited me to their next meeting.

"We're going to shake things up," he said with a smile.

I was not sure I could make it, or if I wanted to get involved, but I wrote down the time and place. Danny had this mesmerizing effect on you. It was not easy to ignore his requests. Maybe it was the intensity of his thoughts and expressions, as fiery as his red hair, or his disarmingly good nature, or that easy smile, but there was something compelling about him.

"Expecting violence?" I asked.

"It depends on what the school administration does. The more they overreact, the greater the chance of violence."

"You're counting on that, aren't you?"

"We're counting on the stupidity of the administration and the police," he said.

"I get it. A couple of bleeding heads, and you'll get the press coverage you need. Very clever."

"That's the lesson of your American Civil Rights Movement," Danny said. "Without that bloody Sunday on the bridge in Selma and the press it attracted, there wouldn't have been a Voting Rights Act, or at least it wouldn't have come as soon as it did."

"Tell me you're not hoping for another Selma."

"No, we hope to keep things peaceful at Nanterre. Our plan is get creative and attract attention without inciting violence."

"Creative?"

"Yes, like the Oxford students who tried to throw Home Secretary Callaghan into a fish pond, or the Sussex students who splattered red paint on a press officer from the American embassy, or the students who turned the water in Trafalgar Square red with dye. That's the kind of cool stuff we plan for Nanterre. Pranks, creative pranks," he continued, breaking out his ten-megawatt smile. "Pranks to make our political points without anyone getting hurt." Danny spoke as if to reassure me, but it felt like he was also trying to reassure himself.

"Why don't you move into the girls' dorm?" I asked. "That would get you plenty of attention."

Danny's eyes widened. "I love it," he responded. "That's perfect! They'll never call in the police for that kind of prank," he reasoned. "Promise me you'll come to the meeting."

"We'll see. How long are we going to wait out here?"

"I don't know. I'm enjoying the conversation."

"Me too."

Just then the door to the apartment swung open, and Terry Barnhart, naked save for a pair of red high heels, hickeys all over her breasts and midsection, emerged, grabbed Danny and me by the arms, and pulled us inside.

Chapter 8

A Walk in the Park

Student life at the American Institute bore little resemblance to my experience at George Washington University. The institute was smaller than GW, more intimate. Everyone knew everyone else. The pace of the day was different too in that I didn't have to fit in a job three days a week. Paris was more my classroom than the rooms at school. Every day I would discover something new about the city, a new street, a new museum, a new monument, a new food and I loved what I learned. But nothing, not even the charms of the city, could distract me from thoughts of My Hanh. I had to see her again.

One of the things I enjoyed most about my life at school was returning after a day of classes to Madame Gueumier's apartment, throwing a Piaf LP on the stereo, running the bath, opening the French windows, and gently lowering myself into the large claw-foot tub in the corner of my room. The cascading warm water caressed and soothed me, fueling my reverie. I would lay there, eyes closed, intoxicated with thoughts of My Hanh.

I relived every moment in the Métro and the garden the day we met: the spark when her eyes met mine, her chiseled face, perfect hands, glowing eyes, her simple and wise words. I glanced at the side of the porcelain tub and saw the luminescence of her skin. I picked up the bar of lavender-milled

French soap and smelled her aroma. I heard the muted sounds of the Gare Saint-Lazare just down the road, the trains whistling, the travelers scurrying, the occasional shout for a taxi, and at last, on more than one occasion, the sound of the needle of the record player scraping at the end of the LP, which had long ago finished playing.

One evening, as I lay in the tub, a hard knock on my door roused me from my reverie. I grabbed a towel, opened the door, and there before me stood Danny, his clothes wrinkled as if he had slept in them, his wavy red hair uncombed, a determined look on his face.

"Well, at least you don't make me wait forty-five minutes like Charlie," he blurted.

I stood before him dripping wet, still not fully alert.

"What, no Terry Barnhart?" he quickly added. "Never coming here again!"

I informed him that the only woman in the apartment was Madame Gueumier.

"Want me to call her?" I asked as we broke into hysterical laughter.

I returned to the armchair next to the tub and continued to dry myself. Danny stepped over the puddle of water on the floor where I had been standing and sat down on the bed.

"You look happy," he said. "Did you meet someone?"

"You're quite a detective. Yes, I met this amazing girl . . ." My voice trailed off, as I realized I couldn't say much more.

"Nice!" he said. "Tell me!"

"I think I'm in love."

"Christ, no, that's crazy."

"What's so crazy?"

"Every time I've fallen in love, it's been crazy."

"This girl seems perfect to me."

"Wow, you're in trouble," Danny responded, a quizzical look on his face.

"I can handle it," I said.

"Really? Is she French?"

"No."

"Where is she from?"

I hesitated and changed the subject. "What's with you?" I asked.

A worried look returned to Danny's face. "My Mississippi moment is coming tomorrow," he said, his expression pensive. I noticed he hadn't shaved and was more unkempt than usual. He looked tired.

"Tomorrow?" I asked. "Did you sleep last night?"

"Not much. Tomorrow I go before the disciplinary board at Nanterre, and I want you to come with me, Robbie."

He spoke as if I had little choice. It was his special way of asking, one part request and two parts command.

"If you want me there, you're going to have to tell me what's going on. What have you done?"

"You know, Robbie. I've done what student leaders around the world have done. I organized a protest to reform the system."

"Reform or tear down?"

"Reform, but if the damn fool administrators don't listen—"

"What happened to getting creative, to the innocent pranks?" I asked. "Did you move into the girls' dorm?"

"Yes, and it went great, just like you said it would. The administration didn't call in the police and we made our point, but I got called before the disciplinary board."

"Oh, so this is my fault?"

"Hey, it was your brilliant idea!"

"So, what's your next move?"

"We want to shake things up. Our group is now a couple of hundred strong. We want to stand up for intellectual freedom, social freedom, sexual freedom. We want better communication between professors and students, between the state and the universities. The system is broken. It should be torn down, but I've got a plan that will make our points and keep the lid on."

"Keep the lid on?" I asked.

"Don't believe everything you read about me, Robbie," he said. "There's a nice Jewish boy under this fiery red hair who wants to change the world without getting thrown out of school and without seeing a lot of people hurt."

"So, the March 22 Movement—that's what got you in trouble."

"Well, that, the move-in at the girls' dorm, and a few other things."

"What else?"

"There was the wisecrack I made to Minister of Youth François Missoffe during his visit to the campus."

"What did you say?"

"I asked him a simple question about housing policy, and he gave me this ridiculous, insulting answer, so I told him his answer was worthy of Hitler's youth minister, and I don't think that endeared me to him!"

"I wouldn't think so!"

We laughed hysterically once again.

"Maybe it's my German ancestry . . . The French haven't forgotten the world wars, and I'm a Jew, so that doesn't help either. Anti-Semitism is still rampant here, you know." Danny looked serious again.

"I've heard that, but it sounds to me like you've been playing with fire with all your *enragé* talk, and that's what's about to burn you, not anti-Semitism."

"The government thinks I march in lockstep with the Trot-skyites, like Alain Krivine and Rudi Dutchke, but I don't. I'm my own guy, Robbie."

"Oh, so you're a communist, too."

"No, Robbie! We reject the communists. We reject de Gaulle and his government. We reject political parties on the left and the right. We reject all claims to authority. We seek a society without authority."

"Is that the speech you're planning to give? Sounds like you're an anarchist, not a communist. Great! That's just great, Danny."

"Robbie, the issues we're raising tomorrow are larger than Nanterre," he said. "We're standing against the corruption of authority in our economy and society, in the trade unions, workplaces, the government bureaucracy, the military, and civil society. Our target is authority itself, which has been abused."

"Another good speech line," I responded, shaking my head in dismay.

Danny ignored me. "And when we stand up to resist the uni-versity structure, we're going to inspire those who are disen-chanted in other parts of society. It will be like striking a match next to an open tank of gasoline."

"That's what I'm afraid of." I thrust my hands outward and made a *kaboom* sound.

"I'm talking figuratively, not literally," Danny insisted.

"So, you're going on the offense before the board, using it as a platform to demand change."

"Yes, and they're going to love me, Robbie, don't you think?" he asked with a wink and that big infectious grin he tossed with innocence to beguile, as if causing trouble were the far-thest thing from his mind.

"Careful, Danny. Your lit match might set off a napalm bomb."

"I don't see that happening," he said. "They're not going to call in the police and violate the centuries-old sanctuary of the university over a protest meeting in the university courtyard."

"Hey, remember Prague," I reminded him. "What could have been more innocent than better heating and lighting? And they were beaten. Are you're expecting television coverage?"

"We're counting on it. It's our megaphone to the world."

"You know, Danny," I reflected, now dry and putting on my clothes, "from everything you have told me, I don't think the administration at Nanterre has a clue about what you are trying to do. I think they are going to freak out if you come on too strong."

"We've got to educate them," Danny said. "Wake them from their complacency. Will you help me?"

"Danny," I . . ."

"Look, we've got too many students in the system right now who have lost hope in their future. We need to shake things up if we're ever going to get real dialog and common-sense reforms."

In the 1960s the number of university students in France had increased dramatically, from one hundred seventy-five thousand in 1958 to five hundred thirty thousand in 1968. Universities became overcrowded, with one hundred sixty thousand students at the University of Paris alone.

Just as Danny had described, the culture at the universities and in the educational system was autocratic and rigid. Decisions were handed down without discussion. The exercise of power was a one-way street—"my way or the highway"—and there was no place for dialog, much less dissent. There was little or no flexibility in the system to evolve based on changing needs.

Hidden from view beneath the ever-charming façade of a tranquil Paris lay an increasingly disaffected, radicalized youth in a nation led by a hopelessly out-of-touch autocrat.

France was ruled by a seventy-eight-year-old general and modern-day royalist (or at least he behaved that way), Charles de Gaulle, or Charles André Joseph Marie de Gaulle as he preferred to be called. Many called him Le General or, like Danny, Le Grand Charles.

Leader of the Free French Forces during World War II, founder the Fifth Republic in 1958, author of its constitution and its first president, elected in 1959, he was a statesman without a parallel in America. He saw himself and France as leading a Third World movement, a counterbalance to the bipolar world of America and the Soviet Union.

Le Grand Charles was not about to allow a rowdy band of students to get in his way. As innocent, insignificant, and disorganized as Danny and his small group were, de Gaulle and his ministers saw them as a threat to stability and the role they wanted France to play.

"In the midst of so many countries shaken by confusion, ours will continue to set an example of order," De Gaulle boldly proclaimed in his New Year's message for 1968. "It is impossible to see how France today could be paralyzed by a crisis as she has been in the past."

"All the rector cares about is the exam schedule," Danny lamented. "He and Le Grand Charles are clueless."

Danny stood up from the edge of the bed, where he had been sitting and walked over to the open French windows. He turned toward me.

"So, come on, Robbie, come with me! It's going to be fun, a walk in the park," he insisted, that determined look back on his face.

"But why *me*?"

"Because I need your help."

"My help?"

"Robbie, you've got no fingerprints over here."

"Fingerprints?"

"There's no dossier on you. You're an unknown and you have an American passport."

"So?"

"If things spin out of control, they won't touch you."

"*Touch* me?"

"Arrest you," Danny clarified.

"Me, on the other hand . . . They know me very well at the rector's office, even at the police and the Ministry of the Interior. If I'm arrested, I'll need a friend on the outside to contact my sister in the Marais and my friends in the movement."

"I thought you said tomorrow was *your* Mississippi moment. You're asking me to make it *our* Mississippi moment."

"Hey, the girls' dorm occupation was your idea," he said, smirking.

"Guilt trip, huh?"

"Whatever it takes. I need your help, Robbie . . . You won't regret it, my friend!"

"Friend, huh? First guilt, then flattery!"

"You are my friend, aren't you?"

"Yes, yes, God help me!"

"So you'll do it?" He held up his fist.

"Get out of here, Danny!" I slapped his fist away and gave him the finger.

"So you'll do it?"

"I don't know, Danny," I said, shaking my head. "I really don't want to get my skull cracked open."

"No way that's going to happen. I guarantee it. I need you, Robbie." He got down on one knee.

"Oh Christ. Get up, you big idiot!"

"So, you'll come?"

"All right, all right. I'll see you at Nanterre in the morning," I said. "And if the board or the police don't kick the crap out of you, I may just do it myself."

Danny smiled and started to leave, but not before turning and raising his right fist in a mock salute. He was practicing his theatrics for the demonstration. I saluted back.

"Walk in the park," he proclaimed, as if there were a hundred people in my room.

"Walk in the park," I repeated as he marched over to the door and turned toward me again.

"Where's she from?" he asked, casting a bemused look at me. . .

"The girl?" I asked, surprised by the last-minute question.

"Yes!" he exclaimed. "You never said."

"Vietnam," I responded.

"Very cool! Not from the North, I hope," he admonished, making a funny face and laughing as he walked out and slammed the door behind him.

I sat on the bed. *What am I doing?* I shook my head. I felt a foreboding, but I told myself it would be okay. She *was* from the north, but it would be okay. Tomorrow would be okay, too. This was Nanterre, a satellite campus outside of Paris. Nothing serious was going to happen there. *Walk in the park. Walk in the park. Walk in the park. . .*

Chapter 9

Revolution

Sleep was not an option that night. I lay tossing, unable to find a comfortable position, my mind on the next day. Danny was my friend. He asked for my help. I wanted to be there for him. His movement was important for the students of France and for all students around the world. I wanted to be there for them, too. I needed to do this. I thought about how life can turn ugly in an instant and how we never see it coming. One moment we're going about our business as usual, and the next, wham! Life drops a bomb that blows our sense of security to smithereens. Would tomorrow be such a moment? A Mississippi moment? I had a premonition, and it would not go away. I also lay awake thinking about My Hanh, thoughts which at last lulled me to a restful sleep and the sweetest dreams.

The next morning I was up at 6 a.m. It was a beautiful Saturday in Paris. I caught the bus for Nanterre, located just outside the city, and before long approached the campus gate, where nothing seemed out of order. The day was warming up, the sun illuminating the narrow streets, filled with students dressed in spring clothes—T-shirts, cutoff jeans, and shirts tied at the waist on buxom coeds, often without the restraint of a bra underneath. The dress code here was "anything goes."

I followed the signs to the administration building and noticed a small crowd just outside the entrance on the university courtyard. *So these are the enragés!* They did not appear unruly and certainly didn't live up to Danny's name for them. They looked more like a fraternity crowd without the beer kegs, which doubtlessly would have been on hand were this an American campus. Perhaps my premonition was wrong and this would, after all, be a walk in the park.

I worked my way through the crowd, across the campus square to the Café Bert, where I was supposed to meet Danny and his friend Pierre, his lieutenant in the movement. I entered the café and spotted a crowd of students huddled around a large rectangular table at the back of the busy restaurant. They were sipping coffees, talking incessantly, and appeared to be a typical gathering of students taking a study break. I spotted Danny. He smiled when he saw me and waved me over. Then rather suddenly, before I could reach him, he jumped up on a chair, his eyes staying on mine as if to say, *Watch this!* I quickly learned why Danny might need my help this day.

"Comrades," he declared to the entire café, casting his words beyond the immediate crowd around his table, "we now march to our destiny to face the pigheaded administrators of our school, but don't think we speak only to them. We also speak to France, to Europe, and to America, to every student and to every worker who is held back, put down, and has no voice. We speak to everyone who aspires to tear down the authority, which on this day, at this time, we no longer need to live, to love, or to prosper!" He raised his right fist in the air.

The café crowd loved it. They roared their approval. I joined in the cheering and the applause as I witnessed the change in Danny from fellow student to inspiring leader standing before me on that rickety chair. *He is remarkable.*

"A world without authority," he went on, "is what we seek. A world where the establishment that holds us back hears our voices. We know they will not listen to one voice, but when all our voices join together as one, I promise you they *will* listen! Let us show today that our dreams can become a reality, and that the aggressor is not the one who revolts but the one who conforms. Let us show that barricades may close streets but they open new paths, paths to a future where we shall no longer live as robots or slaves!" Danny hopped off the chair, a determined look on his face, and came to me, opening his arms as the crowd surged behind him. He gave me a bear hug, held me tight, and whispered, "Stay with me, Robbie; stay with me."

I couldn't tell if he meant that he would be protecting me or if he was asking me to protect him. We exited the café and walked back to the administration building, where the crowd of students had swelled to several hundred and was considerably more agitated. It no longer felt like a fraternity party but something more edgy. Seeing Danny, a sea of people surged around us, and we had a difficult time working our way to the front of the building. Danny worked the crowd like a master politician. Smiling and waving, he stopped to embrace friends and greet strangers, taunting the crowd with cries of "*Vive la révolution!*"

When we reached the front steps, we climbed up to the enormous oak entry door and turned around to face the crowd, who cheered and raised their fists in solidarity. It was then that I first saw at the rear of the courtyard the dreaded instrument of state authority, the CRS, or, as they were known in France, the Compagnies Républicaines de Sécurité. The university rector had called the police to clear the courtyard, afraid that if left unchallenged the students might disrupt the all-important schedule of spring exams.

My heart beat faster at the sight. My breaths grew shallow. I sensed the danger and how easily events could spin out of control. The CRS stood behind us all, dressed in black combat helmets, dark goggles, long black trench coats, and carrying heavy nightsticks and large black shields. They looked ominous, like a Hollywood B-movie version of Space Invaders.

"Danny, what the fuck?" I said. "Why would they send the national police for a university disciplinary board meeting?"

"Watch this!" he exclaimed.

He turned and raised his hands to the crowd, gesturing silence, then climbed down the steps, and walked through the hushed throng, which turned around to face the fearsome CRS. Raising the palm of his right hand, Danny signaled everyone to stay back as he slowly but deliberately walked the two hundred yards which separated him from the line of CRS. Armed with only the mischievous grin on his freckled face, he moved toward the menacing line, slowing only to wave to the television cameras set up on the east side of the courtyard, next to the armored black vans which had transported the CRS to the scene. Inspired by Danny's courage, Pierre and I jumped out from the stationary crowd and hurried to join him, the three of us marching in lockstep.

"This is really nuts, Danny," I said.

"Yes, but you didn't have anything better to do today, did you?" He smiled that smile.

"I would like to survive for my date tonight," I said, the three of us moving ever closer to the danger ahead.

"With your new flame from *North* Vietnam?" he asked.

"How did you know?" I asked, struggling to keep up with Danny, who had picked up the pace.

"I was joking," he said. "You're in love with a commie! Don't worry, I'll make sure you come out of this in one piece."

The time for joking was over. The disciplined cadre of the CRS, batons in hand, stood ahead of us like an impenetrable black wall, any semblance of humanity or empathy obscured by the opaque masks which protected them and hid their faces.

"One for all, all for one!" Pierre joined in, tossing Danny and me a sanguine grin, the three of us marching ahead at a brisk clip.

"I don't think so," I retorted, thinking about saving myself as we closed in on the line of soldiers.

We were now only a dozen steps from getting our heads smashed. I looked over at Danny, who kept that infectious smile, making sure his every move was visible to the television cameras. He was playing the publicity card to protect us, and his doing so was the only thing that might prevent the lieutenant general in charge from ordering the CRS to attack and disperse the crowd. It was a game of chicken, and I prayed Danny was playing it right.

My mouth was dry. I trembled though no one watching could have detected my fear as I continued to march with determination alongside Danny and Pierre. I wondered what My Hanh would have me do at a moment like this. I remembered how bravely she stood as the melee erupted around her on the Métro. *She would want me to be brave.*

As we approached the CRS my confidence grew. I steeled myself for what lay ahead. *Walk in the park! Walk in the park!* We were now so close I could see my face reflected in the heavily tinted polycarbonate visor of the soldier in front of me. We did not slow down. We did not cower. We did not flinch, and when we reached the line of CRS, I closed my eyes and took what I thought would be my final steps before being smashed with a heavy black baton.

The CRS dropped back and opened a path for us to continue, shifting their line to the side of the courtyard.

I opened my eyes. Danny and I looked at each other, thrust our fists in the air, and together with Pierre screamed, "*Vive la révolution!*" elated at our last-second escape from danger. The crowd roared their approval. The television cameras whirred. I breathed a sigh of relief as Danny, Pierre, and I spun around, wove a path through the cheering crowd, which greeted us as conquering heroes, and arrived at the front steps of the administration building. We ran up the steps, our jubilance infecting the sea of rowdy students before us, and stood again in front of the great oak door side by side, our hands waving furiously, our joy in victory fueled by the roar of the crowd.

Danny grabbed the tarnished brass door handle with his left hand and thrust his right fist into the air. Slowly, he pulled the door open, but not before turning again to the crowd to offer one final clenched-fist salute, along with his bright, infectious smile. The crowd roared again, so loudly I thought it could be heard in Paris, even by My Hanh—a thousand fists raised in the air. It was exciting beyond measure.

The victory did not last, however. Unbeknown to Danny, Pierre, and me, after we entered the building to wait for the hearing to start, someone in the crowd picked up a cobblestone from the street and threw it at the CRS, who responded, shields up, by moving forward. Police officials quickly ordered the television crews to pack up and sent them away. More stones were thrown, to which the CRS responded with tear gas, concussion grenades, and a baton-thrashing onslaught to clear the courtyard and restore order. As their forces advanced, still more cobblestones were thrown. There was no shortage of stones, since the courtyard and all the streets around it were made from them. It quickly became what I had feared: a bloody confrontation.

The three of us heard the commotion and watched the battle from a second-floor window, still waiting for Danny to be called into the hearing room. He had stopped smiling. He had been so sure that he could handle things in a way that would prevent violence. We ran back to the front door to re-join the crowd, but by now the police were there and sent us back to the hearing room.

"If I had only been down there, I could have stopped the stone throwing," Danny lamented.

The courtyard was now filled with pockets of wounded students lying on the ground, choking from the tear gas, heads and limbs bleeding, with small groups of students, local residents, and professors around them administering first aid. Passing taxis stopped to offer rides to the hospital. Viewed from the second floor, the scene reminded me of the aftermath of a Napoleonic battle.

"Daniel Cohn-Bendit," a voice called as the double doors to the hearing room opened. "Please enter and take a seat."

Pierre and I attempted to follow but were instructed to remain outside in the corridor. The large doors swung closed. Danny would face his Mississippi moment alone. The violence outside added new impetus for a stiffer penalty.

Pierre and I sat down on the wooden bench in the corridor. The hearing did not take long. In less than a half hour, the doors swung open again, and Danny emerged, his hands in cuffs, accompanied by two officers, one on each side of him. Apparently, the board felt compelled to set an example.

"I'm under arrest," he screamed. "I'm under arrest."

Three more officers followed Danny and surrounded Pierre and me.

"You are under arrest for crimes against the state," the first officer told us as the other two placed handcuffs on Pierre and then on me.

"I'm an American citizen," I protested, to no avail.

The officers dragged Pierre and me down the stairs and locked us in a police van. Danny was already inside. Danny and Pierre were shaking.

"How the fuck did this happen?" Danny asked, tears in his eyes. Pierre was in tears as well.

"My family!" he cried.

The van pulled away from the building, siren screaming, the rear doors locked and the small opening to the driver's cabin closed.

I felt oddly composed. I lifted my cuffed hands to my face, raising my index finger to my lips to hush Danny and Pierre who were openly weeping.

"How can I help?" I whispered. "What can I do?" Danny pulled a crumpled envelope from his jacket pocket, and spoke in a trembling voice just loud enough to hear above the siren, "Here's a letter for my sister in the Marais and the speech I was going to give in the Latin Quarter. If you get out of here before me, deliver the letter and the speech, too!"

"The speech?" I asked.

"Yes, I need you to do this for me, for all of us," he implored with his tone and that look.

He frantically searched his pants pockets and pulled out a second letter, this one for his parents in Germany. "Take them! Deliver them!"

I took the papers, folded them as tightly as I could and stuffed them inside my shirt, covered by my windbreaker.

"What if they don't let you go?" Danny asked.

"Don't worry, Danny. It will be like you said. They had to cuff me and take me for show, but they'll release me. They're not going to hold an American."

"Robbie, you idiot, I just made that up to get you here. I have no idea what they'll do."

"No, they will let me go," I insisted.

"What about me?" Pierre asked.

"You'll be in jail with me, and we'll make our plans there," Danny replied, looking first at Pierre and then at me, lowering his head.

"Well, I guess I got this wrong," he admitted, still wiping away tears.

"Every setback is an opportunity, my friend," I said, putting my hand on Danny's shoulder.

"Ever the American optimist," he rejoined. "It would have been so much smarter for the rector to have sat down with us and talked about the exam schedule and the grievances."

"That's not how things operate in France," I responded.

"It would have diffused the bomb instead of igniting it," Danny added.

"The more the CRS acts to enforce order, the more disorder they create," I said. "The harsher they act to protect authority, the more they play into our hands and undermine authority."

"Our hands?" Danny asked. "You're one of us now?"

"One for all, all for one, my friend."

The van pulled into police headquarters, and the driver turned off the siren. We sat in the back waiting for the doors to open, looking at one another anxiously.

"Well, here we go," I said, offering a final smile.

The doors opened. An officer greeted us with a smirk and led us to a small room on the ground floor. He took off our cuffs and instructed us to empty our pockets and take off our clothes. I felt utter panic as I slowly reached into my pockets.

"Danny," I blurted in a loud voice, "my uncle, Senator Hankie has invited you to visit us in America, at our home in Indiana – Indiana, USA – notre maison aux Etats Unis," I repeated, translating for effect.

"Oh, that's so cool! I always wanted to visit America – and especially your home in Indiana," Danny responded on cue, raising his voice to a near shout. "dans l'Indiana, Etats- Unis!"

Danny and Pierre emptied their pockets, and began to remove their clothes—first their jackets, then belts and shoes, then a slow but deliberate unbuttoning of shirts—all the while glancing at me. I broke out in a cold sweat after taking off my windbreaker with nothing more to hide the incriminating papers from the officer but the buttons on my flannel shirt.

"You're American?" the officer asked at last in broken English. "Let me see your identification."

I pulled out my passport and United States Senate ID card.

He studied them and looked up. "Follow me," he said. By now Danny and Pierre were stark naked and I could see the relief on Danny's face as I put my jacket back on and the officer led me away, the door closing behind us.

Within the hour I was released because of the passport and walked out of the police station a free man, Danny's papers still tucked securely beneath my shirt. I felt an enormous sense of relief and headed for the Métro to catch a train back to Paris.

On the surrounding streets at Nanterre, five hundred more students had been arrested. The rector closed the campus uprooting students who had little choice but to travel to the Sorbonne in Paris to obtain student services. Outraged by the arrests, the violence, and the closing of the Nanterre campus, many of the displaced students joined a swelling army of direct-action revolutionaries.

At the station, I pushed my way through the crowd to the wall map to find the closest station to rue Saint-Jacques, where Danny had told me the enragés would likely gather. Once on the train I carefully studied the speech. I pictured Danny delivering it. I thought about his words and gestures at the Café Bert and in front of the administration building. Whatever doubts I had, I realized I would have to put them aside. I would have to lead as Danny asked me to do and as I now wanted to do. As the train stopped in the heart of the Latin Quarter, I felt my heart beat faster. I ran through the station out to the street, where thousands of students had already amassed on the narrow, medieval rue Saint-Jacques. Any misgivings faded in the excitement of the moment.

All around me, students were digging up cobblestones for ammunition. Two dozen already lay bleeding on the street. The smell of tear gas lingered. The CRS were on the attack. The state had taken the gloves off. The word had spread about summary arrests and harsh sentences meted out without a right to appeal. Thousands of students, teachers, and sympathizers marched on the Sorbonne to protest the police actions. In a show of force by the CRS, hundreds more were arrested. For the moment the CRS had retreated to the interior courtyard of a large walled estate and were out of sight, and it seemed that no one was taking charge for the students, who though leaderless appeared determined to resist.

I walked among the wounded and came upon a girl who lay face down bleeding, and took off my jacket to place it under her head.

"Jan, my God, Jan, you're bleeding!" She was trembling and looked up at me.

"Robbie, help me," she moaned, her voice raspy and difficult to understand.

She had a deep gash on her forehead. I ripped a piece of lining from her jacket and applied it to the wound.

"Jan, let me help you up," I said.

She rolled over and sat up while I held the cloth to her head. I helped her to her feet and walked her to the entrance of the building just across from us. Seeing her wounds, the concierge unlocked the door. We entered and sat on the floor in the foyer.

"Shit, my head hurts."

I removed the cloth to examine the wound. "Looks serious. I think you'll need stitches."

"I'm going to miss all the action!"

"I think you've seen enough action."

"You were great at Nanterre, Robbie."

"You saw me there?"

"Yes. Did you think I would miss it?"

"Why didn't you tell me you were there?"

"I don't know. You were busy with Danny and the CRS. . . I heard you were arrested with him."

"I was, but they let me go."

"Oh, my fucking head hurts."

I placed my hand on her cheek, then took her hand.

"You know, Robbie, if I were available. . ."

"Available?"

"You know. If I were in the market. . ."

"What?"

She smiled. "Robbie, these bastards really hurt me."

"I know. I know." The concierge came over.

"Elle a besoin d'un hôpital," I said.

"I have already called zee ambulance, monsieur."

"Merci."

"But eet will take some time with zee roads blocked."

"Go get the bastards, Robbie!"

"Okay," I said, letting go of her hand and nodding to the concierge to take over.

"Get these bastards, Robbie! Get them."

I turned and headed back to the street. It was a war zone. Jan's blood stained my shirt sleeves. I was angry. The crowd swelled. Suddenly, the CRS reappeared at the end of the road and positioned themselves for a fresh onslaught. My instincts took over. The best defense might be a good offense, so, thinking of Danny, I screamed in French to *enragés* all around me, "Let's charge the motherfuckers! *Chargez! Chargez!*"

"*Chargez!*" the throng roared back, and they fell in behind me.

The ranks of the students swelled from the side streets as I moved ahead, my fist raised in Danny's pose, dodging flying stones and stepping over the wounded, straight toward the assembled CRS, who must have been surprised by the resurgence of a mob they had just mercilessly dispersed. Taking a cue from Danny's playbook, I turned toward the *enragés,* motioned for them to stop, and climbed onto an overturned car. The students cheered as I called on them to do battle.

"*Française, Français,*" I proclaimed as I frantically searched for Danny's message. It was gone. My shirt had come untucked during the melee, and the paper with the speech was lost. I choked, shuddered, closed my eyes, gasped for breath, and began to speak. At first I had trouble forming my words. I stuttered and stammered. The crowd hushed. Somehow, I recovered, finding the confidence to continue. "Today we face the power of the state turned evil on these streets, not protecting us as they are supposed to but harming us, and we must prevail!" The crowd bellowed affirmation. I could see television crews setting up cameras on the sidewalk just ahead. "We are no longer students," I continued. "We are agents of change in a world that cries out for change. From Paris to Prague, from Nanterre to Columbia, from Saigon to Washington, we march to repair this world. We must no longer live at the mercy of the enemies of freedom. We must transform ourselves from students to soldiers, and it is up to us to show our universities, our governments, and the evil CRS that there is a new world on the way. Today that world is watching us, and we must show the way!"

I raised my fist. The multitudes thundered their approval.

"We must think of ourselves as more than we have been," I continued, gaining self-assurance and picking up my cadence. "Our lives must be about more than the pursuit of selfish ends and rampant consumerism. We are not merely the sum of what we have. We are much more than that. Here in Paris and around the globe we must break the power structures that seek to make us cower before their might. We must stand up, and with our courage and our determination we must overwhelm the establishment. We must do this not just for our university but for all the students and workers in our nation and for the progress of our society. It is our generation's turn to man the barricades. The torch has been passed from our brothers and sisters of 1789, 1830, 1848, and 1871. So let us stand today in their names and honor my friend, our friend, Danny, unjustly imprisoned. Long live Danny the Red! Long live the revolution!" I proclaimed, raising my fist in the air as high as my fully stretched body would permit.

The crowd roared, surrounded the car, lifted me off the hood, and passed me above their heads to the front line of the still-growing horde. I took the lead, feeling a power I had never felt before. Students to my left and right shouted encouragement as we marched forward, slowing only to pick up new weapons—broomsticks for clubs, garbage can lids as shields, chains, tire irons, bottles, and more cobblestones.

Thousands strong, spirits high, we surged ahead and approached the line of CRS troops. This time they did not fall back. Shields up, batons swinging, they moved toward us, tossing concussion grenades in our midst. I raised my fist and charged, the crowd following, all of us now in a full run, a frontal assault. I grabbed the shield of the first soldier I confronted and reached to pull his mask as the shield fell to the ground. All around me, students threw cobblestones and grabbed at shields and masks, taking blows from swinging batons. I could hear the cries of the wounded and the loud static of the police radios. Tear gas and black smoke from an overturned car set afire burned my eyes. The students so outnumbered the CRS that our onslaught stopped their forward motion. We had moved so swiftly and in such numbers they could not disperse us. I lay wounded on the ground and watched as the black-clad soldiers regrouped and moved back to the nearby walled estate from which they had come. My spirits soared as they retreated. The streets were ours again!

I was bleeding on the left side of my head, but I picked myself up, fueled by adrenaline and by the power of the moment. The blood flowed over my shirt. I walked a few paces but felt faint and sat down on the curb. A girl in the crowd spotted me and stopped to offer assistance. She tore a piece of cloth from her shirt and examined my wound.

"You are a brave leader," she whispered in French as she patted my forehead, then wrapped it with the cloth.

"*Merci*," I whispered in return.

"*Vive la révolution*," she said, raising her voice and her right fist in a salute.

It was all I could do to get up on my feet to return the salute. She disappeared back into a passing crowd.

I sat back down on the curb to rest. All around me, students erected barricades from trashed cars, stones, lampposts, or whatever they could find. Everywhere there was a sense of excitement fueled by our success at driving back the CRS.

Still woozy and bleeding through my bandage, I got up and walked, stopping to rest again just outside the Odeon Theatre. The building had been taken over by the students and now served as a sort of headquarters, with round-the-clock meetings, lectures, discussions, and heated debates about the meaning of what was happening.

I entered the building and attended a meeting of students who decided to create a new newspaper, *Action*, to report the news and the meaning of the revolution of 1968. I thought of writing an article about this experience as an American in Paris. It was as if I were back in Senator Hankie's office drafting a speech for him to submit to Allen, but now I would be writing for me, to express my thoughts and my feelings and to share my experience. I felt excited, intoxicated!

After the meeting, I walked to the École des Beaux-Arts, where I found artists working on posters with slogans to reflect the meaning of the events. My favorite was a fist with a club, accompanied by King Louis XIV's famous quote *"L' État, c'est moi!"*—"I am the state!" I picked out two posters to put up in my room: "It Is Forbidden to Forbid," and "I Take My Desires for Reality, Because I Believe in the Reality of My Desires."

So, what is the reality of my desires?

Justice! In a world filled with injustice.

Love! In a world filled with hate. I love My Hanh. She is a communist but she is not my enemy. It is forbidden to forbid. I must not forbid. I must overcome.

I continued to walk through the Latin Quarter, stopping at every corner where students gathered to discuss the meaning of the revolution, politics, the police, freedom, government, universities, workers, and most importantly, how to change society. Everything was subjected to challenge under the white-hot light of the revolution. I arrived at the Sorbonne, where students occupied the buildings and had created makeshift dormitories to sleep, eat, and carry on the work of the new order. *"Nous sommes chez nous!"* they cried as if they owned the place.

All around us the police continued to make mass arrests. Anyone found with tar on their fingers was assumed to have dug up cobblestones and arrested on the spot, just like in the final days of the 1871 Commune, when Communards with gunpowder-stained hands were immediately taken aside and shot.

There was also singing, lots of singing. The left sang "The Internationale," the song of the communist party, written during the Commune. The right countered with "La Marseillaise," the French national anthem, though where I walked, I didn't hear much of that.

I continued, energized by the events of the day, until I reached the Hotel de Crillon, where the North Vietnamese delegation was headquartered. I marched to the front desk and asked for Le My Hanh. The clerk was shocked by my appearance and surprised by the request. He denied My Hanh was a guest at the hotel.

"Look, I know she's here! Give her this message." I scribbled a note, 'Meet me at 10:00 p.m. tonight at Shakespeare and Company, at 37 rue de la Bûcherie. Robbie.'

I turned and left the building, continuing my walk to the bank of the Seine. I had no idea if My Hanh would get the note. On the Île Saint-Louis, I found a quiet spot to rest at the end of the Quai de Bourbon. It was called Place Louis-Aragon, a small secluded square at the end of the island overlooking the river. Though my bleeding had stopped, my head still pounded and my clothes were bloodstained. I wondered how I would explain what had happened to Madame Gueumier. No doubt she had seen the coverage on television and perhaps saw me addressing the crowd. I thought about Danny and Pierre in prison and about Jan who I hoped by now had been treated at the hospital.

I walked to a nearby café and ordered a croque monsieur and a Coke. I hadn't eaten all day. I reflected on the meaning of what I had just witnessed and what I had just done. It was overwhelming, as was my throbbing headache. At last I rose, paid my bill, and made my way to Shakespeare and Company. It was nearly 10:00 pm and I longed to fall into the soothing arms of my new love.

Chapter 10

At the Bookstore

Shakespeare and Company was more than a bookstore. It was a literary institution in a nation whose culture valued language and literature, a welcoming place for writers who came to Paris for inspiration and always found a helping hand and genuine interest in their work from the store's owner, George Whitman. Whitman was a tall, wiry man with a goatee, most often dressed in a well-worn tweed sport jacket, baggy slacks, V-neck sweater with holes, and loosened tie. He looked downright shabby, an impoverished man of letters.

I had met Whitman a few weeks earlier when he visited Dr. Nastovich's class. I submitted a poem for the bookstore's quarterly magazine. The store was closing when I arrived just before ten. Whitman was busy tidying up and turning off the lights. He'd been careful all day not to attract the attention of the CRS, which had set up command posts throughout the Left Bank. He had reached out to wounded students and offered them a place of refuge, making available the ten small beds he kept on the upper floors of the shop for visiting writers. I knocked at the door, and Whitman, seeing my wounds, immediately opened it and welcomed me.

"I think we may need to get you to a hospital," he said, doing visual triage on my swollen head. "Let me see that cut." He led me through a short, book-lined passage to an adjacent room, where he asked me to sit down and turned on a floor lamp next to the chair. I could see the front door from here.

He examined the large bump and the deep gash on my forehead, then grabbed some iodine and gauze from a red table, warning "This is going to hurt" as he dabbed it on the wound. I clenched my teeth from the sting.

We heard a knock, and Whitman returned to the front door to answer. It was My Hanh. I saw her through the passage standing at the entry. She was wearing blue jeans and a tunic, and she smiled at Whitman through the glass door. I signaled to let her in. He nodded, pointing to a sign up on wall above the alcove: "Be not inhospitable to strangers lest they be angels in disguise."

"She's your angel in disguise?" he asked, raising his voice so I could hear him in the next room.

"Yes."

Being a master of romantic literature, he needed only glance at my expression to realize how important she was to me.

"You are a friend of the wounded poet, Samberg," Whitman said to My Hanh.

"Wounded?" My Hanh uttered, her eyes widening.

She followed him through the passage to where I was sitting.

"Robbie, *troi oi*, Robbie," she cried out, seeing the blood and iodine all over my head and clothes.

"I forgot to duck," I said. "Nice jeans!"

"Troi oi," she said, kneeling before me and carefully inspecting my forehead. "I wore them for you!"

"Troi oi?"

"It means 'Oh my God!' She stood shaking her head.

"We'll need to take another look at that wound in the morning," Whitman said. "Unless the swelling subsides, you'll need to go to the hospital. For now, though, I have one last bed upstairs, and I think you should go lie down." He pointed to the stairs and told us how to find the small room on the top floor just below the attic. "You'll be safe there," he added, handing us linens and towels from a tiny closet. "And it's a great spot to write a new poem if you're up to it," he added.

I grasped My Hanh's hand as we mounted the narrow, winding stairs and made our way through a maze of tiny, interconnected rooms, each lined with books from floor to ceiling and each a different size and shape, some with nooks, others with crannies, which gave the store its unique personality.

"Let me care for you," My Hanh whispered. We entered the room to find a small cot tucked in a hidden corner, surrounded by bookshelves. The floor was covered with dirty red carpet. There was a darkened mirror on the wall with a worn gilded frame. The bedcover was torn and filthy. We sat on the cot.

"Take off your shoes, my Robbie."

"My shoes?"

She left for a moment and returned with a pan of warm water and more towels. She'd found them in a small kitchen in the hall, which had a gas stove, a refrigerator, and a sink filled with dirty dishes.

My Hanh handed me a torn pillow. "Please take this, place it behind you, and lean back," she instructed.

She brought over a stool from the corner of the room, placed the folded towels on it for added softness and better height, and lifted my feet onto it. She pulled off my socks one at a time and sat down on a chair she had placed in front of the stool. She took a warm, wet cloth and gently washed and dried my feet. Then she lifted and held my left foot in both her hands.

"In my country, when a man is wounded in war or exhausted from hard work in the rice fields, his woman revives him by rubbing his feet. Close your eyes, Robbie."

Back straight, breathing deeply, My Hanh applied gentle, then firm pressure at the precise points of my foot where the nerve endings of my organs terminated. I could feel the stress melt away. My body relaxed. The throbbing of my head subsided.

She massaged every part of the left foot, then every part of the right foot. It was a gift given to me with love that was communicated through her hands. I fell into a deep sleep and dreamed that My Hanh and I were in a magical land filled with cool mountain streams, tall fragrant pines, colorful wildflowers, and magnificent sunsets. It was a land where flowers never wilted and died, where every day began with a meditation of gratitude, and every night ended with a celebration of joy.

We were walking in a cool, green forest, holding hands, when suddenly the skies above us darkened and we could hear a strange whirring sound coming from the clouds. A burst of fire engulfed the forest to our left and then to our right, the lush foliage exploding and turning to ashes in an instant. I looked over at My Hanh and she at me, our eyes filled with fear as everything burned around us. We looked up in shock as an airplane swooped down in a tailspin and crashed in front of us. As we walked toward the wreckage, the charred tail showing the insignia of the United States Air Force, a crew member crawled from the burning fuselage, his left arm hanging by a thread, blood spurting from his neck, his face obscured by the opaque visor of his helmet. He fell before us, raising his right arm, screaming for help. I stopped, frozen by fear, while My Hanh ran to him, leaned over, and pulled up the visor.

"Oh my God. Father!" I cried as another bomb exploded, blowing My Hanh and my father to smithereens right before my eyes.

"Robbie, Robbie, are you alright?" My Hanh asked, gently prodding me.

My eyes opened wide, my bloodied forehead wet with perspiration. I jumped up from the cot.

"A nightmare!" I said.

"I am here," she said, reaching out to comfort me.

"My father!" I blurted, still not fully awake. "The two of you were blown up right before my eyes!" I recounted. "How long have I been asleep?"

"Just over three hours."

"Have you been there the whole time?" I asked.

"Yes, I watched you while you slept."

"What did you see?"

"I saw a young man who changed the world today," she whispered, holding me in her arms.

"What do you mean?"

"My father received a phone call this morning from our ambassador in Prague. He told my father that the Party is changing," she explained. "It is putting a new face on socialism, a face of humanity and democracy. They call it socialism with a human face."

"What does that have to do with me?" I asked.

"Do you know how this change began, my Robbie?"

"No."

"It started with the bravery of students at the University of Prague who marched to Prague Castle to protest conditions at the school and were brutally suppressed by the police."

"Ah, the heating and lighting protest! I know about that," I said. My headache suddenly returned.

"The actions of the students inspired Alexander Dubček to challenge the rigidity of the party under Novotný, and this could show the way for the socialist world to change."

"And what does this have to do with me?" I asked again.

"Your wounds tell me that you battled today like the Czech students, and you showed France and the world there can be a different path. Your words told me—"

"My words?"

"Yes, my father and I saw your speech on the television, and he thought you were brave and that you spoke well. I told him how you rescued me on the Métro. He called you a brave young man, and I have never heard him say that about an American."

"You heard my speech?"

"Yes, and I too thought you were a brave leader. My father asked me to bring you to him. He wants to thank you for helping me and to learn more about the student protests. He believes that student protests will bring pressure on the American political system to stop the war. He would like to meet before the peace talks begin."

"Wait a minute!" I said.

"Are you afraid to meet him?" she asked.

"Yes."

"Treason?" she asked.

"Exactly. I oppose the war, but I'm not willing to commit treason. Helping an enemy in wartime is frowned upon in America," I said.

"Where's the brave leader I saw today?"

"That's unfair!"

"Robbie, how many died in the student protests today?"

"I don't think there were any deaths."

"This morning my father received a report from the village of My Lai that your soldiers murdered more than five hundred innocent men, women, and children."

"Our soldiers are not murderers," I responded.

"They shot the elderly, women, children, even babies," she said, her eyes welling with tears. "One soldier chased a baby crawling on the ground, shooting at him twice with his pistol before finally hitting the target while his comrades laughed at what a bad shot he was."

"That's bullshit!"

"It's not bullshit, Robbie. The soldiers beat women with their rifle butts. They raped and sodomized. They killed livestock and threw the carcasses in the wells to poison the drinking water. They threw explosives into the bomb shelters under the houses, where villagers had hidden. They shot the villagers who tried to escape and burned every house in the hamlet," she recounted, her face covered in tears.

"This can't be true," I insisted, reaching for the towel at the end of the cot and handing it to My Hanh to dry her eyes.

"It is true. While you and your fellow students protest imperfect social conditions in France and march against racism and the war, no one drops napalm on you, and there are no foreign soldiers murdering innocent men, women, and children."

"My Hanh, I had no idea about this," I replied, feeling ashamed.

"This is not your fault, my Robbie, and it does not take away from the importance of what you have done today. I am proud of you for that, but we need to keep things in perspective."

"What you told me about My Lai is horrible," I said. "If it's true, our soldiers behaved like savages. I never thought Americans would do that."

"Will you come to meet my father? Will you speak to him candidly like you speak to me?"

"I'll think about it, as a courtesy to you but only to accept his thanks, if that's really why he wants to see me, but I cannot cross the line."

"I understand," she said.

"May I tell him how I feel about you?" I asked.

"No! No!" she frowned.

"To meet him and not tell him how I feel about you would be to start our relationship with a lie."

"Robbie, it's too soon to tell him about us. He would not understand. You must promise me."

"But if I go, I would like to tell him the truth."

"And what is the truth about us?" she asked.

"The truth is that I have not been able to get you off my mind since the first moment I saw you. The truth is that I think of you every moment of every day, even when I make speeches atop overturned cars and face down the CRS!"

She reached up and placed both her hands softly on my cheeks. "Well, maybe it was a good thing I distracted you today and took your mind off the danger. Otherwise, you might have cut and run, and then you wouldn't be my hero," she said, laughing.

"Or maybe I would have remembered to duck," I responded, laughing too. The more I laughed, the more my head hurt.

"But then I would not be caring for my wounded soldier."

"And I wouldn't have to face your father," I said, breathing a fake sigh of relief.

She laughed again.

"The truth," I continued, "is that you have touched my heart in a way that no girl has before and no girl ever will again. The truth is that I have never felt this way. The truth is that I have fallen in love with you."

My Hanh bowed her head—deeply, slowly—then looked at me and, without speaking, she smiled and kissed me. We embraced and kissed, and after many kisses we sat together in silence. She helped me remove my shirt, cleaning the bloodstains on my chest and arms, and covering me with a blanket.

"Are you afraid of your father?"

"Sometimes," she said. "Robbie, you must understand that a Vietnamese girl does not stand up to her father like girls do in America."

"So, you are afraid."

"It's a matter of respect. I cannot tell him something I know will cause him pain, especially in this moment, where there is so much at stake. He asked me here to help him and to help our country, not to create new problems. I must put him and his work first, and later there will be time for me and for us. Do you understand?"

"Yes," I responded, realizing the wisdom of what she had said and the importance of showing my love by supporting her.

"Thank you, my Robbie!" She reached over to caress my bare chest as she had my feet. "I, too, felt the magic when our eyes met in the train. I knew at that moment our hearts were joined! It is Buddha's will, and we are but the vessels for it."

"But we've just met, mademoiselle My Hanh!" I mock protested, wagging my index finger and playing devil's advocate.

"Ah, my American pragmatist! With a bad sense of humor! There you go again!" She laughed.

She stroked my chest and I leaned over to kiss her, our breaths merging and our bodies joined together. We lay on the cot amid the stacks of books, wrapped in each other's arms, and fell soundly asleep. Hours later, we awakened. The shop was silent, the only sounds the occasional vehicle passing, the clanking of the radiators, and the muffled groans of people sleeping on the floor below.

We spoke of our love of books and learning. We both had loved books for as long as we could remember and had kept every school book from the start of our education. We enjoyed books not just for their content but for their shape, size, and color. We revered them as instruments of communication and learning.

"There's something about the feel of a book in my hand," My Hanh said, taking a slim volume from high atop a shelf.

I understood and smiled at her to acknowledge that I felt the same way. No wonder our favorite places were bookstores and libraries, another thing we shared, despite vast differences in our cultures, upbringing, politics, and geography.

I told her about my library of books on Vietnam, how I collected them, which ones I liked the most, and which ones I didn't like, and how I had packed them in my trunks to bring to Paris. She told me how her father had scolded her for insisting on bringing all her books about America to Paris, also packed in her steamer trunks.

"Đồng thanh tương ứng, đồng khí tương cầu. It means similar people often become friends."

"Like birds of a feather flock together."

"Yes, we are two peas in a pod," she whispered.

"We are," I responded, my eyes wide open staring up at the darkened ceiling.

"I'm wide awake," she said. "Do you want to take a look around?"

"Sure." We got up from the cot, grabbed a flashlight from the table, and wandered about the stacks of books on our floor. The floors creaked, so we walked softly, careful not to make too much noise. My Hanh pointed the light at a wooden ladder leading up to the attic, and we wondered what kind of treasures we might find up there. I took the light from her and climbed the ladder, moving slowly toward the ceiling, and once there, I lifted a worn panel out of the way and gently placed it to the right of the rectangular opening. I shined the light down the ladder so My Hanh could climb up.

I pulled myself through the opening, flashlight in hand, and reached down to assist My Hanh, assuring her I did not see any mice, spiders, or insects.

"Too bad," she said as she climbed up behind me. "In Vietnam we eat mice and insects. They are a delicacy," she said, smacking her lips in the dim light to accentuate the point.

I grimaced to signal my revulsion. Once in the attic, we spotted a single electric lightbulb above us with a thin, rusted chain hanging down. I gently pulled it, illuminating the treasure-house of books and papers that lay before us. My Hanh spotted a mattress in the corner, which we moved toward the light, dusted off by striking it with our open hands, and promptly made our home. We sat quietly for a few moments in this wonderland of old books, stacked high around us, our minds excited by the trove of forgotten volumes.

"You eat insects?" I asked, breaking the silence.

"Yes. In Vietnam dishes such as mouse, bug larvae, and insects are specialties," she said again.

"I hope your father does not invite me to lunch."

"Don't worry, if he does it will be at the Crillon, and they will not serve bug larvae or insects." She added, "Maybe the mouse, though."

"Very funny!"

"I will check the menu, so you need not worry."

"I wonder if there's an old peace treaty up here," I said, looking around.

"Or something left by Jews hiding from the Nazis," she said.

My Hanh had studied the Holocaust and knew that Jews had hidden in attics like this.

We snuggled on the mattress. I pulled the chain to turn off the light and lit a candle. My Hanh caressed me gently as we lay silently. We slowly removed our clothing and lovingly kissed. My kisses found their way to the Y of her body as I showered her with my lips and my tongue, at first gently and then in a torrent of passion that had her shivering and squealing. She reached down to guide me inside her, and together we moved in a rhythm that would go on and on, and every so often she would slow down so the pleasure could be prolonged, until neither of us had the capacity to assert reason on the moment, and the climax of our mutual passion overwhelmed us. We struggled to keep our screams muted so as not to wake those who lay sleeping on the floors below.

In the morning we awakened, looked into each other's eyes—she gently cleaning mine with soft kisses, and I doing the same for her—and we made love again, as if the night had never ended. We fell back to sleep in each other's arms, awoke again, whispered softly, fell to sleep yet again, then slowly rose to dress and climb down the ladder. The other residents had already left, and we searched for Whitman to thank him and tell him we were leaving.

He smiled when he saw us and pronounced that my swelling appeared to have subsided.

"Must have been good blood flow last night," he said, smiling devilishly.

My Hanh turned beet red.

I offered him fifty francs for the night and he accepted it with a smile.

"This will help fund the magazine," he said.

For years, he had struggled to finance the store, in part due to problems with the city, which denied him a business license and forced him to report information about his writer guests daily to the prefecture.

"They don't like my leftist politics or my beatnik clientele," he said. "They closed me down on a technicality."

He would have to submit a detailed report on our stay later that afternoon.

"Do you think you could just ignore the report this one time?" I asked.

He stared at the two of us standing in front of him. "You're from the North?" he asked, turning his gaze to My Hanh.

"My God, young Samberg, you . . ."

"I know," I responded.

He shook his head to sympathize with our plight and invited us to stay for breakfast, which he cooked in his small kitchen as he brought us up to date on the morning news. Things were quieting down in the city.

My Hanh looked at her watch and realized that she had not told her father she would be out all night. She asked for the phone, and Whitman led her to it. After the call, she returned and told us she needed to go back to the hotel immediately, so we hurriedly said our goodbyes and headed to the front door of the shop. Whitman embraced us and said we would be welcome to return any time.

"Here, take this," he said, handing us each a copy of the store's literary magazine.

"And the report to the prefecture?" I asked.

"You were never here," he responded, ushering us out the front door of the shop.

"Thank you!"

I decided to accompany My Hanh back to the hotel. We hailed a cab on the nearby Quai de Montebello and on the way agreed to meet again at 6 p.m. at Jo Goldenberg's, a Jewish deli in the Marais. When the cab arrived at the hotel, we embraced and kissed goodbye in the backseat, and I handed My Hanh a poem I had written in the attic as I watched her sleep. My feelings for her were different from what I had ever felt before in a relationship— stronger, deeper, more profound, while at the same time inexplicably lighter and easier, as if we were meant to be. I was in love and living my life just the way I wanted, filled to the brim!

Chapter 11

Marais

When I arrived at the apartment, Madame Gueumier was there with Marionette Dubois. She took one look at me and raced to the phone to call Dr. Coureau, a surgeon and close friend who lived on the floor below. She had seen me on the news and was furious and immediately began scolding me for "my foolish and immature behavior."

"How dare you interfere in our politics and put yourself in harm's way! You are a visitor here in France, not a citizen," she admonished.

So, it was okay, I thought, for the American soldiers about my age who "visited" Omaha Beach to "interfere" in harm's way but not for this American student at the Sorbonne. I dared not say this, as I knew it would provoke her, and I realized she was only upset because she cared about me.

"You and your hothead *enragés*." She clenched her teeth and shook her head. "Agents of change!" she mocked. "*Mon Dieu*! What were you thinking? You could have been killed out there, and for what? To play revolutionary?"

I didn't respond. My headache returned.

Dr. Coureau arrived and silenced Madame Gueumier with a gesture, waving his stethoscope in front of her scowling face, then examined me, after which he folded the instrument and placed it back in the narrow black leather bag he had brought to this special house call. He carefully removed the blood-soaked bandages from my head and examined the wound.

"I don't like the look of this," he said, insisting we go at once to the hospital for an X-ray. "We need to make sure there's no concussion," he continued, asking me to follow him to the elevator and down to his black Citroën DS, parked in front of the building.

Madame Gueumier accompanied us, her anger having subsided by now.

A short drive later we arrived at Pitié-Salpêtrière, which Dr. Coureau explained was one of the city's largest and oldest teaching hospitals, where he served as chief of surgery. I was whisked through admitting, bypassing a long line of waiting Frenchmen, then placed on a gurney and taken immediately to the X-ray room. The technicians worked quickly to X-ray my head and neck, after which I was wheeled back to an examination room, where Madame Gueumier was waiting.

She walked over to the gurney and gently placed her hand on my shoulder. "You may be a damn fool revolutionary, Robbie," she whispered, "but you're *my* damn fool revolutionary." She smiled and we laughed.

My head pounded from the laughter, and I grasped her hand to show the appreciation I felt for this wonderful woman, who disapproved of my behavior but treated me like a son.

"Thank you," I whispered, continuing to hold her hand as Dr. Coureau entered the room, accompanied by the lab technician holding a sheath of X-rays.

"With a few days' rest, Monsieur Robbie, you'll be fine, but you need to keep the wound clean," Dr. Coureau announced, handing Madame Gueumier a brown paper bag filled with bandages, salves, and special tape he explained would not hurt so much when removed. "You'll also need to retire from the revolution, Monsieur Robbie," he added, looking directly at me and handing me a bottle of large red pills for the headache.

I nodded.

"Where do I pay?" I asked as the technician gathered the X-rays and lab results and placed them into the sheath and handed it to me.

Dr. Coureau, ignoring my question, helped me climb down off the gurney, gave me a cup of water, and instructed me to take two of the pills.

"Today you are the guest of France," Dr. Coureau said at last, "so there is no bill to pay."

"*Merci beaucoup,*" I responded, remembering the taxi ride with Pierre Laboutte, whose card I still carried in my wallet.

"We may have our problems in France, Monsieur Samberg, but a lack of gratitude for America is not among them," Dr. Coureau added. "When my father was not much older than you are, he served in the Resistance, and he was treated by a doctor from Easy Company, and there was no bill for him."

He put his arms around me, gave me two air kisses, one on each side of my face, smiled broadly, and instructed the technician to expedite my discharge.

Madame Gueumier needed to return to work, so she offered to drop me at the Pont de la Concorde, from where it was only a short walk to the apartment. On the way, she begged me to stay out of trouble and to leave the students at the Sorbonne to sort out France's problems on their own.

"You heard the doctor, Robbie. You have a slight concussion, so no more protests, no more revolution! Okay?"

"Okay, I get it! I get it! *Merci.*"

"Home and bed rest is what you need," she insisted, pulling the car to the side of the road.

"Yes, Mother," I said with a smile as I got out of the car.

She laughed, shook her head, waved goodbye, and drove off.

I stood for a moment, watching her car merge with the traffic, and then began to walk across the bridge. It was a beautiful day, and the sun illuminated the buildings along the Seine. By now the red pills had not only eliminated my headache but triggered a nice buzz. I wondered if My Hanh had liked my poem, and I couldn't wait to see her again.

I stopped to look at the sunlight glistening on the river below. It was a beautiful sight. I reached into my pocket and found the crumpled letter Danny had given me to take to his sister. I held it in my hand. I had just promised Madame Gueumier I would retire from the revolution. *What kind of friend would I be if I did not keep my promises? What kind of student would I be if I did not stand up for changing what's wrong with the system? What kind of citizen would I be I did not stand against the war, racism and anti-Semitism? And what kind of partner would I be to My Hanh if I refused to meet her father?*

So much had happened so fast since I came to Paris. All my life I had done what my parents and the establishment expected of me. I took no risks, made no waves. *Maybe I am no longer the Robbie Samberg I have been but the Robbie Samberg I am becoming.* As I walked along the busy bridge, crammed with honking cars and harried pedestrians, my thoughts crystalized. Still clutching the letter, I decided to turn around and head to Danny's sister's apartment at 7 rue des Écouffes, in the Marais. I could rest later.

In Roman times this part of Paris was a marsh, hence the name Marais. In the seventeenth century, it was home to the city's noblemen and a center of elegance and festivities. Great families built estates, known as *hôtels*, like the Hôtel de Sully, where I took My Hanh after the incident in the Métro. Now it was the Jewish quarter of Paris, an area spread across parts of the 3rd and 4th arrondissements on the Right Bank of the Seine. This was where Danny told me he felt most at home, and walking along the narrow old streets I could understand why. There were Judaica shops everywhere, with bearded Hasidic Jews praying or just talking in small groups.

At first glance, the Jews in the Marais appeared very different from the twice-a-year dilettante Jews in my family. These were Jews who spoke Hebrew as a primary language, kept kosher homes, and who strictly observed the Sabbath. As I walked the maze of narrow streets in this Jewish quarter, observed the people, their dress, food, prayer, and ritual, I realized how little I had inherited from my family about my Judaism. I was a Jew by birth but a stranger to the Jews I witnessed here on these streets, but I still felt a connection, no matter how diluted.

I had heard about anti-Semitism in France before my departure, but I took it no more seriously than warnings about the French being rude or hating Americans. I passed Synagogue Beit Yossef just as the worshipers poured out onto the street after services. It was a special sight, the men, in yamaka and tallit, exiting separately from the women, who could not sit with them during the service. I passed the Synagogue de la rue Pavée, built by Polish emigrants in 1910 and designed by Hector Guimard, the architect who also created the Art Nouveau entrances to the Paris Métros, destined to become important architectural symbols of the city. I walked to the end of the street, turned right, and there was Jo Goldenberg's deli, the restaurant where I was later to meet My Hanh.

Outside the restaurant, I ran into a small group of Hasidic Jews, who surrounded me and offered to perform the rites of Tefillin, attaching boxes filled with sacred parchment and connected by leather straps to my left arm and around my head. They moved quickly but delicately so as not to disturb my visible wounds. I could not resist. They were dressed in long black coats, blue and white tallit, tall black hats, and all had long black or brown beards and pigtails, except for one, whose beard and pigtails were bold red, his face obscured by a scarf wrapped around his head. It was Danny!

"The commandments which I command you this day shall be forever engraved in your heart," he said, raising his voice and his arms so all could see and hear.

He stayed in character, and so did I.

"Ah, thank you, Rabbi. I can't wait to hear those commandments. I will obey without question."

"I see you are wounded, so I shall not ask for much," Rabbi Danny responded.

The others had no idea we were speaking in code.

"I hope not, Rabbi, as my head still hurts from my most recent service to God," I said, working hard to suppress my laughter.

"As it is said in Proverbs, blows that wound cleanse away evil, and strokes make clean the innermost parts," Danny said.

He must have had a way better Jewish education than I had.

"Yes, Rabbi, there were definitely blows that wounded. We had a rendezvous with men in black garb a little heavier than yours who did not agree with us, and their rods and their staffs were decidedly not used to comfort us."

I could see Danny was ready to crack up.

"You have been a good soldier, my son, and a very able leader. You have followed the teaching of our sages and stood up for Torah."

The other Hasidim continued to move around me and still didn't have a clue that Danny and I knew each other.

He spoke again, praying and swaying back and forth. "It was King David who said when we praise God, we do so with all of our being. The mind, heart, and mouth express the prayer through speech, and the rest of the body does so by moving, so every fiber of our self is involved in connecting to our creator."

By now they were all swaying back and forth and mumbling prayers at lightning speed.

"I heard your speech from on high," Danny exclaimed in mock prayer, "and God's gratitude shines upon those who do good deeds."

He must have seen me on the television.

"My son, your accent tells me you are American, and as you are a guest in this country I would like to offer you a private prayer," he said, nodding to the others.

They promptly dispersed as Danny placed his hands on my head. He began to chant in what sounded like part Hebrew, part gibberish, and when the others had moved far enough away, he whispered forcefully in plain English, "I escaped!"

"No kidding," I said, making a face, then quickly returning to our masquerade.

Danny continued to hold his hands on my head in a faux blessing. "When they took us for medical checks, they removed our cuffs and leg irons to walk from the police van to the clinic entrance. Pierre pretended to faint, and I managed to slip into a nearby alley and took the Métro to my sister's, where I have been hiding ever since. Did you post the letter to my parents?" he asked, half speaking and half chanting.

"Yes, I sent it yesterday. Why has there been no publicity about your escape?"

"The government would not advertise its failure to keep me locked up. They will send the General Intelligence Directorate to find me, and it will not be long."

"How long?"

"A couple of days."

"When your parents get the letter, they will think you are in jail," I observed.

"That's okay. It's best they know nothing about my escape. It will protect them when they are questioned."

"I was on my way to your sister's. What else can I do?" I asked.

"I need you to buy me a train ticket to Frankfurt. When things quiet down, I'll go to my parents and explain what happened. They'll be angry with me," he added, a troubled look on his face.

"Okay, I'll bring you the ticket, but what about your passport? Won't I need it to buy the ticket?"

"No, if they ask, just show your own," he said, still standing in front of me, his hands on my head as if deep in prayer. "They don't mark passport numbers or names on train tickets. Leave the ticket in a baggage locker at the station and hide the locker key and number on the upper window ledge in the men's bathroom at Le Procope, the one on the second floor. Do not bring it to my sister's or try to see me again, Robbie. It's too dangerous."

"Anything else?"

"That's it, my friend," he said, lifting his hands from my head and stepping back.

"Are you sure?"

"Well, one thing," he said, looking at me. "When you return to America, don't forget the lessons from yesterday, and make that messed-up country of yours live up to its promise!"

"Danny," I said, shaking my head and feeling the emotion of the moment.

He stepped further back, tears in his eyes. "Good luck, my friend," he said as he turned and walked away, never looking back.

I stood on the street, surprised by Danny's last request, and realized I would probably not see him again. His words forced me to think about what I would do when I returned home. There was so much wrong in America and so much to be done before it could live up to its promise. The war needed to end, as well as the pain and suffering it brought to My Hanh's people and to the families of American soldiers. The promise of the Civil Rights and Voting Rights Acts needed to be ful-filled and the barriers of racism that divided blacks and whites brought down. America's rigid anti-communism and the idea that we could somehow solve all the world's problems needed to change.

This is a huge agenda, and I'm only one student. Then I re-membered Robert Kennedy's speech in South Africa where he addressed the evils of apartheid and challenged students to act against it. "Each time a man stands up for an ideal, or acts to improve the lot of others, or strikes out against injustice, he sends forth a tiny ripple of hope, and, crossing each other from a million different centers of energy and daring, those ripples build a current which can sweep down the mightiest walls of oppression and resistance."

I decided right then and there, standing in the ancient, nar-row street of the Marais, that when I returned home I would stay alert for my Mississippi moments, and when they came I would remember Danny's request and call upon that same courage I felt at Nanterre as we marched together into the swinging batons of the CRS.

I continued walking in the Marais, until at the end of rue Vieille-du-Temple I saw one of the Hasidim who had sur-rounded me with Danny and the others. He had a narrow, gentle face, large almond-shaped eyes, and wore wire-rimmed glasses. He looked to be in his mid-twenties. His black pigtails fell all the way to his shoulders and swung back and forth as he walked up to me.

"I'm Robbie Samberg." I extended my hand.

"Ronen Maribor," he responded as we shook hands. He spoke in a heavy eastern European accent.

We turned onto rue des Écouffes. "It means 'street of kites,'" Ronen said, pointing to the street sign, "which also means birds of prey or pawnbrokers."

"Pawnbrokers?"

"There were once many on this street. It's how the nasty myth was born that we Jews became pawnbrokers and money lenders because we are greedy."

"But Jews were money lenders, right?"

"True, but not because we are greedy, but because we were blocked from other professions, and money lending was one of the few things we were permitted to do.

"How bad is the Anti-Semitism here?" I asked.

"Look there," Ronen pointed to a large plaque on the wall of what used to be a school just across the street. He translated. "'To the memory of the director of personnel and students of this school, arrested in 1944 by the Vichy police and the Gestapo, deported and exterminated at Auschwitz because they were born Jewish.' I think that plaque says it all, Robbie." He explained that during the German occupation and the Vichy government, twenty-five percent of all Jews in France were transported to German death camps, either dying in transit or in the gas chambers. He shook with emotion.

"What about Dreyfus? When did that happen?" I asked.

Ronen stopped, an unsettled look on his face. He grabbed at his right pigtail and held it.

"Dreyfus," he whispered. "Dreyfus," he repeated, gazing off into the distance. He turned to face me. "Let's go sit down." He took me by the arm and led me across the street to a café. We ordered coffee. Ronen clasped his hands in front of his chin, closed his eyes for a moment, then started to speak in a somber voice.

"Alfred Dreyfus was a well-respected captain in the French army, a dedicated patriot. He came from a wealthy Jewish family in Alsace. After the loss of Alsace to Prussia in 1871, he and his family moved to Paris to escape living under Prussian rule, and he joined the army, motivated in large part by a desire to seek vengeance against Prussia."

"So he was a patriot."

"Yes, but in October 1894 he was arrested and thrown into prison for passing military secrets to the Prussians. A few weeks later he was convicted of espionage by a military court and sentenced to life in prison."

"What?"

"The key evidence at his trial was a handwritten letter called the bordereau, written on tissue paper, unsigned and undated, stolen from the Prussian embassy in Paris. The handwriting in the letter bore no resemblance to his own. The rest of the evidence was locked in a dossier, which the government classified as top secret and would not disclose."

I checked my watch, showing it to Ronen. It was getting late.

"Next, the anti-Semites used the fact that Dreyfus was a Jew as a way to vent their suppressed rage and fear, pointing out that he belonged to the same tribe as Judas and like Judas had turned traitor for money. 'The scum was not French,' one wrote. 'We understood everything in his deed by his looks, by his face!'"

"By his face?"

"Yes, you know, the caricature of the crooked-nosed Jew. Dreyfus looked Jewish, so he must have been guilty," Ronen said, his voice dripping with sarcasm.

"Shit."

"This was how these people thought," Ronen said.

"Shit," I whispered again.

"As the venom poured forth in the press, Alfred's brother, Mathieu, quit his job as director of a textile business and devoted himself full-time to proving his brother's innocence."

Ronen paused and motioned to the waiter for more coffee.

"Mathieu hired a new attorney and found an expert, who not only showed the handwriting in the letter used to convict was not Alfred's, but also identified the writing as that of another officer, a Major Charles Ferdinand Esterhazy. That same year the chief of the army's intelligence section, Lieutenant Colonel Georges Picquart, proved that the letter used against Dreyfus was written by Esterhazy, but Picquart was promptly demoted, and a military court acquitted Esterhazy and sent Picquart to prison.

"What kind of shit?" I poured myself more coffee and leaned in closer to Ronen, whose face and voice were now animated.

"These sentences exposed the blatant corruption in de military court system. Liberal politicians became more vocal, calling for a retrial of Dreyfus. Then in January, 1898, the celebrated writer Émile Zola published an open letter in the newspaper titled 'J'accuse! . . .'" The letter was written to the president of France. It was scathing and prompted a libel lawsuit, which was exactly what Zola intended. He knew that a public trial in a civil court might force the military to reopen the Dreyfus case and expose the military cover-up. However, Zola lost and was convicted of slander. He was forced to flee France.

"Shall I go on?" Ronen asked.

"Go on!"

"It got worse from there," Ronen continued. The growing tension resulted in riots throughout France. Inspired by Zola, another great writer, Anatole France, spoke out, as did the leading doctors at the Pasteur Institute and senior professors at the Sorbonne. Marcel Proust, whose mother was Jewish, joined the cause. The Jewish journalist Theodor Herzl became so alarmed at the outbreak of anti-Semitism that he proposed the idea of establishing a Jewish state."

"So the idea of Israel was born from Dreyfus," I observed.

"Yes, the anti-Semites who perjured themselves to destroy Dreyfus could never have imagined it!"

"Poetic justice?"

"Yes, you could say that." Ronen took another sip of his coffee. "In September 1898, it was proven in court that the evidence against Dreyfus had been forged by another officer, a Major Joseph Henry, who confessed, was sentenced to prison, and shot himself. Henry's motive was to protect the honor of the army, and Dreyfus, a Jew, was the perfect scapegoat. The French military had been humiliated by the loss to Germany in the Franco-Prussian War, and there was institutional pressure to protect the army from further humiliation. At this point the government finally ordered the military to conduct a new trial, but when Dreyfus was called back from prison for that trial, the military court found him guilty again."

"What the hell? This is unbelievable!"

"The French army could not expose the corruption in its ranks," Ronen explained. "The rigid chain of command held. But this time the political pressure outside the military was so great that the commander in chief, the president of the Republic, pardoned Dreyfus."

"It was finally over?"

"In July 1906, twelve years following his arrest, the French Supreme Court of Appeal finally found Dreyfus innocent. He was restored to his rank and once again named head of a battalion."

"Justice prevailed."

"It did, Robbie, but when you think of the pain caused to this man, to his family and friends, and to France, which was torn apart, its social fabric smeared with anti-Semitic venom for more than a decade, you can hardly conclude this was a happy ending."

"But there was also the courage of Mathieu rising up to defend his brother, and of the artists, writers, and political leaders who stood up for Dreyfus, and the courts, which eventually brought forth justice. In this otherwise-sad story, the forces of anti-Semitism lost, and from the pain and suffering they sowed came the idea for establishing Israel. There was a silver lining after all."

"You are such an optimist, Robbie."

"I guess it's the American in me.

"I'm not and maybe that's the French in me."

"I'm learning to stand up for justice in my life," I added, as I signaled the waiter.

"Is that how you got those wounds on your head?" he asked. "At the Sorbonne?"

I nodded.

"I'm also learning something about myself I never knew, the Judaism inside me, the Judaism that connects me to this place and to the history of our people."

We both sat at the table in silence. The waiter arrived to pour a final cup of coffee for each of us and left the check.

"That's why we Jews need to remain vigilant so it doesn't happen again on our watch. Sometimes humanity's darker impulses become so unglued, as they did with Dreyfus, that there is no redeeming value—it's just all bad, all evil—and to ignore this . . . is to invite more evil things to happen again."

"I think the lesson is that we need to protect our politics from extremism on the left or the right. Isn't that it?"

"I guess you could say that, Robbie, but, as I said, I'm not an optimist. I know too much to be an optimist."

"You do, and I thank you for sharing it with me. It's getting late and I must meet my girlfriend at Goldenberg's. Would you like to join us?" I asked, thinking My Hanh would enjoy meeting him.

"No, thanks. I have a meeting at the temple. I have enjoyed this time with you, Robbie. Please take whatever lessons you feel are important from this history and use them to heal the world where you can," he said, reaching out to shake my hand and say goodbye. "And get to know your Judaism," he added. "It will add comfort and meaning to your life."

"*Tikkun olam*," I responded, rising from the table to offer Ronen a hug.

"Yes, *tikkun olam*," he repeated, embracing me.

"Shalom."

"Shalom." We left money on the table for our coffees and walked off in opposite directions.

Despite my optimism, I wondered how the France of Voltaire could have become the France of Vichy and whether the battle for the soul of this nation or my own would ever end.

Chapter 12

Meeting with the Enemy

I walked to Goldenberg's deep in thought about the tortured history surrounding me on the dark, narrow streets, about Dreyfus and the lives shattered by the hateful anti-Semitism of the Nazis. Ronen's plea for vigilance resonated with me. My family's abandonment of Jewish culture and tradition bothered me. *Maybe part of being vigilant about anti-Semitism is maintaining those traditions.* I wondered if My Hanh knew about Dreyfus, and if Vietnamese history had its own chapters where fear, intolerance, and cruelty ran amok. I realized these are human faults that have no national or cultural boundaries.

By now the sun had set, the temperature dropped, and people walked more quickly along the crowded streets, their coats buttoned up, their scarves wrapped more tightly. I was struck by the similarities between racism at home and anti-Semitism in Europe. Both were a form of intolerance of those who were different. I thought about our civil war and the fifty thousand soldiers killed, wounded, and missing at Gettysburg in a single battle on a summer day to end slavery and preserve the union. I thought about Goodman, Schwerner, and Chaney, for whom there were no plaques on walls to celebrate their bravery, but who died no less heroically and tragically than the thousands of French who joined the underground to help defeat the Nazis, or those who hid Jews in their cellars and attics to save them from deportation to death camps.

I thought of Sheriff Bull Connor of Birmingham and his attack dogs, sent against the civil rights protesters. Would justice one day prevail for Negroes in America, or would racism merely fade from the headlines and lurk beneath the surface, just as anti-Semitism had in France after Dreyfus, only to rear its ugly head on another day? What was it about this human failing that allowed it to embed in and darken the hearts of men, lie dormant for a week, a year, or a millennium, only to rise up again and drag us back into a cesspool of hate? I questioned and questioned again, my thoughts a Socratic dialog as I walked along the dark streets at a brisk pace.

Suddenly, I heard a familiar voice, and I stopped and turned around. It was Dr. Nastovich walking just behind me with Jan, who, like me, had a bandage on her head.

I was shocked to see they were holding hands. The moment I noticed this, Jan dropped his hand. She looked pale and embarrassed.

"Hey!" I smiled and reached out to hug her. "You're looking a whole lot better than the last time I saw you. How's the head?"

"Probably hurts as much as yours."

"Ouch! You made it to the hospital?"

"I had to wait forever for the ambulance, but they eventually came."

"Stitches? Let me see."

"Yes, and it hurt like a son of a bitch."

"Robbie, please understand . . ." Jan whispered, her back to Nastovich.

"There's nothing to explain," I said, concealing my shock about the hand holding.

Nastovich stood back silently watching the two of us talk. He seemed nervous, shifting his weight from side to side.

"Hi, Doctor, really cool to see you outside class," I said, waving to him. He moved closer. "What are you guys doing here?"

"We were about to ask you the same thing," he said.

Jan and Nastovich together. . . I just don't get it. I looked at her as if to say I was not into judging her, though, in fact, I was freaked out.

"Samberg," Nastovich interrupted, "yesterday I was visited by an embassy second secretary, who asked me about you."

"Second secretary?"

"He was CIA," Nastovich said, "and that's not paranoia."

"Now what would the CIA want with me?" I asked, feigning surprise.

"He asked a lot of questions and wanted to know who your friends were. He went to the office and asked for your school records. I told him nothing. I don't know what you're up to, Robbie, but you better be careful."

That was the first time he'd called me by my first name.

We stood together for a few more moments in silence.

Holy fuck, the CIA! No way I can meet with My Hanh's father – they're already on to me!

How am I going to tell her?

"I need to be going," I said.

"We do too," Nastovich said. He explained they were meeting someone for dinner.

"Thanks for the heads-up about the CIA. It's cool," I added. Maybe they saw me on TV at rue St-Jacques and want to interview me. I'm sure it's nothing."

"I'm not so sure," Nastovich replied, with Jan nodding in agreement.

"I'll stop by the embassy tomorrow. See you at school."

"Bye." I walked away, a picture of nonchalance, but far more alarmed about the CIA visit than I had let on. Maybe they tracked me visiting the Crillon when I left the note for My Hanh, or when I met her at the bookstore. This was not good.

I arrived at Goldenberg's and entered the colorful, noisy restaurant, filled with neighborhood residents catching up on gossip and feasting on an endless supply of Middle Eastern fare. I could smell the pungent odor of the spices as the cooks worked at dipping chickpea balls in a fryer and filling pita breads to bursting with crunchy cabbage, roasted aubergine, tahini, and hot sauce. Everybody was busy eating, juggling savory food with knives, forks, and spoons and in animated conversation. It was a wonderful sight, though it could not distract me from the nervousness I felt about the warning I had just received from Nastovich.

There in the far corner, watching me search for her, I saw My Hanh, who lit the way with her incandescent smile. I was, as they say in France, *follement amoureux*, or "madly in love," and I felt better the moment I laid eyes on her shining face. She got up to greet me and wrapped her arms around me, pulling me close. We kissed, oblivious to the hubbub of the busy restaurant.

"My Robbie, it is good to see you," she whispered, continuing her embrace as people walked around us, taking little notice. This was France, and public displays of affection were commonplace and accepted, even between Americans and Vietnamese.

We continued our embrace.

"I like being in your arms," I said, kissing her face all over.

We were making a spectacle of ourselves, but we did not care.

"I adored the poem!" she said.

"I adore *you*," I responded, nibbling her ear.

By now we were trying the patience of even the most romantically inclined French waiters, each of whom was forced to navigate around us as we stood in the middle of the narrow restaurant floor.

"I have a surprise for you," she said, still not letting go, her arms squeezing me against her body.

"You want to make love right here in the middle of the restaurant, right?" I asked with a naughty smile.

"Ah, my incorrigible optimist," she murmured wickedly.

"What is it?" I whispered as I nibbled her ear.

She pulled away. "My father has sent his car for us. It's across the street." She pointed to the restaurant window, beyond which I could see a black ZiL limousine with a police escort, the motor running. He has arranged a special dinner for you."

"My Hanh, I can't do this."

"But you said you would think about it."

"I have just learned that I am under surveillance by the CIA.

"You won't take the risk?"

"My Hanh, what do you expect from me?"

"I expect the man I love to stand by me and to keep his word." She looked at me with disappointment and disapproval.

"You've cornered me here," I responded, starting to feel my resolve weaken as I looked at her face.

"Please, Robbie!" I paused, my brain working overtime.

"Okay, I'll go, but we're going to have to do this my way."

"Your way?"

"Yes. You leave first and take the limo. I'll leave a half hour later and walk to the hotel. Meet me in one hour at the rear entrance in the alley near the trash cans and make sure no one sees you. And tell your father there can be no one else in the restaurant. I'm not taking any chances."

"Thank you, my Robbie!" She wrapped her arms around me. "I'll be there." She headed outside to the limousine.

I braced myself for what I could not find a way to avoid. I was about to meet with the foreign minister of North Vietnam, Le Duc Tho. I ordered a coffee. The half hour passed in a moment. I walked through the crowded restaurant, and stopped to pay Jo Goldenberg at the register. I exited the restaurant and headed across the busy street to a smaller, side street which ran in the direction of the Crillon. I moved from one side of the street to the other, my eyes peeled for anyone looking suspicious.

Led by a police escort, the Citroën carrying My Hanh sped toward the Hôtel de Crillon, next to the American embassy. When it arrived, two uniformed men opened the car doors, greeted My Hanh with deference, and ushered her inside.

A half hour later, I arrived at the hotel and turned into the dark alley which ran behind it. I spotted the trash cans and the rear door. There was no one there. I stood in a small alcove next to the door and waited for My Hahn. It was silent except for the sound of passing cars on the street a few hundred feet away. The longer I stayed still, waiting, the more my nervousness returned. At last, the door swung open and My Hanh emerged. She smiled at me and took my hand. I squeezed hard. We walked through the interior corridors of the hotel remaining on a lower floor to avoid guests and staff. A stairway led up to the restaurant, Les Ambassadeurs, a grand, ornate room with gilt ceilings and cozy nooks along the east wall with large picture windows overlooking Place de la Concorde. It was intimidating—a bit like being ushered into the Hall of Mirrors at Versailles.

We were the only people in the restaurant, except for the staff of servers, in dress uniform, who tended exclusively to us. We were seated at an oval-shaped table set with magnificent china, a rich linen tablecloth, matching napkins, and heavy, elegant silverware in front of the large window at the center of the room. The waiter poured pink champagne into our cut-crystal glasses as we waited for My Hanh's father to arrive.

I looked at My Hanh sheepishly and in mock formality lifted my glass to propose a toast "To surviving the interrogation!"

"And the CIA," she added.

We laughed and clinked glasses. "Remember, not a word about us" she warned.

My shirt was wet with perspiration from the walk and my palms sweaty. My Hanh smiled as the elaborately carved double doors opened at last and her father entered the room. He was a tall, stately man, dressed in a black silk tunic with a split turtleneck collar opened at the front. As he moved closer, I noticed his gait, a slow but confident stride with little variation. He smiled at My Hanh and turned his gaze on me. He gave no indication of feeling in the look. It was antiseptic. It was all I could do to keep my teeth from chattering.

"So, you're the American who rescued my daughter," said Le Duc Tho without emotion, more a statement of fact than an expression of appreciation.

Not sure what to do, I thrust my arm forward to shake his hand and knocked over the crystal tumbler in front of me, spilling ice water all over the table.

"Oh no!"

"It's okay, Robbie," My Hanh responded as she grabbed her napkin and began to sop up the water.

Tho sat in his chair and said nothing as the waiters responded to the spill with a fresh white cloth to cover the wet spot.

"Rescue? Well, I think it was more that I was in the right place at the right time, sir," I said, trying to regain my composure.

"He rescued me, Father!" My Hanh insisted. "You are too modest, Robbie."

Tho gave his daughter a stern look and turned to me. "My daughter has not yet learned to allow a young man his modesty," he said in a lecturing tone, speaking perfect English.

"He did!" My Hanh protested, her eyes trained on her father as if to convince him.

"There is little I can say in a favorable way about America or Americans, but I am grateful to have my daughter safely back, and I want to thank you."

Tho stood up and reached over to shake my hand. I stood and did the same. His grip was tight but lasted only two shakes before he pulled away and we both sat down again.

I noticed his eyes studying My Hanh and me as the maître d' approached and two waiters brought out the first course, a traditional Vietnamese noodle soup. I wondered what he was thinking. His face was opaque.

"We offer you this evening some samples of Vietnamese cuisine that I don't think you will find in America," the man announced.

I tasted the soup, which was spicy and delicious, and signaled my approval to My Hanh, who now seemed a little on edge, too. *Happily, the first course contains no mice, spiders, or insects.*

Tho spoke in a soft voice, "I see you were wounded in the street battles." He eyed my forehead, which still showed signs of the wound. "My Hanh told me about this, and I saw you speak on the television. When I was your age, I suffered wounds in battle as well."

I kept thinking that sitting next to me was the man who founded the Indochinese Communist Party in 1930, who led the Viet Minh to victory against the French, and who was a key leader of the Vietcong insurgency now at war with the United States.

"Thank you for inviting me," I said. "This is my first Vietnamese meal."

Tho smiled briefly and nodded. In him I could see My Hanh's patrician look, her fine, clear skin, and her regal manner. *How could a hardened communist and sworn enemy of America appear so gentle? Perhaps it would not be so difficult to tell him how I feel about his daughter.*

I wondered if he had already sensed something between My Hanh and me from our body language. Here was an enemy of America, and I was in love with his daughter and dining with him, something it was likely few if any other Americans had done. My Hanh had told me he had not yet met the American envoy sent for the peace talks and that it was not entirely clear that the talks would even take place, much less be fruitful.

"My Hanh tells me you are interested in our history," Tho said.

"Yes, very."

"She told me you brought all your books about Vietnam from America to Paris," he said. "Did she tell you she brought all her books about America to Paris?" he added, looking at her with lingering consternation.

"Oh, Father," My Hanh replied. "He knows."

"You know it costs a great deal to ship that many books from Hanoi to Paris," he complained, looking again at his headstrong daughter.

"Father!" she responded, silencing him on the subject with a serious look.

"As a young man," Tho continued, "I joined our revolution. It was a natural part of the idealism of my youth. This was during the Japanese occupation, and in time I earned my place in the Party's leadership."

My Hanh looked surprised by her father's candor. It was almost as if she were learning things about him for the first time, too.

"It's difficult for Americans to understand what it's like when your nation is occupied by a foreign power," Tho explained. "This is not something America has experienced since your war for independence against the British two centuries ago. No one alive in the United States remembers what it's like to have foreign troops on your soil."

"We don't think about that, because the oceans have always protected us," I responded.

Tho paused to consider my observation. "After the defeat of the Japanese empire in 1945, which ended their occupation of our country, we thought at long last we would have our independence. For a thousand years, our country had been occupied by China and then by France, and you just cannot imagine the excitement we felt at this moment. I remember looking at the face of our leader, Ho Chi Minh, as he read the declaration of our independence as the Democratic Republic of Vietnam. He looked so content, so happy that we would no longer have to suffer the humiliation of foreign occupation, but the moment of joy did not last. The French government sought to reestablish its colonial empire and occupied our country again. Your American government financed eighty percent of the French occupation so the struggle continued. I was a leader in that struggle, and I was arrested, just like your friend Danny."

"How many years were you in prison?" I asked.

"Too many. Let's see. I was jailed by the French from 1930 to 1936 and again from 1939 to 1944. This was a dark time for me."

"Father, this is the first time I have ever heard you speak of this," My Hanh said.

"These are memories I would rather forget, My Hanh," he said, studying his daughter for a moment. "But I share them as a courtesy for our guest, for his appreciation of our history," he added.

"Danny is the only friend of mine ever imprisoned," I said.

"When you find out where he is, you may want to visit him," Tho said. "This is when a friend needs you the most. I had friends who helped me when I was in prison, and I have never forgotten their loyalty and their kindness."

I thought about telling them about the help I was about to provide to Danny, purchasing his train ticket to Germany, but I decided not to speak of it. I would tell My Hanh later, in private, but I needed be careful about what I said in front of her father. *Maybe the hotel is bugged?*

"After we defeated the French at Dien Bien Phu," Tho continued, "we thought again we would finally have our independence. But the Geneva Accords following our victory divided our nation. Our fate became entangled in the Cold War. America stepped in to support a puppet regime in South Vietnam. To achieve independence, we now had to defeat the most technologically advanced military on the planet," he said, peering at me and pausing for effect.

"David and Goliath," I said hesitantly.

"And what a cruel, bloodthirsty enemy you are," he said, studying me again with steely eyes and an awful grimace.

I sat up in my chair, my body suddenly on alert.

"You know, sir, we have nuclear weapons, and we have not used them," I said, realizing the moment the words poured out of my mouth that I had trodden on dangerous ground. Thankfully, the maître d' and waiters arrived at the table to clear away dishes and place new ones before us. The table fell into an awkward silence.

"These are sugarcane prawns and lemongrass chicken skewers," the maître d' explained as the waiters gracefully laid the dishes on the table.

My Hanh took the plates one at time and, in the tradition of a Vietnamese hostess, served her father first and then me before she served herself.

"I have studied Vietnam's painful history. I know how many decades you have been at war," I said, attempting to salvage the conversation.

"So, Robbie, are we supposed to be grateful that your government has not annihilated us with a nuclear holocaust?"

"Well, no . . ."

"Are we supposed to be grateful that your war machine has limited itself to burning countless people alive in storms of fire tossed upon them from passing aircraft? Is this the restraint of a great nation?" he asked, raising his voice ominously. "Is this how you deal with a small Asian nation seeking its independence?"

My Hanh placed her right hand on her father's sleeve. They sat motionless for a few moments.

"Robbie, we did not seek this war with America! Who in their right mind would wish for such a thing? And your side has suffered, as we have. Twenty-five thousand American soldiers have died, more than eighty thousand wounded, according to your government's statistics, and soon you will have a half-million soldiers fighting in our small country in what I assure you is a very lost cause," he said, his voice again lowered but fiercely passionate.

My Hanh looked at me as if to stealthily send her support to endure what had become a more difficult conversation.

Tho continued, as if rehearsing what he would say to the American delegation: "If after two million tons of bombs and napalm have been dropped upon us—more, I think, than your air force dropped on Germany during World War Two—we have not already given up fighting for our dream of unification and independence, then what more could you possibly do to make us give up?" He paused for a second, jaw clenched, eyes opened wide.

"Nuclear holocaust? Another Hiroshima?" he demanded, pounding his fist down on the elegant tablecloth.

The waitstaff scurried over, thinking that we needed attention, and Tho waved them away.

"Did your President Lincoln give up on preserving your union because of the great losses at Gettysburg and Antietam? And what if he had? How would history have judged him? What makes anyone in America think we would ever give up?" he said, his tone angry, his expression resigned.

I turned to My Hanh, who wore a similar look on her face, then back to her father.

"How do you think it will end?"

Tho paused, seemingly surprised by my question. My Hanh remained silent.

"Victory," Tho responded emphatically. "Your Goliath is about to be slayed by our army of Davids."

"We've got a Pentagon with endless resources and battle-tested generals who would disagree," I said.

"They will lose, Robbie, because your nation's reach has exceeded its grasp. It may take more time before it becomes apparent, but I assure you I am correct," he said, his tone now calmer, though equally determined.

"Is this ever going to heal?" I asked.

"Never fully," Tho answered without hesitation. "The mothers who lost sons, the soldiers who lost limbs, the brothers and sisters of those killed and wounded, the hundreds of thousands whose lives were ruined by this war will pass their pain and suffering to future generations on both sides. I don't think these wounds ever heal."

"What will it take to stop this?" I asked.

Tho thought for a moment. "We are practical men, Robbie. We simply need a guarantee of unification and independence and this war will end. After that we'll open our wounded hearts to reconciliation—perhaps not right away and perhaps never completely, but we'll encourage the healing to begin."

"What you said reminds me of Lincoln, who could have ordered death for the surrendering soldiers of the South after our civil war but instead instructed his generals to disarm them and send them home to their farms. He understood the importance of promoting reconciliation following a brutal war, how that would accomplish so much more than vengeance," I observed.

"That's the first time anyone has compared me with Lincoln, and I take that as a great compliment, Robbie," Tho responded.

My Hanh raised her glass. "To healing."

"To healing," I rejoined, clicking our glasses.

Tho did not join in the toast. "Healing comes after victory, and we are not there yet." He looked at My Hanh, as if to rein in her optimism. Then, looking to lighten the mood, he looked at me and added, "I hope the wound on your head heals soon, because judging by how it looks it must really hurt!"

Tho and My Hanh smiled at last, and to my surprise the three of us laughed. I began to relax.

"My daughter tells me you have become a leader in the student movement!"

"Well, yes, but it was quite by accident. A happenstance. The true leader, Danny was arrested and I was the stand in."

"Ah, my daughter exaggerates about you again! I think with all this exaggeration, she must like you," he observed. He turned to look directly at My Hanh. "Now, my daughter, let's not lose our objectivity, for without that we may lose our way," he warned with a look and a wink, half in jest, half seriously.

"Don't worry, Father, I inherited my objectivity from you and it never leaves me. But I tell you, Robbie is all that I have said and more," she added, looking at me. "He's just very modest. In the battle on the streets of Paris, he *was* the leader, and I know that when he returns to America he will be a leader there, too. Remember the brave speech he gave standing on the wrecked car on rue Saint-Jacques? You saw it on the television, Father."

"Yes, I did speak to the crowd, standing in for Danny. The words were mine. They just poured out of me. The ideas were those of the movement, a movement that is happening across the globe. I really can't take credit for this."

My Hanh kicked me under the table and threw me a disapproving look for contradicting her. I squinted, realizing I deserved it.

"Ah, more modesty from our dinner guest," Tho responded, and turned to me. "I understand you acted for your friend, but those were your words, and you had the courage in the heat of battle to stand up and share them, and you motivated the crowd and acted as its leader in place of your friend, and therefore I think My Hanh is correct about this. She has not exaggerated. And at the end of your speech, you said, 'Long live Danny the Red,' which greatly impressed me, because it meant you put your friendship with Danny above the stigma of openly praising and supporting a leftist leader—something that Americans never do."

"Well," I admitted sheepishly, "we call him Danny the Red because of the color of his hair, not his politics. I don't think he likes anybody's politics at this point, so I think again you give me too much credit, sir."

"No, Robbie," Tho rejoined, "I don't think you give yourself enough credit. Just as the power of your words inspired the crowd yesterday to stand up against the power of the state, which was much stronger than the group of unarmed students, the power of our idea, the idea of a unified, independent Vietnam, must inspire us, a nation of simple peasants, to stand up to the United States of America."

I winced, betraying that Tho's words made me uncomfortable. I feared the conversation could become tense again.

"But I must tell you, Robbie," Tho quickly added, "that we harbor no ill-feelings about Americans as a people. The American political system is not operating wisely in your policies toward us, but I think in time your system will correct itself. You once traded in human slaves but later outlawed slavery and in the past decade have changed your laws to discourage racism. You have shown a willingness to change, and that gives us hope."

"What about communism?" I asked. "Many Americans who support the war do so because you are communists, not because they wish to deny Vietnam its unification and independence."

"That's a good point, Robbie," Tho responded, looking at me, then at My Hanh. "My daughter tells me you are from New Jersey, the son of a capitalist who sells music."

"Yes, my father owns a Muzak franchise and leases music played in offices, restaurants, and factories. We call it a background music company. He is more like the small farmer who owns his own plot than what you might think of as a wealthy capitalist."

"Does he own the means of production?" Tho asked.

"Well, not exactly. He leases the music that is owned by a larger company, which recorded it, and under an exclusive agreement he re-leases that same music to local companies in the area of his franchise for a fee."

"Then he is a capitalist—a small capitalist, but a capitalist," Tho said, looking as if he was still trying to decipher my explanation.

"Is that bad?"

"We do not believe individuals should own the means of production, only the state should own them, and all people in an enterprise should benefit from the enterprise according their needs," Tho said.

"So, you would have someone who contributed little to an enterprise gain more from it because of their needs than another who contributed much more but whose needs were not as great."

"Yes, exactly," Tho replied, smiling.

"How do you define what somebody needs?"

"That's decided by the Party. But it's wrong for one person to own the means of production and benefit way beyond their needs at the expense of others whose contributions are equally if not more important to the success of the enterprise and whose needs are not met."

"You are a nation of idealists," I observed, attempting to mask my skepticism.

"Is that bad?" Tho asked.

"No, it's just that ideologies can sound really great in theory but fall short in practice," I observed, wondering if the conversation might be wandering again into dangerous territory.

"Well, Robbie," Tho said, looking pensive, "it's true that our society is not perfect, but then you must admit that neither is yours." I felt as if I were having one of my exchanges with Nastovich.

"The problem is that people are not always wired to act for noble purposes, but more often from self-interest," I explained. "But when people are allowed to act from self-interest, their collective decisions largely result in the most efficient distribution of goods and services. That's what makes a free economy work so well." I looked at Tho and My Hanh, whose expressions were impassive.

"Yes," Tho replied, "but almost always at the price of great inequality. We think men and society can do better than that. We think great concentrations of wealth and power in the hands of a self-interested few can be dangerous. This is why we have chosen communism. It's not the only reason, but it's an important one."

"In my studies of America's involvement with your country, I have concluded that our problem has been more with your communism than your nationalism. Were it not for that, I don't think we would be at war with you," I said, gaining confidence.

"Robbie, communism is the path we chose to organize our society, and it helped to move us beyond the Confucian roots of our past, which had kept our society static for centuries. Our historical circumstance led us to adopt the socialist path, but that does not mean we are a threat to other nations, and especially not to America. Besides, there are many nations, some even in Europe, which have chosen a socialist path, but you do not drop napalm on them," he added emphatically.

"So, you are saying that your communist government has no designs on neighboring nations."

"That's right, Robbie," Tho responded. "We needed to break free of old models in our society to build a modern Vietnam that could sustain its independence, where progress could be made for all citizens, and that could coexist peacefully with China, our large, powerful neighbor. The Chinese example was an important one for us, and it influenced our evolution. But the important thing, Robbie, is that our communism is a communism with Vietnamese characteristics. It is not a system designed to be imposed upon others. It is not part of a plan to accomplish hegemony in Southeast Asia or in any part of the world, and most importantly, it is not a threat to the United States of America."

"The leaders of our antiwar movement might believe that, but the men who make our foreign policy do not," I said.

"Well, then," Tho responded, "I must find a way to get your president to understand that what I have told you is true. If I can do that, the war could end quickly." He waved his right hand for emphasis. "Are you enjoying your meal, Robbie?" he asked.

"It's delicious," I said, happy to talk again about the food.

"Vietnamese cuisine is considered one of the healthiest in the world," My Hanh added, returning to the conversation after an uncharacteristic silence.

"I loved the pork and vegetable dish," I said, pointing to the serving dish in front of me. "How did you get a French kitchen to cook all these Vietnamese dishes?"

"When we travel on diplomatic missions, we take along our own kitchen staff and ingredients so we can eat as we do at home," Tho explained.

"The pork dish is called *gỏi*," My Hanh explained. "It's what you call a salad, but unlike in the West, it does not contain lettuce." She ate a mouthful. "Our cooks use only the finest pork spare ribs and the freshest herbs and vegetables to create this taste." She spoke with greater animation now that the conversation had moved away from politics.

"Robbie," Tho continued, "we have no natural enmity for America or Americans. Yours is a society eight thousand miles away, and once we are unified, North and South, we shall pose no threat to you. But this war can only conclude with our unification and our independence. We cannot settle for less, just as your Lincoln would not settle for less than the preservation of your union."

I imagined him leaning over a conference room table and telling our diplomats the same thing. I wondered who they might be and when that might take place.

"You admire our President Lincoln?"

"The first thing I did before coming to Paris was to reread the letters and speeches of Abraham Lincoln. What better way to prepare to meet the Americans? My Hanh has studied Lincoln, too, and admires him. I also admire the great general of the South, Robert E. Lee. He was a reluctant warrior, which is part of what made him a great warrior. You know, some of the greatest warriors—Yamamoto from Japan, even your own Eisenhower—abhorred war, but when called upon to defend their nations, they applied their talents to the fight with objectivity, common sense, and bravery. I think of myself as that kind of warrior."

"But Lee and Yamamoto lost," I said.

"Robbie!" My Hanh interrupted.

"I told you this war will end in our victory," Tho said. "We are reluctant warriors, but history is on our side. Even if your military machine kills most of us and enslaves the rest in what would have to be a brutal colonial occupation, you could not sustain it. Such a victory would crumble under its own weight and we would eventually accomplish our dream of national unity and independence."

"I think that's the way Lincoln saw slavery in our country," I said. "He believed it would eventually end of its own decay, because it was morally wrong. He had hoped the South would agree to ban slavery only in the new territories in our west and was willing to allow it to continue in the deep South."

"But his views changed, and he eventually freed the slaves everywhere in America," right?" Tho asked.

"Yes, but it took the bloodiest war in our history to create the conditions for him to do that."

"A hundred and three years have passed, and the wounds of your civil war have not fully healed," Tho observed.

"Perhaps the healing will come sooner between America and Vietnam with the distance between us," I responded.

"You are wise for such a young man," Tho said, smiling at me. "Despite Lincoln's actions, the heritage of slavery in America continues and racism persists, right?"

"Yes, we have racism, just as here in France and in Europe there is still anti-Semitism."

"Fear and hatred for people who are different is not purely an American phenomenon," Tho said with a hint of sarcasm in his voice. "I notice you have a certain fondness for my daughter, who is very different from you," he added unexpectedly with a laugh and a smile, raising his eyebrows. *Perhaps it was the rice wine that let loose this levity.*

"Maybe we are not so different as you think, Father," My Hanh offered to his, and especially my, surprise. I looked at her. *This is moving into dangerous territory.*

"Maybe, my educated daughter, you are right, but I don't think Mr. Samberg has had much experience with girls from our part of the world, right?" He gave me a studied look.

"Right," I replied, thinking of how I might change the subject back to Vietnamese cooking. I was about to ask about the mice, spiders, and insects when Tho continued with enthusiasm.

"Well, let me explain. In Vietnamese culture there is a strong tradition of male superiority. The highest status in a Vietnamese family belongs to the man, the father. He has absolute authority in the household. His position as provider for the family is unchallenged. He is not expected to do housework, to cook, or to clean. When he returns home from work, he relaxes. As head of the household, he has the final decision in all matters. Although he might consult his wife or children, he is not expected to do so."

I concluded that Tho was not onto us and continued to listen intently. My Hanh looked uncomfortable in her silence.

"Sounds like a man's world to me," I observed, darkening My Hanh's reaction even more. "It also sounds like America in the 1950s, only our men came home and turned on the TV to watch football. But what about your women? Do they accept this?"

"Ours is a patriarchal society," Tho said, "so women have limited rights, and they take a secondary place in the family. They are brought up according to a strict discipline, and they remain in the home. Since most women do not enter the job market, there is less importance attached to their education."

I glanced at My Hanh, who was now agitated.

"Father," she interrupted, her voice insistent, "you neglected to explain to Robbie that my generation is changing all this."

Tho reluctantly concurred with a nod. I sensed the distance between him and his daughter on the subject and suspected this was not the first time it had come up between them.

Tho continued as if to underscore how different things were in Vietnam.

"There is a saying in our country: 'If you have a son, you have a descendent, but you cannot say so even if you have ten daughters.'"

My Hanh instantly flashed a look of disapproval, although she still did not respond. As the table was cleared for the next course, Tho told me that he never imagined he would be having such a conversation at this dinner. "I hope I can speak as freely to your American diplomats, if we can ever get them to come to the table."

Then he turned to My Hanh and looked at her with affection. He saw the discontent and discomfort on her face. "Of course, My Hanh is an exception," Tho added without missing a beat. "She has been well educated in our socialist schools and has studied here in France and now in China, and thanks to socialism, there are no longer official barriers to prevent her or any girl from taking up an important profession."

"Father, let's not give Robbie the impression this is true for all girls in our country," My Hanh added. She looked at him sternly, and he returned a look of surprise at her contradicting him.

"Alright," Tho conceded, "there is, as my well-educated daughter is suggesting, a difference between the aspirations of our party and what we have achieved."

"Especially when it comes to women," My Hanh added, her voice lowered, as if she were sneaking in the observation so as not to be noticed making it.

"Progress takes time and perfection is elusive," Tho observed in a lecturing tone.

"Sounds like a conversation I could have at home around the kitchen table," I said.

"What do you mean, *around the kitchen table*?" he asked.

"It's just an expression about where American families have conversations about politics, community or family issues, sitting around the kitchen table having their breakfast or dinner."

"I like that idea," Tho responded. "Maybe we should have our negotiations with your country's diplomats around a kitchen table."

"If my mother were here with us, she would tell you that the traditional role of women in America, until recently, was not so different from that of Vietnam, but the feminist movement is changing this. Women are now seeking equality with men."

"American women did not have the right to vote until 1920, right?" My Hanh asked.

"Ah, the Nineteenth Amendment," Tho exclaimed with a note of restrained admiration. "This was a struggle that was good for the women of your country, as I think the struggle for the Voting Rights Act will be good for your Negroes, but our system is less dynamic. We don't change so quickly," he conceded, looking over at My Hanh, who nodded.

"Vietnamese women need a Susan B. Anthony!" she added, clenching and shaking her right fist for emphasis.

"Vietnamese women need for their men to win this war and unify our nation, and then we can worry about progress for women," Tho responded, his tone an admonishment.

Just then the waiters brought the desserts, platters of banana coconut tapioca pudding, and mini–coconut crème caramels, served with a sweet wine.

"Ah, Château d'Yquem," Tho said. "I know you will enjoy this, Robbie."

The waiter poured a small amount in his glass. Tho picked it up and swished the wine, carefully observing the ring it left. Then he breathed in the aroma, placing his nose just above the rim to take it in.

"Excellent," he declared as the waiter filled all our glasses.

It was sweet and delicious, and I wondered if he was going to offer a toast. He did not, eager to continue his lecture about Vietnamese culture.

"You know, Robbie, in Vietnam boys and girls are not free to court. Girls date under strict parental supervision. Western-style romance is considered inappropriate for unmarried girls. Parents arrange marriages because they can be objective and make better judgments," he said, looking at My Hanh and at me.

"In my grandparents' generation, there were matchmakers," I responded, "but today parents leave decisions about marriage to their sons and daughters. But it is still important for a boy to ask for the hand of his girl from her father."

"So, are you asking me for my daughter's hand?" Tho asked with a mock-serious look. "The rice wine is strong," I said. "Maybe too strong!"

My Hanh almost fell off her cushy, red velvet chair. She gasped, her eyes widening, her lips drawing tightly together. Tho suddenly looked shocked as he noticed her reaction and mine. Her gasp told the story. The table went silent.

"I'm joking, of course," Tho said, his eyes scanning us both, "but I see on my daughter's face there is more going on here than I have been told." He paused for a moment that seemed to last longer than it actually did, as his mood transformed, his tone chilled, and he cast a disapproving eye on My Hanh. This was headed downhill fast.

"My Hanh." He said her name slowly, the anger in his voice building.

"I am sorry, Father!" she blurted. "I did not know how to speak to you of this," she added, her voice breaking with anguish.

Here is her Mississippi moment . . . and mine.

"Sir," I interrupted to run interference, speaking slowly, "My Hanh and I have found something special in each other."

"I don't want to hear more," Tho exploded, holding his right hand in front of my face.

"Please let me just say that I feel love and respect for your daughter," I insisted, ignoring the hand.

The color drained from My Hanh's face as it had on the Métro. We sat silently, waiting for Tho to say more. He looked at each of us with resignation, shaking his head, and began to speak slowly.

"The path for a mixed couple in Vietnam or in America is an impossible one. It defies our history and our culture, and it will bring shame on our family and on our nation."

I reached for My Hanh's hand under the tablecloth. She was trembling.

"My Hanh." Tho turned to look directly at her. "We have serious matters to address with the Americans here, and we must keep our minds clear to accomplish this."

She burst into tears. "Father, I need to excuse myself," she said, quickly getting up from her chair and fleeing the table.

As soon as we were alone, Tho turned to me, his look troubled. "Robbie, I know in matters of the heart we don't control when and how such things happen, but your timing could not be worse."

I looked down at my half-eaten plate of dessert, unable to raise my head to face him.

"Look at me, Robbie," Tho said as I slowly lifted my head. "You know, I could forbid My Hanh from seeing you." He paused to gather his thoughts, continuing to hold me in his gaze. "As a father, this is very hard for me. As a diplomat, it is harder because you are from the nation with which we are at war," he said, his tone analytical rather than emotional, his voice firm but soft.

"It's a brody," I responded.

"A what?"

"A brody—that's when your car skids off the road with the brakes locked," I explained. "A bummer."

"Bummer?"

"Yes, bummer—that's when something gets so complicated it brings you down," I explained.

Tho paused, looked at me, and spoke in a fatherly tone. "Robbie, I can see that you mean well, but please listen to me. This relationship has great risks, and there could be grave consequences for you both." He reached over and placed his hand on my forearm.

"I know," I said.

Tho paused again, opening his eyes wider, then leaned in to continue. "You both need to be sure this is what you really want," he whispered. "You need to take time to know each other. It is never a good idea to rush in matters of the heart, but especially in this case."

"Will you allow me to see her?" I asked.

"I think it's a little late to be asking my permission," he said, a resigned look on his face.

"This is the first time I have fallen in love. I did not expect it and I don't understand it, but I feel it. Nothing in my heart tells me to slow down—in fact, the opposite—but I will follow your advice. I will go slowly, and I will influence My Hanh to go slowly."

"You must keep this relationship a secret," Tho added. "You can't tell your parents, your friends, or anyone," he admonished. "The risks are too great."

I nodded.

"You need to have a cover."

"A cover?"

"Yes. Maybe a study for one of your classes on Vietnamese history and culture, sponsored by a professor, something that will explain the time you spend with My Hanh."

"A study?"

"Yes, you can ask your professor Nastovich to sponsor it," he suggested. "My Hanh told me about him."

"I don't think he will do it."

"Then you will need to find someone who will."

"That may be difficult."

"The first of many difficulties." He shook his head. "Now please go find my daughter and bring her back to the table."

I rose, and we looked at one another. We had crossed some boundary, finding ourselves in unfamiliar territory.

"Now go," he admonished, waving me away.

My Hanh was just outside the restaurant door, sitting alone in an alcove, still sobbing. I approached her.

"This is your fault," she said.

"My fault?"

"Your face when my father joked about asking for my hand—it gave us away. You will never succeed as a diplomat," she added, her tone scornful.

"My Hanh . . ."

"I told you not to tell him about us. I told you he would not accept it."

"My Hanh, I didn't mean for this to happen. It's okay. He has given his permission for us to see each other. It's not so bad."

"What? I thought he would forbid me from seeing you," she said, wiping the tears from her eyes, her anger subsiding.

"No. He sees how much we care for each other. I think he is torn, but he only asked that we slow things down to make sure this is right and that we keep our relationship a secret."

"But we already know it's right," she said.

"Yes, but we must give him time to understand and adjust. We must slow down for him, not for us," I said, kissing her cheeks. She did not resist but did not return my kisses.

"You don't know him as I do."

"Let's take him at his word, My Hanh," I said. "We need to do this."

"Robbie, I want to feel better about this, but I know my father, and he often does not reveal everything he thinks and feels. I fear that his skepticism about us runs deeper than you realize."

"He only asked that we slow things down, so let's give him that and meet his skepticism head-on with something more powerful."

"With our love?" she asked, throwing her arms around me and showering me with kisses, her mood lightening. "Oh, Robbie, forgive me my dark clouds."

"There is nothing to forgive," I whispered, taking her hand and holding it tightly. "Let's get back."

We returned to the table, holding hands. Tho greeted us calmly and with affection. He comforted My Hanh with a comment that he hoped he would find as fine an American to deal with on matters of state as she had found to explore what he simply called matters of the heart. My Hanh smiled, and Tho quickly changed the subject back to why they had come to Paris.

"I wish to speak to you more about our two countries, Robbie, and to seek your advice," he said. "Are you willing to help?"

"My advice?" I asked, feeling some discomfort.

"Don't worry, Robbie, I won't expect you to spin a brody," he said, smiling.

My Hanh looked puzzled. "I don't know this *brody*," she said.

"I will teach you," I responded, looking at Tho, who grinned and laughed, then raised his glass.

"To peace," he toasted.

"To peace," I responded.

"To peace," My Hanh repeated.

Just then, the waiters placed in front of each of us the final course, elegantly presented on ornate dishes, each covered with a polished silver top.

"Ah, the mignardise," I said.

"Better!" Tho responded as the waiters lifted the sliver covers in unison. "We conclude our meal with the rarest Vietnamese delicacies—dog meat, snake meat, and water rat!"

Chapter 13

Sunday

Sunday has arrived!
I'm glad I am alive!
Sweet hyacinth aroma
Repels the humdrum
Platitudes give way
To blessed latitudes
Anticipating solitudes
Remarkable delays!
Breathe power
To Sundays.
—Robbie Samberg

In the quiet of early Sunday mornings, the streets of Paris told their stories. All you had to do was look, listen, and use your imagination. The clop-clop of horse-drawn carriages passing by; the panting of a nobleman dashing through a dark alley after a duel; the cries of a mob rising up against the order of the day.

The city's slower pace invited exploration, and My Hanh and I would start Sundays at Café Procope, in St-Germain-des-Prés, each of us arriving excited to share all that had happened since our last time together, and each bringing a new book or article. To conceal our relationship, we always covered our heads, me with a hooded sweatshirt and My Hanh with a scarf, and we always varied the hour of our meeting. We avoided visiting the same places at the same times or on the same days, and I set up a special study project for extra credit on the history of Vietnam, sponsored by Dr. Nastovich. I didn't think he would do it, but when I told him about my passion for Vietnamese history, he readily agreed. If I were ever questioned about spending time with My Hanh, the study project would serve as my cover.

Nestled at a cozy table at Café Procope, My Hanh and I would talk about what we had learned during the week with excitement and passion, always over steaming hot coffee and warm croissants spread with butter and preserves. We dissected everything. She introduced me to Buddha, the health benefits of becoming a vegetarian, and the power of meditation, and I introduced her to the concept of the neighborhood barbecue, the American fascination with baseball, and the strange habit of chewing gum. We spoke endlessly about the war and about politics and history.

It was a nonstop ad hoc cross-cultural seminar on the serious and the not so serious, with the added benefits of romance and sex—yes, happily lots of sex—wherever and whenever possible. My Hanh's education in France and her Buddhism had combined to help her throw off the puritan constraints of Confucianism. Unlike most Vietnamese girls, who were expected to remain virgins until marriage, she saw herself the equal of men, who were free to engage in sexual exploration without shame.

As we spent time together, we discovered more things we shared in common. We learned that our immediate and mutual feelings of attraction were underpinned by shared interests that crossed geographical boundaries and more often than not were inexplicable, given the vast differences in our cultures. That we were so alike was a mystery, a beautiful mystery!

It was the second Sunday in May, a glorious spring day in Paris. We arrived at Café Procope early and sat at a cozy corner table.

"I read a book this week about your Benjamin Franklin," My Hanh offered, sipping her coffee and taking a bite of croissant, "and I loved him. He is, I think, my favorite American." She quickly corrected herself, grabbing and tightening her grip on my hand: "My second-favorite American."

"What do you like about Franklin?" I asked, wondering if she realized that we were sitting at a café he frequented when he served as minister to France from the upstart American Continental Congress. *Perhaps he took his morning coffee at this very table.*

"He used to eat here," she said.

"I know."

"Franklin was romantic, inventive, brave, and wise," she said. "And sexy! What more could a woman ask for in a man?"

"What about kind and funny?" I inquired. "And rich?"

"He was kind and funny, too," she said, "and very popular with the ladies, and yes, I think wealthy from his patents and his land holdings, but you know we socialists are not impressed by wealth. But come to think of it, maybe he is again my favorite American, and you, my Robbie, have fallen to second place!"

I was amazed at her interest in Franklin because he was also among my own favorite figures in American history. In my last semester before coming to France, I wrote an independent study paper on Franklin and his service as the ambassador to France during the American Revolution. I too found him to be inventive, brave, and wise, and I described him in my paper with almost the same words used by My Hanh.

"Who else do you admire?" I asked.

"Napoleon Bonaparte," she responded without hesitation. "Now there was a man of great ambition, driven by inner demons, who channeled these into amazing accomplishments for his nation and the world."

She spoke like a professor.

"You admire the former emperor of France? That's a strange choice for a Vietnamese communist. I'm not sure too many of your countrymen would share your admiration."

"There was more to Napoleon than most people realized," she said, putting down her coffee and waving her right hand for emphasis. "He was a strong leader who worked tirelessly to accomplish great things for France. He understood that it would take a strong leader to govern the French, and he was dedicated to spreading the ideals of the Revolution throughout Europe, taking a stand against inequality, intolerance, and feudalism."

Now she sounded like she was making a political speech.

"And I thought you Vietnamese communists weren't interested in spreading the gospel," I responded, reminding her that she and her father had assured me of this. "All you want is unification and independence, right?"

"Ah, my Robbie, you are not playing fair!"

"If you admire Napoleon for conquering Europe to spread the ideals of the French Revolution, why should I not believe you harbor the same ambition for socialism in Southeast Asia?"

"No, Robbie. Just because I admire Napoleon, doesn't mean that the Vietnamese Communist Party seeks to spread our political ideology beyond our borders." She sounded annoyed. "I have my own mind and my own way of thinking about things. Do I take everything you say as the policy of your nation's government?"

"Good point, but I am not the son of the secretary of state."
She ignored my comeback.

"I think in Napoleon's time, following the chaos of the Revolution," she continued in the same professorial tone, "it was
necessary for France to have a strong ruler, just as it requires
having a strong ruler today."

"You also support de Gaulle?"

"Well, no, but Robbie, not all societies can adopt your ideal-
ized Greek concept of democratic rule. In fact," she added with
a twinkle in her eye, leaning toward me and placing her hand
on mine, "your so-called democracy in America is not really
democratic at all, with your Electoral College and your system
which allows the open buying of political influence."

It's a full-court press! "Now wait a minute . . ."

"Isn't it true that in certain states the electors can still vote
for a presidential candidate even if that candidate has lost the
popular vote? Is that what you call democracy?" She let go of
my hand, tossing it away to accentuate her point.

"Yes, that's true," I replied, adding that I was no expert on
the Electoral College. "Okay, the big secret is out . . . Our American system of government is not perfect . . . Perhaps we could
use a civics lesson from your communist party in North Vietnam."

"Robbie, you are infuriating me, talking like a brainwashed
bourgeoisie," she barked.

"So, I am nothing but a bourgeoisie and brainwashed?" I
asked, stung by her words.

My Hanh's expression suddenly changed, her annoyance
subsiding.

"Robbie, I apologize. I got carried away. I must learn to
control myself and not to call you names just because you
act—how do you say in America? —like a jerk." She smiled
broadly. "I confess that the American system of government

has its good points, too, and we communists have our bad points."

"All right, and I believe you when you say North Vietnam is not out to conquer Southeast Asia, like your friend Napoleon conquered Europe."

"But he was more than just a despot who conquered Europe," My Hanh insisted. "Don't forget, Robbie, that he established a new system of law, built roads and canals connecting all parts of France, settled historic issues with the Catholic church, built grand monuments to French history, and promoted the idea of France as a force for the advancement of civilization."

She spoke as if from a speechwriter's talking points.

"Very impressive. Too bad all those people had to die on battlefields just because he was only five feet two inches tall," I observed sarcastically.

"Ah, you are again showing your ignorance, my Robbie. The Napoleon complex has been disproven! Five feet two inches in old French units is actually five feet seven inches by today's standards, and the average height of a Frenchman in Napoleon's time was five feet five inches. This so-called Napoleon complex, that he was aggressive as compensation for his small physical stature, is a myth, just like the attack by North Vietnamese torpedo boats on the USS *Maddox* at the Gulf of Tonkin."

"You got me there!"

"And what is my handsome, though still second-favorite American going to do for his country? How about ending your country's obscene and foolish war in my country? Then you'll have the resources to spread your perfect ideology of self-governance to all the less fortunate peoples around the world. End the war, and I'll forget about my affections for Bonaparte and Franklin."

She smiled her wicked smile and we laughed. We did a lot of laughing. We had decided never to miss a Sunday together after her father gave us his blessing to date. No matter what might happen around us—strikes, demonstrations, student protests, setbacks in the peace talks—we would keep our Sunday dates. It was our time together and it was sacred.

We kept a list of places we wanted to visit on Sundays, and after sorting through a half dozen or so, we decided this day to visit the Church of the Dôme at Invalides, designed by French architect Jules Hardouin-Mansart for Louis XIV, and later converted to Napoleon's tomb. It seemed like the perfect place to continue our conversation.

As we passed over the Pont des Arts, My Hanh stopped midway across the bridge and pulled me over to the low iron railing that faced the Eiffel Tower. I thought she was going to take a picture with the Kodak Brownie I had around my neck.

"It's time for our ceremony," she said, reaching into her purse and pulling out a handwritten note. She held it up.

"Ceremony?" I responded quizzically.

"Yes," she said. "I think we should declare our love, and I have written a ceremony for us to do it." She moved close to me, holding up the paper for us to read.

"Alright, but I think your father would say this is going too fast."

"I don't always do as my father asks. Do you?" she asked, again fielding the wicked smile.

"Definitely not."

She took my hand as we faced the Eiffel Tower and we read aloud together.

"Now we shall feel no rain, for each of us will be the shelter for each other. Now we shall feel no cold, for each of us will be the warmth for the other. Now we are two persons, but there is only one life before us. We promise to love, respect and honor each other, sharing our plans and interests, ideals and emotions, through the trials of life and the joyous times, caring for each other forever."

My Hanh reached into her purse to pull out a small brass padlock and key. The lock had a hand-drawn heart on each side. She placed the lock on the rail, turned the key to lock it, and handed the key to me. "Now please, my Robbie, throw the key into the River Seine."

"How are we going to take the lock off if I throw away the key?"

"We are not taking it off. No one is ever taking it off, and that's the point."

"We are going to leave the lock here?" I asked, scanning the rail from one end to the other to confirm that there were no other locks on the bridge.

"The lock will stay here forever, as we shall love each other forever," she said.

I threw the key as far as I could and kissed My Hanh, who had once again surprised and delighted me with this moment of romance.

"When did you think up this little ceremony?"

"Yesterday afternoon as I passed a hardware shop."

I wondered if others, seeing our lock, might be inspired to place one of their own to symbolize their love. *This is an idea tailor-made for Paris and perfect for a Sunday.*

We continued to walk hand in hand toward the Church of the Dôme and soon arrived at the foot of its front stairs.

"Sure you can handle the competition?" My Hanh teased as we were about to climb the stairs to visit *Napoleon*. "You know, I'll be standing right next to him, and you have yet to conquer your first country."

"Good thing he's dead," I said.

"And in seven layers of coffins," she added with her infectious grin, holding up her *Michelin Guide.*

"That's not funny, it's creepy."

"You're right, my Robbie! I must be spending too much time with you. Your really bad sense of humor is rubbing off on me."

"I see that the Dôme is the second-tallest structure in Paris," I said, ignoring her taunts and reading from my own well-worn guidebook.

"No, I did not know this," she said. "Let's climb to the top!"

We ran up the stairs to the entrance. The church was built in 1706, its façade symmetrical, ornate, and towering. In 1840, it was converted into a tomb for Napoleon, a majestic setting for the larger-than-life emperor. We walked through the rotunda, peeking into the rooms on either side, which housed the remains of France's greatest war heroes. At the center of it all was a huge circular hole in the floor, with a wall about chest high running the circumference, and on the floor below sat Napoleon's massive green sarcophagus, said to be constructed of seven or eight separate coffins, of increasing size, each placed within the next and finally encased in the great outer coffin of shining green stone. Without the interlocking, multiple coffins, it was feared someone might steal, or worse yet, desecrate the emperor's body, not an implausible thought given the tumultuous history of France.

The magnificent building and massive coffin set in the rotunda evoked the scope and significance of France's First Empire.

There was a special exhibit on Napoleon at the adjacent Musée de l'Armée, and we walked there, meandering through the rooms, replete with everything Napoleonic—hats, swords, furnishings, documents. We stopped in front of a glass case to view the Napoleonic Code, the extraordinary work of jurisprudence that won Bonaparte his place in the frieze on the ceiling of the United States Supreme Court, alongside the other great lawgivers in the history of man. My Hanh did not know that Bonaparte's name had been placed on this frieze, which I triumphantly explained to her, shattering her claim of knowing more than me about Napoleon.

"You really can't expect me to know what you Americans paint on your walls," she contended, throwing up her hands, "but I still know more about Napoleon than you!"

"It's not painted; it's a relief, a sculpture," I said.

"Ah, same idea! Of course, knowing more than you is not saying much." My Hanh poked me, a devilish look coming over her otherwise-beautiful and glowing face. She snuggled up to me, ran her hands down my back, and rested them squarely at the center of my butt. And as if on cue, we strolled into a corner room, which housed Napoleon's bed, the one he used in the imperial palace, small by modern standards, but adorned with a luxuriously thick red velvet spread and crafted from rich mahogany, with four carved posts topped with golden cups on one side and onyx busts of women's heads on the other. We were the only people in the room.

My Hanh whispered, "That's the bed where Napoleon made love with Marie Walewska and Desiree." She moved closer and slipped her arms around me. "And with Hortense!"

There being no guard and no one else around, she kissed me, sliding her tongue into my mouth, and without warning pushed me down onto the bed.

"Is this your idea of a demure, submissive Vietnamese girl?" I teased as our lips locked and our bodies rolled across the imperial bed. "What happened to going slow?" I whispered, succumbing.

"It must have been the French nannies," she taunted breathlessly, "and I have diplomatic immunity." She thrust her right hand deep into my trousers, whispering, "*Vive l'Empereur!*"

Suddenly an elderly couple from Brooklyn, judging by their accents, entered the room.

"Guard!" the lady called out in dismay. "Guard!"

We jumped off the bed and ran to the nearest exit, laughing uproariously.

"You're a wild one," I observed as we reached the safety of the street.

"You are getting to know me better, my Robbie, just like my father asked." She paused. "And you still love me?" she said sheepishly.

"More each day! More and more each day!"

We kissed lustfully as passersby smiled with approval.

"Robbie," she whispered, "I wish to live with passion in each moment. I come from a place where life can be stolen in an instant. We must enjoy our time while we have it."

"Yes, and I think you are doing a pretty good job at it, jumping my bones on Napoleon's bed in a museum! And I thought the Vietnamese liberation movement was about geography and politics," I said, rolling my eyes.

She took my comment as criticism.

"Are you threatened by my spontaneity or my sexuality?" She placed her right hand on my butt, giving it a hard squeeze. "You, the leader of students trying to tear down authority and move society into a future of free expression, afraid of sexuality, afraid of spontaneity! How American! Maybe you will one day become just like that elderly couple at the museum." She laughed. "But I won't be with you. I'll grow old with my Napoleon or my Franklin."

"I was just kidding!"

"You Americans bomb us, burn us, kill us, and when we steal a moment's enjoyment of life, you criticize us for violating your stupid puritanism."

"Wait a minute!"

"No, I'm not waiting a *second*!" She turned her back to me.

I was surprised by her outburst, but as always, she got me to thinking. I walked over, stood behind her, whispering in her left ear, "Maybe you're right. Maybe I am threatened by spontaneity and sexuality. Since I left home for Paris, I've had more spontaneous sex than I ever imagined, but this is still new for me. I would never admit it to anyone, and until now, not even to myself, but it's not always comfortable," I confessed. "I told you, I may have led the protest for Danny, but that, too, was a new role for me. At home I only wrote articles to oppose the war and stayed away from protests. Here it's as if there's a new me with something to prove, but the old me, Robbie Samberg from Trenton, is actually pretty old-fashioned and maybe a little afraid."

My Hanh turned around. "I understand, my Robbie." She took my hand and softened her tone. "What you heard my father say about Vietnamese girls and our culture is what I have inside me, too. But I am more than the values I got from him and my mother. I have become my own woman, and I am having fun with you, enjoying things I cannot do at home. This is my first time for this, my first time for love and to live like a liberated woman. In my country, only men can live this way. I don't accept that. But you know, Robbie, a part of me, too, is just like you—old-fashioned. I think my spontaneity is how I show my newfound freedom to myself and to the world. It's my rebellion."

"I can relate," I responded, admiring My Hanh's honesty and amazed to learn again how similar we were. "We are just alike."

"Yes, exactly. You, the freshly minted radical, and me, the freshly minted sexpot," she said.

We laughed hysterically.

"Two peas in a pod!" I exclaimed. "Do I still need your permission to reach over to your side of the pod."

"Yes, you do!" she exclaimed. "Boundaries, my Franklin, boundaries," she replied suggestively, thrusting her hand yet again on my butt and pulling me close.

"Ahhh, so that's your idea of boundaries."

"What's the matter, my American puritan? This Vietnamese wild woman too much for you?"

"Perhaps, but as we are in France I'll rise to the occasion—no pun intended."

We laughed again.

As the day progressed on that special Sunday in May, the air warmed and the sun shone and we continued our walk. The skies were clear and the streets filled with people. It felt like a festival.

"A penny for your thoughts," My Hahn said as we walked together. She had adopted that expression ever since I used it in the garden of the Hôtel de Sully on the day we met.

"I'm thinking about Danny and the movement. It's been a week since I last saw him and I wonder—"

"You didn't expect to hear anything, did you?"

"No, but nothing in the papers, no word from his friends in the movement, nothing about Pierre either. It doesn't feel right."

"I also can't stop thinking about when I led the movement at Nanterre with Danny and especially afterward on rue Saint-Jacques."

"You were amazing."

"I felt so alive doing that. What is that?"

"I think it is the feeling we have when we meet our potential, when we do what we were born to do," she said.

"Was I born to lead student revolutionaries on the streets of Paris."

"No, you were born a natural leader and when you lead, no matter where you are, you are going to feel exhilarated."

"You think so."

"I know so."

We arrived at a great park near the Louvre called the Jardin des Tuileries, where we could see in the distance model boats racing on a huge fountain at the center. Model boat races were the rage in Paris, and on Sundays the hobbyists would congregate around the fountains and sail their crafts with great precision. This was a competitive and serious business. My Hanh and I decided to enter the competition, renting boats from a nearby vendor, and to our mutual delight took first and second place in the main event of the day!

We were treated as heroes and were accepted as a racially mixed couple in a way we could never be in America or in Vietnam. As we returned the boats to the vendor, I suggested we celebrate our victories.

"What did you have in mind?"

I pulled a bottle of Bordeaux from my bag, along with two glasses and a corkscrew. "How about this?"

"Beautiful!"

"And I know just the place to enjoy it," I said. "There's a great oak tree with a large hole in its trunk in the park. I learned about it in my studies of Franklin and the American War for Independence. It was used for espionage, so it must be secluded, or at least it was in the eighteenth century. Let's find it."

"Yes, my spy." She smiled.

"Not funny," I replied.

We set out to examine every tree in the park until we found this special oak, moving deeper into the garden and away from the main paths. It took us more than an hour to find it.

"There!" I exclaimed, at last spotting the great oak with a deep hole at the base of the trunk. It was tucked away in a remote corner next to a stone wall with dense shrubs all around that afforded privacy. "That's the tree! That's the tree!"

We ran to it and sat down, leaning up against the great trunk just next to the hole, which was positioned between us. I quickly opened the wine bottle and poured our first glass.

"To Franklin!" we toasted.

"What about the espionage?" My Hanh asked.

"You're sure about that diplomatic immunity?"

"You said this happened in the eighteenth century, so I think the statute of limitations would cover us both."

"I'm worried about what I'm doing in the twentieth century."

"No, no," she said. She discouraged me from bringing up the fear I felt about the CIA and getting caught.

"I can see the headline in the *Trenton Times*: 'Local Boy Hangs Out with the Enemy.'"

"Yes, you should be more careful about the company you keep. You should stay away from that reactionary Charlie Siebel."

"Very funny!" I turned toward her, placing my hand on the knotty bark that surrounded the entrance to the hole in the tree trunk. "This is the place where Franklin's secretary, Dr. Edward Bancroft, passed secret messages written in disappearing ink, rolled up tightly and placed inside magnum wine bottles, leaving them in this hole for British agents to pick up during the American War for Independence."

"Go on." She smiled, clearly amused. "Don't worry. I know how to keep state secrets."

"I'm sure you do. Bancroft was a double agent and Franklin knew it," I explained, "and he used Bancroft to leak messages to the British on just how close he was to concluding an alliance with France. He wanted them to know, because he knew they did not want war with France and might sooner conclude a favorable peace with the American colonies. I discovered this doing my research on Franklin and Bancroft at the Library of Congress."

"And how do you know this was the tree?" My Hanh asked.

"Because there is no other oak with a hole large enough to hide a magnum bottle," I said. "I have read Bancroft's papers, in which he described the oak tree next to a stone wall. This must be the tree."

"How cool!" My Hanh exclaimed. "Double agents, spies, a war for independence won right here at the base of this tree. I drink to victory in the American War for Independence," she offered, refilling our glasses from the bottle then carefully placing it inside the tree. "I drink to victory in Vietnam's war for independence." She raised her glass again.

"Let's just drink to America coming to its senses and electing a leader who will pull us out of Vietnam."

"You are such a diplomat, my Robbie," she protested. "No wonder my father likes you. But okay, I can drink to that." We toasted again.

We sat at the base of the tree, oblivious to the world, absorbed in each other, our every thought, word, and gesture as the daylight ebbed and the air grew cooler.

As the sun set and the shifting light altered the colors and the shadows in the tranquil garden, we toasted again and again, covering everything from Napoleon's now partially messed-up bedspread to the success of her father's coming negotiations with America. We finished the wine and lay beneath the tree, finding warmth in each other's arms.

"I'm going to show you an old Vietnamese tradition, My Hanh whispered, moving her head next to mine until our noses touched.

"Like the Inuit tribe of Alaska," I said, enjoying the feel of her warm nose rubbing the cold tip of mine. "This must be how they kept warm," I added.

"I think it is so cold in your Alaska they had to do more," she responded, giggling.

"More?"

She took my hand and moved it across her chest, massaging her breasts as she reached around to unhook her bra.

She moaned with pleasure at the touch. "Now we can make love like the Taoists."

"So, they did it in the woods, too?" I asked, wondering what would come next.

"No, my Robbie, they did it slowly, very slowly," she whispered, her hands reaching down to touch me. "Never striving, never judging . . ."

"Like we did at the bookstore."

"Yes." She stroked me slowly. "The pleasure you feel is the buildup of yang. The longer we can wait, the greater the heat and light and the closer you will be to heaven."

"I'm already in heaven."

"Tell me when you are close and I'll slow down," she said. "The idea is to prolong the pleasure."

I kissed her and moved my hand inside her pants, which she quickly unbuttoned, then reached for her navel, my fingers lightly caressing its concave interior on their way down to the shaven Y between her legs. She was the only girl I had ever met who shaved below, which she explained was more beautiful to touch and to taste.

"The ancient Taoists swallowed each other's sexual secretions," she explained. "Do you want to try it?"

"Do you have to ask?"

"The Taoists believed it would prolong life."

"I want to live forever," I mumbled amidst unintelligible groans.

She laughed, and I moved my fingers deeper inside her.

"Robbie, you must go slowly, too, so please stop when I tell you," she said, breathing heavily. "The slower I go, the greater my yin essence," she said, squealing, our noises penetrating the otherwise dark and tranquil garden.

She closed her eyes and breathed more deeply, and we continued stroking and resting at a steady pace, always stopping just in time, then building the yin and yang again, until at last, taking a quick look around in the darkness, My Hanh took me in her mouth as I slid around and took her in mine, and alternating between light flicks of the tongue and deep devouring, we each came uproariously and swallowed the results in a single gulp.

"You did that like a porn star," I said as we caught our breaths and began gathering our things to move on.

"What's a porn star?" she asked.

"You don't know what a porn star is?"

"Like a shooting star?"

"Yes, just like a shooting star."

By now the garden was illuminated by moonlight and lanterns on iron poles strategically placed along its paths. We decided to head to Les Halles, the outdoor marketplace of Paris, for a dinner of French onion soup, which My Hanh loved and wanted me to try. She knew a restaurant there, Au Pied de Cochon, which was celebrated for this dish.

But first we needed to return to My Hanh's hotel to pick up the car assigned to the delegation. She wanted to make sure we had a way to get home in case we finished dinner after the Métro closed at 1 a.m. Hand in hand, we emerged from the garden out onto the Place de la Concorde and walked over to the Hôtel de Crillon, which was located just off the great square. We were greeted warmly by the doormen, who knew My Hanh well and exercised absolute discretion about keeping our meetings away from prying eyes.

"Good evening, Ms. My Hanh," the doorman said, tipping his hat. "How can I help you?"

"We need the delegation car," she responded.

"Why not let us take you where you are going like your father has requested?"

"No, no, we can handle a little evening ride in Paris."

I lifted up my red map book to show him we were well prepared.

"Oh, Ms. My Hanh," he said, exasperated. "Let me at least give you an umbrella."

He handed it to her and waved for his colleague to bring the car around to the front of the hotel. It was a maroon Deux Chevaux, a car with a funny round shape. It was a little difficult to drive, but I quickly adjusted as we took off for Les Halles.

We drove among the structures of iron and glass built under Napoleon III to house the great outdoor market. I looked over at My Hanh.

"What's the one thing you couldn't forgive *me* for?" I asked.

"Do you mean what would make me stop loving you?"

"Oh, maybe you'd still love me but not forgive me."

"I don't think I could still love you if I did not forgive you," she said.

"Really?"

"Whatever you might do, I would say you must have had a good reason and I would forgive you. I forgive because of who I am, not because of what others do."

"What if I betrayed you?" I asked.

"I trust you would not, just as you trust I would not."

We arrived at Au Pied de Cochon, whose name in English was "At the Foot of the Pig." It was just before 9 p.m., still well before the food trucks were scheduled to arrive from all parts of France to unload their gastronomic treasures. Les Halles operated all night, and this was my first visit. By day the area was a regular part of the city—streets and sidewalks—with the only sign of the nocturnal marketplace being the numerous elegant steel-and-glass warehouse structures, which were transformed at night into the epicenter of food distribution not just for Paris but for food lovers throughout France.

As we parked the car, nothing I saw prepared me for the adventure which was about to unfold. Dinner was delightful. More wine, escargot, again more wine, a different vintage, a tray of seafood stacked on ice—lobster, oysters, clams, shrimp—more wine of yet another variety, and at last the steaming bowls of French onion soup with melted Gruyère cheese on a piece of toasted French bread at the top, the cheese falling in a bountiful pattern all around the edge of the ceramic bowl, which was still scorching hot from the oven. I don't know which was more fun: eating the soup, with its delicious onion broth and large chunks of softened fresh onion, or picking the cheese from around the sides of the bowl, really a Crock-Pot, until the last smidgen was gone. It was such a treat, and we both enjoyed it heartily, lingering with yet another bottle of wine, more toasts and animated conversation.

"Check, please!" I asked the waiter, who promptly brought it to the table.

"Let's see: five francs for the onion soup, fifty francs for the seafood platter, fifteen francs for the escargot, and thirty francs for wine. That's a hundred francs, split between us, okay?" I asked.

"That's half my pay!" She looked surprised and withdrew her foot which had been caressing my leg under the table.

"For an unforgettable dinner." I moved my foot to touch her leg.

"In America, doesn't the guy pay for his date with the girl?"

"Used to be, but that's changed."

She moved her leg away and frowned. I raised my hands and my eyebrows as if to ask what she expected.

She grinned. "Okay. Okay. I'll share like one of your liberated girls." She moved her foot to my leg again and caressed me.

"*Merci.*"

After dinner we emerged from the restaurant satiated and tipsy—or let's just say quite drunk—and crossed the street toward where we thought the car was. To our astonishment, the street was transformed. There were scores of trucks unloading produce everywhere around us. Men in blue cotton frocks had taken over every square inch of the sidewalk. Crates of oranges, apples, and pears were piled high on all sides of the street, and the Deux Chevaux was nowhere to be found. My Hanh and I worried that it had been stolen. What would her father say? Would we cause an international incident? What if the delegation's secret presence in the city was uncovered by the press? The situation began to turn from amusing to disconcerting, although we were both sufficiently drunk to cast our worries to the wind and continue celebrating.

We approached a city police officer walking his beat, who surprised and delighted us with a salute, raising his hand to his head. Unlike American police, the French officers, called *gendarmes*, did not have guns but carried batons and wore long blue capes down to their ankles with matching caps, which, I thought, endowed them with a certain charm. Their look embodied the idea of Paris from a bygone era. They saluted every citizen they met. It was very special.

"We have lost our car," I explained as the officer lowered his hand to his side.

"Monsieur, madame," he said, "it is easy to become disoriented in the market, but until the streets clear in the early morning, there is not much I can do for you. It's best that you just search the area on your own, and I am sure you will find your car," he offered, overlooking the obvious signs of our inebriation. This was Paris! We were lovers! This was routine!

My Hanh and I searched, and we searched, and we searched. We stopped for coffee at an all-night café. After, we searched again, ever more hopelessly lost, and we continued to talk about our families, friends, schools, politics, everything that came to mind. Soon the night began to fall away and the darkness turned to dawn. At last, at about 5 a.m., having searched the streets around every food booth in the market, we spotted the Deux Chevaux, rising like a mirage from beneath a shield of produce crates, on the very same street where we had arrived hours before, just across from Au Pied de Cochon. The farmers, unloading their crates of produce and unable to move the car, had simply built the marketplace around it. We laughed and hugged each other for joy. A feeling of relief came over us as we reentered the car, corn husks and chunks of lettuce scattered across its hood, started the engine, and pulled away.

As the sun rose, the Deux Chevaux sped across an almost-empty Place de la Concorde to the Hôtel de Crillon.

I reached out for My Hanh's hand as we pulled up to the hotel and whispered, "I love you."

She smiled at me as two doormen approached the car, one on each side. We got out and walked to the circular entry for a final embrace and goodbye.

"À bientot, mon amour," she said as she turned to enter the hotel.

I watched her disappear into the ornate lobby and stood for a moment. I was tired but so deliriously happy that I didn't feel the fatigue. This was the girl of my dreams. I didn't care if she was a communist or that her father was an enemy of America. I just loved her, worshipped her, adored her, and the heat and light of that love was blinding.

The sun was rising across the Place de la Concorde, bathing it in a golden light, and I could hear the water splashing in the two great fountains on either side of the ancient stone obelisk at its center. Although coming off a night without sleep and more than a bit hungover, I decided to walk home from the hotel, still energized by the excitement of the day and the night and my feelings for My Hanh. I was walking on air! By now the wound on my head was healing, the throbbing had stopped, and my spirits soared from the love in my heart and the adventure of loving her in Paris.

As I walked the still, quiet streets, my thoughts turned again to my family and how upset they would be if I told them about My Hanh. *They'll never accept my falling in love with her!* I imagined explaining to them that she was the daughter of the foreign minister of North Vietnam. I could see my father carrying on about what a mess this would make of his business. And my mother sobbing in her bedroom . . . And my sisters blaming me for screwing up our family and their futures.

I also thought about Danny. It had been a week since I had last seen him in the Marais, and I needed to buy his train ticket. I decided this could not wait any longer, so I entered the Métro and headed for the Gare de l'Est, stopping at the first ticket booth. Danny was right. The ticket agent did not ask for a passport, and the only choice I needed to make was the time of departure, which I chose, feigning consideration of a busy schedule. I tried to appear nonchalant as the agent looked me over from behind the thick glass of the ticket booth. I feared he might recognize me from the news coverage of the demonstrations. There was a long line behind me, but the agent took his time. He acted as if he were doing me a favor selling me the ticket, which added to my suspicion. The French did not share the American notion of customer service. At home, the customer came first; in Paris, the salesperson came first. Finally, the agent got around to handing me the ticket and my change through the window. I quickly stepped away from the booth.

I placed the ticket in a baggage locker and took the Métro to Café Procope to leave the locker key on the window ledge in the second-floor men's room, as Danny had instructed. I put it in a small envelope marked with the locker number. Emerging from the bathroom, I decided to stay and have some breakfast before continuing my walk home. I took a seat in one of the second-floor dining areas just below an etching of Ben Franklin from the days of his ambassadorship in Paris.

I thought about Danny having to tell his parents about his expulsion, arrest, and his role in the student movement. That would be a tough conversation. Things had quieted down on the streets for the moment, but they were soon to mushroom into something far greater than any of us could imagine. I also thought about my obligations at school, the schoolwork that had fallen by the wayside as I got caught up in the student revolt, and my romance with My Hanh.

Paris was proving far more than a distraction from the issues I had left at home, which were nothing compared to what was unfolding around me now. I was living a life that just weeks before I could never have imagined. *"How are you going to keep him back on the farm once he's seen Paree?"* I laughed out loud. I paid my check and continued my walk, the air clear and the sun shining. Another beautiful spring day in Paris.

At the other end of the Pont de la Concorde, I came upon the Louvre, which I had not yet visited, though it was high on My Hanh's and my list. Despite my fatigue I decided to go in, but first I had to find the entrance, which was not so easy. After much searching, the entrance turned out to be a nondescript side door marked only by a wooden sign. I purchased my ticket thinking the entrance did nothing to convey that I was about to enter one of the world's greatest art collections, much less the former palace of the kings of France.

As I walked among the Greek and Roman statues, I thought about the changes in the governments of France. The origins of Paris were Roman, and the evolution of France as a nation was marked by violent clashes over centuries. Between the Revolution in 1789 and 1955, when de Gaulle founded the Fifth Republic, France was governed under two empires, two different monarchies, and five different republics. It had a total of thirteen written constitutions! Upheaval was the order of the day, and street battles were commonplace. What was happening in May 1968 had cultural and historical roots. It was part of a pattern. It was as if something in the French DNA compelled the reoccurrence of political instability. No wonder the motto of the city of Paris was *Fluctuat nec mergitur.* "She is tossed by the waves but does not sink."

I arrived at the Denon Wing of the Louvre and entered a grand hall with a high, arched ceiling, lined with Italian art and sculpture. I don't know what it was about this hall—its great length, the ceiling height, the tall windows through which you could capture a glimpse of the street outside the palace and, just beyond, the boats on the River Seine—but something got to me as I walked its length, transported to another time and place, engrossed by dreams about the past, about glory days gone by. It was a reverie.

Again, I thought about My Hanh, and I knew she would feel the same way. I couldn't wait to take this walk with her beside me. I thought about Danny and wondered when he would get the envelope with the locker key, and about Jan and her holding hands with Nastovich. It was all so crazy. I thought about my sisters, Lorraine and Dottie, and how their lives might be changing at home. Would they understand what I was experiencing here? Not likely. And, of course, I thought about my parents, alternating between gratitude for their having made this trip possible, and sadness that they would probably never understand or accept the love I felt for My Hanh.

On the left, midway down the great hall, I came to the room where the *Mona Lisa* was displayed. It was placed on the right side of the large room, just another painting among many on the wall. There was no special protection, no enclosure or guard, nothing except for a small sign just under it that read "No Flash" to protect its finish from discoloration.

I joined the small group surrounding the painting. This was Lisa del Giocondo, or *La Joconde* as they called her portrait in French. It occurred to me that the famous smile was no smile at all but rather a transitory look of contentment, as if she had yet to decide whether the thought that provoked the smile could sustain it, her lips upturned slightly, but the effect far too constrained to be described as a smile. My Hanh. . . now *she* had a smile! This woman had a contented smirk, leaving you to wonder how her look might change in the very next moment. *Maybe this prospect of change is the magic that generates so much interest in the painting.*

As I studied the *Mona Lisa*, I recognized a voice from behind me. Suddenly I felt a tap on my shoulder, and I turned around, pleased and astonished to see none other than Christine René, my masseuse from the *Queen Elizabeth*. I had not seen her since our date on the ship. She looked wonderful, dressed in baggy, beige slacks, a blue flannel shirt, and carrying paintbrushes and an easel.

"Robbeee," she said, smiling and giving me a warm hug and a lovely kiss on both cheeks. "*Comment vas-tu?*" she inquired, then quickly said again in English: "How are you?" She stood and looked at me with surprise and pleasure. "What happened to your head?" she asked, noticing the scab and the spot where my hair had been trimmed back. "Oh no!" she exclaimed. "Tell me you were not hurt in the demonstrations!"

"Yes, and it's a long story."

"Well, you must tell me," she insisted.

She had just finished her painting class and invited me to walk with her to her locker to put away her brushes and easel and to have coffee in the museum restaurant. I recalled the last time she had instructed me to follow her to the crew's quarters on the *Queen Elizabeth*.

"You are in art school," I said.

"Yes, at the Sorbonne," she said. "We often come to the Louvre to copy the masters. It's a great way to learn."

She looked rested and even more attractive than the last time I saw her on the deck of the ship.

"Remember the night we met?" I asked, smiling.

"I think we broke all the rules that night," she said, laughing.

"Yes, and maybe a few rules not yet written."

"It is good to see you again, Robbeee," she said, moving closer and taking my arm as we walked. "Tell me about the demonstrations. How did you get caught up in that?"

"It's complicated," I responded, "but I'm all right now."

Christine shook her head sympathetically. "Those damn fool *enragés* closed down the university," she said scornfully, "and I had just finished paying my tuition! Now I don't know if the classes I paid for will continue, and I don't think there will be a refund. I worked hard for that money." A look of displeasure clouded her otherwise-beautiful face.

"So, you don't support the demonstrators?"

"Support them? I think they are a bunch of idiots who probably never worked a day in their lives," she said, her voice a near-volcanic eruption. "I had better get credit for the canceled classes, or I am going to start my own revolution," she added, seething. "Or maybe I'll join the CRS so next time I can club the bastards."

"You are really angry about this," I said, stating the obvious.

She pulled away. "I am, as we say, *énervée*, which roughly translates to 'very pissed off.'"

"But it was the school administration that closed the Nanterre campus, not the demonstrators. They could have kept it open, and you would not have lost a cent of tuition."

"Robbeee," she rejoined, more agitated, "they closed the school *because of the demonstrators*, so how can you blame the school? I blame the damn fool *enragés*."

"Christine, the demonstrators were only trying to get the administration to be more responsive to the needs of students, but they responded with CRS batons instead of dialog, and that's when things flew out of control."

"How do you know so much about this, Robbeee?"

"I was there with my friend Daniel Cohn-Bendit."

"You're a friend of Danny the Red?" she asked incredulously. "I'm shocked, Robbeee! What business did you have joining French students in the Latin Quarter? You're an American, and you don't even attend the Sorbonne."

"Danny asked me to speak for him after he was arrested."

"You cross the Atlantic first class on the *Queen Elizabeth* to arouse civil strife in France among our students, most of whom, like me, are poor!" she exclaimed with unrelenting agitation.

"Christine, please let me explain," I said. "First, about the ship—"

"There is nothing to explain," she said curtly, walking away from me. "I am sorry I massaged you, sorry I made love to you, sorry I met you, and sorry, but I won't spend another minute with you."

"Christine!"

She stopped, turned around, and walked back to me. We stood face-to-face in the middle of the grand gallery.

"Look, Robbeee," she said, trying to contain her anger, "my parents are in the military. They work hard and obey authority. They instilled in me the idea that we all must work to get ahead in life, so I spent two years at sea to raise the money for my university education. And you"—she paused—"you who have had everything handed to you, you come over from America and ruin everything I am trying to accomplish." She shook her head in disgust. "You and your talk of *lutte prolongée* and *CRS* SS and *le cancer gaulliste*—you are all idiots," she fumed, turning again and storming off, but not before delivering a final epitaph: "Get out of France. Don't come back!"

Chapter 14

Anna Chennault

By the time I reached Madame Gueumier's apartment at 54 rue de la Bienfaisance, it was raining, and I was surprised to find Le Duc Tho's black limousine parked out front, the wiper blades swishing back and forth. I had not slept, and was upset about what had happened with Christine. I was exhausted and looking forward to a hot bath, my soft mattress, and some sleep. From the windows of the Louvre and on my walk back to the apartment, I'd seen evidence of renewed demonstrations in the city, large crowds of people, and protest signs freshly painted on buildings. Something big was afoot.

As I approached the car, My Hanh jumped out, waving to me and struggling to open her large black umbrella. She ran toward me, a look of distress on her face.

"Robbie," she cried, reaching out and putting her arms around me, "the streets are a mess. There are new protests, and my father asked me to come here to bring you to him. There is something important happening with the peace talks, and he would like to speak to you about it."

"What is it?"

"I don't know, but he's upset, and he asked me to find you and bring you to him right away."

"Here we go again! This does not sound like a social visit," I said, shaking my head back and forth. "I just came from the Louvre, and I have so much to tell you."

"You went to the Louvre after you dropped me off this morning?" she asked. "Poor boy, you have not slept! Well, I did not sleep either. I spent the day thinking about you, my Robbie, thinking about us, and then my father called and asked me to find you. He was so agitated. I have never seen him that way," she said. She reached out and placed her right hand on my cold, wet cheek, raising the umbrella so I could fit under it.

"We're both exhausted, and right up there," I said, pointing to the french window of my room just above us, "is a hot bath and a bed, but it looks like that will have to wait, right?"

"Right," she responded, casting me a look that gave me no choice. "We must go now, my Robbie."

We hurried into the limo, and the driver headed back toward the Crillon, zigzagging and taking side streets to avoid the demonstrations. Once in the car, My Hanh explained that her father had spoken on the phone with a friend in China, a wealthy businessman who had contacts in America and knew a Wall Street banker who was very close to a woman named Anna Chennault, a Chinese expatriate who lived in New York City. All My Hanh knew was that what her father had learned about Chennault upset him.

"I think that's why he wants to speak to you—something about Chennault," she said.

"My Hanh, I have never heard of Anna Chennault. I do not know her, and I have no idea why he would want to speak to me about her."

She shrugged her shoulders, shook her head, and looked at me. She reached over and took my hand.

"You're frightened," she observed as she moved closer to me.

"Yes. If I one day have to explain my social contacts with your father, the father of the girl I love, even if he happens to be the foreign minister of North Vietnam, I think most people would understand. But if I assist him in matters of diplomacy or affairs of state, that would be something different."

"I understand, my Robbie, and I'm sure my father understands," she said, squeezing my hand. "If you do not wish to come, I will ask the driver to turn around."

"You read my mind," I responded. "I was just thinking about asking him to take me back to my hot bath and warm bed."

"I can see the worry on your face and the fatigue," she said. "We are both tired, right? And I'm frightened, too," she added, furrowing her brow.

"My Hanh, there are so many reasons we should turn this car around," I said.

"Please, Robbie, trust my father, see what he has to say," she said imploringly. "What did you see at the Louvre?" she added, changing the subject.

"Oh, I saw your best friend."

"Franklin or Bonaparte?"

"Bonaparte, and you were right: he was average height for his day, but still much too short for you," I said. "I saw his life-sized statue."

"And you missed my statue standing right next to his?"

"Must have missed it," I said with mock disappointment.

As the limo sped toward the Crillon, I told My Hanh about seeing Christine, about how she opposed the demonstrations at Nanterre and the Sorbonne and how she criticized me.

"This woman, Christine, was thinking only about her personal situation, and important as that may be to her, it is not as important as reform of the educational system in France," My Hanh said. "You must not doubt yourself when others doubt you, Robbie. You must trust yourself and support whatever you do, and I will always support you, too."

The car pulled up to the hotel and the doormen approached. We could see the main part of the demonstration ahead of us on the Avenue des Champs-Élysées. A butler led us upstairs through a maze of rooms, and at last to a large, ornate corner sitting room, where Le Duc Tho sat on a couch with another Vietnamese man. He was dressed in a black tunic with the top button undone, his gray hair combed straight back, a worried look on his face. They both stood when My Hanh and I entered the room.

"Thank you for coming, Robbie," Tho said, offering me a restrained smile and a polite handshake. "This is Xuan Thuy, who is assisting me in our negotiations."

Thuy was short and squat and dressed in the same black tunic as Tho.

After the handshakes, we sat down, and Tho offered me coffee or tea. I asked for black coffee. My Hanh greeted Xuan Thuy and kissed her father but did not join us for coffee. Instead she left the room, telling me she would see me after the meeting. The three of us were alone.

"Robbie, I heard you had a somewhat frustrating visit to the Paris market," Tho said. "You almost lost the car, and that would have been unfortunate."

"Yes, it was a night of surprises, quite an adventure."

"Well, I have another surprise for you, Robbie, and this one may make you uncomfortable," he said, speaking the latter part of the sentence slowly, ominously.

"I am already uncomfortable," I said, "but I have decided to listen to any request you may have, so please go on."

"Yes, fair enough," Tho responded. "Do you know Mr. Allen Hoffers?"

"Yes, I know him. He was my boss when I worked at Senator Hankie's office. Why do you ask about Allen?"

"Robbie, diplomats use networks of people. Sometimes they are purely social contacts or even family contacts, and sometimes they are paid spies to exchange information. Do you understand?"

"Now I'm really uncomfortable," I said. "Look, Allen is my friend, but I really cannot be a part of anything that—"

"Please hear me out, Robbie, and you can choose to help or not, okay?"

He sounded like My Hanh when he said "okay." She had a habit of ending her sentences with "right?" and "okay?"

"Okay," I responded, my nervousness evident in my shaky voice.

"We know that Hoffers admires you, promoted you, and trusts you. You were his protégé at the senator's office, right?" Tho asked.

"How do you know this?"

"We know."

"Right, that's right," I said.

"We know that he was the one who gave you the opportunity to answer correspondence about the war for Senator Hankie, right?"

"Yes, that's right."

"We know that he is close to Senator Hankie, right?"

"Yes, that's right, too."

"We have read the letters you wrote. We have read your columns in the university paper."

"How did you get—"

"We have our sources, Robbie," Tho said. "Is there anything I have said so far that is not correct? If so, tell me; if not, do not say anything," he said, his voice steady and serious.

I sat silently—on the verge of teeth chattering, knees knocking, and hands shaking. I could not imagine how he knew these things.

"So now, Robbie, please allow me, as you say in your country, to cut to the chase," Tho continued in a sinister tone. "Today I learned something disturbing, and it affects our goal to conduct meaningful peace talks with your government and the puppet regime of South Vietnam. As you know, we have been in Paris for several weeks. The puppet regime has diplomats here as well. Secretary Rusk's staff is here, too. So are the Russians, who have leaned on us to have serious talks. We had preliminary exchanges about a site for the talks, the shape of the table, the number of translators allowed, and other details required for such talks to take place. At first, things went smoothly. Then suddenly it changed. We would agree on something like the venue, and then we would learn that the puppet regime's delegation had changed its position and preferred someplace else. We agreed on a round table and they changed again, insisting on a rectangular one. We agreed on one translator and they changed yet again, asking for three. It became apparent the puppet regime was stalling. So I made inquiries"—he paused—"and today I learned why the puppet regime is monkey wrenching this way. Have you ever heard of Anna Chennault, Robbie?"

"No, I have not, sir," I said emphatically.

Tho turned to Xuan Thuy and conferred in Vietnamese. Their exchange was heated, as if they disagreed about what to say next.

"Well, Robbie," Tho continued slowly, "you are about to be one of only three people in France to know that this woman, Anna Chennault, is a secret liaison between the South Vietnamese ambassador to the United States, Mr. Bui Diem, and a man called John Mitchell."

"So?"

"Do you know the name John Mitchell, Robbie?" Tho asked.

"No, I do not."

"Do you know what Mr. Mitchell does for a living?"

"No, I do not."

Tho paused and conferred with Xuan Thuy. Their words were again heated.

Now Xuan Thuy spoke for the first time, leaning toward me as if to signal that what he was about to say was extremely sensitive, and he whispered in broken English, just loud enough for Tho and me to hear him.

"He is the campaign manager for Richard M. Nixon, the Republican candidate for president of the United States."

"Mr. Nixon was once your vice president, right? Isn't that correct, Robbie?" Thuy asked.

"Yes, he served as vice president under President Eisenhower. Where is this going?"

"Where do you think it is going?" Thuy asked.

"I don't know where it is going! That's why I asked."

"Robbie, according to the Constitution of the United States, who is in charge of United States foreign policy?" Tho asked, taking over the conversation from Thuy.

"What?"

"Who is in charge, Robbie?" he asked again. "According to the Constitution?"

"That would be Lyndon B. Johnson," I responded as if I were taking a grade school civics class.

"And he is?" Tho asked. "I mean what is his title under the Constitution?"

"Surely you know that he is the president of the United States," I said.

"Do you know the president of the United States?"

"I met him once at a reception at Senator Hankie's office. He stopped by to congratulate the senator on his appointment as chairman of the Foreign Relations Committee. They were very close before LBJ became president, when he served as the Senate Majority Leader."

"Are they still close?" Tho asked.

"Yes, very close I believe."

"You know the president?"

"I was briefly introduced by Allen," I said, "who once worked for the president when he was a senator, and we spoke for a few minutes about the radio business. His family owns radio stations in Texas, and my father is interested in purchasing a station someday, so we got to talking briefly about this, but I don't think he would remember me, and I really can't say that I know him, not in the sense you are asking about."

Tho and Xuan Thuy looked puzzled and again broke off the conversation to confer in Vietnamese. This time they continued for some time, after which Thuy got up and left the room. He did not say goodbye to Tho or to me.

Tho and I were left alone in the room.

Tho got up to pour himself some tea from a silver pitcher resting on a hot plate. "Would you like more coffee?"

"Yes, please."

He brought the coffeepot over and filled my cup. "Black, right?"

"Black."

"Robbie," he continued, "I am going to need for you to trust me."

"You want me to trust the foreign minister of North Vietnam?" I asked.

"I want you to trust My Hanh's father, Robbie. Can you please do that?"

"If I do, I'll betray my own father, my mother, most of my friends, and all my countrymen," I responded.

"You must decide," Tho said quietly.

"Go on," I replied, doubts beginning to fill my head the moment I uttered the words.

"I need you to deliver a message," Tho said, "and for your protection, we are going to need a way to communicate with you that no one can trace."

"If it must be kept secret, it must be disloyal," I said, "and that is—"

"Trust me unless and until I do something untrustworthy, Robbie, okay? How can I get in touch with you in a way no one would ever suspect and no one could ever discover?"

I thought for a moment. "Well, this is going to sound crazy, but there is this tree in the Jardin des Tuileries."

"A tree?" Tho said incredulously. "Spies on both sides use wire taps, listening devices, ciphers, and hidden cameras, but trees?"

I explained the history—Franklin, Bancroft, and Lord Carmarthen in the British Foreign Office. Tho listened intently.

"Perfect! How do we find this tree?"

"My Hanh knows it."

"You know you are being watched by your CIA because you have come here twice, and because you are dating My Hanh."

"Yes." I nodded.

"Seeing how you two lovebirds carry on, they have probably concluded that your relationship is purely social. This is good, for as long as that is all they think it is, they will keep careful records but leave you alone."

"Dr. Nastovich told me the CIA visited my school."

"Aaah, your Nastovich! He has been a CIA informer for the past five years," Tho said.

"Nastovich, CIA?"

"He hides it well behind his leftist American expatriate ve-
neer."

"Wow! I would have never thought . . ."

"Now, you must not give them reason for suspicion, Robbie,
so there must be no apparent change in your behavior. You
must continue dating My Hanh just as before."

"You know, I am not sure . . ."

"Just stay with me, Robbie, okay?"

"I'm not making any promises."

"No promises." He nodded his understanding. "But I think
you should not come to the hotel again. I also don't think we
should meet again."

"How will it work my seeing My Hanh?"

"After today My Hanh will meet you wherever you go on
your dates. Our delegation car will bring her and will take her
home alone," he explained.

"How will I know when you need to reach me?"

"I'll write a letter, put it in an empty wine bottle, and have
the bottle placed in the hole at the base of the oak tree."

"Just like Dr. Bancroft," I said.

"Yes, and just to be certain," he added, "the only authentic
messages will be in empty bottles of Château Margaux, vintage
1947, and any note from me will be written in French and
signed with a code name that only you and I will know. The
code name will be Monsieur X. When you receive a message in
French from Monsieur X, it will be a message directly from me.
Do you understand, Robbie?"

"Yes, but how will I know when the bottle is there?"

"My Hanh will tell you," he said. "She will use another code.
She will say—let me think of something . . . Aaah, 'Free Dreyfus,' the French Colonel unjustly imprisoned whose story My
Hanh told me captured your imagination, and when she says
that, you will know that a message waits for you. To signal that

you will get it, you must repeat 'Free Dreyfus,' but if you do not repeat it, we shall know that you have changed your mind about helping."

"I'll have to risk that brody, after all," I said.

"Ah, going off the cliff, right? That will be up to you."

He got up slowly from his chair. "I think this concludes our business today. Thank you for coming, Robbie. Now go home and get some sleep," he said, walking over to the phone to call My Hanh to accompany me down to the lobby. "Robbie," he added, "I am grateful that you were the first American I met here in Paris. Do you want the car to take you back to your apartment?"

"No, I'll take the Métro," I said.

"Yes, that is a better idea. But be careful. The city is erupting in protests."

My Hanh returned to the room, bowed to her father, and reached out to take my hand. As we walked out together, she squeezed it hard, responding to the troubled look on my face.

"How was it?" she asked.

"I'm still trying to figure that out."

"You are going to help us?"

"It depends on the message in the bottle."

"What?"

"Speak to your father. He'll explain," I said.

"A bottle in the oak tree?"

"Yes, we are going to use the tree."

"That's so cool," she said. "Like spies in the eighteenth century."

"Not so fast. I'm not a spy yet."

We arrived at the hotel lobby and agreed to meet for dinner the following night.

"My Robbie, there is something I need to tell you," she whispered as we hugged just outside the doorway.

"What is it?"

"Tomorrow," she said, her lips touching mine for a final kiss goodbye. "I'll tell you tomorrow."

Chapter 15

Jazz under Paris

"Did you turn in your paper," Nastovich asked Jan, leaning over his podium after class the next morning. "It was due yesterday." I stood next to her.

"I have a few more footnotes to add."

He looked at her and responded with a silence that screamed.

"Okay! I'll have it this afternoon." I could feel the discomfort between them.

"I did mine on the Velodrome d'Hiver, when the French police rounded up thirteen thousand Jews in 1942 to ship them to Auschwitz."

"Good choice," he said. "Some like to forget that story."

"There are thirteen thousand reasons not to forget it."

"Robbie, I heard something from a friend at the Ministry of Justice. The moment they find Danny, he's going to be out of here, deported," Nastovich said. This was news to Jan and me and to the rest of the world.

"Not unexpected," I said.

"Another Jew deported from France," Jan said.

"Oh, is he going to play that up? I can see him now, posing before the cameras, smiling and crying anti-Semitism all the way to the German border."

Jan and Nastovich had no idea that I had provided a ticket out for Danny.

France in 1968 had not fully reconciled with France in the 1940s. There was a disconnect between de Gaulle's portrayal of heroic resistance to Nazism and the disgrace of the Vichy collaboration. Danny was just the one to exploit it, and the French authorities knew it. But with his train ticket safely in place at Le Procope, I was confident he would make it back to Germany on his own.

What happened in France after the demonstrations at Nanterre became the envy of other student movements around the world. On May 13, the day I met with Tho and Xuan Thuy, and the anniversary of de Gaulle's return to power ten years earlier, all of the major trade unions of France called for a general strike, and the entire nation began to shut down. Soon Parisians found themselves in a city and a nation closed for business. Unlike the student demonstrations in New York, Berlin, Warsaw, and Rome, the French students were now joined by French workers, and that created the illusion of a worker–student coalition.

In reality, as Nastovich had told us in class the week before, it was not a coalition. He explained that although some of the younger workers may have been sympathetic to the students, the trade unions, especially those backed by the Communist Party, were not. He told us these were in fact two different movements: workers who wanted radical reforms in the workplace, higher wages, and more benefits; and students who wanted a radical change in the French way of life, the tearing down and rejection of authority at all levels of society.

As I walked to the Métro after my meeting with Tho, I saw evidence of the demonstrations and the strike on the streets. Student slogans adorned the walls, including a silk screen poster with Danny's face which read, "We are all Jews and Germans." It reminded me of Danny bragging that so many of the student leaders in France and around the world were Jewish. He used to tell a joke: "If the Maoists wanted to have a dialog with the Trotskyites, what language would they speak? The answer: Yiddish." For the first time in my life, I felt proud to be a Jew.

I grabbed one of the last Métros before the strike took effect and made it back to Madame Gueumier's apartment. I couldn't get the meeting with Le Duc Tho off my mind. When I entered the apartment, I opened the French windows, turned the brass knobs to fill the tub, and sat on the edge of the bed. I felt overwhelmed and uncertain about what lay ahead. With noise from the demonstrators wafting up through my open windows, I shed my clothes, walked over, and gingerly placed my left foot inside the tub to make sure the water was not too hot. It was just right, so I slithered down into the warm, protective cocoon and felt relieved. My body submerged, my head just above the water, I could see the steam rising around me as the cooler outside air filled the room. *There are no tubs like this in prison.* I could be convicted of high treason for aiding the enemies of the United States. I shook my head and shrugged it off, but the truth was that I was on very uncertain ground, and I was afraid. *Am I allowing my love for My Hanh to cloud my judgment? What is it she wanted to tell me?* After a long, hot soak, I got out of the tub, dried off, put on the baggy blue pajamas my mother had bought me for the trip, and headed over to my desk to catch up on work. In a few minutes, I felt too sleepy to continue, and I lay on the bed and closed my eyes. I slept through the rest of the evening and the entire night.

The next morning, I raced to make my morning classes and returned home right after to catch up on schoolwork and write letters. I had completed Nastovich's paper on time, but I was behind in almost every other subject. There were papers coming due and tests looming. It felt like a big mess. I decided to write a letter to my parents, and in thinking about what to say I realized how much my life had changed and how much I could not tell them. I could not tell them about My Hanh or about my conversation with her father. They would never understand. Yet these were the two most important things in my life. I felt alone.

After writing the letter, studying for a French exam, and writing outlines for two papers, I decided to telephone My Hanh to arrange for dinner. As her phone rang, I detected an extra click on the line and thought it was CIA surveillance. I felt paranoid, and with good reason.

"My Hanh?"

"Yes, my Robbie."

"Hi! How are you?"

"I slept well last night."

"Me too." I heard more noise on the line.

"Did you hear that?"

"Hear what?"

"Just calling to arrange our date tonight." More static.

"Did you hear de Gaulle is in Romania?" she asked.

"No, no, I don't know anything about that."

"Father says he's recruiting for his Third World Movement."

"I don't know about that."

"How were the demonstrations by your place?"

"I didn't see anything."

"I heard that Pompidou is about to set the arrested demonstrators free, withdraw the CRS from the Sorbonne, and reopen the university."

"Oh. . ."

"Our friends in the French party tell us he is about to offer the unions a ten percent pay increase, an increase in the minimum wage, a decrease in working hours, and more benefits."

"Really. . ."

"And the puppet regime is still stalling about the table shape. It's maddening."

"Yes, that *was* a terrible puppet show! I was mad about it, too!"

"What?"

"My Hanh, I can't understand you. There's too much static on the line." I coughed hard two times.

"Oh yes, yes, that—static. Where shall we meet for dinner?"

"How about Chartier, say nine o'clock?"

"Okay, see you there."

Le Bouillon Chartier was one of our favorite restaurants. It had been in business since the nineteenth century, with its high ceilings, wood balustrades, and mirrored walls, all of which remained as they were originally constructed. It was an authentic French bistro, although they called it a *bouillon*, a throwback to the early days of restaurant development, where working-class Frenchmen could enjoy a multicourse meal at a reasonable price.

The French valued good food and wine and a lifestyle that cherished and protected the time to enjoy them. A four-course dinner was about ten dollars—fifty francs—including an appetizer, main course, salad, and dessert; not exactly first-class *Queen Elizabeth* cuisine, but well prepared with fresh ingredients at a reasonable price. The waiters, like those at most restaurants My Hanh and I visited in Paris, were older men, career professionals, not the kids or part-timers who worked at restaurants at home. In France, working as a waiter or any job in the restaurant industry was a long-term vocation, not just someplace you stopped to pick up a few bucks to survive on a career path elsewhere.

Many of the waiters at Chartier had been there since the Second World War. Their stories were amazing, although they worked so quickly to keep up with the turnover in tables, writing orders and tallying bills on the white paper tablecloths, there was not much time for talking. Our favorite waiter was Pierre, a large, jovial, mustachioed Frenchman from Nice, who had just celebrated his twenty-seventh year at Chartier. "Monsieur Vietnam," he would call out whenever he saw me. Mr. Vietnam was my nickname, since he almost always heard me hotly contesting the war, to which his attitude was always "Been there, done that." And he had. "We already had our Vietnam fiasco," he would say with a smile on his face. "Now it's America's turn!" It also delighted him that I had fallen in love with My Hanh, whom he adored and fussed over like an older brother. I had the feeling he, too, had once loved a Vietnamese girl, although he never spoke of it.

Many of the French I met felt the same way as Pierre about Vietnam. They understood from their nation's experience that America was going off the deep end, driven by the twin evils of self-righteousness and a technological-superiority complex. "You Americans are so naïve," Pierre would say, rolling his eyes and in that one gesture ripping apart all the hypocrisy and self-delusions of our so-called great power. I did not disagree with him, even as he poured the scorching-hot criticism all over me. I was on the receiving end because I was an American, but he was preaching to the choir.

"You think your napalm and your jet planes can destroy the power of an idea, but they cannot, and you will fail, especially in a primitive society like Vietnam, unless you are prepared to annihilate every last Viet Cong and stand guard over a subjugated people for decades," he would say again and again with absolute certainty.

As usual, Pierre welcomed My Hanh and me with a few teasing jabs as he showed us to a table, recited the menu specials, handed us the wine list, and joked about our status as an

American-Vietnamese couple, labeling us *une salade mixte.* As an added surprise, he invited us to join him after dinner at a jazz club in a cavern under the city.

"My Hanh, you're going to love it! I don't know about your tone-deaf American," he teased.

"A cavern?" I asked.

"You don't know about underground Paris?"

Pierre explained that beneath the city lay hundreds of miles of tunnels, part of a dense system of abandoned canals, reservoirs, crypts, bank vaults, wine cellars, and limestone quarries.

"It's a treasure-house of history, Robbie!"

"Sounds like a plan to me," I replied, looking over to My Hanh for her approval. She had heard of underground Paris but had never been there.

"It's also the hippest jazz spot in Paris, but you need a guide, or you may not find your way back up."

My Hanh and I enjoyed the dinner—leeks vinaigrette, hard-boiled eggs with mayonnaise, vegetable soup, followed by beef bourguignon, salad, cheese, and chocolate ice cream with the best Chantilly cream I had ever tasted. We waited for closing time, drinking a second bottle of Bordeaux and talking about Vietnam, the protests at Columbia, and the latest demonstrations and the strikes. We placed our money on the table just next to where Pierre had calculated the bill by hand on the paper tablecloth.

"You realize our call was tapped," I said, looking around the room for anyone who looked like they might be CIA.

"Yes, I finally figured that out, my Robbie. I'm sorry I spoke so freely. I was excited to get your call—"

"The unions are going to turn down the government's offer of that ten percent pay increase," I predicted, responding to what she had told me earlier on the phone.

"How do you know this?" My Hanh asked.

"They know they have the government's back to the wall. De Gaulle needs to put an end to the chaos, so he will agree to whatever the unions ask," I observed.

"You're right, my Robbie," she said. "One day you are going to be a political leader," she blurted, tossing me a look of pride for no apparent reason.

"There's a lot to think about," I responded. I looked at her and realized how important everything she said and thought had become to me.

"You'll see! I know these things," she said.

"Your very own Bonaparte?" I said, and laughed.

"No, my very own Samberg! Robbie, what I have been wanting to tell you—"

"Robbie." Pierre stopped at our table, bottle in hand. "Have more wine." He filled our glasses again. He had finished work and was ready to go.

It occurred to me that drinking two bottles of Bordeaux may not have been the best preparation for climbing down into the underbelly of Paris, but the damage was already done.

My Hanh and I followed Pierre outside the restaurant through a narrow alley, where we came upon a large iron manhole cover. He quickly removed it, revealing a deep hole with a view straight down into the darkness and a small ladder attached to the side of the vertical drop. He pulled out a flashlight that flickered and threw off scant light.

"Is that all we have to see down there?" I asked.

"Relax, Robbie," Pierre said. "My Hanh's smile will light your way."

She laughed heartily.

The three of us began the long descent as Pierre explained the life of the *cataphile*, which, he said, he was proud to be, spending most of his time off duty exploring abandoned mushroom farms, catacombs, German bunkers, and headquarters for the French Resistance during the war. On the eve of D-day, Pierre explained, Resistance fighters moved into position in these same caves to carry out sabotage against the Germans.

My Hanh and I were excited by the history and the adventure. As we climbed down, feeling our way in the near darkness, the air began to smell of mold and dampness. Water droplets appeared on the ladder rungs at the lower levels, making them slippery and more dangerous.

At last we arrived at the bottom, and Pierre lit a torch that he pulled from an iron bracket on the wall. It spewed black smoke which added to the eeriness of the scene. We were standing in a chamber surrounded by skeletons stacked like firewood, femur upon femur, skull upon skull, their eye sockets pointed in our direction as if they were a ghostly welcoming party to a world of the dead.

"There are six million bodies buried here," Pierre said solemnly.

"Six million?" I asked, astonished. "That's how many Jews the Nazis murdered in the Holocaust."

He picked up a parchment-colored skull, pointing to its enlarged nasal opening, telling us that this was likely a sign of leprosy. He handed it to me. I wondered how long the germs for leprosy remained potent and was happy to place it back on the pile and quickly move on. It was spooky beyond measure.

We walked through chamber after chamber, each filled with skeletons of people long since forgotten, until we heard the faint sound of echoing voices, laughter, and music in the distance. Pierre explained that the skeletons were people formerly buried and later exhumed from overcrowded cemeteries in the eighteenth and nineteenth centuries. They dated back to the France of Charles VII, Henry II, Louis XIV, the Revolution, and even as far back as the founding of the city some two thousand years ago.

"I can feel the souls," My Hanh said, closing her eyes for a brief meditation. She clasped her hands and breathed deeply. It was as if she left us for a moment.

"You believe in the afterlife?" I asked after she had reopened her eyes.

"I believe the life energy of these people has joined with the energy of the universe. They live on in that energy and in the memories of those who loved them," she said.

"These bones are so old that no one who loved them is still alive to remember," I observed.

"My Robbie, the life force of their energy still exists in the pure potentiality of the universe. I can feel it. And the energy of love is timeless, immortal, and immutable. True love does not die with the body. It lasts forever."

"Some must have been poor," Pierre added, "some rich, some powerful, others powerless, some healthy, some sick, some content, others miserable, but now in death they are all equal and all anonymous. I have seen this hundreds of times, but I am always moved by the sight."

My Hanh nodded her understanding.

We moved on and the music grew louder, until we reached a large smoke-filled chamber packed with people sitting at tables, drinking wine, listening to music, and doing what the French loved to do—talking and arguing about politics, love, life, history, everything and anything. Pierre led us to a table in the back corner where four Negro men were smoking and talking in hushed voices.

"Hey, soldiers," Pierre greeted them. "These are my friends Robbie and My Hanh."

They remained silent and looked at us suspiciously.

"You can trust these two; they are my friends."

They still did not respond. Pierre had apparently misjudged our acceptance.

"Robbie is a student leader against the war, and My Hanh is from North Vietnam," he said, thinking this would break the ice.

"I'm Robbie Samberg," I offered, stretching out my hand to the man sitting closest to me.

He did not raise his hand or say a word. The others sat motionless, hushed up.

Pierre could see that this was not working, so he quickly wrapped his left arm around My Hanh and his right arm around me, pulled us close, leaned over the table, and said sternly, "Trust these two! They are my friends!"

"Huey Newton, Monroe, Louisiana," came the first response, "but we don't hang with white boys, even if they ag'in the war and pussy-whipped by da Viet Cong bitch"—a nod to my holding hands with My Hanh—"but since you're tight with our French bro Pierre, sit down."

Newton told us he had just lost his younger brother in Vietnam. He squinted as he spoke, his eyes nearly closed, his mouth in a frown. He wore a black leather jacket with a matching beret pulled down just above his left eye.

"Nothin' about America makes sense anymore," he said.

The others nodded in agreement, then they introduced themselves: Stokely Carmichael, H. Rap Brown, Eldridge Cleaver. They called themselves the Black Panthers, and Pierre explained that they were on their way to Algeria to purchase weapons. He had helped them with his military contacts and had met with them several times over the past week.

"King's civil rights thing be dead," Newton said. "Black Power's where it's at!" The others nodded their approval. "We ain't beggin' whites to shit on the same pot or be sat in the front of the bus, and we don't give a fuck about voting in their elections," Newton continued. "As long as Whitey lives, none of that shit gonna make a difference. Things only change when we kill Whitey, get it?" he growled.

"More blacks in jail today than schoolin'," Carmichael said. "It's Whitey's fault; they all be racists every one. The Whitey government sells arms, trains killers, even helps drug smugglers. It's poison, man. They even do radiation shit on our own people like the Nazis." His large round eyes bulged as he spoke. He wore a tight black T-shirt and blue jeans, a red bandanna tied around his head.

"That's pretty radical shit," I responded, looking to Pierre for support. "You guys are going to screw up all the progress made by King and the Civil Rights Movement if you carry on like this. You're wrong about the vote. The vote can change everything. For all his stupidity escalating the war, Johnson deserves some credit on voting rights. He risked pissing off his Southern base to make that happen, and over time, you Negroes—"

"Blacks," Newton interrupted.

"Okay, blacks over time can tip the balance of voting in America in every election at every level. This is huge, and you guys are going to piss it all away if you carry on like this."

My Hanh looked at me with pride for challenging them.

Ad-libbing, as I'd done on rue St. Jacques, I continued. "Robert Kennedy is running for president against Johnson, and if he wins it will be a chance for Negroes—I mean blacks—to bring America back to its senses and then—"

"White boy," Brown interrupted, "we spell Amerika with a *k*, and it's not a *k* for Kennedy, it's a *k* for 'kill Whitey'!" He scowled, raising his bushy eyebrows above the dark sunglasses that lay crooked on his face. He wore a jeans jacket, black slacks, and an open shirt with a large collar.

The other Panthers raised their fists and whooped their approval.

"No, no, you don't get it," I shot back. "Your loose talk of violence is going to alienate every white middle-class man and woman in America and send them running for protection to George Wallace or Richard Nixon. Don't you see that you are working against what you want for your own people?"

"Fuck you, white boy," Brown snarled.

"Okay, shoot me right here right now," I rejoined, "but you are fools, and you're going to get yourselves killed and kill any hope of progress for blacks, and I don't give a shit how you spell 'America'!"

"Hold on!" Pierre shouted, no doubt realizing it was time to shut me up before he might have the unpleasant task of lugging my dead body up the ladder to the street. "I think we need to cool it. We're here for the jazz, not for a race war."

"You want to die tonight, Samberg?" Carmichael taunted. "You're a Jew, aren't you? I can tell by your crooked nose and your big mouth, which if you don't shut I'm gonna fill with the barrel of my .45 and do some changes to that white face of yours right here right now!" He reached into his jacket in slow motion.

"*Alors! Alors!* Men." Pierre stood up, raising his hands. "There will be no shooting in this room tonight, not if you ever want to see those guns from Algeria. Now mind your manners!"

To emphasize his point, Pierre remained standing over the table. He was huge, a retired ranger with the French Foreign Legion who had fought in Algeria and at the Battle of Dien Bien Phu, where he was one of the last Frenchmen standing.

"Now, let's have some wine," Pierre continued, following a menacing pause and filling the glasses all around, lifting his for a toast. "To jazz!"

My Hanh and I raised our glasses.

"We'll drink to that," I said.

The Panthers paused, then reluctantly lifted their glasses. "To jazz!"

"We done with King and the nonviolence shit," Newton said. "It done left us with nothin', and the progress you white liberals brag about is your thing, not ours." He looked at me. "You pat each other on the back at cocktail parties, but we who be in the ghetto are still poor and we still ain't goin nowhere, except to Nam to die. Only a gun to Whitey's head gonna change that."

"Look, I get your anger about the war," I jumped in, remembering my visit to the draft board, and how blacks don't get the deferments given to whites. "I get it."

"You don't get shit," Newton countered. "There are brothers dyin' out there every day, forced to fight Whitey's war with them Viet Cong, burnin' homes and villages, kill'en or done be'en killed and do'en smack to escape the hell. Dig this, man: you don't get shit, Samberg!"

"Glad you got it that blacks doin' most of the fightin' over there and the dyin' while you middle-class Whiteys get a pass from the Whitey draft boards," Carmichael said. "We done with that shit, too. We gonna burn down those draft board offices!" he cried, raising his right fist in the air once again.

"Yes, I get that. Now you get this: as sure as we're sitting here, you're not gonna change shit if you scare the middle class into voting for Nixon or Wallace. That will only make things worse. It will play into the hands of the right-wing law-and-order types, who will smash your dumb heads."

"Who you callin' dumb, Whitey Jew?" Newton shot back.

"I'm trying to get you to hear me!" I said, raising my voice. "You're not hearing me."

"Robbie." My Hanh reached out, placing her right hand on my shoulder and gently pulling me back in my chair.

"And I can do without the Jew talk! I get it; the war is wrong! I get it! Being a black man in America sucks! I get it! You're pissed!"

Newton tossed me a mean look. "You white motherfuckers have no idea," he seethed. "We no longer believe a single word the white man says. We've been fucked and fucked and fucked again, and we're done bein' the fuckees; from now on we be the fuckors." His face suddenly broke out in a smile.

The other Panthers erupted in laughter, raising their fists in the air.

"Look, Newton," I said, leaning toward him, "I'm against the war, I'm against racism, but I'm not ready to give up on America. I think we can get through this. We've got the political leaders and the political process to get through this."

"Political process," he interrupted. "What the fuck you talkin' about?"

"What process?" Newton asked again. "The one that killed off red men, took their land, and locked up the rest on reservations, or the one that stole Africans, sold them as slaves, and today locks us up in economic and political chains as thick as the chains we wore as slaves?"

"You are livin' bullshit, white boy," Brown said. "You ain't never felt the pain. That's why you ain't ready to give up on America. You're just one more privileged fat cat. One more Whitey that needs killin'."

"Hey, man, the America that made you slaves also gave us Lincoln and the Northern soldiers who fought to end slavery," I said, my voice lowered but steady and passionate.

"You're hopeless, white boy," Newton responded. "If you love your enemy in America, they gonna eat you alive."

"No more hopeless than you," I said.

"Can you men please calm down so I can enjoy the music?" Pierre slammed the table and spoke a loud voice that meant business. The musicians came on stage and began to play.

There was a gulf between us at that table as broad and dangerous as the deepest fissure between blacks and whites in America, between those who supported the war and those who opposed it, between those who welcomed the liberation of women and those who were threatened by it.

As the dissonant sound of jazz filled the room, My Hanh put her head next to mine and whispered, "Robbie, I'm proud of you. I love you."

She kissed me and snuggled up to enjoy the music.

The pianist was a Canadian black man, Oscar Peterson, who poured his soul onto the keyboard. His fingers moved with lightning speed, unleashing powerful music that for the moment transcended the enormous gulf in our politics. At a time when America seemed to stand for nothing but strife in the world, jazz music, created by blacks in America, was one thing we could all be proud of, and something loved and appreciated in France. I looked at Pierre and My Hanh and Carmichael with his red bandanna, and I wondered if the ills that now bedeviled Vietnam, France, and America might ever heal. *In all three places, it will be a long time coming.*

Then, at a soft passage in the music, with Peterson lightly touching the higher keys at the right of the keyboard, as I noticed the coiled intensity of his passion in the sweat which poured down his neck onto his soaked collar, My Hanh tilted her head and whispered in my left ear.

"You're what?" I gasped, my world forever changed.

Chapter 16

Free Dreyfus!

For My Hanh, Oscar Peterson and his trio were a revelation. Jazz did not exist in the music culture of North Vietnam. It was something new for her, and she loved it, and I loved watching her as she moved to the music. Pierre loved jazz, too. The Panthers were also into it but didn't allow themselves to show their enthusiasm, lest it appear to dilute the ice-cold animosity that underpinned their raison d'être, this notwithstanding Pierre's plying them with bottle after bottle of Bordeaux.

Not so with My Hanh and me. We were loose as could be and grooving to the music, our hands and body movements telling a story of alcohol-induced abandon—that was until My Hanh told me she'd missed her period.

"I'm pregnant," she whispered, her soft voice masked by the melodies of jazz.

"My God," I responded, taking her hand.

"I have been praying to Buddha," she said. "It's in his hands."

"This complicates everything," I said, looking around the table to see if Pierre or the others had heard us. They were transfixed by Peterson's piano, their eyes following his hands moving across the keyboard at lightning speed just a few feet away.

"I have been wanting to tell you," she whispered, keeping her head next to mine so we could not be overheard. "We'll deal with it," she added, squeezing my hand.

"Deal with it?"

"I know in the West when a girl gets pregnant she can go to a doctor and have an abortion," she said. "This is what we must do."

"Is that what you want?" I asked.

"It's not what I want but it's what we must do, Robbie," she said, touching my face and looking into my eyes to gauge my reaction.

"My Hanh . . ." I looked at her but could not find words to respond. The room spun around, the music faded to the background and I suddenly felt isolated by fear.

"It is sad because our child would be so beautiful," she mused.

"My Hanh, My Hanh," I said softly, staring ahead, still at the table but no longer *of* the table, collapsed in a darkening world, the only thing holding me up the feel of My Hanh's hand in mine.

"I can ask Dr. Coureau," I said. "He is a friend of Madame Gueumier, but this is not what I want. This is not what I want for us."

"If you tell him, Madame Gueumier will know, too," she said.

"He is French," I responded, "and the French have understanding hearts in matters of love. He will protect our privacy."

"How do you know that?" she asked.

"The way he treated me at the hospital. . . I think we can trust him."

"This is not happening!" I whispered in My Hanh's ear, looking perhaps to any who saw us like I was nibbling on it with affection.

"We must stay calm, meditate, and take what action we can," she responded, whispering in my ear as if she were returning my affections.

"Think about your father, my parents . . . This is not really happening," I said again.

"It is happening," she responded, still whispering in my ear, but if we cannot end the pregnancy, we'll create a beautiful child from our love, and that is something wonderful, too."

"I'm not ready for this," I said.

"My Robbie, nobody is ready for what life—"

"Hey, you lovebirds," Pierre said. "What are you whispering about over there? I'm trying to enjoy the music."

It was 2 a.m., time for the trio to take a break. When the music stopped, the Panthers rose from their chairs and took off. They didn't say goodbye, just stood up, nodded, and walked out.

Pierre remained at the table with us, and during the break two thin, bearded men and a woman dressed in a long madras dress with beads down to her waist joined us, filling the empty seats. They were Americans and even more wasted than My Hanh, Pierre, and me.

"Welcome to the table," Pierre said. "I'm Pierre, and this is Robbie and My Hanh."

"I'm Jim, and this is Pam and Van," Jim slurred, "and we're deep into Oscar Peterson, man."

I had the feeling Jim was a musician.

"Play an instrument?" Pierre asked.

"Nah, man, just some bits on the maracas, tambourine, and harmonica, but I sing, man, and I whistle."

"Hey, you played the grand piano on 'Orange County Suite' and the Moog on 'Strange Days,'" Pam corrected him.

"Very cool," Pierre added. I sat silently, still in shock about the pregnancy. "Very cool," Pierre said again as the waiter came to refill our glasses.

I didn't have a clue about the music Pam mentioned.

My Hanh glanced at her watch and asked the waiter if there was a phone. "My father asked me to call before midnight."

"How cozy," Jim slurred, eyeing her in a way I did not care for.

Pam looked as unhappy as me.

My Hanh excused herself to make the call. As she got up, Jim ogled her again, and I became more uncomfortable, though I was still too shaken up to say or do anything about it.

"Where is she from?" Jim asked.

"North Vietnam," Pierre responded, looking over at me. I could see that he detected the change in my mood.

"Wow, extremely cool," Jim said. "She is so beautiful!"

"Jim, what songs do you sing?" Pierre asked.

"Anything that moves me! I like to write poems and turn them into lyrics, but I really don't want to talk about my work, man. Can you just dig that?"

"Sure, I can dig that," Pierre said, still looking at me.

I could see the concern on Jim's face.

"Hey," Pam interjected, "Jim had a horrible gig this past December, and it really shook him up. He's not being rude; it's just that we're here to get away from all that."

"Okay, we get it," Pierre said. "No harm done."

My Hanh returned to the table, grabbed her glass of wine, and drank it down in a single gulp.

"You okay?" Pierre asked as the band returned from its break and began to play.

She did not respond. Then she turned to me and delivered a second blow. "Free Dreyfus," she whispered.

I did not respond.

"Free Dreyfus," she said again, looking at me and raising her voice enough so Pierre and the others could hear.

"Dreyfus? Alfred Dreyfus?" Pierre asked. "The Jew? The spy? My grandfather thought he should have been hanged."

"Well, I think he should never have been arrested," she responded, looking sternly at Pierre, then at me. No one else at the table had any idea what she was talking about or why she was saying this.

"What does a girl from North Vietnam know about Dreyfus?" Pierre asked, puzzled and annoyed. She did not let on that I had just told her about Dreyfus, having recounted everything I had learned from Ronen.

"He was a Jewish colonel in the French army unfairly imprisoned years ago in a terrible act of anti-Semitism," she explained. "I believe he was a patriot, not a spy. That's why I say 'Free Dreyfus,'" she proclaimed, eliciting blank stares from Pam, Jim, and Van.

She cast her luminescent eyes on me, begging for my response. I sat silently.

"Not everyone thought he was innocent," Pierre said. "My grandfather was in the military at the time and he thought Dreyfus was guilty."

"Hey, that's cool," Jim said. "My old man is military—Admiral George. He commanded a carrier group during the Gulf of Tonkin thing," he said, slurring his words. "I never talk about him," he added, looking to My Hanh for a reaction.

"Free Dreyfus," she repeated, looking at me and raising her glass.

"Yeah, free Dreyfus, and 'Long live the King of May,'" Jim said, raising his glass. "That's Allen Ginsberg," he said, "and I love his poetry! Free Dreyfus!" he repeated, his voice breaking into song.

Pam, Jim, Van, and My Hanh lifted their glasses and joined in the toast. Pierre and I remained silent.

"Pierre," My Hanh asked, "how about it? For Buddha?" He shrugged. "For me then?"

"Well, it was a long time ago," he said. "We military don't easily forgive spies."

"And you, my Robbie?" My Hanh sensed my anxiety and looked into my eyes like that first day in the Métro.

I knew I had to decide.

What message would Tho ask me to deliver and to whom? Would it be about Chenault? About Nixon's interference with the peace talks? Would it be treasonous? Could it affect the presidential election? Harm my family? End my career? Ruin my life?

"Spies, I really hate spies," I finally offered, shaking my head.

"Me too," Pierre rejoined.

I was out of time. My Hanh was asking for my support out loud with her words and silently with her eyes. I had no idea where this would lead—first a child, now an act of treason? It felt like more than I could handle, but despite my fear and my shock, I saw in her eyes a love that buoyed me. *Our love will get me through this. Our love will get us through anything.*

I raised my half-empty wineglass and turned to My Hanh. "Free Dreyfus!"

Pierre, Van, Jim, and Pam raised their glasses. "Free Dreyfus," they repeated, laughing and unaware of the saga that was unfolding.

My Hanh grabbed my hand. "Robbie, I'm suddenly not feeling well," she said loudly enough for all to hear. "Do you think we could leave after this set?"

"Of course," I responded, playing along to get us to what we both knew had to come next.

"No problem," Pierre said. "I'll get the check, and we can head out."

The others at the table turned their attention back to the music, which again filled the room. I felt a strange calm come over me. Perhaps it was because I had made a decision to risk all for My Hanh, and if fate would have it, to be a father to our child. The ground had shifted and I felt resigned to handle whatever lay ahead with the pregnancy and in that bottle in the Jardin des Tuileries.

I could feel the fatigue as My Hanh, Pierre, and I climbed our way out of the catacombs at 4:30 a.m. Once back on street level, we entered a café, which had just opened for the new day, and ordered three *cafés express*, the ultra-rich coffee of France. The streets were still empty and dark. No people. No cars. I was exhausted.

My Hanh used the café phone to call for the delegation car. I pulled Pierre Laboutte's card from my wallet and called him. I told him it was urgent and he promised to come immediately. I stood on the dark street next to My Hanh.

Pierre asked that we not speak to anyone about the weapons from Algeria. He said he was going to back out of the deal with the Panthers and tell his contacts to do so.

"I don't want American blood on my hands," he said.

As My Hanh's car pulled up, Pierre bid us goodbye.

"Whatever happened with you two tonight, I trust you will handle it," he said, offering a hug to My Hanh, then to me.

"*Merci*, Pierre. *Merci pour tout*," we responded, speaking together as one. He turned and walked away down the narrow, winding Paris street.

"Pierre," I called out as he walked off. "Dreyfus was innocent, a good Jew, and a good Frenchman."

"Alright," he responded, looking at me and at My Hanh. "For me the Dreyfus Affair ends tonight." He waved goodbye.

I walked My Hanh to her car. The uniformed driver got out and opened the door for her.

"Robbie," she said, turning toward me, but before she could speak I placed my index finger on her lips. Then I leaned in to kiss her lightly on each cheek and offered a final lingering kiss on the lips.

She slipped into the backseat of the car, and it pulled away.

Chapter 17

Unraveled

"Allen, can you hear me? It's Robbie from Paris . . . ROBBIE FROM PARIS . . ."

The connection was poor, so I hung up, ran down the hall to the postal clerk, and asked her to place the call again.

In 1968, you couldn't make a phone call from Paris to the United States on a private phone or a pay phone. You had to visit a post office and have the call put through.

I explained to the clerk that I was calling the chief legislative aide to United States Senator Lance Hankie, but she was unimpressed. She had never heard of Hankie and made me wait in line again before assigning another tiny soundproof booth to take the call.

As I stood in line, I thought about the night before and the shock of learning My Hanh was pregnant. It was as if someone had hit the fast-forward button on my life, speeding it up to a moment I was not prepared to handle. The earth shook beneath my feet; familiar surroundings looked different, and the fabric of my thoughts turned a dark color. My Hanh was resigned to the need for an abortion, but I wanted to take some time to consider the alternatives. We had never discussed marriage or having children, and suddenly, wham, they were both on the horizon before us, with no clear path forward to make either possible. I worried about what I had already done for My

Hanh's father and what I was about to do. I had gone to the tree, I had retrieved his message, and now I was about to follow his instructions, an act that once undertaken could not be rescinded, and an act that might ruin my life at home as much as My Hanh's pregnancy with an American child might ruin her life in Vietnam.

As if this were not enough, I couldn't stop thinking about the violent divisions between blacks and whites in America I had experienced the night before at the jazz club. I thought about the Black Panthers and how far they had strayed from the principles of nonviolence. These guys were at war, I thought, and the enemy was all white men. It felt like the America of 1968 was becoming the France of 1789, 1830, 1848, or 1871, a powder keg of revolution, with angry minorities ready to pour onto the streets and man the barricades. The antiwar movement and the Civil Rights Movement were both becoming more extreme, and if things didn't change, the violence advocated by the Panthers could spread to the thinking of the equally angry antiwar leaders. *That's what happens when people with deep grievances and powerful convictions are not heard. Either they shut down in apathy or they turn to violence, with no regard for the consequences.*

I knew that in America, violence by a radical few would beget fear in the majority of the middle class and that this would be exploited by the right-wing law-and-order types to kill off the progressive movement. I knew that if that happened, it would be goodbye civil rights, goodbye Great Society, goodbye liberal politics, goodbye Democratic presidential victory, goodbye Democratic majority in Congress, goodbye economic development for the inner cities, and so on. It would mean hello draconian law and order and repression, and beyond that the equally great danger of a return to apathy and indifference. While I had long thought about these things, the idea of bringing a child into this world, *my* child, suddenly gave me motivation to do something about it. I could no longer play safe as an observer. I could no longer stand on the sidelines. The time for debate and talk was over. I needed to act.

Waiting in the new phone booth, I suddenly heard a clicking noise on the line.

"Allen, is that you?"

"Yes, it's me, Robbie . . . What's wrong? Why are you calling me in the middle of the night?"

"Allen, is your phone secure? Can you pick up on the secure line?"

"Secure line? Is that necessary? Wait a minute, Robbie. I'm going to put you on hold and pick up in the other room."

Allen was one of a select few Senate staffers assigned to the Foreign Relations Committee with a security clearance high enough to warrant a secure phone line at his house.

The line went silent, and the few minutes I waited for him to pick up again felt like forever. I couldn't bear the thought of waiting in line again if we were disconnected. The booth had no ventilation, and it was hot and stuffy and reeked of the body odor of the many who had used it before. *What was I about to do?* The phone booth began to feel like the third steam room on the *Queen Elizabeth*.

I pulled off my coat and took off my sweater. They dropped to the floor.

"Robbie, I'm back. Now what the hell is going on?"

"Can you hear me?"

"Yes, I hear you!"

"Allen, have you ever heard of Anna Chennault?"

"Of course. The Dragon Lady. She's the Chinese Republican big shot from New York who's been out raising money for Nixon. She's the darling of the ultraconservatives, the reigning empress of the China lobby, and a real looker! What about her?"

"I have learned that she is not only raising money for Nixon, she is conveying private messages from him to the government of South Vietnam," I said, speaking slowly to make sure he heard every word.

"What kind of messages?"

"On Nixon's orders, she told President Thiệu that if the South Vietnamese government scuttles the peace talks about to begin here, a Nixon administration, once elected, would offer them a better deal than they would get from Johnson," I said, again speaking slowly for emphasis.

The line went silent.

"Allen, are you there? Did you hear what I just said? She has told them that Nixon will be harder on the communists than Johnson and will give away less to end the war. She has also told North Vietnam that unlike Johnson, Nixon would not be encumbered by all that has gone before and would be more flexible with them than Johnson, so he is playing both sides to scuttle the peace talks. He's afraid a last-minute deal will cost him the election, and he is not going to let that happen."

The silence continued, and I could almost feel Allen thinking through the phone line across the Atlantic.

"Robbie Samberg, are you into drugs or something?" he finally blurted. "Maybe like too many tabs of LSD? I think you are hallucinating, my friend."

"No, I am serious, Allen," I said in my clearest and firmest voice. "This shit is actually happening."

"How do you know this, Robbie?"

"Allen, I know this is going to sound crazy, but—"

"It already sounds crazy."

"I know, I know. It started when I helped rescue a North Vietnamese girl in the Métro," I began to explain.

"You *are* doing drugs."

"No, no, Allen, hear me out. Her name is My Hanh, and I happened to be there when she was accosted by a drunken French soldier, and I helped her and I had no idea who she was. I later learned she is the daughter of Le Duc Tho, the foreign minister of North Vietnam—"

"Christ, Robbie!"

"Allen, for God's sake, hear me out. Tho is in Paris to secretly meet with Rusk's people and the South Vietnamese about a bombing pause and a settlement. Surely you must know about this."

"Go on," he said, sounding like he was at last listening.

"The problem is that Rusk's team has not been able to get the South Vietnamese on board. They have been dickering for weeks over minor issues like the size and shape of the conference table and the meeting place, the same way they dickered for weeks over the city in which to meet."

"Where did you learn this, Robbie?"

"Tho told me," I said.

"Fuck no, Robbie."

"Fuck yes, Allen."

"You met with Le Duc Tho in Paris?"

"My Hanh introduced me to him, and he told me about Chennault and Nixon. He shared his sources, and he is convinced that Nixon is behind the delay in the peace talks."

"Do you have proof of this?"

"I have photos of John Mitchell entering and departing Anna Chennault's apartment in New York City, and I have transcripts of wiretaps of Anna Chennault's phone. The calls are between her and Bui Diem, the ambassador of South Vietnam to the United States. They confirm Tho's suspicion."

"And how did you get this?"

"Oh, I knew you would ask me that. Remember my master's thesis on Dr. Edward Bancroft?" I asked.

"The double agent who worked for Franklin? The tree with the hole in the trunk in the Jardin des Tuileries? You've got to be kidding."

"This is no joke," I said. "Tho needed a way to communicate with me that could not be traced, so I told him about Bancroft, and he used the same tree just a couple of centuries later," I explained. "The photos and wiretaps were copied to a tiny piece of silicon called a chip, taped to a single sheet of paper, and left for me in a 1947 magnum bottle of Château Margaux. The bottle was left in the hole at the base of the same oak tree that Bancroft used to exchange messages with British secret service chief William Eden in the eighteenth century."

There was stone silence at the other end of the phone. "Allen, are you there?"

"Let me see if I've got this straight," Allen recapped, as he used to do when we had lunch in the Senate cafeteria. "While you're over there studying at the American Institute, you rescue a North Vietnamese communist damsel in distress, who just happens to be the daughter of the foreign minister of our enemy, who just happens to be in Paris for secret peace talks, and upon her introducing you to her father, he confides in you about political skullduggery that if revealed could result in Mr. Nixon's arrest for treason, which, of course, would also have a profound impact on the next US presidential election, not to mention the prospects for peace in Vietnam. Did I miss anything, leave anything out?" he asked matter-of-factly. "Other than the fact that the North Vietnamese have stolen our latest integrated circuit technology."

"Well, yes. Allen, there's more."

"More! How could there be more?" he asked, raising his voice. "Ah, tell me you have not fallen in love with the commie girl and want to defect to Hanoi to marry her," he deadpanned.

"No, no, not the defecting part . . . but I have fallen in love."

"My God, Robbie! You have really stepped in it, my boy!"

"And she's pregnant!"

The phone went silent again. I wondered if I should have said it.

"Allen? Allen, are you there?"

Suddenly he thundered, "What the fuck have you done?"

"Yes, I have really stepped in it and deeply, but I feel better having told you."

"Just why *are* you telling me all this?"

"Because you are my friend and . . ."

"And . . . ?"

"Because the sheet of paper to which the chip was attached had a handwritten note from Tho, explaining the contents of the chip and asking me to send the documents to you and you alone. The note was signed by Monsieur X, the code name Tho told me he would use in his secret communications. He and I were the only two people who knew this name, and now you are the third."

"Mr. X asked you to tell me what Nixon and his people are up to?"

"Yes, he knew we were friends."

"Were friends—good choice of words," Allen said, laughing nervously. "I don't think I want to know you anymore," he added with a sigh that was partly humorous and partly dead serious. "He also knew I would be honor bound to report this to Hankie, and that Hankie would be honor bound to report this to the boss. He's pretty clever, that commie."

"These guys are so well informed, Allen, it wouldn't surprise me if they had pictures of us in the Senate cafeteria slurping our bean soup," I said, reminding him of our friendship.

"Aaah, Robbie, you know I miss our lunches."

"I do too. I'm such a wreck from all this."

"My God, Robbie, I don't know where to start. This is such an overload. I thought things were crazy here and out of control, but you have raised the bar, my boy."

"What's happening at home?"

"Haven't you read the papers?"

"I don't have time to read papers here."

"McCarthy's write-in campaign lost to LBJ in New Hampshire, but only by seven points. He walked away with more delegates than Johnson, and that prompted Kennedy to finally get off the fence and jump in and Johnson to withdraw, so we now have two antiwar candidates duking it out, the poet and the pro," Allen explained, his voice echoing from the transatlantic connection.

"What about the Republicans?"

"Romney is going nowhere, while Reagan is waiting for someone to place the crown on his head. Rockefeller is running around waving the polls he bought and paid for showing that he, not Nixon, is the one to defeat the Democrats. He's also spending a ton of money on ads, but he's also going nowhere."

"And Nixon?" I asked.

"From what I hear, he has been quietly working the delegates. He has a lot of IOUs and he has learned a lot from his loss in 1960 and his run for governor. He appears to have his act together, or at least I thought so until this phone call."

"Can you believe it, Allen?" I asked.

"It really doesn't make sense, Robbie. If Nixon is trying to scuttle the peace talks to get elected, he's violating the Logan

Act and committing treason. With a half-million American soldiers on the battlefield and thirty thousand killed, the things you have described reveal a side of him that knows no boundaries in order to win." I could hear him calculating, weighing his thoughts carefully, just as he used to do in the Senate cafeteria while fidgeting with the rims of his wire glasses.

"I don't get it either. If Nixon is already ahead for the nomination and looks strong in the general election, why would he take the risk?" I asked.

"Maybe it's 1960, when the Kennedy's screwed him in Chicago . . . Maybe that fire has not gone out. Maybe it has fanned an even hotter flame. Maybe he will do anything to make sure he is not screwed over again. Or maybe he's got a loose screw or two we just don't know about."

"If Johnson settles the war, that would do it, right?"

"It could, but that's not how I hear Johnson is playing this. He's no saint, Robbie, but from what I know, now that he has dropped out, he's trying hard not to favor anyone."

"How do I get you the wiretaps and the photos?"

"I need to think about that and talk to Hankie, and I'll get back to you. Maybe we can arrange for a CIA jet. However we do it, we need it done fast, and we need it done securely. Once Johnson learns about this, he'll have Hoover tapping phones all over the place, including Nixon's. Johnson is going to come down on Nixon like a ton of bricks."

"Did you ever think it would get this crazy?" I asked.

"No, and my instincts are pretty good on this stuff."

"But won't the Johnson withdrawal just hand the nomination to McCarthy or Kennedy?"

"Those guys look good in the press and to those who don't really understand the process, but Johnson continues to control seventy to seventy-five percent of the Democratic delegates, and he will hold them for Humphrey no matter how many primaries McCarthy or Kennedy wins. There's no way anybody is going to get the Democratic nomination without Johnson's blessing."

"Even Kennedy, with the legacy and all his contacts from 1960?" "The half-life of a political machine in short. Nineteen sixty was a long time ago. Kennedy is going to have as much trouble in the South as he did in Oregon. If he makes a deal with Daly in Chicago, like his brother did, he's going to alienate the young idealists in his base. This is not going to be easy for him—in fact, it may be impossible. I'm betting on Humphrey, and I'm betting when Johnson finds out about Nixon's treason, all hell will break loose!"

"So, what am I supposed to do now?" I asked, the sweat now pouring off my face in the cramped, hot booth.

"This is tough, Robbie, but you're going to have to ditch the girl and the baby," he said emphatically.

"No fucking way."

"Think about it, Robbie, and think with your brain, not your pecker or your heart."

"I can't do that," I said, my voice quivering.

"Robbie, for God's sake, stay away from the commie girl-friend and her father! I'm sure you're already under CIA sur-veillance. If you cut it off now, when you return I'll get my hands on your dossier and see if we can fix things. Nobody but Hankie is going to know about this call, but I can't help you unless you cut things off with the girl and her father. Do you understand?"

"Allen, there's just no way I can do that," I responded em-phatically.

"Robbie, you need to hear me on this!" Allen screamed into the phone. "You, your family, your father, and mother, your sisters, their future, your future—it's all at stake in how you handle this. Do you know what happens to a mixed-race child in Vietnam when the father is American? Do you honestly think you can bring her here, have a child and a normal life? Do you think your father will ever get an FCC license to operate a radio station if his son is arrested for espionage in Paris? Do you want to end up in prison? Really! Put the chip and the note back in the bottle, and put the bottle back in the tree, and do it as soon as we hang up from this call. Do you hear me? You don't want that stuff anywhere near you!"

"I hear you! I hear you!" I repeated, feeling crushed by the consequences Allen had made so abundantly clear.

"Make sure to wipe the note clean with a cloth and wipe the bottle, too. I'll get back to you as soon as I can. Now go be a student and stay out of trouble, will you?"

He abruptly hung up the phone.

My shirt was soaked with sweat. I sat in the steamy booth looking down at my coat and sweater crumpled on the floor at my feet and glanced out the tiny glass window in the door of the booth. I could see the line of impatient wannabe callers now stretched halfway across the room. *Cut things off with the commie girlfriend*, Allen's words reverberated. *Cut things off!* I sat immobilized on the tiny stool in the cramped booth.

The woman at the desk walked over and knocked on the door. "Monsieur, you must leave now," she instructed, but I could hardly hear her voice through the soundproofing.

I knew that once I opened that door I would have to face up to what Allen had asked me to do, and I knew that I could not do this. *Allen does not understand. What does he know about love or children? He's a bachelor married to politics. Easy for him to say cut things off!* I needed to see My Hanh, and together we would figure out what to do. We were strong together; we would find a way.

I could not ask her to come to America, and I could not go to North Vietnam, but I could take another year to study abroad in Peking. We could go together. Maybe our child would not be shunned there as in Vietnam or in America. But America had no relations with the People's Republic of China, and there were no organized study programs. Perhaps My Hanh could get her father to help us. *Yes!* He loved his daughter and would want to protect her happiness. Once he learned I was going to be the father of his grandchild, he would come around. He could use his influence with the communist party to get me into a Chinese university. I could teach English and learn Mandarin. I loved languages. It would work out. I was certain of it. *Yes, this is the plan, and together in school in Peking, My Hanh and I will have a life of our own and a family.*

But what about my parents? I clenched my teeth at the thought of my father learning that I had defected to Red China. He would never understand. I shook my head. Maybe with the passage of time, he and my mother would acquiesce even if they might never approve. At first, they would be shocked and angry, but if one day they learned the truth—how much I loved My Hanh, how much becoming the father of our child meant to me—they would change their thinking. They would likely cut me off financially, but if they did I could find work and I would find a way to live. Tuition in China was probably cheap. I would find a way. Eventually, they would forgive me, and one day, when they met My Hanh and hugged their grandchild, they would accept us!

I grew more determined as I mustered the courage to step out of the booth. There waiting for me was the postal clerk who had knocked at the door, along with a crowd of very unhappy Frenchmen who knew nothing of the issues I wrestled with and showed their impatience with sour looks. I followed the woman to the desk, paid the overtime on the call, which took nearly every franc I had in my wallet, and headed out to find a cab, wondering if I had enough money left to get home.

As I flagged down a cab outside the post office, I noticed a black car parked on the street with two men in dark suits and sunglasses in the front seats. *My CIA tail?* Allen was right, but I didn't care. I had to find My Hanh!

Chapter 18

The Visit

At six the next morning the doorbell rang at 7 rue de la Bienfaisance, and there, smiling his six-megawatt smile, his rounded, cherubic face aglow, stood Allen Hoffers.

"I'm looking for Robbie Samberg," he told Marionette, who had dutifully opened the front door in her bathrobe.

She smirked at him and, eyeing not one but two black Cadillac limos just outside the door, motors running and chauffeured by bulked-up men in dark suits and sunglasses, decided to personally escort Allen to Madame Gueumier's fifth-floor apartment.

"You're kidding," I said in broken French as Marionette informed me through my closed door about the visitor.

I threw on a pair of jeans and a flannel shirt and followed her to the foyer, wondering how Allen could possibly have gotten there so quickly. It felt like we had just hung up the phone.

"Allen, what the—?"

"Well, I was in town and thought I would take you to breakfast. I hear they have some great croissants next door at the Gare St-Lazare," he added in a casual tone that belied my shock.

"What the—?"

"You remember my telling you I'd get right back to you. What?" He paused and grimaced for effect. "Did you forget?

Still have that problem listening, don't you?" he admonished as an afterthought fired from a slingshot.

"What?"

"Why don't you put on some nice clothes, and we can spend the day?" he said as I stood next to him, bewildered. "I have a few places I'd like to take you, but put on a jacket and tie, okay?"

Madame Gueumier entered the foyer, awakened by the ruckus, and, seeing I had a guest, offered coffee, but Allen said we needed to get going. I quickly changed, while he waited in the foyer with Marionette and Madame Gueumier.

"I think our student has been hanging out with the wrong crowd," he told the ladies in broken French.

Madame Gueumier raised her eyebrows as if to agree.

"I'll make sure he mends his ways," Allen added with a smile.

I returned in my three-piece suit. We said our goodbyes and headed toward the small cage-like lift at the center of the hallway, just outside the apartment.

"Okay," I said as soon as the apartment door closed. "What the fuck is going on?"

"The CIA black ops guys are taking us for a little ride," Allen said. "And heads up, they're going to cuff you when we get to the car."

"What?"

"It's standard operating procedure for suspects of treason," he said.

"Treason! Allen!"

"I know. I'll try to get them to loosen up as soon as I can, but right now

you're as hot as napalm in Nam," he said, shaking his head.

"Allen, please!" I placed my right hand on my forehead and sighed. We entered the car and the agent on the passenger side demanded that I hold out my hands. I looked at Allen, trembling.

"Do it," Allen admonished.

"But I've done nothing wrong!" I said.

"Do it," Allen repeated.

I paused and shuddered feeling the sweat pour through my glands and slowly lifted my arms. The agent grabbed my wrists and slapped on the cuffs.

"Allen!" We drove off merging into the busy morning traffic of Paris.

"So why are you here, and how the hell did you get here so fast?" I asked as our two-car convoy raced along the bank of the Seine.

"You really dropped a bomb with the Chennault thing."

"I told you, but I never thought it would come to this." I raised my arms and held the cuffs in front of Allen's face, grimacing.

"I didn't know when we spoke yesterday, Robbie, but twenty-four hours ago the North Vietnamese agreed, in return for a bombing pause, to let the South participate in the talks, to halt shelling in the cities, and to stop abusing the DMZ—the terms Johnson has been seeking for months."

"Tho is making his move?"

"Yes. This is the first time they have agreed to negotiate with the South. It's a big step forward, but we need to clean up the Chennault thing, he said, signaling the driver to take the exit to the Jardin des Tuileries.

"We?"

"Yes, we are going to get the proof about Nixon and Chennault, and we're going to take it home. You did put it back in the tree, Robbie."

"Yes, I put it back last night—exactly like you told me. What do you mean, we're going to take it home?"

"As soon as I told Hankie about Chennault, he picked up the red phone and told LBJ, and LBJ wants to see that X file like yesterday," Allen said. "Your Mr. X really played this one brilliantly."

"X file?" I said.

"That's what the CIA is calling the file with the photos of Mitchell and the intercepts. According to Hankie, Johnson has been playing it straight with Nixon. He was determined to keep the negotiations in Paris above domestic politics, and he assured Nixon there would be no surprises and no tricks, so he's furious about the Chennault thing. He feels betrayed bigtime!"

"Tho's move is the first real chance for meaningful talks and a settlement. Nixon's subterfuge with Chennault and the South Vietnamese threatens everything," he said.

"How did you get here so fast?"

"He wants to see the file and he wants to see you, Robbie," Allen said, ignoring my question. "He isn't satisfied with the intelligence he's gotten through regular channels and he's not sure what side you're really on. Oh, and did I mention? He wants all this to happen today."

"What side I'm on? Shit!"

"You were a fool to meet with Le Duc Tho, and a bigger fool to fall in love with his daughter," he said. "What did you think would happen?" he added, pointing to the cuffs and shaking his head back and forth.

"Today?" I mumbled.

"Yes, today!"

"He's got the CIA, the FBI, the NSA, and he wants to talk to me?"

"Robbie, there aren't a whole bunch of Americans out there who have met with Le Duc Tho, and you're the one Tho trusted to disclose Nixon's monkeywrenching."

"From LBJ's vantage point, your role in this is pretty muddled. Believe me, Hankie and I vouched for you, but he wants to judge himself.

"Oh shit," I muttered, realizing how far things had spun out of control.

"We're going to fetch that Margaux bottle, head for Le Bourget, and fly to Andrews," Allen said. "The chopper will meet us there to take us to the White House."

"You're telling me I'm going meet with the president today? Today?" I repeated, looking at my watch. "That's not possible. Even if we left now, we wouldn't arrive until the middle of the night."

"We're not flying commercial," Allen said.

"Even if it's a military jet, it's not going to get there today," I said, glancing again at my watch. The twin limos pulled up to the front gate of the Jardin des Tuileries. "Drive along the alley just past the Orangerie," I instructed the driver. "How are we flying?"

"Blackbirds," he said.

"Blackbirds?"

"SR-71 Blackbird. It's a top-secret jet that does Mach 3.2 at eighty-five thousand feet. We should be at Andrews in about two hours, depending on how the air-to-air refueling goes."

"Allen, I don't do roller coasters, and you're telling me we're going to cross the Atlantic at Mach 3.2?" I said, my eyes wide open, my voice trembling.

"Robbie, the commander in chief has directed—"

"Allen, I'm not military. I'm a student, a civilian, remember?"

"You're a student in handcuffs and in big trouble, and I'm taking you to the only person on the planet who can get you off the hook," he lectured. "Besides, I took the Blackbird here this morning, and it wasn't that bad," he added with a smile.

"Not that bad?"

"Well, except for the takeoff; that was like a rocket launch," he said, his smile quickly disappearing.

"Rocket launch?"

"Yes, when the afterburner lit, it got a bit hairy, but you're in better shape than me, and you'll get used to the space suit and the pure oxygen pretty quickly."

"Christ, Allen, are you for real?" He handed me a handkerchief to wipe the sweat off my brow, which was no easy task in the cuffs. "Pull over there," I pointed to a clearing at the side of the alley. "Take off the cuffs and I'll get the bottle," I said, thinking this was my moment to escape.

"No way," the agent in the front seat spoke up. "The cuffs stay on until you suit up for the Blackbird. We'll go with you." He glanced at the agents from the second car who by now stood alongside our car. I looked over at Allen who offered zero comfort or support

"Don't even think about it," Allen said.

We jumped out of the car and one of the agents jimmied the lock on the small gate. We moved quickly through the park to the place where My Hanh and I had made love only four days earlier. There was the oak tree, and the bottle just as I had left them the night before. An agent grabbed the bottle and we headed back. I thought again about escaping. *If I could dash off and lose them among the trees. . . but where will I go from there?* With the resources of the CIA and the NSA mobilized to catch me, I would not get very far. *Christ, I'm in handcuffs and the agents are packing colt pistols!*

"Glad you decided to return," Allen said as we jumped back in the cars. The agent handed him the bottle. He struggled to pull out the cork to retrieve the tightly rolled-up paper and the chip. He examined both before slipping them into a red file.

"Allen, I need to talk with you before we meet the president," I said as the cars sped off toward Le Bourget. "I need to talk through how I should handle this, okay?"

He cast me a blank stare.

"Allen, please!"

"I'm flying in a second Blackbird right next to yours. We'll have a radio hookup, so we can talk on the way."

"I'm scared, Allen."

"You should be," he responded. "You really fucked up."

The driver radioed ahead of our impending arrival. Allen explained that before the flight we would eat a low-residue meal of steak and eggs, and a military doctor would examine us. After that, we would suit up in the same suits used by astronauts and begin the process of adjusting to breathing pure oxygen.

"Allen, I really don't think I can handle this," I said, growing more nervous about the flight. "I've never told you, but I'm phobic about airplanes. I've never taken one. Only boats and trains!"

"Samberg, cool it, man . . . You're not going to die! I'll be up there too, so just relax, will you?"

"No way," I mumbled as the car sped through the morning mist and pulled into Le Bourget.

We drove to a remote corner of the airport, through two sets of barbed-wire gates with checkpoints, and out onto the runway, pulling up to the twin Blackbirds, which ground crews were preparing for takeoff. We entered a flight trailer sitting next to the planes, where at last, the cuffs were removed and we were checked by a doctor, and served a meal just as Allen had described. We donned our flight suits, climbed aboard the planes and fastened the safety belts. I could feel myself breathing the oxygen in my helmet as I watched Allen's Blackbird blast down the runway and lunge straight up as the afterburner lit.

In a moment the plane disappeared, and it was our turn. I prayed and held my breath as the J58 engines roared their thirty-two thousand pounds of thrust, enough to drive an ocean liner. The sky was clear and the weather good, and my heart pounded. To get off the ground, the Blackbirds took off with a limited amount of fuel, so moments after takeoff they had to rendezvous with a KC-135Q Stratotanker to take on the fuel necessary to cross the Atlantic at supersonic speeds. I watched as Allen's Blackbird filled up next to us and a second tanker pulled up to rendezvous with our plane. The four planes lumbered in the air as if in a warm-up lap before the flag would drop and the race would begin.

I heard Allen's voice crackling through the headphones: "Robbie, you still alive over there?"

"Alive but scared shitless."

"Good preparation for meeting the boss."

I could hear him chuckling over the radio.

"Okay, so let's start with what you'll need to know," Allen began, trying to comfort me and raising his voice to be heard above the roar of the engines. "First, the important stuff: he's a rabid UCLA fan, so if all else fails, tell him you think they're a sure bet for the NCAA championship . . . and he likes Ohio State for college football."

"Are you nuts?" I asked, clinging with my gloved hands to the metal console in front of me. "Allen," I screamed through the intercom as the afterburners in both jets lit again and shot us through the sky to supersonic speeds.

"Mach Two," Allen screamed back.

"Oh my God." I was crushed into the seat by the g-force.

"Steady, Robbie boy," I heard Allen say over the static.

"Get me the fuck out of here!"

"Mach Three," Allen yelled as the planes rose above seventy thousand feet and the curvature of the earth appeared below.

We leveled off, and my body began to adjust.

"You calming down a bit?" Allen asked.

"Oh, calm as can be," I responded.

"All right then," Allen said. "Hankie is worried about the president."

"What do you mean?" I asked, my eyes dazzled by the sight out my window. "I'm nauseous," I added.

"It will pass."

"Great. It better."

"It's the stress. Hankie told me that since he dropped out of the race, he's been working himself to death, trying to turn things around. He has positioned himself above politics in the pursuit of peace. He wants that for the country and to rescue his legacy."

"He must be under incredible pressure," I said.

"You know he has a heart thing, and Hankie said he hasn't been sleeping well. The last time Hankie saw him he was miserable, fighting off a lingering cold, and short-tempered as hell."

"Sounds like how I'll feel if we ever get off this damn spaceship," I said. "It's hot in here!"

"Considering the fuselage is about five hundred degrees right now, you're not doing badly." I could see the glow surrounding the titanium skin of the aircraft.

At an hour and a half into the flight, the pilot came on the intercom to announce that we were beginning our descent to Andrews. He warned it would be steep, and I felt more extreme nausea until the wheels finally touched down and the parachute deployed to slow the plane. When the Blackbirds rolled to a stop, the ground crews pulled back the canopies, and we climbed down in front of the waiting helicopter, emblazoned with the seal of the president of the United States. I felt like kneeling and kissing the runway, but there was no time.

We entered a trailer identical to the one at Le Bourget, which was parked next to the helicopter, for another med check and a quick change of clothes. My suit, which had been packed in the plane, was wrinkled, but I was relieved to put it on again.

A tall man in a dark suit entered the trailer holding a set of handcuffs and approached me. "We need to cuff you again, Samberg," he said.

"Oh no, please, no!"

Allen reached out and grabbed the agent's arm, pulling it down and handed him a telephone receiver. The agent listened, uttering "yes, sir" several times, then turned and left the trailer.

"Thank you!" I looked at Allen. He nodded and we hurried to the chopper. As soon as we boarded, the motor revved, the blades whirled, and we lifted off for our final destination, the White House.

"Welcome aboard Marine One," a voice announced through the intercom. "This is Captain Spiars. Our flight time is approximately one-half hour. Please let the steward know if you need anything."

Quaalude!

Allen and I sat in the comfortable leather chairs and continued to talk. I was still feeling sick from the changes in altitude and the shock to my body of supersonic flight. My head hurt. My breathing felt funny. I was a mess.

"Thanks again for the handcuff thing," I said.

"Now that we're back in the States, the CIA has no authority to cuff you," he said.

"Look, can we please get real? All I did was fall in love with a girl from the wrong part of Vietnam!" I had to yell to be heard above the noise of the rotor blades.

Allen responded with a blank expression. "I deserve credit, not handcuffs for letting you know that Nixon was monkey-wrenching with the peace talks!"

"Let's hope LBJ sees it that way," he finally responded. "But sometimes innocent men are found guilty, Robbie. Remember Dreyfus." He held up the red X file.

"You know about Dreyfus?" I asked incredulously.

"Every serious student of European history knows about Dreyfus and the letter he didn't write which was used to convict him."

"The bordereau, the French letter written on tissue paper, unsigned and undated," I gasped, recollecting my conversation with Ronen in the Marais.

"Yes," Allen said. "Dreyfus never wrote the letter, but when a French housekeeper at the German embassy brought it to French counterespionage, they used it to convict an innocent man. If this X file falls into the hands of those looking for a scapegoat . . ."

"They found an innocent Jew to blame for the leaks at the French Military Intelligence service, the only Jew the French general staff had ever promoted," I said.

"You need to be prepared for anything, Robbie, especially if LBJ doesn't buy your story, and who knows what will happen if Nixon gets elected?" he warned. "I've heard from a friend inside the Nixon camp that he is anti-Semitic—he often talks about not trusting Jews."

"I met a Hassidic scholar in Paris who told me about Dreyfus and anti-Semitism," I said.

"I hope he's praying for you," Allen said, shaking his head as the helicopter rolled to the right, making its turn from Virginia to the District of Columbia. "Robbie, I'm not sure where this is going, but we're about to find out."

Allen was being kind, I knew. The risk I'd taken by falling in love with My Hanh and helping her father hit me now as it never had before. I was about to hand over documents to the president of the United States that could send Richard Nixon to jail and rock the politics of the nation. If the wrong people learned of my involvement, there was no telling what they might do to me and to my family. And like Dreyfus, I was a Jew in a nation where anti-Semitism still existed.

The helicopter swooped in low over the Potomac River, passed the Jefferson Memorial, and, just before the Washington Monument, swung left and quickly set down on the White House lawn, where two uniformed ushers waited to escort us inside. We had been in Paris just two and a half hours before. It was 5:30 a.m. Washington, DC time and we had left Le Bourget at 9 a.m. French time, so adjusting for the time difference, we had arrived before we departed.

"Mr. Samberg, right this way," the usher said, reaching out to greet me as I stepped down from the helicopter, the blades still whirling above.

I followed, my head pounding from the Blackbird flight and the abject fear I felt about my circumstance and meeting the president of the United States. *Great moment to be suffering an awful headache.* Allen had warned me about Johnson. Under the best of circumstances, he could be earthy, moody, and hot tempered, and these were definitely not the best of circumstances.

We walked across the lawn toward the Oval Office, Allen just behind me carrying the red X file in his right hand and accompanied by the second usher.

Senator Hankie met us outside the French doors in the Rose Garden and pulled Allen off to the side just out of earshot. I waited nervously with the ushers as the two of them spoke privately, taking in the beauty of the lawn we had just crossed and the VH-3 helicopter now sitting silently on its pad, the sun illuminating the presidential seal and the words "United States of America" written in navy blue on the side. It was an impressive sight.

"Robbie, the president wants to see you alone in the residence," Allen reported after breaking away from Hankie and returning to me.

Hankie disappeared via the French doors.

"Alone?"

"If he's meeting you in the residence, he'll probably go easier than if he met you with the boys in the Oval . . . Lady Bird is up there, and that's good. He's generally on his best behavior within earshot of the Bird."

"The Bird?" I asked, recalling that My Hanh's name in English was Lucky Bird.

"That's his nickname for Lady Bird. Her real name is Claudia, but you won't hear him call her that. Here, take the X file," he said, handing it to me.

"Oh great, Allen, just great," I responded, my teeth chattering, my wrinkled suit soaked with perspiration.

One of the ushers led me through a white exterior door farther down the walkway, and we continued through a maze of hallways to a private elevator—smaller than I would have thought for a six-foot-four president of the United States. There was room for just the two of us. The elevator quickly climbed two floors and opened into a small rectangular den with a large window overlooking the Old Executive Office Building next to the White House. The window was round at the top and flat at the bottom, covering the entire wall, with billowing lace drapes opened to afford a spectacular view.

The usher led me to an armchair just across from a plush, comfortable-looking blue couch. He poured me a coffee in a gold-rimmed porcelain cup, offered me cream and sugar, and departed. I sat alone in silence, looking at every detail of the room, the rich, dense, pale-blue carpet, the inlayed mahogany coffee table between the chair and couch in front of me, the lace curtains offsetting the windows, and the bright-red telephone sitting alone on a side table against the wall. Next to the phone was an electronic device with a typewriter keyboard and a screen.

"Young man," bellowed a throaty voice in a Southern drawl as a tall man with large ears, furrowed brow, thin greying hair and clear-rimmed glasses sauntered into the room and sat down on the couch just in front of me. "You mind telling me why in the hell you were hanging around in Paris with the North Vietnamese delegation?" he asked, looking directly into my eyes and leaning toward me, his head almost touching mine. He was dressed in a dark-blue silk robe with matching slippers, the presidential seal on the upper-left-hand pocket of the robe. He gave a half smile and waited for my response. There appeared no need for introductions or pleasantries.

"Mr. President, sir," I said, teeth chattering, mouth dry, wiping my palms on my pants and responding slowly, "it was not really that I was hanging around with them; it was just that I happened to fall in love with My Hanh, the daughter of their foreign minister."

"So, you hung around long enough to fall in love . . . Is that it, son?" He raised his bushy eyebrows as if to debunk what I had just told him.

"Sir, I swear I didn't know she was from North Vietnam when I saw her in the Métro and I fell in love with her at first sight. She was in distress. I helped her to escape from a disgruntled French soldier, who was seeking to harm her, and after that—well, you know what happens when you meet the girl of your dreams. It all just snowballed, and the next thing I knew I was seeing stars and lost all sense of proportion about everything. All I could think about was her and, you know, when I finally learned who she was and where she was from, I didn't give a damn about it. I just knew that I loved her, and the thought of losing her, never seeing her again, breaks my heart." Somewhere in there, my teeth had stopped chattering.

"And her father told you to tell Hoffers that Anna Chennault was delivering messages from Nixon to the South Vietnamese and that she was telling them to scuttle my peace overtures because he would get them a better deal. Is that it, son?" he asked, looking into my eyes.

"Yes, that's it, sir."

There followed an uncomfortable silence, during which his gaze continued to bore straight through me, seeming to size me up and take the measure of what I had said.

"Let me see that file, son."

He took the paper from the red X file, removed the silicon chip, and carefully placed it in a small tray which ejected from the side of the machine on the counter. The machine lit up, and the transcript of Chennault's conversations appeared on the screen. He stood for a few minutes scrolling down and reading the documents. He looked carefully at the photos of John Mitchell entering the Chennault apartment.

"Damn, that two-timing SOB," he snarled.

He pressed a button on the coffee table and sat down. An aide quickly entered the room.

"Get me Dick Russell at home," he told him.

"You know what, son?" he said, leaning even closer to me and placing his large hand on my right shoulder. "I happen to know you didn't have time for breakfast this morning, so why don't you grab some of that White House French toast up there on the counter"—pointing to my right—"take some more coffee, and we can continue our little talk? Head hurt? That's a rough flight on the Blackbird. I understand from Hoffers you're planning a career in government. Is that right?"

"Yes, sir. Maybe politics."

"Well now, that's my profession and it was my daddy's, and I know something about it, and I will tell you right off that falling in love with a communist was probably not the best thing you could have done for a political career. Don't you agree, son?"

"Yes, sir."

The red phone rang and Johnson picked it up.

"Good morning, Dick, is that you? Now I've got someone here, but I've got a good one for you. Remember our conversation about our friend from California? Well, you were right. You are always right about people, my friend. Remember what I told you about the China lobby, the Chennault rumor? Well, I now know it's true. I have seen the transcripts. While our friend has said all the right things to my face, he's been sticking it to me behind my back. He's got this Chennault woman visiting the embassy and telling them I am going to sell them out, like Yalta and Potsdam, and warning them not to let me take away their liberty just months before he will be elected and will protect them. Can you imagine that? The SOB is a real two-timer, Dick. Now I cannot go into more right now, but I wanted you to know and I want you to call Dirksen and tell him he needs to get to Nixon and stop this shit, and he needs to do it right now. You do that and call me back when you're done."

He hung up the phone and turned back to me. "Tell me about the meetings and dinners you had with Le Duc Tho and Xuan Thuy. What did you learn?"

"I didn't have dinner with Thuy, only with Tho, who wanted to thank me for helping his daughter in the Métro. He was very nice, very smart, and very well informed."

"Don't you think when he saw you on TV that he also wanted to learn about the antiwar movement, to gauge its strength?"

"I told him I wasn't really the leader of the French student movement. I was filling in for a friend, but those images on television were very powerful."

"Yes, I saw the tapes. You certainly acted like the leader. So what did you learn?" Johnson asked again.

"From the demonstrations?"

"No, son, from Tho."

"I learned that Tho is more nationalist than communist. He's motivated by a centuries-old desire for independence and unification, long denied Vietnam by the Chinese, the French, the Japanese, and now America. That's why they fight."

The president nodded, leaned close again, and placed his large hand back on my shoulder. "Son," he said in a soft voice, "last night I was on the phone with Kosygin, and he's sending troops into Prague to crush the Prague Spring, so you really can't trust these communists. You're thinking with your pecker, not with your brain."

"No, Mr. President."

"Listen to me, son. Nobody wants to end this war more than I do, and I'm ready to do some big things to get it done. I see the turmoil and strife all around. I've got the deaths of boys like you on my mind all the time. Every morning I look out these windows and I don't like the landscape I see—McCarthy and Kennedy second-guessing me, and now Nixon undercutting me. I've got my boy Chuck fighting over there, and I feel what all parents feel about war. I want it to end, but my job is to end it in a way that won't give the green light to communist aggression around the world. It's a harder job than anyone can imagine. Whether you believe me or not, I don't want the death of another boy on my watch." He removed his hand from my shoulder and rubbed it across his forehead as if to wipe away what looked to me like genuinely felt pain.

"Are you okay, sir?"

Somehow the question just dropped from my lips, and I feared it might not be well received, but instead he warmed to me.

He grabbed a tissue and blew his stuffed nose. Then he rubbed his bloodshot eyes. "Son, I am trying to negotiate a bombing pause and get peace talks started, but I need to do it in a way that works for the United States. We can't just cut and run on this, and I know this country is tired of war, but I must hand this off to the next president without hell breaking loose somewhere else," he said, looking down at the floor in a more vulnerable way than I had ever seen him on television.

"Do you think that could be Nixon?" I asked.

"I hate to say it, but it's looking that way. He's a dishonest shit, but he probably has the best grip on his party and their delegates, and he's going to be tough to beat for the nomination. I used to get along well with Dick. He was there for me when I returned to the Senate after my heart attack. He put the country first after we roughed him up in the 1960 election. I respected the guy, but this Chennault thing . . . What scares me is that this time he wants to win so badly, he's willing to interfere with my peace negotiations."

"Are you angry enough about it to run again?"

"You know, son, I have told the country I will not run, and I can still beat any Republican, but I'll let you in on a little secret: I'm tired here, and this country I love is in a crisis, and the best thing I can do now may be to keep out of politics to get everybody on board to end the war."

"But will you think about—?"

"Son, I don't think anyone can run for president and at the same time run a war in its fifth year and negotiate a complicated peace. It's a big job, and you've got to be on top of the Congress, the candidates, Hanoi, Saigon, the Paris delegation, the Russians, and so on and so on."

"You haven't exactly left any Democrat with an easy road forward."

"Look, son, I'm talking straight here. This job is a lot harder than anyone realizes, and while you're here you just want to do the right thing, but presidents don't control as much as people think. There's a lot of shit in the barn right now—the war, the Cold War, the Black Power movement, the antiwar movement, the violence in the streets, the fear . . . I don't think anybody could have shoveled all that and come out smelling like a rose. There are days I want to take Bird's hand, march on out of here, and head back to the ranch, where we can mind the herds and play with our radio stations."

"Radio stations?" I remembered the first time we met at Senator Hankie's office, when he told me about these. "That's my father's dream—to own a radio station," I said.

"Well, they don't belong to me. They belong to Bird, but I kind of help them along where I can—you know, for our retirement. That's your daddy's dream?"

"Yes, sir. He wants to buy a radio station in Florida. He sees it as higher calling than his jukebox business—you know, being a local broadcaster in the community. The president moved his head next to mine again and replaced his hand on my shoulder. "Son, with that nasty dossier following you around, and the good fortune of having a father with his own business, I don't see that there's much choice for you but to finish school, get down to Florida, and let your ole man show you how to make money."

"I just can't imagine working for my father," I said. "We don't get along at all."

"Son, I don't give a rat's ass about whether you get along! You may fight with your father, compete with him, and you may wound each other and it may hurt, but you are still blood, and if you do your job, he'll come around to understanding and appreciating you. They always do."

"I tell you he just doesn't get me and he doesn't like me," I insisted.

"Son, your talking like a child!" he scolded.

"It's complicated!" I said.

"You know, son, a lot of people urged me to stop the bombing without preconditions, but the generals told me that would put our boys at risk, and I was not going to do that. So, I've taken a lot of flak. I've been hit and hit again, even as I've been working to get the bombing halt done right. I finally got the North to agree to stop infiltrating along the DMZ, to stop shelling the cities and to sit down and talk to the South in return for the pause. Those are big concessions, and now this Chennault thing has thrown a monkey wrench into the works. Talk about complicated." He shook his head.

"How would your father have handled this?"

"I think he would have sent the FBI to arrest Nixon and thrown his ass in jail for treason."

"Seriously?"

He looked up at me, bowed his head next to mine, placing his other hand on my shoulder. I could almost feel him thinking through his tightening grip. "Damn that Nixon," he whispered. "He works through intermediaries. Even with the transcripts and photos you brought today, we still don't have his fingerprints on a smoking gun."

"So?"

"On second thought, he continued, "if my daddy was sitting in the Oval Office and saw the problems the country faced today, I think he would find a quieter way to deal with Nixon.

He wouldn't want to upset the nation with another shock at a time when belief in government has already been so damaged. I think he would work behind the scenes to get Nixon to stand down." He paused, then smiled at an epiphany. "He would have made sure that somebody would be secretly left in the government to keep an eye on the bastard after he left office, maybe a mole deep inside the FBI."

"I wonder if allowing a man like Nixon to take power might be worse than confronting him now and preventing the damage it's a sure bet he'll do in the future."

"That's a good question, Robbie. But I won't decide how I'll deal with Nixon until I speak to my closest advisors, and the last time I looked, you are not one of them," he said, closing the subject. It was clear by the look on his face that he was angry, and that whatever he chose to do would have the desired effect.

The president lowered his head and let his large body droop down, as if to convey he was out of steam, and in the moment of silence that followed I realized that I had just witnessed a side of him that few had ever seen. LBJ looked up, his eyes on mine like lasers, and yet again moved his head just next to mine, and in a whisper said, "Son, when you came here today, I really thought you might be leaving in hand cuffs. There's an FBI team downstairs waiting for the word from me to arrest you. But that's not going to happen." I sighed deeply, the sword of Damocles lifted from above my head.

Lady Bird entered the room. We both stood. She wore a bright-red dress with a single strand of white pearls around her neck, her jet-black hair coiffed to perfection. "Bird, this is Robbie Samberg, who used to work for Lance Hankie and Allen Hoffers at Foreign Relations. He's just visiting from Paris, where he's had some interesting experiences he shared with me."

"So very nice to meet you," Mrs. Johnson said turning to the president and glancing at her watch as if to underscore that they were running late.

"Funny," I blurted. "My Hanh's name in English means Lucky Bird. Maybe I'll start calling her that when I return to Paris."

"Now that's a real coincidence," LBJ said, slapping me on the back. Lady Bird left the room.

"Robbie, when you get back, there's something I need you to do for me.

"What sir?"

"I want you to deliver a personal message to Monsieur X."

Here we go again!

"From what you have told me, I think Tho likes you and trusts you. Please tell him I'm willing to meet him half way to get this war stopped. Tell him if we can establish some trust, we can get a bombing halt in place by Christmas. It will be our Christmas gift to the people of America and Vietnam.

I sat down, dumbfounded.

"Now not a word about this to anyone," he warned, "not to Hoffers or Hankie or anyone."

"Mr. President, I'm—"

Lady Bird Johnson entered the room again. "Lyndon, we have breakfast with the Fulbright's in forty-five minutes, and you have to get ready," she said.

"Bird, how are the radio stations doing?" the president asked.

"Now Lyndon, you know we're number one in every market, and revenues are up forty-three percent over last year," she said.

"Now that's what I like to hear, son," he said, looking at me.

I must have appeared ghostlike, the blood having drained from my head, the empty capillaries in search of replenishment to bring the color back to my vacant face.

"Time to move along, son," he said.

Lady Bird left us again as quickly as she had come in. The president stood up as if getting ready to leave. I did the same.

I reached out to shake hands and say goodbye, and he again put his arms on my shoulders and pulled me close to him.

"Before you head back, Rostow will give you my message for Tho. Just deliver it, son, and tell him what I told you. Speak from your heart. I'm going to keep this X file, and I'll make sure one day it's made public at a time when the country is ready to hear about the real Dick Nixon."

"Yes, sir."

"You do this for me, and you won't have to worry about Mr. Hoover's dossier on you. I'll make sure it goes away."

"And what about My Hanh?" I asked. "What about my Bird?"

LBJ paused and looked at me. "Well, you'll have to work that out on your own, son. I know she's pregnant, and that complicates the thing. I have determined that your love for this girl is no threat to the security of the United States. I may be the only politician in the country willing to give you a pass on that, but until January 20, I'm the only one you need. You stay with her, and while I'm president you'll be left alone—I'll even help you get someplace where you can both live in peace—but there's no way you can stay with her and return home for a career in government or politics. You must make that choice for yourself, and it's a hard one. Next time, son, try falling in love with a capitalist. And don't be a fool: finish college and help your father buy that radio station," he admonished, turning away and handing me off to a White House usher.

Chapter 19

The Letter

The Cadillac pulled away from the traffic at Place de la Concorde and veered over to the entrance of the Hôtel de Crillon. I asked the driver to park and wait, and watched him pull up in front of the American embassy next door, where he was quickly admitted to the grounds. Thanks to President Lyndon B. Johnson, I was the only student in Paris with a government limo and embassy driver. Such were the perks of returning to Paris on a secret mission for the commander in chief.

The Blackbird had landed at 5 p.m. at Le Bourget, and I suffered a powerful jet lag from the two flights in one day. My body clock was scrambled and I was still a mess. I still wore the same crumpled suit I had put on the morning before.

I entered the ornate lobby of the Crillon, the president's personal message safely tucked in my jacket pocket. As instructed, I would hand it directly to Tho and tell him what LBJ asked me to say. "No one else," Rostow had admonished, handing me two sealed envelopes, one for Tho and the other a letter from the president to me.

I approached the front desk, looking from side to side, searching for My Hanh. I longed to see her, to embrace her, and to tell her what had happened. With LBJ's promise of protection, I was confident we would find a way to stay together. She would be happy I was bringing the letter, and her father would be grateful. He would help us, too. This was our ticket to stay together, I thought.

I rang the ornate bell sitting on top of the front desk and waited for the clerk to return. The lobby was quiet, which was unusual for the early-evening hour. I recalled from my prior visits the crowds of well-dressed Parisians and foreigners coming and going, men in black tie, ladies in elegant gowns, on their way to the countless social events held each night in the city of light. At last the clerk returned and greeted me, and I asked her to announce my visit to the fourth floor, to see My Hanh, just as I had on my prior visits. I gave her my full name and handed her my passport, expecting her to accompany me to the private elevator.

She studied the passport but asked me to wait before she disappeared into a back office. A moment later, the clerk returned with another woman, who introduced herself as Madame Cybele, the front desk manager. She, too, carefully examined my passport. She looked me over and invited me to follow her, but instead of taking me to the private elevator or the stairs I had used on past visits, she led me in a different direction.

"Is this the way to the suite?" I asked.

Madame Cybele didn't respond but continued down the corridor, turning into an ornate corner office. On one side I could see the American embassy just across the street through the large, partially opened French windows, and on the other the windows looked out onto the front portico of the grand hotel.

"Please sit down, Mr. Samberg," Cybele said graciously. "I have a letter for you."

I sat on the richly upholstered couch across from her desk.

"A letter for me?"

She handed me an envelope with the name Hôtel de Crillon embossed in gold.

"I am very sorry, Monsieur Samberg," she quickly added, "but the guests on the fourth floor have checked out. They left late last night. Mademoiselle My Hanh left this letter for you," she said, gazing at me now frozen before her, the letter dangling from my right hand.

I could not move. My lungs deflated, a sensation more intense than anything I had felt on the Blackbird. I turned my head toward the tall windows on the far side of the office next to the hotel entrance, where I had embraced My Hanh so many times. I slowly rose from the couch and walked in a trance toward the windows and, reaching them, sank down onto the thickly carpeted floor amid some bags left there next to a brass tree planter, my body limp, my hands shaking as I gripped the letter, short of breath. I tore open the envelope.

My Robbie,

Without warning father has decided to send me back to Peking to end my pregnancy and continue my studies. For security reasons, he has moved the delegation to a new hotel. I am so sorry I could not tell you in person, but he did not tell me until the last minute, when all the arrangements had been made and I could not reach you. If I had, I think it would only have caused us both more pain, so maybe your reading this letter is the best way for us to say goodbye.

As a Buddhist, I try to live my life doing no harm, but I find in this moment if I abandon my family to stay with you and have our child, I do them great harm, and if I abandon you to be an obedient daughter, I do you and me great harm. There is no decision here that I feel good to take, but I know you, too, have a family and a home in America, and I thought about how your family would react to your bringing home a girl from North Vietnam. Surely they would not accept me or our child. Surely your

prospects for employment, especially in government and poli-
tics, would be ruined. Few would understand and fewer would
accept us.

I know in my heart as you do in yours that our love is real and
strong, but we do not live in a world of just the two of us. We
live in a world connected to others and connected to our pasts
and to our futures. Now is not the time for us to damage the
worlds from which we came by thinking only of ourselves and
our love and the pain we wish to avoid. We must think of the
greater good, and that means I must return to Peking, and you
must return home to America.

I see the day coming when your Robert Kennedy will win the
election for president, and I fully expect you to return home and
help him get elected. Then I hope you will serve in his govern-
ment and help end the war. I know one day you will become a
great leader yourself and help restore your nation to its highest
ideals.

If I came with you and bore our child, none of that would be
possible. I would only be in your way, and that's something I can-
not do. So now I must go, even though there is so much I have
not yet said, so much we have not yet done, but please know as
you read this letter that you will always occupy a special place
in my heart, as I know I occupy a special place in yours. No mat-
ter where life takes us, no matter how many decades we may be
apart, one day, if not in this lifetime, then in the next we shall
be together again, and until that moment comes I shall hold you,
my Robbie, and I shall never let you go. Hold me, too!

I love you!

My Hanh

I sat motionless on the floor until Madame Cybele, seeing
how I suffered, kneeled down to assure me I could stay as long
as I needed. She placed her hand on my shoulder and held it
there for a few moments. Then she left and moments later re-

turned with a tray of hot tea and pastries, which she placed on the table in front of the couch. She helped me get up and led me back to the couch. I could not speak.

Thinking back to that early evening at the Hôtel de Crillon, reading My Hanh's letter, collapsing on the floor of Madame Cybele's office, I have no idea how long I sat there on the carpet or on the couch, or whether I drank the tea she brought to me or ate the pastries from the silver tray beside the teapot, but at some point, when the shock and fog had lifted, I recall that Cybele sat down beside me, placed her hand on my arm in consolation, and led me back to the lobby. I remained in a state of shock, feeling confused and empty, observing everyone and everything around me but unable to formulate my thoughts, much less articulate them.

Madame Cybele tried to console me, offering me more time, perhaps a drink or dinner or anything I might have asked for. She was incredibly kind and patient. She volunteered the hotel limo to take me home. I couldn't remember where home was—last time I felt conscious, I had been in the White House talking to the president of the United States. Now I was back in Paris, and it took a moment for me to recall my room at Madame Gueumier's apartment. I realized that was where I needed to go, and I remembered that I had a driver waiting outside to take me.

It was the saddest ride I had ever taken, looking out the car window at the sidewalks crammed with couples walking hand in hand, embracing by café tables, kissing passionately at corners waiting to cross the busy streets. Every public display of affection exploded the sadness I felt at the loss of My Hanh and the child I would never know. For a long time, I could not be consoled, and the darkness in my shattered heart remained, immune even to the charms and distractions of Paris.

Chapter 20

Heading Home

As a high school student, I had idolized John F. Kennedy and was seduced by his charisma. I used to love to watch his nationally televised press conferences. He was the first president to use television in this way, and he had the intelligence, wit, and charm to pull it off. He inspired an entire generation to get involved and created hope that young people working for their country could make a difference. Amidst the tumult of 1968, with the ship of state tossed by heavy seas, unmoored from the anchors of optimism created by Jack Kennedy, I found myself turning to the candidacy of his brother Robert.

As I slowly recovered from the shock of My Hanh's departure, the words of her letter resonated, and I decided that upon my return home I would volunteer for the Kennedy campaign. *He and Martin Luther King are the keys to changing the direction of America.* Only they could keep us from falling off the cliff of social unrest toward which we were headed. Kennedy and King would come together, I thought, as moderate voices to appeal to the majority of whites and blacks and create a message of unity and hope instead of division and fear.

Then one fateful day, as I waited for Nastovich's class to begin, a student rushed into the classroom to tell us he had heard on the radio that someone had shot Martin Luther King. My heart broke as I thought of what this would mean for America.

311

How can a country endure so much damage? How can anyone turn the Black Panthers away from violence after this? We are heading off the cliff.

Nastovich digressed from his scheduled lecture that day to talk about the assassination and what it meant. His assessment was more optimistic than I expected.

"It will be tumultuous for awhile as black people vent their rage, and they will likely strike out and the credibility of the radicals will be enhanced," he predicted. "But communities recover. The vast majority of blacks are not radical and will not be radicalized even at so great a blow."

I listened to him making the same argument I had made to the Panthers at the jazz club, but with King shot dead, I was no longer buying it. I wondered if Nastovich would feel the same way had he been with me that night, had he known about the guns the Panthers tried to buy from Algeria. For the first time, Nastovich was the optimist and I was the pessimist. I prayed I was wrong, but I saw nothing but danger ahead.

As Paris degenerated into mass pandemonium, I found myself increasingly sidelined from participation in what I felt was a world coming apart. I walked the streets with my Kodak Brownie and my tape recorder, interviewing protesters and capturing the sounds of a hundred thousand people marching through the streets. This time they marched not to oppose de Gaulle but to support him and to oppose the chaos that had ensued after the workers had joined the students in shutting down the nation.

De Gaulle secretly flew to Baden-Baden to get the support of General Massu and the French army in Germany. He told Massu, "I cannot fight against apathy, against the desire of a whole people to let itself break apart." Massu assured de Gaulle that the army would remain loyal and struck a deal of support in return for de Gaulle's granting of amnesty to soldiers jailed since a 1961 coup attempt in Algeria. The next day de Gaulle returned to Paris and addressed the nation by radio, as he had from London during World War Two. *"Française, Français, je ne me retirerai pas,"* he declared—"I shall not resign."

He rallied a nation tired of chaos and longing for stability. He mocked the demands of the student protesters as *chienlit* "shit in bed," and accused the communists of seeking "an international autocracy." He dissolved the National Assembly and announced that a general election would take place in June. He demanded that workers return to work, or a "state of emergency" would be called and "appropriately tough" action taken.

As he spoke, army troops moved toward Paris, and tanks were stationed on the ring road surrounding the city. The march of support that followed the speech was a sight to behold, thousands of French flags waved in a kaleidoscope of red, white, and blue. I witnessed the mass demonstration and heard the roar of a hundred thousand people chanting in unison against the communists and the radical students.

For the remainder of my time in Paris, I could not stop thinking about My Hanh, but I had no way to contact her. She'd left no forwarding address or telephone. The only portal to reach her was the hole in the oak tree in the Jardin des Tuileries, where I'd left the president's message for Tho. I knew Tho would get it, but I also knew any letter from me to My Hanh would not be forwarded.

Perhaps it was for the best. Perhaps, as My Hanh had written, this clean break, this guillotine-like severing—so abrupt, unanticipated, and painful—was the best way for us both to recover from the heartache. I knew she was suffering as I was, and no distraction could lessen the pain. I grieved every time I walked past a place we had been together or thought about what she had said or done, or what she might say or do. It was as if a part of me had been cut off but I could still feel it as it once was, like a soldier in war who loses a limb but can still feel it. My Hanh and our child were gone, but their presence lingered in my heart and mind, and it hurt badly.

In late May, I ran into Christine René again and told her the truth and apologized for deceiving her on the ship. She had calmed down by then and, hearing that I was more middle class than first class, she warmed to me and listened sympathetically as I told her about My Hanh and my broken heart. She had completed her art classes and did not lose her tuition. She spoke again of the loss of her first love, killed in the LA riots, and her struggle to get over it. We talked about the process of grieving and what a strange and unpredictable journey it could be. In our mutual consolation, we grew closer and became friends.

Madame Gueumier also consoled me when I told her about My Hanh. She, too, had lost her true love, and she understood how I felt and how long it might take to heal. Her support helped me get through the rest of the school year.

After the King shooting, riots broke out in Boston, New York, Newark, Baltimore, Pittsburgh, Cincinnati, Detroit, Chicago, Nashville, Memphis, Kansas City, Oakland, and even in my hometown of Trenton. I worried about my parents and my father's office, which was not far from the inner-city neighborhood in Trenton. I worried about Mary Anderson, the black woman who had worked as our housekeeper for thirty years and who'd lovingly raised my sisters and me.

Robert Kennedy was in his chartered plane in Muncie, Indiana, when he learned the news of King's shooting. He took off for a previously scheduled campaign rally in Indianapolis and upon landing there learned that King had died. His wife, Ethel, asked him to cancel the appearance, but he refused, and he drove with a single aide, Fred Dutton, to the black wards, the inner city of downtown Indianapolis, where a thousand people, still unaware of King's shooting, waited to see and hear him.

"I have some bad news for you," he told the crowd in a hushed voice, amplified by a portable speaker mounted to the flatbed truck on which he stood. "Bad news for all our fellow citizens and for people who love peace all over the world, and that news is that Martin Luther King was shot and killed tonight."

The crowd murmured in shock as Kennedy's words sank in, and cries of grief echoed throughout the cold night air. Speaking extemporaneously, Kennedy continued solemnly: "Martin Luther King dedicated his life to love and to justice for his fellow human beings, and he died because of that effort. On this difficult day, in this difficult time for the United States, it is perhaps well to ask what kind of a nation we are and what direction we want to move in. For those of you who are black, considering the evidence there evidently is that there were white people who were responsible, you can be filled with bitterness, with hatred, and a desire for revenge. We can move in that direction as a country, in great polarization—black people amongst black, white people amongst white, filled with hatred toward one another. Or we can make an effort, as Martin Luther King did, to understand and to comprehend, and to replace that violence, that stain of bloodshed that has spread across our land, with an effort to understand with compassion and love.

"For those of you who are black and are tempted to be filled with hatred and distrust at the injustice of such an act against all white people, I can only say that I feel in my own heart the same kind of feeling. I had a member of my family killed, but he was killed by a white man . . . We have to make an effort in the United States; we have to make an effort to understand, to go beyond these rather difficult times." Then he quoted the poet Aeschylus. "'In our sleep, pain which we cannot forget falls drop by drop upon the heart until, in our own despair, against our will, comes wisdom through the awful grace of God.'

"What we need in the United States is not division; what we need in the United States is not hatred; what we need in the United States is not violence or lawlessness but love and wisdom and compassion toward one another and a feeling of justice toward those who still suffer within our country, whether they be white or they be black. So I shall ask you tonight to return home, to say a prayer for the family of Martin Luther King, that's true, but more importantly to say a prayer for our own country, which all of us love—a prayer for understanding and that compassion of which I spoke."

The crowd of black Americans applauded, warming to Kennedy's sincerity and his sensitivity. He continued to speak from his heart, calmly, thoughtfully, his voice steady.

"We can do well in this country. We will have difficult times. We've had difficult times in the past. We will have difficult times in the future. It is not the end of violence; it is not the end of lawlessness; it is not the end of disorder. But the vast majority of white people and the vast majority of black people in this country want to live together, want to improve the quality of our life, and want justice for all human beings who abide in our land. Let us dedicate ourselves to what the Greeks wrote so many years ago: 'To tame the savageness of man and to make gentle the life of this world.' Let us dedicate ourselves to that and say a prayer for our country and for our people."

There were no riots that night in Indianapolis. And when I read this speech the next day in the *International Herald-Tribune*, I knew what I needed to do. I could not wait to get home and work for the Kennedy campaign. There was no other American politician who could have spoken that way at a moment like that. He was special, and those remarks that night touched my heart and cemented my loyalty.

I imagined My Hanh reading those words, and saw the magnificent smile of admiration that I knew would come to her face. She would understand how I felt and know what it meant to me. With a newfound focus I completed the school year. I looked forward to seeing Allen again and resuming my life in Washington. I looked forward to seeing my family.

I boarded the *Queen Elizabeth* once again on June 1, just a week before the California primary, having settled my affairs in Paris and enjoyed a farewell dinner with Madame Gueumier. She put her arms around me the morning of my departure and handed me a precious gift. It was a book on French Indochina, autographed by her late husband and given to her before his final tour. It must have meant a great deal to her, and I was touched beyond words that she gave it to me.

The boat was as grand as ever, and my cabin on the way home was a great improvement over the one I had occupied with Bernie O'Higgins almost a year before. That was because I took my father's advice and handed the steward a fifty-dollar bill. He promptly upgraded me from third to second class. I spent the days on board walking the decks for exercise, reading in the ship's library, and wondering how things were going for Kennedy in California. *This will be a make-or-break primary.* In 1968, ships' newspapers at sea were about activities on board, and there was no way to learn about what was happening in the world. So I speculated and hoped Kennedy would recover from his loss in Oregon, bringing together the moderate white middle class and the disadvantaged blacks and Hispanics, who had not yet turned to radicalism or apathy.

After six days spent pleasantly at sea, I watched from the upper deck as the great ship passed the Statue of Liberty, a gift from the people of France to the people of the United

States. My year in Paris had taught me how much our nation owed to French culture and history. I had learned that without Lafayette and the French fleet, the American experiment in democratic government might not have survived. The French were there at the birth of our nation, and they gave us the republican ideals that became the foundation for our Declaration of Independence.

I thought of Madame Gueumier and her husband as we passed the statue, and I thought of Christine René, Dr. Nastovich, and my friends Danny, Jan, and Pierre from the restaurant Chartier, and the generosity of the taxi driver, Pierre Laboutte. I thought about French history, the periods of chaos and upheaval from which France always managed to recover, and that gave me hope that our nation would find its way as well. If they could, we could.

The boat passed Ellis Island, where my father's parents, Ida and Abe, had landed a century before. The life they led as immigrants in New York was tough, and I thought it wise to remember that. They had nothing, and their son, my father, had nothing. They had to earn everything on their own. They struggled and worked hard so I could stand on the deck of this great ship and spend a year studying abroad, the first member of my family to do so. My father was not affectionate, I thought, but one day I would show affection to my children, and that was all that mattered. I could learn from the past and not be a slave to it. My eyes teared at the thought of the child I had lost.

The tugboats pulled up as the ship approached New York Harbor, where I noticed that the flags were at half-mast. My family was again at the dock and greeted me warmly. My sisters looked well, Lorraine more animated than ever, Dottie looking healthier, both now in therapy thanks to my mother, who finally realized that her dwelling on thinness was not a good thing. *Hallelujah!* I thought when I learned this.

Strangely, unexpectedly, seeing the changes in my family got me to thinking about Andi. I wondered whether she still had feelings for me and whether she might, as Christine had, forgive me for acting like a jerk before I left. Facing her would be a Mississippi moment of another kind, and I decided to call her. I thought about My Hanh's words "to do no harm," about the lotus flowers cleaning up the mud. I would clean up my mud.

To my pleasant surprise, my father put his arms around me on the dock and whispered, "Welcome home, son," carrying on about strange men in black cars watching him from across the street, and finally, it was my mother who held me in her arms, tears in her eyes, and told me that my hero, Robert Kennedy, had won the California primary the night before but had been gunned down at midnight by a disgruntled Arab named Sirhan Sirhan.

"Oh my God!" I screamed. "Oh my God!"

Soon after I left President Johnson's note in the tree, the United States and North Vietnam agreed to begin negotiating. Hanoi announced that Xuan Thuy would head the North Vietnamese delegation at the talks. LBJ chose Ambassador W. Averell Harriman to represent the United States. LBJ and Nixon, two masters of the black arts of politics, continued to eye each other warily, Nixon determined not to have the election stolen by an October surprise, and LBJ furious about Nixon's subterfuge with Anna Chennault.

When news of LBJ's bombing-halt efforts became public, Nixon, with utter insincerity, released the statement, "In the last thirty-six hours I have been advised of a flurry of meetings in the White House and elsewhere on Vietnam. I am told that top officials in the administration have been driving very hard for an agreement on a bombing halt, accompanied by a ceasefire, in the immediate future. I have since learned these reports are true. I am told that this spurt of activity is a cynical last-minute attempt by President Johnson to salvage the candidacy of Mr. Humphrey. This I do not believe."

Johnson was outraged. He received a new NSA intercept of a phone call between Ambassador Diem and President Thiệu. "I am still in contact with the Nixon entourage," Diem told Thiệu, "which continues to be the favorite despite the uncertainty provoked by the news of an imminent bombing halt."

LBJ called Senate Republican Minority Leader Everett Dirksen and said, "It's despicable, and if it were made public I think it would rock the nation!" He raged at Dirksen about Nixon's holier-than-thou "this I do not believe" line. "I thought Dick's statement was ugly the other day, like he had been told that I was a thief, and a son of bitch and so forth, but he knew my mother, and she really wasn't a bitch," he told Dirksen, his voice dripping with sarcasm.

Johnson plotted revenge while manipulating Nixon through others to back off. In a phone call with Nixon and Humphrey, he signaled Nixon that he was onto him. He mentioned some "minor problems" from the "China lobby" and said, with the same utter disingenuousness Nixon had shown him, "I know that none of you candidates are aware of it or responsible for it." But he did know. He had another FBI intercept from the South Vietnamese embassy. This time Anna Chennault was heard to say she was delivering a message from "her boss," and the message was to "hold on, we're gonna win."

Johnson called Senator Dirksen again and cut to the chase, his voice howling, "This is treason!"

Chapter 21

Epilogue

Twenty-Two Years Later

Andi entered my office, not expecting to find me there so late.

"The book?"

"Yes"

"I've done the logs for tomorrow. I have your ticket for the broadcast conference in Singapore and the program. Want me to bring them in?"

"And the side trip to Vietnam?"

"I have that too."

"Anything on Tho?"

"It's throat cancer. He's in an army hospital for treatment."

"Oh my. And My Hanh?"

"Nothing. I've searched everywhere. You'll have to ask him."

"Okay. Let's send the telegram and check the weather in Hanoi. I'll need to know what to pack. Leave it all in my box on your desk."

"Okay, boss. . . until we get home!" She gave me that look.

"Right!" I smiled.

"I'll leave you to your story. Want me to run your bath?"

"No. I don't know how long I'll be."

She closed the door behind her and soon thereafter I heard the sound of her car pulling out of the parking lot. I was alone again—*I remember the day she stormed out of my bathroom in Washington twenty-two years ago.* I never dreamed when I called her again after Paris that I would end up marrying her and that we would go into the radio business with my father. *LBJ, may he rest in peace, is happy!* I looked up at my office wall and saw the photo of a younger me—I hardly recognized him—posing in the Jardin de Tuileries with My Hanh, standing before the great circular fountain, holding our winning sailboats and looking like we owned all the happiness in the world.

The black Volga sped from the airport through noisy streets filled with hundreds of city dwellers on bicycles and almost as many motorbikes, all competing for space with filthy, rusted buses, powered by overhead electric lines that zigzagged over the street like a vast spider web. I was amazed to see what people loaded onto bikes—huge baskets of fruit, vegetables, chickens and ducks, stacks of fish traps, logs, bags of rice, even a slaughtered pig tied to a sling. The scene bore little resemblance to what Americans would think of as a nation's capital in 1990.

Tho's secretary responded to my telegram, inviting me for tea the day of my arrival, just three days following his seventy-ninth birthday. She made no mention of his illness. Twenty-two years had passed since I had last seen him in Paris. I wondered if he would even remember me or the message from President Johnson I had left for him in the oak tree. Mostly, I wondered about My Hanh. *Will I see her? How will that feel?*

The Volga sped on and we passed a tall woman wearing an *áo dài* just like the one My Hanh had worn two decades earlier on the Paris Métro. I remembered her face and figure frozen in time at age eighteen. *What will she look like at age forty?* I was certainly different, my hair cropped short, my face and body fuller. *Will she recognize me if she sees me?*

It was October 13, 1990, the end of summer in Vietnam. It had rained all morning and the Volga did not have air-conditioning. The humidity was insufferable and I sweat right through the light-weight tan suit I'd worn for the occasion. We passed the Imperial Citadel of Thang Long and the Old City Gates. The red bricks at the base of the gates reminded me of the wall surrounding the Nanterre University courtyard where Danny had led the charge against the line of CRS.

After Paris, I did not see Danny again until I ran into him by accident in a Frankfurt bookshop in 1977. He was working there. Andi and I were in Germany on vacation, shopping. Nine years had passed. He recognized me standing in the travel book section and tapped my shoulder.

"The books on Paris are over there," he quipped, his smile lighting up.

My mouth dropped. *"Danny!* My God, Danny!" We hugged and carried on for a few moments and Andi came over and I introduced her. He invited us to dinner, and we spent the evening sharing memories about Paris and the counterculture in 1968.

"I have been working on environmental issues," he said. "You?"

"After Kennedy was killed, I lost hope, spent a few months in limbo, then decided to go into the radio business with my father."

"What, no politics? Any volunteer work?" he asked.

"I'm a Rotarian, but most of my time is spent on the business."

"Too bad! I was counting on you to change the world."

"Right!" I smiled.

Over the years, Danny's views had changed, too. He was more conventional and centrist, not even a remote facsimile of the Danny I knew back then. He talked about writing a book, and I told him I was working on mine.

Then, following a pleasant dinner of Wiener schnitzel prepared by his wife, as he walked us to the door to say goodnight, he told me Jan Miller had died. Charlie Siebel had told him that she died of leukemia shortly after returning home from Paris. *So that's the secret!* He said she told no one about her illness because she didn't want to be pitied in the short time she had left. *So Jan!*

After meeting in Frankfurt, Danny and I corresponded occasionally and when his book came out in 1988, he sent me a signed copy. He wrote an inscription: "We cannot change the past, but we can change the future." *So Danny!*

The Volga arrived at the stately home of Le Duc Tho. It was located on a quiet street that showed no signs of the fierce American bombing that had rocked the city at Christmas time eighteen years before. To force the North Vietnamese to negotiate, Nixon had ordered twenty thousand tons of bombs dropped on Hanoi and Haiphong, killing 1,600 civilians. I clutched the invitation to tea sent to me by Tho's secretary, walked to the entrance, and rang the bell. The driver waited in the car.

"Mr. Samberg? We are expecting you." An elderly housekeeper greeted me at the door with a somber look. She wore a black cotton dress with a large floppy collar. Her pitch-black hair was pulled up into a bun. She led me to the living room, where Tho's secretary waited, rising to greet me warmly, but also with a sad look on her face.

"I am Le Thi Suong," she said, holding out her right hand. She too had black hair pulled straight back and also wore a black dress. She wore large round glasses.

"Mr. Samberg, I am so sorry to tell you that Le Duc Tho passed away last night. There was no way to reach you."

"My God. I am so sorry," I choked.

"In the tradition of our country, there is a public ceremony to honor him today at the Mai Dich Cemetery."

"This is such a shock. I was hoping to see him again."

"He knew you were coming today and on his deathbed, he requested that I ask you to speak at his ceremony. Will you?" she asked.

"Speak . . . at the ceremony . . . today?" I choked again.

"Actually, we must leave now. He wanted you to do it," she repeated.

What will I say?

There was no time for tea. She took me by the arm and led me back outside. The driver got out of the car and walked toward us, surprised to see me again so soon.

"Shall we take my car?" I asked.

"Yes, that would be helpful."

I told the driver to take us to Mai Dich Cemetery. She explained that this was a special resting place for party leaders and celebrated revolutionaries.

I was anxious. I had no time to prepare. I thought about my library on Vietnam. I still had all the books I had read twenty-two years before. I thought of the conversations I had had with Tho. It was so long ago. *Why me? Why would he want me to speak at his funeral?*

The cemetery was not far. We parked and walked through an archway along a narrow path leading to the ceremony. There was a large crowd, with many people in traditional costume wearing conical hats with silk chin straps. We moved through the crowd and stood beside the grave site. Suong spoke and the crowd hushed. She introduced me.

"Before he died, our venerable leader, Comrade Le Duc Tho, asked that we hear today from an American, Mr. Robbie Samberg," she announced. Then she nodded to me. The crowd murmured its surprise. *That was the shortest introduction, ever!*

I looked out at the sea of faces. *What can I say? How will they understand me?* I remembered the day I spoke for Danny on rue Saint Jacques—no script; only the passion of the moment to gather my thoughts and create the words. I had studied this nation. I knew its history. I held great sympathy for its cause and the suffering of its people and great sadness that my own country had done so much damage here. I remembered Tho, his kindness when he learned of my love for his daughter, his carefulness and consideration when he asked me to deliver the X file to Allen. His love and admiration for My Hanh. *Speak from your heart! Speak from your heart!*

"I am honored," I began.

The crowd fell silent. Then my eyes cast down to the first row in the sea of faces and there, rising from a chair, tall, proud, beaming—just as youthful as she was at eighteen—stood My Hanh, looking at me as if nothing had changed in twenty-two years. I gasped but could not stop the crumbling of my emotions, my eyes catching hers again exactly as they once had on the Métro. My heart stopped as I saw her glance to her left—ever so slightly, as she used to do when she spoke volumes with her eyes—and there next to her, tall like her, dignified like her, stately like her, stood a strapping young man. I saw my face in his and I wept for joy.

Acknowledgments

I want to express my admiration and gratitude to the late Allen Hoffard and Rosemary Rorick, whose mentorship will always be treasured.

Thanks, too, to my fellow students in Paris: Richard Kennedy for his enduring friendship and for prompting my memory about events and reviewing early drafts, and to Bill Valenti, Mike Dumez, Mary Rebecca "Reynolds" Weary, Valerie Lofland, LTC, John Wilkins-Wells, and Cynthia Hebert for sharing their recollections of the American College in Paris.

Thanks to my skilled editors, Amy Belding Brown, Marcus Trower, Chris Noel, and Ellen Brock who helped bring this work to life with their talent and advice and to my friend Jang Eun Mi for her encouragement and inspiration.

I also thank the Honorable Linda Dessau, Governor of Victoria, Australia, for making possible my amazing workplace in Paris at 17 Place des Vosges, where most of this book was written. My gratitude as well to Marie-Laurence Marco, librarian at the Maison Victor Hugo, 6 Place des Vosges, where I also worked, and to Brigitte Grosset-Janin, in whose charming apartment at 52 rue des Franc Bourgeois I completed this book.

Special thanks to the first wordsmiths in our family, Leslie Pearl and Deborah Pearl and to Jay Neugeboren for his invaluable assistance.

Greatest thanks to my wife, Dr. Joann Hendelman-Pearl, whose love, support and devotion made the writing of this book possible.

Reading List

This novel takes place in the context of social, political, and historical events at play during 1968 in France, Europe, and the United States, including the war in Vietnam, the Civil Rights Movement, the women's liberation movement, the events of May in Paris, the history of anti-Semitism in France, and the 1968 American presidential election. Readers who want to learn more about these topics will find good instruction in the following:

Paris and France

Barba-Negra, Paul. *Symbolism of Paris, The Sacred Dimension, The Myths*. Paris: Les Editions du Huitieme Jour, 2004.

Barrault, J. L. *Souvenirs Pour Demain*. Paris: Editions Du Seuil, 1972.

Bazin, Germain. *The Louvre*, London: Thames and Hudson, 1966.

Beevor, A., and Cooper, A., *Paris After the Liberation*. London: Penguin, 1994.

Bernstein, Richard. *Fragile Glory, A Portrait of France and the French*. New York: Penguin Group, 1990.

Bizardel, Y. *Sous l'occupation: souvenirs d'un conservateur de musée*. Paris: Calmann-Lévy, 1964.

Bredin, J.-D. *The Affair: The Case of Alfred Dreyfus*. New York: Plunkett Lake Press and George Braziller, 1986.

Cobb, Richard. *Promenades*. Oxford: Oxford University Press, 1980.

Cobb, Richard. *The Streets of Paris*. London: Gerald Duckworth & Co Ltd., 1980

Cobb, Richard. *Tour de France*. London: Gerald Duckworth & Co Ltd., 1976.

Dallas, Gregor. *Métro Stop Paris: An Underground History of the City of Light*. New York: Walker Publishing, 2008.

Horne, Alistair. *Seven Ages of Paris*. New York: Vintage Books, 2002.

Jouve, Daniel and Alice; Grossman, Alvin. *Paris: Birthplace of the USA*. Paris: Grund, 1995.

Kerper, Barrie. *Paris: The Collected Traveler, An Inspired Companion Guide*. New York: Vintage Departures, 2011.

Landes, Sonia; Landes, Allison and Landes, Rebecca. *Paris Walks*. Washington: Owl Books, U.S., 2005.

Lauriston Boubers, Thierry de. *The Kings of France*. Paris: INPI, 1981.

McCullough, David. *The Greater Journey, Americans in Paris*. New York: Simon and Schuster, 2011.

Maisel, Eric. *A Writer's Paris, A Guided Journey for the Creative Soul*. Cincinnati: Writer's Digest Books, 2005.

1968 Michelin France. Paris: Pneu Michelin, 1968.

Middleditch, Michael. *The Paris Map Guide, Fifth Edition*. London: Penguin Random House UK, 2012.

Platt, Polly. *French or Foe*. London: Culture Crossings, 2005.

Procope, Francois. *Le Procope*. Paris: Le Procope, 2015.

Paxton, R. *Vichy France: Old Guard and New Order*. New York: Knopf Doubleday Publishing Group, 1981.

Pryce-Jones, D. *Paris in the Third Reich*. London: Holt, Rinehart, and Winston, 1981.

Queneau, R. *Zazie Dans le Métro*. Paris: Gallimard, 1959.

Servan-Schreiber, Jean-Jacques. *The American Challenge*. New York: Atheneum, 1968.

Shea, Neil. "Under Paris, Secrets Beneath the Streets." *National Geographic*, February 2011.

Steele, Ross. *The French Way*. New York: McGraw Hill, 2006.

Trouilleux, Rodolphe. *Unexplored Paris*. Paris: Parigramme, 2002.

Tuilier, A. *Histoire de l'Université de Paris et de la Sorbonne.* Paris: Nouvelle librairie de France, 1994.

Wenzler, Claude. *Genealogy of the Kings of France and Their Wives.* Rennes: Editions Ouest-France, 2003.

White, Edmund. *The Flaneur.* London: Bloomsbury, 2001.

The War in Vietnam

Appy, Christian G. *Patriots: The Vietnam War Remembered from All Sides.* New York: Viking, 2003.

Falk, Richard A. *The Vietnam War and International Law.* Princeton: Princeton University Press, 1968.

Minh, Ho Chi. *Ho Chi Minh on Revolution, Selected Writings, 1920–1966, Fall, Bernard B., Editor.* New York: Frederick A. Praeger, 1967.

Fall, Bernard B. *The Two Viet-Nams, A Political and Military Analysis.* New York: Frederick A. Praeger, 1967.

Fitzgerald, Frances. *Fire in the Lake.* New York: Random House, 1972.

Gettleman, Marvin E. *Viet Nam, History, Documents and Opinions on a Major World Crisis.* New York: Fawcett Publications, 1966.

Goodwin, Richard N. *Triumph or Tragedy, Reflections on Vietnam.* New York: Vintage Books, Alfred A. Knopf, and Random House, 1966.

Gordon, Bernard, K. *The Dimensions of Conflict in Southeast Asia.* Englewood Cliffs: Prentice-Hall, 1966.

Greene, Fred. *US Policy and the Security of Asia.* New York: McGraw-Hill, 1968.

Johnson, Lyndon B. Viet-Nam: *The Third Face of the War.* Washington: Department of State Publication, 1965.

Johnson, Lyndon B. *We Will Stand in Viet-Nam.* Washington: Department of State Publication, 1965.

Langguth, A. J. *Our Vietnam: The War 1954–1975.* New York: Simon & Schuster, 2000.

National Security Action Memoranda (NSAM), Lyndon B. Johnson Library

Oberdorfer, Don. *Tet! The Turning Point in the Vietnam War.* Baltimore: Johns Hopkins University Press, 2001.

Worro, Robert S. *Vietnam Peace Proposals.* Berkeley: World Without War Council, 1967.

Zinn, Howard. *Vietnam, The Logic of Withdrawal.* Toronto: South End Press 1967.

Raskin, Marcus G., and Fall, Bernard B. *The Viet-Nam Reader.* New York: Random House, 1965.

Reischauer, Edwin O. *Beyond Vietnam, The United States and Asia.* New York: Random House, 1967.

Shaplen, Robert. *The Lost Revolution, The US in Vietnam, 1946–1966.* New York: Harper & Row, 1966.

Civil Rights Movement

King, Mary. *Freedom Song: A Personal Story of the 1960s Civil Rights Movement.* New York: William Morrow & Co, 1987.

Lester, Julius. *Look Out, Whitey! Black Power's Gon' Get Your Mama.* New York: Dial Press, 1968.

Pearson, Hugh. *The Shadow of the Panther: Huey Newton and the Price of Black Power in America.* Reading: Addison-Wesley Publishing, 1994.

Women's Liberation Movement

Davis, Flora. *Moving the Mountain: The Women's Movement in America Since 1960.* New York: Simon & Schuster, 1991.

de Beauvoir, Simone. *The Second Sex: The Class Manifesto of the Liberated Woman.* New York: Vintage, 1974.

Evans, Sara. *Personal Politics: The Roots of Women's Liberation in the Civil Rights Movement and the New Left.* New York: Vintage Books, 1980.

Events of May 1968

Andro, P., A. Dauvergne, and L. M. Lagoutte. *Le Mai de la révolution*. New York: Julliard, 1968.

Ardagh, John. *The New French Revolution*. New York: Secker and Warburg, 1968.

Aron, Raymond. *La révolution introuvable: Réflexions sur les événements de Mai*. Paris: Librairie Arthème Fayard, 1968.

Aron, Raymond. *The Elusive Revolution: Anatomy of a Student Revolt*. New York: Praeger, 1969.

Aron, Raymond. *La révolution introuvable*. Paris: Fayard, 1968.

de Beauvoir, Simone. *La force de l'âge*. Paris: Gallimard, 1967.

Feenberg, Andrew, and Jim Freedman. *When Poetry Ruled the Street: The French May Events of 1968*. Albany: State University of New York Press, 2001.

Gitlin, Todd. *The Sixties: Years of Hope, Days of Rage*. Toronto: Bantam Books, 1987.

Karnow, S. *Paris in the Fifties*. New York, 1997.

Kurlansky, Mark. *1968, The Year That Rocked the World*. New York: Random House, 2004.

Les grands événements 1968. Paris: Solar et Presses de la Cité, 1969.

Marwick, Arthur. *The Sixties: Cultural Revolution in Britain, France, Italy, and the United States c. 1958–1974*. Oxford: Oxford University Press, 1998.

Ross, Kristin. *May, '68 and Its Afterlives*. Chicago: University of Chicago Press, 2002.

Witcover, Jules. *The Year the Dream Died: Revisiting 1968 in America*. New York: Warner Books, 1997.

1968 Presidential Election

Califano, Joseph A. Jr. *The Triumph and Tragedy of Lyndon B. Johnson: The White House Years*. New York: Simon & Schuster, 1991.

Goodwin, Richard N. *Remembering America: A Voice from the Sixties*. Boston: Little, Brown & Co, 1988.

Highlights from LBJ's Telephone Conversations, May 1968 to January 1969, www.lbjlib.utexas.edu/johnson/archives.hom/dictabelt.hom/highlights/may68jan69.shtm

Lyndon B. Johnson Library

Parry, Robert. *America's Stolen Narrative*. The Media Consortium, 2013.

Thomas, Evan. *Robert Kennedy: His Life*. New York: Simon & Schuster, 2000.

Thomas, Evan. *Being Nixon*. New York: Random House, 2015.

Farrell, John, A. "Nixon's Vietnam Treachery," *New York Times,* December 31, 2016.

About the Author

Bill Pearl is an American author who lives in Palm Beach County, Florida.

Bill's novel *Hearts on Fire, Paris 1968*, was inspired by his experiences as a student in Paris in 1968. He attended the American University in Paris, Colby College, Waterville, Maine and the George Washington University, Washington, D.C. (B.A., M.A.)

Formerly, Speech writer to the Administrator, Federal Energy Administration (FEA), Washington, DC '75-'77, Bill wrote the column "Energy Sense" for 800 weekly newspapers in the United States for former FEA Administrators John C. Sawhill and Frank Zarb.

Prose & poetry published: George Washington University Hatchet; Time Magazine; Paris Voices, Paris, France; Fiesta Magazine, Boca Raton, Florida; Encore Magazine, Albuquerque, NM; The Poet, Peu a Peu, Mishawaka, Indiana, The Advocate, Prattsville, New York.

Author of "Heart Songs" Second Place of 34 books entered in 2003 Annual Poetry Book Competition sponsored by Poets of the Palm Beaches; Author of "China Heart", Inspirations of Chinese Characters, a book of poems published in 2012.

Bill is a Rotarian and three times president of the Rotary Club of Palm Beach, Florida. He has also served as Chairman of the Rotary Foundation for Rotary District 6930. His proudest moments

in Rotary have been in organizing professional exchanges between America and France, two countries he loves very much!